NOT IN BRONXVILLE

A Suburban
Mystery Novel

BY RITA K. FARRELLY

CHICAGO SPECTRUM PRESS
4848 Brownsboro Center
Louisville, Kentucky 40207
800-594-5190

ISBN 1-886094-83-7

Printed in the U.S.A.

10 9 8 7 6 5 4 3 2 1

For our Decatur Avenue
Family of Six

Prologue

....

In forty-six years of life, Luke Plisky had killed dozens of people. Today, there would be one more.

Only four of those were murders.

The rest were "killed in action" in the Vietnam War. What difference did that make to those who loved them? None, he thought. Death has no modifiers.

A quarter of a century later, thousands of miles from the battlefield, Luke still remembered them, those his country sent him to kill.

Today, in a pre-dawn April fog, he stood near a tree, north of the graveled running path that circled the Bronxville Lake.

He'd been there for almost an hour. "Start out early," his mother had told him in East Lansing, years ago. "You never know what you might run into. No one wants to listen to excuses."

All that time, the advice had served him well.

This morning, he'd done a little two-step in place, to ward off the chill. His jogger's suit, a nondescript gray, fit his lean six-foot body snugly. Black running shoes. A navy baseball cap pulled down very low over a high forehead and deep-set ice blue eyes. Aviator glasses, darkly tinted; a thick wreath of curly, auburn hair peeking out from under his cap.

His long, thin face had a trim mustache.

From time to time, Luke focused his binoculars on a six-story slate building a half-mile across the water: Lake View Co-operative. It stood at the end of a cul-de-sac, with five other apartment complexes, up on a grassy hill.

If all went according to plan, Dan Horgan would soon exit from Lake View's rear door. A few pushups on the grass, then a slow lope down the incline to the path. There, he'd pick up his stride and begin jogging around the lake. Luke had observed and timed this routine more than a dozen times. Horgan, a fit sixty-three-year old, would circle the lake in about eight minutes.

Luke had waited for the perfect day. This was it. The trees were starting to bloom, partly obscuring the view of the track from nearby apartments. Fog clouded the view of drivers from the scenic Bronx River Parkway that ran parallel to the lake.

At 5:45 he sighted his quarry coming out of the rear door of Lake View. At 5:50 Dan Horgan started his first lap. There were no other joggers in sight. Luke Plisky moved out from behind the tree, and walked the short distance down to the lake's path. Once there, he began jogging slowly toward Horgan. He ran steadily with a barely discernible limp in his left leg. In about three minutes, they'd meet.

Just before they did, Plisky grabbed his chest and fell to the ground, face first. Horgan, seeing him, picked up his pace, stopped and bent over to help. "You O.K., buddy?"

No answer. When Horgan leaned over to turn Plisky on his back, Luke opened his eyes and mumbled, "Weak ankle. Just give me a hand, I think I can make it up." Horgan reached down, extending his right hand. Plisky grabbed it to steady himself. With his left, he reached into a pocket, pulled out a small pistol, and shot Horgan once in the heart.

Horgan's eyes filled with shock and pain as he fell. "Dear God," he murmured. Then his eyes rolled back in his head. When Luke checked his pulse, there was none.

Cars were swishing by on the Bronx River Parkway, and cicadas were chirping in the trees, when he left Dan Horgan in the dirt. Luke walked slowly back through the brush and the park area, then to Tuckahoe Road. By 6:35 he was back in his white-shingled house in the Crestwood section of Yonkers.

He removed the wig and jogging outfit, showered, shaved and dressed for work. Navy blazer, gray slacks, blue shirt, paisley tie, black moccasins. He ate his usual breakfast: orange juice, a toasted raisin bagel, coffee. At 7:30 he got into his royal blue Taurus and took the Deegan Expressway south, exiting in the South Bronx. After parking his car in a nearby garage, he crossed the busy street and walked through a large yard. Small groups of children were shrieking outside the main door of the old three-story brick building. A whispered, "Here come the duke…"

Just after eight o'clock, he stood in front of a fifth grade classroom at P.S. 807.

Luke Plisky was a teacher.

The Prior November...

1

....

Their union contract gives New York City's teachers one prep period a day. The time is to be used for class-related work: planning, lesson preparation, contacting parents and guardians, things like that.

Teachers call it their mental health break.

On this mild, rainy Thursday before Thanksgiving, six are gathered in the teachers' room at P.S. 807 in the Highbridge section of the Bronx. Prep period.

One is doing *The New York Times* crossword puzzle. A second is explaining to Harriet "the Hat" Noble why Harriet's turkey dressing was never moist. Still another is analyzing the latest shift in New York City's School Chancellors: "By the time they find their way to the Bronx, they're gone."

Two are working. Enid Gomez, a student teacher in her mid-twenties, is busy with a plan book. Luke

Plisky, a seasoned fifth grade teacher, is quietly coaching her.

Luke ("the Duke") Plisky is a legend at P.S. 807 and in this community where he's worked for more than a decade. When Enid Gomez looked at Luke Plisky, she saw a tall, slender, middle-aged man with a high forehead, thin blondish-gray hair, just a trace of a light mustache, and ice blue eyes with a two-inch scar below the right one. Unlike many on the staff, Luke took great care to dress well. "I tell the kids to look their best, so I do, too," he'd said when asked. Years ago, the kids had christened him "the Duke." Now, few knew whether his name was Luke or Duke.

His name was not the only mystery about Luke Plisky. Enid Gomez had heard that he was a Vietnam war hero, but didn't like to talk about it. That apparently accounted for the facial scar and the slight limp. Word was that he'd been married once, but that his wife had been killed by a mugger; he never talked about her either. Mild-mannered and gentle, he spoke softly but was a superb disciplinarian.

Only once had he been known to get angry. On Parents' night three years ago, two neighborhood toughs had tried to rob him outside the school. He'd already handed over his wallet, but when told to remove his sterling silver identification bracelet, Luke had appeared to comply and then knocked the thug unconscious with one karate chop. The thief's partner had fled, but not before Luke had retrieved his wallet. A patrol car had arrived shortly thereafter and delivered the grounded man to the hospital, under arrest. His buddy had been picked up within the hour, claiming "that meek skinny guy was like a Ninja turtle."

One thing Enid Gomez did know: he was a superb teacher. Luke held out hope to his kids. Working with him, Enid felt that she too could make a difference in their lives; that, for a time, she could insulate them from the poverty and meanness of the streets.

She was not alone.

Later, when all was known, Selma Einstein, school secretary at P.S. 807, said of Luke: "He was centered. Never ruffled. Not with parents. Not with kids. Not with the stupid bureaucracy in this system. Do you know what that's like around here? What can I say? We never really knew him, but you know what? He was loved."

Selma was Queen Bee at P.S. 807. Chancellors, School Boards, Principals and Assistant Principals came and went. Selma Einstein stayed. One fourth grader had said of her: "Miz Einstein, man, she's like …she IS who IS 'roun heah."

But that was later, the following autumn, when all was known.

Now, Luke checked the clock: fifteen more minutes till class. He finished talking with Enid Gomez, stood up and walked out of the room, down the quiet hall. The plaster on the ceiling was chipped and the walls needed a paint job. He made a mental note to talk with the principal about that.

Stopping at the computer room, Luke took out a key and unlocked the door. The room was off-limits to students, except when a teacher was there. Today it was empty. He sat down at a terminal and keyed in an ID and password. There was one E-mail message, from "Loot."

The message read:

100 D #4

Luke erased the incoming message, acknowledged its receipt to "Loot," and signed off. Tonight, in his Crestwood home, he'd key in a numbered Swiss bank account and verify a $100,000 deposit. It was just a formality. The money would be there, payment for killing a Fort Lee junkie who'd sold drugs to kids.

He left the computer room and walked slowly down the dingy corridor, back to his home room. His fifth grade class would return from the library in a few minutes. The last period before lunch was a challenge for most teachers, but not for him.

In September, Luke Plisky had received the Community School Board's "Teacher of the Year" award. The recognition pleased him. He loved teaching, worked hard, and was very good at it. The schedule allowed him to moonlight at a second job, one that required similar skills: planning, patience, resourcefulness. Today it had paid him $100,000. That would buy a lot of plaster and paint, maybe a few computers. Not bad for a "Teacher of the Year."

One who moonlighted as a contract killer.

2

Later that same day, Shannon O'Keefe entered Grand Central Station from the Vanderbilt Avenue entrance.

The scene reminded her of a gigantic temple. Tonight, crowds are more frantic than usual, rushing from all directions, single-mindedly heading for home or getting an early start on Thanksgiving travel.

Like the native New Yorker she is, Shannon navigates quickly and deftly through the throngs. The express train to Bronxville is on schedule, departing from Track 38. Time for a quick stop at the women's restroom.

When she comes out, a violinist is serenading the crowd: AVE MARIA. Not quite Isaac Stern, but not bad, not bad at all. She drops a dollar in the open violin case. Where but in New York do you get serenaded by Schubert outside the ladies' room?

Down the ramp to the train, which is already in the station. Ten minutes to departure; it's almost full. She enters the fifth car. The window seats and most of those on the aisle are taken. Looking toward the back of the train, she spots her Bronxville neighbor and friend Dan Horgan. He's reading, probably the agenda for the Lake View Co-op Board meeting they'll both attend tonight. As Board president, Dan will run the meeting. Looking up, he waves. She waves back, but sits down several rows ahead of him. Long ago, Shannon's father had trained her in commuter etiquette. Another train—the "D" on the Independent subway line from the Bronx to Brooklyn, by way of Manhattan. His golden rule: "Don't start gabbing with people you know; commuter time is private time, often the only free time a person has in the day." Then, it had seemed a prickly commandment. Now, she followed it religiously, fighting hard to act friendly when someone sat down next to her and began chatting.

She sees what appears to be an empty seat on the aisle. Nope, it's occupied. A laptop computer. Gesturing to its apparent owner in the windowseat, she asks to sit down next to the mid-twenties tortoise-shelled glasses ad for Banana Republic, a trendy casual wear chain that dots the New York landscape. A heated cellular phone conversation is underway. Mouthing "sorry," her seatmate points to the overhead compartment, where Shannon can move the laptop.

Great, she thinks I'm the stewardess.

Too tired to argue, Shannon lifts the computer to the berth above. Once seated, she breathes deeply. The mile walk from Columbus Circle has taken a toll on her forty-eight year old body. Time to start jogging again. Taking out her compact, she checks herself out. Her short, fashionably cut brown "do" is still in place; liquid brown eyes are still serious, but the dark lines under them are gone; an aging spot or two has been camouflaged by light makeup. A little lip gloss and she's set. Not bad, kiddo. Settling her five and a half feet into the seat, she pulls out the Board's agenda from her attaché case.

The motorman's voice comes over the loud-speaker: "Good afternoon, ladies and gentlemen. This is the Harlem line's 5:10 express to Bronxville; no stops in between." Ms. High-Tech groans, mumbles an obscenity and stands up hurriedly. After tripping over Shannon, she grabs the cellular phone and attaché case, along with the laptop from the over-head rack, and runs from the car as the door is closing. Shannon slides over to the window seat, looks out and sees the woman dashing along the platform, screaming to a conductor: "Greenwich, which way?" A lovely moment. At times she was in awe of the next generation. This made up for it: virtual reality, all geared up for the future, but not for day-to-day living.

The train starts to move slowly, quietly. The half-hour ride home to Bronxville is a quiet gift at day's end. Tonight she'd read the Board's agenda and attachments one more time. A few months ago, in a weak moment, she'd agreed to serve as Vice-President. Dan Horgan had told her: "It's no big deal, a lot like the Miss America contest: Will the runner-up step in, if the winner can't perform her duties?"

She'd laughed and said: "Yeah, but look at the dethroned Vanessa Williams today, and who remembers the one who replaced her?"

"Relax," he'd answered. "I'm in great health, and have never posed in a compromising position!"

She wasn't sure about that, but about the job he

was probably right. That was August. Like most
Vice-Presidents' jobs, it was mostly ceremonial and a
back-up when the President was traveling or ill. Dan
Horgan, a trim and vigorous sixty-three year old widower, looked physically fit. Often out of town on legal
business, he prided himself on staying in touch. At
the office, he'd been nicknamed Iron Horse Dan; no
one could recall his ever being ill. A jogger with the
body of a forty year old and energy to spare. A bookie
would bet on his living to be a hundred. Or more.

....

F. Daniel Horgan, seated several rows behind
Shannon, felt like Methuselah.

His muscular frame was sweating from every
pore; he was tired and his head ached. He'd left his
Park Avenue law firm, Horgan & Stern, early. The
train was unusually warm for November. Brushing
back a thinning strand of iron gray hair, he'd removed
his Burberry trench coat and the navy pinstripe
jacket of a London-tailored suit, folding them carefully and placing them in the overhead compartment.
Vest opened and tie loosened, he removed the Board
agenda from a thick portfolio and put on his reading
glasses.

God, he hoped this meeting would go smoothly.
Nothing else had in the past several months. There
might have been worse years in his life. At the
moment he couldn't think of one.

Was it Ernie Pyle who'd said, "War is hell?" So
was downsizing. Not just on the people who lose

their jobs, but on the guys who have to do it. He was lucky. Lou De Femio, his principal assistant, had handled the details; and Lou was an iceberg. Well, by tomorrow it would all be over. Dan was looking forward to the weekend and to next week, when he'd fly to California for Thanksgiving Day with his son Chip.

Looking up, he saw Shannon O'Keefe enter the car and waved. What a gem. He'd gotten to know her when she moved to Lake View a few years ago. They'd even dated for a time, and who knows where it might have gone? But Shannon had been through a difficult separation and divorce. She had no current interest in marriage, even to Dan Horgan, whom most women considered a very attractive widower, a great "catch."

They'd remained friends, and invited each other to social occasions. He'd encouraged her to join the Lake View Board, and then to become Vice President. Impressed with her broad corporate experience, he'd retained her as a consultant to work with Lou De Femio on his law firm's re-structuring. It was a match made in heaven. De Femio wanted to offer her a permanent job when the six-month stint had ended in August. Dan had guessed she'd say no and was proved right. Shannon had left the telecommunications industry's corporate treadmill and liked being a temporary executive. Who could blame her? There were times when he wished he could do it himself, sell the firm, give up the management headaches, return to what he did best: litigating high-profile cases.

The train moved out of Grand Central Station and Dan began reading the minutes of Lake View's last Board meeting. Why bother? Perfect, as usual. Gwyneth Fielding, Recording Secretary, was an ex-nun. Lake View had the only board minutes in Bronxville with no split infinitives.

Lots of routine stuff tonight. The big agenda item was filling the open building superintendent's job. Dan re-read the résumés and applications of the three top candidates. All good. One, Max Schneible, was even a college graduate.

He looked out the window as the train passed the Fleetwood Station. Next stop was his. Standing, he took his gear from the overhead compartment and walked down to Shannon O'Keefe's seat. "Home again to Brigadoonsville." It was their private joke. Shannon had once told Dan, a Bronxville native, that nothing much had changed there since its founding in 1898. She smiled, stood, and together they approached the exit. The train glided smoothly into the station.

The night was soft with the time-honored happy shrieks of small children, some with mothers, some with nannies, a few with fathers, all welcoming the commuters home. Dan and Shannon walked down the platform and the short stairway. Crossing Kraft Avenue, they headed for the managing agent's office, a few doors away from a triplex movie theater.

Bronxville, tonight as it was almost a century ago, was a quiet sanctuary from city life.

3

....

"Let's do it," said Dan Horgan to Lake View's Board of Directors.

It's 6:05 at the real estate offices of Davidson and Kryhoski on Kraft Avenue. Rich Kryhoski is short and hefty, balding and moon-faced. He's managing agent for Lake View and three dozen other cooperative buildings in Westchester County.

His office resembles the man himself, peripatetic and perpetually disheveled. Not your nineties paperless work space.

Kryhoski had inherited his father's half of the business more than twenty years ago. When his partner Kirk Davidson retired in 1988, Rich had bought out his share too.

Brokerage fees still accounted for most of the firm's income. The managing agent business was a sideline that many real estate agencies had given up years ago. Margins were small and the time commitment large. "They put a nickel in, and expect a dollar song," a friend sang about co-op and condo clients. Dithering, indecisive Boards with too many litigious shareholders.

On his father's advice, Rich had kept the managing agent business going. "When the real estate market's down, and brokerage fees are trickling in, you'll have a source of steady income." That had allowed him to ride out a dry period in the early nineties when many of his friends had gone out of business or consolidated with larger firms.

Good managing agents developed strong contacts with Boards, and those often led to brokerage fees when residents sold their apartments. Now in his early sixties, Rich prided himself on being the best in the business.

Tonight, when Dan Horgan and Shannon O'Keefe arrived at 5:50, the formica-top conference room table was littered with paper, ashtrays, a half-eaten ham sandwich and an unopened granola bar. Several incoming faxes were piled up in the tray. Shannon helped Rich to clear the table while Dan reviewed his notes and prepared for the meeting.

By 6:04, Kryhoski and all but one of the eight Board members were in their seats. Gwyneth Fielding, board secretary, readied her laptop computer, Robert's Rules of Order at the ready.

Tonight, predictably, Val Thomas dashed in the door at 6:05. Thomas apologizes, mumbling something about a late emergency at the office. The Board knows otherwise. The Bronxville parking meters don't function after six. Val, a thirty year old C.P.A., has saved another quarter for his retirement fund.

Dan begins. "A full agenda tonight, folks. Let's move quickly through the routine stuff, and spend time on filling the building superintendent's job."

Nods all around. The Board quickly approves Gwyneth's minutes of the last meeting. Most have not read them, trusting Gwyneth's 'ex cathedra' reputation for accuracy and fairness. Val Thomas, treasurer, summarizes the financial statements: "Expenses-to-date are running about five percent below budget, but we still have two months to go. We can't get cocky." No one was about to.

Rich Kryhoski began a detailed update on improved security procedures, re-paving of the parking lot, and the new boiler pump. Rich is good on detail, less so on the big picture. Now he's serving up detailed diagrams of Lake View's heating system, boiler, pumps, pipes, valves, air flow, etc. Just hitting his stride, like a late evening news weatherman, he's interrupted by Elmer Brick. Elmer is one of Lake View's oldest residents, fount of institutional memory and common sense.

"So we're installing the latest system, Rich. Two questions: will we be cool in summer and warm in winter? And will the pipes still sound like there's some little ghost in there, wailing to get out?"

Rich smiled: "Yes to the first question; no to the second. Even better…"

Horgan interjected: "Thanks, Rich. I think we know all we need to know for now. Anything else, Rich?"

"Just one informational item for you. Had a complaint that the Foster baby is screaming at three o'clock in the morning, disturbing the Arnolds. Told them that I didn't think the Board could reasonably construe the House Rules on noise to apply to one-month-olds."

Val Thomas, whose wife was expecting their first child, nodded appreciatively. The rest shared a "now-we've-heard-everything" look, happy that Rich had handled the problem.

"O.K., let's get to the main event," said Horgan. "Rich has lined up interviews for the three top candidates for our building superintendent's job. You've each received a copy of their applications. Rich, will you check if they're in the reception area, while we cover a few basics?"

"Yup."

Dan proceeded: "I've asked Shannon, our resident human resources pro, to give us a few pointers. One thing we don't need is an EEO complaint. The only thing tougher than hiring a building superintendent is firing one. Shannon?"

"It's actually pretty simple. Rule #1: focus on the job requirements. Anything that bears on that is relevant; anything that doesn't isn't. Rule #2: when in doubt, return to Rule #1. That's it."

"O.K., anyone want to sum up the job requirements?" asked Dan.

Jay Shapiro, a reedy and tweedy young architect, did. "The doorman said it best: Please all seventy-two owners, twenty-four hours a day."

Horgan smiled. "Agree, Jay. Anybody with a few more specifics?"

Hester Harrington, a sixty-something doyenne of "old Bronxville," volunteered. "Well, we need someone just like George. A good family man, willing and able to do most minor repairs, cheerfully; fill in when the doorman or porter is sick; mediate neighbors' problems with each other; police the parking lot; tide things over when someone acts inappropriately. You get the picture."

Shannon O'Keefe blanched at the "good family man" part, but kept quiet. George Perkins, like all the recently deceased, had achieved a kind of sainthood he'd never experienced in life. "Don't speak ill of the dead" had turned into "Light an eternal flame for them, and keep it burning brightly." The month before George died, at least three residents had clamored for his dismissal. Wherever George was, he must be laughing out loud.

Elmer Brick chimed in: "All we need is a combination of Mother Teresa and Houdini!"

"With a dose of Arnold Schwarzenegger," added Val Thomas. "Strong guy, soft heart, like Kindergarten Cop."

"I can see it now in the Bronxville Review Press-Reporter," said Elmer. "The Terminator hired to run Lake View."

Horgan used one of his natural talents, a withering stare, to bring the group to order. Shannon was certain that this was in the genes of certain people: judges, nuns, service reps at the Department of Motor Vehicles, mothers. Others, like Dan Horgan, picked it up along the way.

The stare shut off the silly talk. Horgan then summarized the superintendent's job: "How about this: someone who's knowledgeable in building repair, with managerial and social skills to relate to residents, outside contractors, the local Police and Fire Departments, and the rest. Does that cover it?"

"Sounds good to me, Dan," said Elmer. "Just one question for Shannon. Are you saying that if a one-legged nonagenarian shows up, wearing an earring, we have to hire him?"

"Nope. I'm saying that you can't use his disability, perceived age, or sexual orientation as a reason NOT to hire him. You CAN mention that in the event of a fire, the job may require a person to dash up six flights of stairs to help residents on the top floor, and ask if that poses a problem."

"Sounds like a no-win situation for the guy, Shannon. If he says 'Yes,' we tell him he's nuts; if 'No,' no job."

Shannon nodded: "Well, those may be our conclusions, Elmer, but we don't need to tell him anything until we've made our hiring decision. Then we get to use reasonable judgment. That doesn't guarantee we won't get sued, but does allow us to claim that we only did what that old standby, any reasonable man, would do."

Val Thomas looked up from his spreadsheets: "Do you think that they never use the term 'reasonable woman,' because there are none?"

The meeting was heading downhill when Rich Kryhoski returned, stating that two of the three building superintendent candidates were in the reception area.

Horgan nodded: "O.K. If there are no further questions, bring in Henry Gonzales."

"Sounds like a quiz program," said Jay Shapiro.

Kryhoski returned with Gonzales, who was not a Schwarzenegger look-alike. Lithe; about 5 feet, 9 inches tall; fifty-ish, with tiny tufts of hair around his ears and little anywhere else. Dressed in a dark polyester suit, he wore wire-rimmed glasses and appeared neat but nervous, soft-spoken, and eager to please. His qualifications were impressive, with a community college degree and twenty-seven years' experience as a building superintendent in a rent-controlled Brooklyn apartment complex.

No earring.

"Why would you move to Westchester?" asked Dan.

"Two reasons. Our Brooklyn neighborhood's overrun with drug lords, and then there's the schools. My youngest is twelve and my wife and I checked out high schools. Bronxville High School is way up there."

Nods and a few more questions. Several times, people asked him to speak up so he could be heard. Finally, Horgan thanked him and promised a decision from Rich Kryhoski's office within a few days.

"Next up, Rich."

Kryhoski brought in the second applicant, Dominic ("Call me Dom") Rizzuto. Forty-something, tall and husky, well-groomed, sportily dressed in a brown Ralph Lauren blazer, yellow Izod sport shirt and khaki corduroys. Confident and smooth, very smooth, a born extrovert.

No earring.

Rizzuto had obviously done his homework, and after quick introductions, was addressing each Board member by name. He made a point of telling Hester Harrington how much he admired her work on The Bronxville Beautification Committee. She beamed. Shannon seethed.

He discussed arriving from Milan, "northern Italy," as a small child. The family had first taken up residence in Mount Vernon, just south of Bronxville, where his father worked as an electrician. During World War II, several building superintendent jobs had become available, and they'd moved to Queens in New York City. The job meant a rent-free apartment, with regular income. Rizzuto Sr. had many of the skills needed. What he didn't know, he learned quickly and passed on to his son. On his death in 1975, Rizzuto Jr. had graduated from community college and taken over on an interim basis. He'd stayed ever since, but now wanted to move out of the city.

"Family, Mr. Rizzuto?" Shannon cringed at Gwyneth Fielding's question, but the applicant was not flustered: "One wife, two kids, one off the family payroll and out on her own, thank God! My wife's an emergency room nurse and thinks she can probably get work here at Lawrence Hospital."

Elmer Brick had appeared comatose since the interviews began, but now perked up: "Better yet, taking care of some of us older folks at Lake View, Dom!"

"And younger ones, Mr. Brick," quipped Rizzuto. He winked at Shannon, who wanted to throw up.

"Like Bill and Hillary, you'll get two for the price of one," he added.

Others peppered Rizzuto with questions. Finally, Horgan thanked him and he left. "Rich, there's one more: Max Schneible, right?"

"Dan, let me make one final check. He wasn't out there with the others." Kryhoski ambled back in short order.

"Sorry, but it looks like Schneible's a no-show."

Just then, a figure appeared behind Rich. "Sorry, Mr. Kryhoski, I've been out there for an hour. Guess you didn't see me. I'm Max Schneible."

When Schneible entered the room, Shannon knew she was in the middle of a "photo-op." Five foot eight with a body a tad short of chubby. About thirty. A head of curly, medium-length black hair; navy corduroy suit; tailored light blue shirt; aerobic shoes; wide, friendly face; open manner.

Not one earring. Two.

Max Schneible was female.

Horgan recovered quickly and ushered her to a chair. Shannon stifled a giggle. Hester looked like her scarlet "A" for "aplomb" was about to stand for "angina." Elmer Brick almost popped his glass eye. Jay Shapiro and Val Thomas lunged for their reading glasses and became passionately interested in her job application. Gwyneth Fielding began pointing and clicking her mouse feverishly.

Only the newest Board member, Dr. Evan Doubleday, seemed to take it in stride. Doubleday was quiet, thin, owl-eyed, and jug-eared. Shannon saw him as a Woody Allen minus twenty years. Now, he stood up, removed his round eye glasses, and offered his hand across the table to Max. "Welcome," he said simply, and then sat down.

The rest seemed catatonic.

"Is it Ms. Schneible, or Mrs?" asked Horgan.

"Max is fine."

"Max it is. I must tell you, we weren't expecting…"

Max smiled: "Yeah."

Hester whined: "Then Max stands for Maxine?"

"No, Mrs. Harrington. It stands for Max. My parents were expecting a boy, and the family name was picked out beforehand. They stuck with it."

Gwyneth Fielding asked, "Why would you want a job like this?"

"Pretty simple. I got my degree in civil engineering at City College, and have worked for Con Ed for eight years. I'm tired of working for someone else, and want to start my own construction business one day. This job offers experience, contacts, and a rent-free apartment till I get the capital to run my own show."

"Uh, do you have family, Max?" asked Elmer Brick.

Shannon looked down one more time, but she'd underestimated Max.

"Yup, parents and two brothers. They're great, but it's time to get my own place."

"What makes you think you can do this job?" chirped Hester. "You have no experience as a building superintendent."

"Righto. But my dad taught shop at a vocational high school in the Bronx. When he built a little vacation place in the Catskills, I helped him put in the foundation, plumbing, electric wiring, stuff like that. He taught me all he knew and that's a lot."

Shannon jumped in. "Max, what do you do at Con Ed?"

Damage control, mostly. I direct line crews that check out transformer problems, repair feeder cables when manholes explode, respond to power outages. The works, I guess."

"Is there no end to your talents, Maxine?" Hester Harrington had regained a bit of her aplomb, though her perfectly knotted silk scarf was now askew. But sarcasm was lost on Max Schneible.

"Max. Yeah, sure is. Paperwork. Hate it. Call it desk-phobia. You know the old Think and Do books? Me, I like doing, not thinking about doing."

Horgan sensed it was time to end discussion. "If that's it, I think we can let Max go. You'll hear from Rich within a few days, Max. Thanks for stopping by."

Max stood up. "You're welcome. See ya."

A silence settled in. Horgan checked his watch and noticed it was close to eight o'clock. "O.K. Let's get a sense of the group, and see whether we agree on a candidate tonight or need to sleep on it."

Elmer summarized the options. "Seems to me that the choice is Casper Milquetoast, Rambo, or Rosie the Riveter."

Horgan pushed on. "O.K., let's start with Hank Gonzales. Anybody want to speak for him?" No one did. The consensus was that he needed an assertiveness training course, and Lake View was not the place to learn on-the-job.

"Moving on," said Horgan. "Rizzuto?"

"I liked him," said Jay Shapiro. "Confident, well spoken, good experience, tough but seasoned. He's our man." Hester Harrington agreed: "I vote for hiring him as soon as possible."

"Something bothers me," said Shannon. "I'm not even sure what it is. Maybe he's a little too smooth." She was embarrassed to mention the wink. Besides, maybe he had a tic in his eye.

"I, for one, don't know what you mean, Shannon." Hester was adamant. "After all, he'll represent Lake View to the public. And image isn't everything, it's the only thing!"

Horgan wondered if that was what Vince Lombardi had in mind when he talked about winning.

"Good point, Hester," said Elmer Brick. "But we're not hiring a Minister of Protocol here. Just a building superintendent."

Horgan intervened. Arguments at eight o'clock on empty stomachs were the worst kind. "Final candidate: Max Schneible. Anyone favor her?"

Shannon hesitated for a moment, hoping someone else would take up the cause. Dr. Evan Doubleday did.

"Yes."

"Care to elaborate, Doctor?" asked Horgan.

"We agreed on the qualifications. She has more of them than the other two. Period."

"But she's never been a super, Doctor," whined Hester. If Evan Doubleday had not been a physician, Hester would have said, "Ridiculous." As it was, her words dripped with contempt.

Evan answered: "Well, for every surgeon, there's got to be a first patient."

Shannon broke in. "I agree with Evan. Max has the best qualifications. So she hasn't been a super. She's done all the things a super does. So she's a diamond in the rough. We've hired them before and they've worked out."

Hester was not surrendering, though her Gucci scarf had. It was now completely unraveled. "She's more like carbon, Shannon, and she lied on the application."

"Where?" asked Shannon.

"Right here, where it says SEX. She left it blank."

"Maybe she has none," offered Elmer.

"Well, it's better than one I saw where the guy wrote: Occasionally," answered Val Thomas.

Shannon laughed: "No, Hester, she didn't lie. We all saw the applications in advance. Any of us could

have picked up the blank item, and asked beforehand. We didn't. Let's face it, if she'd written in
Female, do you think she'd have made it to the final
three?"

Horgan looked wary. Time to hold or fold:
"Should we vote now or sleep on it tonight? Tomorrow, I can phone you and take a vote: Rizzuto,
Schneible, or continue the search. If necessary, we
can convene over the weekend."

Shannon paused for a few moments, then spoke.
She sensed that Dan wanted to do what he always
liked to do: please everyone, arrive at a compromise.
A telephone vote would allow him a secret ballot, and
she wanted to know where he stood. If individual
minds were made up, there was little point in delay.
"Dan, we're all moving into a hectic holiday season.
Not a great time for ad hoc meetings."

"I second that, Dan." Hester too was ready to
vote. "Why do we need to think about it?"

"O.K., then, we'll vote." Dan asked for a show of
hands: "Dom Rizzuto?"

Three hands went up quickly: Hester Harring-
ton, Elmer Brick, and Jay Shapiro. Dan Horgan, Val
Thomas, and Gwyneth Fielding were wavering. Then
Gwyneth and finally Dan raised their hands. Val
Thomas did not.

"Max Schneible?" Three hands went up: Shannon's, Evan's and Val's.

"Well, it's five to three for Rizzuto. Unless we
want to re-open the search, that's it," said Dan.

Kryhoski winced, but was lucky. No one thought

that was a good idea.

"O.K.," said Dan. "Rich, offer him the job. That's it for tonight. Happy Thanksgiving, everybody." The group had already begun scooping up papers, and Jay Shapiro was almost out the door, when Gwyneth Fielding tapped her ergonomic mouse gently on the table: "There was no motion to adjourn!"

Jay turned and shouted, "Motion to adjourn!" It was seconded by Elmer Brick, and approved unanimously. Gwyneth nodded happily, checked her digital watch and keyed in the time to her laptop. 8:09 P.M. Another perfect set of minutes would be in everyone's mailbox by the weekend.

Shannon and Evan walked out into the starless autumn night. He looked at her and she was smiling. "A dime for your thoughts, Shannon?"

A small step for womankind, Doc. Max Schneible lost out tonight, but her day will come."

"Absolutely," said Evan.

They had no idea just how soon.

4

It was close to 8:30 when Shannon and Evan Doubleday parted in Lake View's lobby. Evan lived on the second floor in the middle section of the building. Shannon's apartment was on the third floor in the back, with two views of Bronxville Lake.

The Board meeting had cheered her after a frustrating day. One negative about being a temporary executive was that you got to do what no one else wanted to do. Her current job was director of human resources for an international consulting firm on Central Park West, just north of 59th Street. This morning, she'd held exit interviews with two employees who'd been fired; listened to another's sexual harassment complaint; and drafted a company guideline on "dress down" days. Her boss Burke Parker, senior vice president, wanted a "win/win policy, one that will please the clients and allow Generation X to do their thing, whatever that is." Parker made every working cliché an art form.

She'd told him that maybe the company was not ready for "dressing down," but he'd just smiled and said he had confidence in her ability with words.

This afternoon he'd showed her a draft of a letter he was sending to the executive vice president. Did she have any comments? The letter focused on what a great job his Human Resources Department was doing: dowsizing, reducing employee benefits, extending working hours, more win/wins, the works. Shannon almost lost her lunch at his conclusion: "In spite of these unprecedented changes, morale continues to be high." She'd wanted to ask him whose morale he was talking about, and how did he know? He left his office only for two hour "business lunches," for strategy and team-building sessions with bosses and peers, and at quitting time. He had his own bathroom, so no one got to see him in the john. The line on Burke Parker had always been: "What does he do and when does he do it?"

Wasted energy. She settled for telling him that he'd spelled his boss's last name wrong on the memorandum. "Oops," he'd answered, "that's what happens when you're a big picture kind of guy like me."

Oh well, the best thing about "temping" was that you could always say good-bye.

She walked through the dining room to her eat-in kitchen and checked for phone messages. One: "Hi, Mom. Maria. Just wanted to ask if you'd bake a cake for dessert on Thanksgiving Day. Oh and, uh...Dad can make the dinner, too. Call when you can. Luv'ya."

Maria was Shannon's twenty-six year old investment banker daughter, giving her mother notice she'd be celebrating Thanksgiving with her ex-husband again. So Tony Caruso was giving up a couple of liposuction and tummy tuck surgeries to bond with his ex-family on Thanksgiving Day in Scarsdale. What a guy!

The choice of meals in the freezer was limited. There was pizza with pepperoni and pizza plain. No house specials. She settled for plain, stuck it in the microwave and prepared a green salad. With a glass of white zinfandel, she walked into the living room and flipped on the TV. A mindless sitcom, but a relaxing diversion.

The microwave pinged and the phone rang. Together, natch. She'd screen the call. "Shannon, it's me, Ceecy. If you're there, pick up, will you? I'll be brief."

Ceecy Caruso Cohen, former sister-in-law and still loyal friend. Shannon picked up the phone.

"Ha, gotcha!" hailed Ceecy.

"Well, hello to you too. How are you?" This was not a good opener with Ceecy, who was never good. If you had pneumonia, she had double pneumonia.

"Well, Arthur has chronic fatigue syndrome. Lucy's boyfriend thinks he's gay but wants to maintain their relationship until he knows for sure. David's into Scientology and Madonna's allergic to cat food."

In short order, an update on Ceecy's whole clan: husband, kids and new kitten Madonna, who had fit right into the dysfunctional family. Ceecy continued: "Anyway, how about breakfast on Saturday?"

"Sounds good. Usual spot at 9:30?"

"Great. See you there. Gotta run and whip up something in the blender for Madonna's dinner. *Ciao.*"

Shannon hung up the phone, smiled, and opened the microwave door. Her pizza now looked like it had come from the consignment shop. She reset the dial to warm it up. When it was ready, she brought it to the living room, and lifted her wine glass: "To the sometime joys of single life!"

5

It's four o'clock on Friday, the following day, at the New York law offices of Horgan & Stern.

Dan Horgan has cleared his calendar, preparing for an early departure.

He swivels his black leather chair, looking out the window of his plush corner office. As the sun dips, Park Avenue's pedestrians are already into their holiday hustle. There are more cars, whose drivers honk louder and more often.

His thoughts drift to an earlier Thanksgiving season, thirty-three years ago and his first meeting with Jake Stern in civil court. Jake represented the plaintiff, a twenty year old African-American woman, in a malpractice suit against one of New York's premier hospitals; Dan represented the hospital.

Thirty years old, Dan already had a national reputation. A superb trial lawyer, he'd never lost a jury trial.

Until then.

He'd underestimated Jake Stern, whose baggy suit looked ten years old. A fortyish man in an old man's body. Small and craggy like a macaroon. Jake had enough thick black hair for two people and it regularly fell down into his eyes. Dan wanted to recommend his own tailor and barber to him.

Much of the time, Jake's wizened face had a "what's going on here?" look, reminiscent of the movie actor Barry Fitzgerald in his best roles. Chronic befuddlement.

By the time Dan realized that Jake Stern knew more than he did about the law, Dan's own client, and the jury, it was too late. He'd missed the man's doggedness, his erudition and competence, his fundamental decency, his understanding of human nature, and, more than anything, his passion.

The jury had not, and awarded the plaintiff a $2 million verdict for malpractice.

Dan was stunned. The next day, he called up Jake Stern to invite him to lunch at the Harvard Club. Jake said yes, but only if he could pay. It was the least a winner could do. And the lunch would be at *his* club, which turned out to be a hot dog stand in the garment district.

That day, they'd become an odd couple. Dan was Bronxville born and bred, schooled there for 12 years, Princeton University and Harvard Law. Jake came from New York's lower East Side, Stuyvesant High School, City College and Brooklyn Law School, where he'd graduated first in his class.

After Harvard, Dan had received offers from the top law firms in New York. He'd picked the largest and most prestigious. Jake had applied at the same firms, but received no offers. He'd gone to work for Legal Aid, serving the poor for a decade. Then, he set up a practice of his own in a small office on 39th Street, off Eighth Avenue.

There were several more lunches, some on park benches and a few at the Harvard Club. Dan had gotten Jake there by reminding him that all men are equal before the law, and that Jake had been discriminating against the rich.

Six months later, Dan left his law firm and set up a partnership with Jake, who'd joked: "We'll corner the market. You take the Wasps. The Jews are mine. We'll split up the Catholics between us. They don't have much money anyway."

Even now, Dan smiled at the innocence of that early, happy time. They worked from early morning till late at night, six days a week. Jake took off Saturday; Dan, Sunday. Overhead was kept to a minimum. It was a year before they could afford a full-time secretary.

In five years, the partnership prospered and they rented a suite of offices in the Empire State Building. In time, Jake became a nationally prominent criminal defense lawyer, and Dan an expert on corporate and securities law. They added attorneys and support staff slowly, and only when the work load screamed out for it. They were a top pair, both professionally and as friends. Jake watched over the firm's internal operations: expenses, taxes, employee matters, and the like. He parceled out money like it was his own. Dan oversaw the external parts of the business: government affairs, Bar Association matters, community relations, and pro bono work.

When their kids were grown, both sold their homes and moved to the Lake View co-op in

Bronxville. Their apartments were side by side on the top floor of the rear of the building. They shared a terrace and breathtaking views of the Bronxville Lake and park. Their wives, Minnie and Julie, were best friends.

In 1985, Jake's wife Minnie had finally persuaded him to take his first extended vacation in ten years. He did, and suffered a massive, fatal coronary in Antigua.

For a few months, Dan was paralyzed by the loss. Ever so slowly, prodded by Lou De Femio, a senior attorney, he took hold. De Femio, with his work ethic, street smarts, and drive, became a highly trusted second-in-command. New lawyers were hired, along with paralegals and support staff. Jake had pioneered in law office automation, and that part of his legacy prevailed for a time. Horgan & Stern was still on top. The firm expanded quickly, and, against Lou De Femio's recommendation, Dan moved its offices to more luxurious space on Park Avenue.

The turn came in 1990. Business failures, downsizings, belt tightening were everywhere. For a while, that meant more legal business, to usher firms through the change. But restructured companies emerged with leaner budgets for staff services. Many made drastic cuts in outside counsel, opting to do the work in-house. The work they sent outside was highly specialized in nature.

It was also work that too few lawyers at Horgan & Stern were now qualified to do. Expenses were up and revenue down. The place began to take on the aura of the Titanic.

Lou De Femio had finally confronted him last January. The Four Seasons at 52nd Street on Manhattan's East Side was Dan's favorite restaurant. Lou, a workaholic like Jake Stern, normally ate a pastrami sandwich, occasionally a cheeseburger, always in his office.

That day, over filet of sole, Lou's message was forthright and simple: "Dan, we're in trouble. We're just not getting the business we used to. Revenue's been off for the last two years. I spent the weekend looking at year-end results. Not good. Our bonuses were level, but next year you're going to look like the Grinch who stole Christmas."

De Femio was not always as polished as Horgan might have liked, but Dan respected his candor and integrity. A solid guy. Neither a schmoozer nor a boozer; never one to "cry wolf." Dan's reaction was his usual "I'll think about it." Translation: "Enjoy the sole."

Lou let him sleep on it for a few days, then popped into his office and said: "Dan, I love this place. But the ship's going down, and I've got to think about Nina and the kids. If you don't hear me out, I'm leaving."

Dan gave in, knowing that Lou meant it. There was no better all-around lawyer in the city than De Femio. Dan also realized he was blessed in having an assistant he could trust. The man was an ace. "O.K. You've got my attention."

Over several more lunches and a couple of late dinners, Dan and Lou had talked, argued, and reviewed the problems in some detail. The bottom line was that Horgan & Stern had lost its edge as one of New York's top law firms. There were more than enough lawyers and support staff on hand, but not enough with the right skills. And the pipeline was no longer full. There were too many older guys (the older ones were almost all men) who arrived late, sat in their office, read *The New York Law Journal* and the latest briefs from the circuit courts. They'd argue about them in the corporate dining room over French cuisine. Rarely did one invite a paying client. Some acted like they were still in high school debating societies. Afternoons, they would see a client or two to update a will, provide estate counseling, or do pro bono work.

There were too few rainmakers bringing in new business.

Last year had been the worst in the firm's history. They'd eked out a profit, but a small one. Associates' salary increases had been held to the rate of inflation. Two of the best, a twenty-eight year old black woman from Brooklyn Law School and a thirty-year old white man from Rutgers, had left for better jobs. The firm once had a track record of recruiting bright people from the best local schools, kids from blue collar families. They'd work for lower starting salaries than the Ivy League crowd, learned just as quickly and put in equally long hours. The quid pro quo, however, was that they were monitored by partners who were pros in their fields, and who offered superb training.

Now, too many of the mentors could be mentees. Some had not litigated a case in years. Others had limited knowledge of the increasing legal complexities of multi-million-dollar corporate deals: mergers, acquisitions, divestitures. There was little depth in areas that were hot: taxation and environmental law. Old clients dropped Horgan & Stern for newer, cutting-edge firms. The "straw" came when Lou asked a senior patent lawyer, Morgan Templeton, for a quick update on software patent law. Templeton said he'd get back to him in a week.

"Dan, you've got to move before it's too late," Lou had argued. Dan sensed he was right, but backed off from Lou's proposal. Lou wanted the firm to tackle its own problems: "Let's give our best associates a mandate to go through the place with a top-to-bottom review and forward their recommendations to the management committee."

Dan lacked confidence that any internal group could pull off an objective study. He also liked to distance himself from bad news, and favored hiring an outside management consulting firm. Many had done business with Horgan & Stern in the past. What better time to reciprocate, keep his network going, maybe pick up some new business in the process?

De Femio reluctantly got proposals from three of the major firms. At the time, all were doing a landmark business. The presenters were mostly expensively tailored young MBA's in pin-striped suits, who came armed for a total media experience. There were computer-generated colored slides, pie charts, and a carefully indexed loose-leaf binder for all six members of the management committee.

For hours on end, Lou listened. There were strategies, visions, competitive analyses, computer simulations, extrapolations, new paradigms and some other things he didn't understand, and had no wish to. In each case, the studies would take several months, and the costs would be in seven figures. "We know you want our first team here," more than one had said.

When the third top-of-the-line team had left, Lou De Femio felt like he was being hoisted on his own petard. The effort he'd envisioned involved several weeks of concentrated, low-cost analysis of the business: a couple of senior partners, flanked by the firm's top associates. He went back to Dan Horgan, arguing for his simpler and cheaper approach. "My God, Dan, if we hire these guys, we'll have to file for bankruptcy before we execute the solutions."

Dan's response: "Let's think about it some more." Lou went home in a funk.

What Dan had done was talk to his neighbor, Shannon O'Keefe. He knew she'd had extensive business analyst experience, and had worked with Brett Halliday Temporary Executives following her departure from corporate life. Over dinner at Palmer's Restaurant in Bronxville that Saturday night, he described the project: "Is this something you and Brett might be willing to tackle?" It was and they would.

Lou De Femio was not overjoyed when Horgan presented him with this alternative. He'd never met Shannon O'Keefe, but figured she was some bimbo having an affair with Dan, happy to mix business with pleasure. He was wrong, about both the affair and her competence.

Shannon and Brett Halliday had sat down with De Femio and mapped out a plan that was not unlike his original idea. The two consultants would direct the project, provide analytical skills and training, and set up work teams, using the fast-track associates at Horgan & Stern. There would be no slow-motion time to debate visions and strategies. No color slides or slick presentations. Just thorough analyses, following structured interviews with every person who worked for Horgan & Stern, and with major clients.

The group worked overtime and delivered its report to Horgan and De Femio in May. Lou had expected few surprises. There were many. Horgan & Stern was over-staffed by about forty people. Many lawyers were doing what paralegals could do faster and cheaper. There was lots of computer equipment, but it was underutilized.

One lawyer's office had three personal computers and four printers. When questioned, her secretary answered huffily: "I've got bad feet. I use the extra printer to rest them on in the afternoon."

Shannon O'Keefe reported that at least three senior secretaries were still using typewriters, one her old trusty Smith-Corona manual. "It's served me well over the years, and got us through the '65 power blackout. Why dump it now?"

Brett Halliday stated that "one senior lawyer went on and on about *The Firm* and *The Client,* citing technical errors he'd identified in the novels. Unless John Grisham is your client, the guy ain't producing anything worth a tinker's damn."

Another attorney had dismissed paralegals as "wannabe lawyers who couldn't make it." She certainly was not going to trust anything signed by one of them, and proudly announced she checked all their work from scratch.

A tax attorney, asked to identify the firm's principal strength, offered up "the mailroom."

"You mean their efficiency?" asked the astonished associate.

"Good grief, no. They're slow as molasses. But they send all your holiday packages out free. And," the associate added, "most of the packages were going to the guy's family in Bologna, Italy."

The task force had analyzed the firm's phone bills: Twenty-five percent of long distance costs were to places where the firm had neither clients nor other law firms on retainer. "Well, they sure took that 'Friends and Family' commercial to heart," said Horgan.

"For chrissakes, Dan, can't they find a few friends and family in this country?" moaned senior attorney Irv Kassler.

"They can and have, Irv," was the response. "We've analyzed the local phone bills as well. Out-of-pocket costs there are modest, compared to the long-distance bills, but get this: 20 percent of the calls are to their own home phone numbers, and 32 percent of the time spent on the phone is to those numbers as well."

"Isn't there any good news?" asked Kassler.

"Not a whole lot. There's one more item, though. Want to guess the most frequently called number by your employees?"

No one did.

"The Weather. Runner-up is Dial-a-Joke."

And so it went. A Band-Aid approach wouldn't work. The firm needed major surgery if the patient were to survive this decade, much less the next one.

The management committee took several weeks to lay out a plan, review the legal points, decide who and what would go and what would stay. In a few cases they opted to give capable people a choice: learn new skills or leave. They hammered out new rules by which the firm would operate. Horgan insisted that the severance policy be liberal and that the new organization not be draconian. It was, after all, reputation and relationships, both internal and external, that had brought them success. He was not prepared to play Ebenezer Scrooge, who never had the dream.

What the management committee came up with, was, by industry standards, generous. The principals worked hard to be fair, to push sentiment to the background, to treat employees with dignity and respect. All would receive severance, based on length of service. Those who were interested would get outplacement services, personal counseling, and retraining. Professionals would have use of their offices and support services for a temporary period. The usual termination benefits and more were provided.

In August, Lou distributed a memorandum to all employees, announcing the program in general terms. Within twenty-four hours, every person affected was notified personally by a supervisor. Professional counselors were on hand for those who wished it.

The execution went flawlessly, but was still an execution. The reaction was numbness, then incredulity, and finally anger. Those who'd agreed that something needed to be done, those who would benefit from a leaner organization, those who would now be thrown into new jobs with commensurate opportunities and compensation, all were frozen. The consultants, Brett Halliday and Shannon O'Keefe, had prepped Dan and Lou to anticipate this: survivors' guilt syndrome.

For weeks, it was fire and ice.

Dan hoped that, when the battlefield was cleared, it all would have been worthwhile, that he'd live to enjoy the firm's resurrection from its ashes.

Well, today was D-Day for the final three impacted by the downsizing. By Monday, Brian Palmer, Walter Donohue and Margo Stern would be gone.

The decision to terminate Margo, Jake and Minnie's granddaughter, was the toughest of all, and unrelated to the study. It was as convenient a time as any for Dan to deal with a nagging personnel problem. He was sure that Jake Stern would have supported it. Once, when Jake had fired an older attorney for incompetence, Dan had told him: "I think you'd fire your own grandmother, if she couldn't cut it, Jake."

"Damn right," he'd said. "Lucky for her, though, she's dead." They'd had a good laugh.

Margo Stern had come highly recommended three years ago. Top tenth of her graduating class at New York Law School. She'd aced the Bar Exam first time. Street-smart, aggressive, and addicted to work. In the last year, though, she'd also become addicted to vodka. Margo's legal research, once thorough, was now scattershot. Her briefs, once the best of any associate, had often been used with little or no change. No more. There were still many peaks in her performance, but there was slipshod work as well. She was often in a dreamlike state. Once it was hard to get Margo Stern out of the office. Now, her attendance was sketchy, her hours, irregular.

Several attempts at counseling had produced a temporary improvement, then another plateau, followed by a dip worse than before. Margo Stern would admit to no problem. Without that, there was no solution. Performance reviews, once superior, were now barely satisfactory. Vince Patten, her boss, did not see her as a future partner in the firm; nor did anyone else.

Dan had talked to her personally, once Patten delivered the news of her termination. He'd put the best face on it: a clean slate, and the rest. She barely acknowledged what was happening, took no opportunity to afford herself outplacement assistance or counseling, and began coming into work on time, every day, and staying late.

Dan had talked with Minnie Stern, Jake's widow, to express his concern. "She's in denial, Minnie. She's got to move forward."

"What can I do, Dan? I can't fire a grandchild. Don't worry. This may be the jolt she needed. She'll come back. She's done it before." Dan wasn't so sure, but, with the welter of things on his plate, pushed it out of his mind.

Now, the bloodletting was over. Horgan & Stern could get on with its business, recapture past glory. He put on his jacket and trench coat, wished his executive assistant Jacqueline Sheppard a good weekend, and left for home.

6

....

Two hours later, Lou De Femio was preparing to leave the office.

At forty-nine, Lou was a hefty, olive-complexioned man with dark hair flecked with gray. A meticulous and conservative dresser, he had a no-nonsense demeanor that often reminded Dan Horgan of Jake Stern. Had Dan Horgan not known Lou before Jake died, he'd have bet that Lou had been Jake in a former life.

Tonight, he walked down the pinewood-paneled hall, knocking softly on the open door of Margo Stern's office. Margo was just over five feet tall, and her raven curls were barely visible behind a foot-high pile of papers. "Just stopped by to wish you luck, Margo. You'll land on your feet. You're a first-class lawyer. Remember that."

Margo gave him what Lou later described to Dan as "a spaced-out look, like I was the Loch Ness monster," and responded confidently: "Oh, I'll be here Monday, Lou. In fact, I'll be working this weekend. Dan has one of those complicated merger deals coming up. I promised him an outline of our client's options. It's half done, not something I can turn over to someone else."

Lou knew it wasn't so, that this was still another

delaying tactic. How often had he told Dan that Margo Stern would have to be ushered out by the security guards? Well, Dan would have to deal with this one himself on Monday. Lou was tired of playing hatchet-man. More than once he'd heard the office gossip. "Dan hires; Lou fires." "Dan promotes 'em and Lou demotes 'em." *Basta!*

He waved good-bye and left her office.

....

Down the hall, Brian Palmer was removing a few final things from his workstation. He still found it hard to believe he'd been terminated. Fifteen years ago Brian had been hired at Horgan & Stern right out of Columbia. Law Review, top quarter of his class. But Brian couldn't pass the Bar exam. Three tries and you're out was the standard. After coming close the first time, he took a cram course. The second outing he lost track of time, barely completing eighty percent of the questions. By the third, his brain was so muddled with information overload that he froze completely, leaving before the exam was over.

Ordinarily that would have meant "resignation by mutual consent." But along the way, Brian had picked up another skill: computers. Long before anyone else in a law office knew much about them, he'd spotted the opportunities. After his third failure at the Bar exam, he'd gone to Jake Stern and proposed a short-term trial for himself as a systems analyst. Jake said he'd think about it overnight. Allowing Brian to stay, even temporarily, would set a precedent. Who got a shot at a fourth strike in baseball? Besides, Jake had no patience with intelligent people with no drive. There had to be standards! He never bought into the "poor test taker" excuse. Brian crammed only before an exam, and his work hours were shorter than most. Around the office, his nickname was "LIFO." Last in, first out.

But Jake had read in the professional journals about new efforts to streamline office administration through computers. He had never had any interest in gadgets, and had none now in technology. He did watch office expenses like a hawk. As the business grew, so did overhead. Maybe it was time to give automation a shot.

The next day, he spoke to Brian and offered him a six-month reprieve, promising to support his efforts. That was all Brian needed.

He remembered that time as hell on earth, with fourteen-hour work days and seven-day work weeks. The attorneys treated him as a failed lawyer, a mechanic. What relevance could newfangled machines have to their hallowed profession?

Secretaries and support staff pegged him as a threat to their own job security. There was even talk of bringing in a union. Brian got Jake Stern to make a commitment: no one would lose a job to automation. Overstaffing would be managed through attrition.

That won over a few adventuresome secretaries and paralegals. Brian worked tirelessly with them. He pushed, pulled, bribed and cajoled until they realized how routine functions could be automated; how long, boring boilerplate contracts and other documents could be produced in a fraction of the time; how legal research could be accelerated through LEXIS and other information retrieval systems. Overtime costs were reduced and people actually got to take lunch hours.

Before long, Horgan & Stern had a reputation for being on the cutting edge of technology, a place where talented lawyers and support staff wanted to work, where clients could count on superb work delivered on time. Business increased dramatically and profits soared by 50 percent, after inflation, in a three year period.

Brian's six-month trial was extended indefinitely. He fell comfortably into the role of office nerd. His own reputation grew and he'd been invited to speak at several Bar Association meetings on the subject of law and technology. Years passed and thoughts of the Bar exam receded.

Then Jake Stern died. He'd been more than a supporter of Brian's. Jake was his godfather in the firm; the person to whom he could go for funding or support on still another leap into the future. In spite of Brian's achievements, change still brought fear to people. With the business recession of the early 90s, the firm's partners were no longer willing to guarantee job security. And Dan Horgan was no Jake Stern. He was always cordial to Brian, appreciative of his successes, but he'd removed himself from daily operations.

Whoever got to see Dan Horgan first got what he

wanted. That was usually a partner, never a lowly systems analyst. And partners built fiefdoms. Brian Palmer, mechanic, threatened their turf.

Last winter, when Dan Horgan had hired a management consulting team, Brian thought the tide had turned. What better chance for professionals to see what needed to be done? He was open with them, acknowledging that the firm's technology was no longer cutting edge; that duplication existed; that equipment was incompatible.

With hindsight, he realized he'd been naive. He'd told the consultants what the problems were, then saw them parroted as their own conclusions. He felt that he wasn't the first messenger to suffer the consequences. If systems were faulty, why did you need a systems analyst? And even if you did, this one was not up to the job. There were hackers out there who were younger, smarter, and really "state-of-the-art." What's more, they'd work for half of Brian's salary. Lou De Femio had given him the news, laying out a severance package and outplacement services. That was in August, three months ago. In a half hour he'd walk out of Horgan & Stern an ex-employee. Who would hire a man just turned forty? An average man at that: medium build, a bit shy, prematurely balding. A gay man with an HIV-positive lover.

And not even a good-bye handshake from Dan Horgan. "Fuck 'im," said Brian to himself.

....

On the ground floor, Mailroom Supervisor Walter

Donohue was checking that all outgoing packages were out before the weekend. There was a time when that simply meant working through the post office. Now there were all sorts of new methods: domestic priority mail, global priority mail, express mail, Federal Express, Air Express, UPS, same day delivery, the works.

Decisions, decisions.

What was next? A service to get the mail there before it was sent? Now there's an idea! Maybe he'd become an entrepreneur, start his own service. Call it YDS, Yesterday Delivery Service. The thought made him smile.

Walter's assistants Myrna Scheflin and Conan Kelly had invited him out for a farewell toast at Rosie O'Grady's, a local watering hole. He'd said no.

Even without a drink, he felt light-headed. Damn it anyway. What did he expect of an out-of-shape sixty-eight year old who was suddenly useless?

Long before the axe fell, he'd contemplated retiring. But that was different. Then, he'd have called the shots. Now, having given the best years of his life to Horgan & Stern, he was being tossed out like an old shoe.

He tried to think positively. For the first time in his life, he wouldn't have to rise at six o'clock. His Bronx cronies were always telling him about the pleasures of retirement: traveling, fishing, playing cards and checkers in Williamsbridge Oval, going to the library, babysitting for grandchildren, watching them grow up.

Well, he was happiest "staying put." Even as a

boy in Belfast, he'd thought fishing was cruel. As for the rest, well, they might be good weekend activities, but a man's work was his life. Was it Camus who said that "when work is soulless, life dies?" He thought so. His job in the mailroom might not have been much to others. To him, it was life. The lawyers might do all the brainy work, but without him, it never went anywhere. More than once, hadn't Jake Stern told him he'd "saved the day" by pulling out all the stops?

Once the ball carrier at Horgan & Stern, he'd be just another old guy filling up a park bench, drawing a Social Security check.

Walter took one final walk around the mailroom. Then, as he'd done every night since they'd been married, he telephoned his wife Edna at their Bronx apartment. "I'm leaving now; see you in an hour or so."

After putting out the lights, he walked out the door and trundled slowly to the Independent subway train across town. Who was he, anyway? A hulking old man without a job, without value.

When Walter was a boy in Ireland, his mother had read poetry to him. He still read poems, and some of his favorite lines came back to him at critical points in his life, like tonight when he waited for the traffic light at Sixth Avenue. He thought of that old whiner J. Alfred Prufrock, measuring life out "with coffee spoons." Make it decaf and that's me.

Yessir, just another old boyo whose work was done, wending his way home from the fields.

7

By 8:15, Edna Donohue was worried.

She'd looked out the window of her third floor apartment on Parkside Place in the Norwood section of the Bronx, just up from 207th Street. The streets were quiet, with no sign of Walter on this muggy November night.

Edna walked out to a cheerful yellow kitchen to turn down the oven. The pot roast was done, the potatoes roasted. String beans were cut and ready for the stove, and a mixed salad awaited tossing. Two cups of fresh shrimp cocktail were in the fridge, along with two bottles of Lowenbrau for Walter and chilled chablis for her. His favorite meal for this special night.

Edna had primped and even gotten a "do" in the beauty parlor today. Her mid-length naturally wavy gray hair had never looked better, she thought. And she had on Walter's favorite dress, a red designer number from Loehmann's. Three years old, it tugged at the middle just a bit. After the holidays, she and Walter could both eat right, slim down.

Then they could do things together, maybe take a few trips, take a course or two. She'd have to work on him a bit, first. Walter always said, "I hate change."

The walk to the subway usually took him about fifteen minutes. That should have gotten him home by 7:30 at the latest.

There were no reports of accidents or subway delays on TV or the radio.

Would anyone still be at Horgan & Stern? Edna didn't want to be a "nervous Nelly." At 8:30, though, she made the call. She got that nice Margo Stern. "She treats me like an equal, not like some of those other fancy-schmantzy lawyers who think mail room people are just off the boat," Walter had said.

Tonight, Margo promised to check with the Security Guard and call her back. Ten minutes later, she did. Walter had left the building at 6:10. They talked for several minutes; then Edna thanked her and hung up the phone slowly, pensively.

Sometimes, on Friday nights, he stopped off for "a small one" in the neighborhood. Not often, though, and even then, he was always in by eight. Should she call the police? Not yet. They had murderers and rapists to catch, not dilly-dallying husbands.

At nine, Edna telephoned her son Buddy, a Bronxville neurosurgeon. When the answering machine came on, she hung up.

She had just walked out to the kitchen to check the oven again when the doorbell rang. "Mrs. Donohue, it's Joey. Officer Joey Rodriguez, and my partner. May we come in?"

She looked out the peephole, and quickly opened the three locks on the door. Little Joey Rodriguez, whom Walter had taught to play baseball fifteen years ago, was now big Joey Rodriguez. Walter's and Edna's own son Buddy preferred chess to baseball. Joey had no father, so Walter had "pinch-hit" for him, often taking him to Yankee Stadium on 161st Street in the Bronx.

Now Joey stood at her door in the blue uniform of a New York City police officer. There was an older male cop with him, but Edna focused on Joey's kind, troubled face.

"It's Walter, Joey, isn't it? Something's happened to Walter!"

The two cops entered the door. Joey spoke quietly, a slight choking in his voice. "Yes, Mrs. Donohue. Please sit down." He ushered Edna to a fading, flowered sofa in her spotless living room. Her eyes were pleading.

"Mrs. Donohue," Joey began softly, "Walter had a massive heart attack on the train, near Fordham Road, on his way home from work. A fireman was on the train, and administered CPR. It was bad, though. He never came out of it. They got him to Union Hospital, but he was already dead."

A long pause. Then Edna simply nodded. "I knew in my bones something had happened. First, I've got to turn the oven off. Then I'll call Buddy."

Joey could see Edna in the hall dialing her son, who was now home. "Buddy, it's your father. He's gone, Buddy. Your father is dead." She dropped the phone and Joey heard her sobbing. He walked over and ushered Edna back to the sofa, where she wept on his shoulder.

His partner, Officer Ray Hawkins, picked up the phone and gave Buddy Donohue the details. Buddy would drive down to Union Hospital, identify the body, and make arrangements.

Joey then made Edna a cup of tea. She sipped it slowly. "Well, Joey, my man didn't have much of a retirement now, did he? And I won't have to worry about having him home for lunch, after all."

Joey smiled, and for a long time, the three sat there wordless, drinking tea.

8

"A slam-dunk, Babe."

Just before midnight on Friday, the door to the Rizzuto ground-floor apartment in Queens banged loudly.

Ida's husband Dom was shouting in the hallway: "Well, I nailed it good! Didn't I tell you last night's interview was a breeze? Kryhoski called this afternoon to offer me the Lake View job. Told him we'd move there within three to four weeks."

Ida had arrived home a short time ago from her three to eleven emergency room nursing shift at St. John's Hospital. A pot of coffee was perking on the stove, and she was about to bite into a grilled cheese and tomato sandwich.

Tonight, as usual, Dom's world revolved around himself. She hated it when he talked in sports analogies; it made her feel like a basketball. Calling her "Babe" was even worse; it was cheap and common. Ida could tell by his voice, and then by looking at him, that he'd been celebrating at Maury's, a local bar where Dom and his friends hung out, drank beer, watched "Monday Night Football," hockey and NBA basketball games, and made small bets. They hooted during the action, slamming huge paws on the bar when the home team scored. During the breaks, they told each other crude jokes and stories of how life had cheated them.

"Dom, you should have talked with me first."

"What's to talk about, Ida? Jobs like this in a great neighborhood, rent-free apartment and utilities, they don't pop up every day. You gotta take 'em when they come along. It's time for us to move up in the world."

"But Rudy's still in school, Dom. And then there's my job that I just happen to like. Our friends and family, all our roots are in the city." Ida was tense but firm, surprising even herself.

Dom was not in a listening mood. "The problem with you, Ida, is that you never want to take risks. You know what your tombstone will read? Born, Raised and Died In Queens. Is that what you want?" His voice was louder now. He was speaking faster, slurring his words.

"Dom, I want what's best for all of us, not just you and not just me. All of us, as a family."

"Shut up, Ida! You think I don't care about family? Didn't I agree to let you start up your career again? We'll talk details in the morning, Ida. I'm tired. But we're going! That's that. We're going! And now, I'm going to bed." And off he went.

Ida was tired, too, but wanted to wait until he was asleep. Dom was difficult to talk to, sober; when he was drinking, he was impossible. She read *The Daily News,* made out the week's shopping list, and poured a cup of coffee to help her think.

As a young girl, Ida had everything going for her. Only this fall, she'd gone to her 25th year high school reunion and someone had brought out a yearbook. There she was, prom queen, "Most Likely to Succeed," and headed for nursing school.

When she returned from the reunion, she'd gone to the mirror. What she saw surprised her, maybe because she was comparing herself to her classmates. The once bourbon-colored hair, worn shoulder length and straight, was now short and permed, with only a few shades of gray. Her strong, fine-boned face with a patrician nose was lined but still handsome. A five-foot, nine-inch body, once a sculptor's dream, was still firm after two kids. At her tenth high school reunion, a single friend has asked her if she "worked out," and Ida had said: "No, I work in."

"Oh, you have a personal trainer?"

"No, said Ida. "I work in, washing dishes and scrubbing floors."

At the reunion, she'd found herself confiding in an old friend, Claudia Golden. Ida hadn't seen her in five years, not since Claudia's messy divorce. Just before that, Claudia had looked like Cinderella in her pre-fairy godmother days. Now, she positively glowed. "Ida, it sounds dumb, but for years I thought it was me. Forget the fact it was Harry who was sleeping around, spending half his salary on tits and ass, neither of which were mine; that I had to work part-time just to pay the bills; that it was me who had to go to school every time one of the kids had a problem. When that dirtbag did come home for dinner, he expected to find House Beautiful with Kathie Lee Gifford at the door, and a golden goose on the dining room table. Goose, schmoose, I cooked his all right!"

Ida had listened in awe as her once mild-mannered friend continued: "What did you do, Claudia?"

"Well, first I joined a women's group and went for counseling. It sounds dopey, Ida, but on a scale of one to ten, my own self-esteem was minus five. Anyway, that gave me courage to ask Harry for a divorce. The schmuck acted hurt and shocked. He didn't fool me, though. His law firm is big on community service and Harry was getting ready to run for town supervisor. A divorce wouldn't suit his image. You know, they all gotta have pictures of the great one at home with loving wife and kiddies curled up by the fire."

"And so?"

Claudia beamed: "I hired a private detective, who followed Harry and got pictures. Lots of 'em. Wonderful Kodak moments, but not the kind Harry wanted to give out at the train station with his campaign literature. Floozies of every stripe. Got an uncontested divorce, alimony and child support. Good-bye Harry! I went back to college on the alimony, and now, would'ja believe it, I'm working on Wall Street as a broker!"

"Of course I'd believe it, Claudia, and I'm glad for you. I just wish I had your guts."

"Hey, Ida, who was it who scored the final jump shot for the state championship in '71? You! Hell's bells, you just gotta get out there and do it again!"

"Join the NBA?" laughed Ida.

"Of course not. But if Dom is still playing the gigolo and gambling his paycheck away, he'll never change. You've gotta do something, and soon."

"Like what?"

"Get counseling, for starters. I know, I know," added Claudia, seeing Ida's reaction. "Our generation was taught to work out our own problems. Well, look where that got Nicole Brown Simpson!"

"Hey, Claudia. Things aren't that bad. So far as I know, Dom sees himself as a ladies' man, but he's not running around. And I sure as heck have no time to!"

"So what's his problem?"

"Dom thinks he should have been born a mover and shaker, instead of a shoemaker's grandson. You wouldn't believe his ego. To keep it going, he lives beyond his means, beyond all our means! And lately, well, he's been drinking too much, even gambling a bit. The old story, first you're hot, then you're not."

Ida was embarrassed to mention that Dom had hit her a few times. She'd been brought up to believe that some things were best kept private. Besides, the morning after the last time it had happened (he'd come home with flowers), she'd placed them on the table and said: "Dom, no more. Next time, I'm leaving you." That had been five months ago and he hadn't touched her since.

"Why do you put up with it?" asked Claudia.

"Well, my job helps us to make ends meet. Even more, it gives me something for myself, a life apart from him. It's helped, but it's not the answer. Lately, part of my salary is going to pay off his gambling debts."

"And there's no end in sight?"

"Not even a fork in the road. If anything, the more he owes, the more he bets. Forget about college for our kids. Catherine moved out after high school, and is going at night. And Rudy will probably do the same thing in a few years. I wanted something better for them, Claudia."

"Look, Ida. You're not a kid anymore. If he won't help himself, he'll drag you into the poorhouse with him. You need to get help."

"And you've got just the person, right, Claudia?"

"Yup, the one who helped me work things out. Her office is in Westchester. A little drive from here, but you're less likely to run into your neighbors."

"Well, let me think about it. Give me her name and number, O.K?"

A week later, Ida had called and made an appointment with Ceecy Caruso Cohen. Since then, she'd seen her every other Saturday.

Ida finished the newspaper and coffee, shut off the TV, and went into the bedroom where Dom was snoring loudly. She'd talk with him in the morning, but was not hopeful. Whatever happened, she'd keep her therapist's appointment on Saturday.

The more she thought about it, the more she realized it was not just that Dom was out there slam-dunking, but that he treated her, an all-state center, like she wasn't even a bench-warmer.

9

Saturday was the week's first clear, blue-skied day in Bronxville. Shannon O'Keefe woke at seven, picked up *The New York Times* outside her apartment door, put on the coffee machine, and read. By eight, she'd showered and dressed. Living alone had many minuses and at least one plus: carte blanche to the bathroom.

She wondered if you could trace a family's history by studying its bathrooms. Hers might read, "In And Up From The Outhouse." When her grandmother had arrived from Ireland, she'd lived in a railroad flat, with one outside facility for several families. When Shannon was growing up in the Bronx, there were two adults, five kids and one bathroom in her parents' rented apartment. Marriage brought an upgrade with a one-family house in Riverdale, two adults and two kids. Two bathrooms.

Now she had one and a half all to herself.

It seemed a little obscene, when so many were homeless. She'd give a little extra money to O.K. Sampson, a bag lady on East 42nd Street, outside Grand Central. So what if O.K. shamelessly fingered Catholics and Jews, playing on their guilt?" It was easier than Confession.

Showered, dried, sprayed and dressed in a lemon jogging suit, she felt like an off-season daffodil. Ice cream colors had been fashionable last fall. This year, it was neutrals. Once, that would have influenced her wardrobe. No more.

She exited from Lake View's rear door, down a patch of brown grass to the graveled road that circled the Bronxville Lake. There were two pedestrian bridges, one at the lake's north end, just below the neighboring village of Tuckahoe, and one at the south, in Bronxville. She usually did about four slow laps.

A few years ago, a racing biker had shouted, "Coming through, on the left, granny!" She'd looked around for granny, and realized she was it. Not too long after, she dyed her graying hair back to its original brunette color.

Today, on her first lap, she was surprised when Dan Horgan passed her. Dan usually jogged shortly after sunrise, even on weekends. Now he waved and shouted, "See you later!" She nodded, having promised to stop up to his penthouse apartment for a pre-holiday drink tonight.

Better focus on jogging. Already there were bikers, in-line skaters, aerobic walkers, dog walkers and joggers, running mothers and fathers pushing three-wheeled baby strollers. A few happy children were racing small wagons and scooters, taking advantage of the unseasonable warm weather. There were just plain walkers, of course, but not a whole lot. Many of these early-morning buffs had

Walkmans, a few had beepers, some had both. On mild, sunny week-ends, you watched your flanks.

Shannon jogged without Walkman or beeper, wanting to escape the world, not connect with it. Simple things pleased her: the beautiful morning, her good health and new freedom. Reaching the north side of the lake and crossing the bridge, she turned south along the footpath that ran parallel to the Bronx River Parkway. Traffic was already heavy.

Looking up, she could see Lake View in the distance. The handsome slate building of 60s vintage was still a premier co-op. Its outer Tudor facade had been cleaned and washed down a few months ago. Freshly caulked terraces glistened in the early morning sun.

"A virtual kibbutz."

That had been her real estate agent's description of co-op living when she'd moved here. Shannon now had experienced both the "virtual" and the "kibbutz" parts.

The woman had gushed that "co-op living combines the best features of individual and joint home ownership." Shareholders own shares in the corporation, with title to their own apartments. They elect a Board and a managing agent to provide day-to-day services. "No muss, no fuss. Believe me, Lake View is *la crème de la crème.*"

The agent hadn't mentioned a couple of things, including the fact that each resident had a different idea of what was in the common interest. Then there were expectations, like the level of maintenance each was willing to pay for. The two were rarely the same.

And ownership was a double-edged sword. In the rented Bronx apartment of her childhood, the landlord was the common enemy. There was always too much heat or not enough; corridors were either too dark, or lit up like a discothèque. Stoops and back yards were either too kid-friendly or off-limits to children. The super was the conduit for most problems, but the landlord was arbitrator and judge.

Once, Shannon had met the landlord, and was surprised to find him soft-spoken, even kindly. Her mother had agreed, but suggested she not spread the word: "When we need an extra egg or run out of sugar, you knock on the neighbor's door, not the landlord's. No reason to upset the apple cart." The reasoning seemed convoluted at the time. What had apple carts to do with it?

Now she knew.

In a co-op, with everyone an owner, everyone was also a landlord. Walt Kelly's Pogo had it right: "We have met the enemy and it is us."

Since this was Shannon's first shot at living on her own, she'd evaluated all the alternatives. House? Condo? Co-op? Lease or buy?

Her skills in mechanics, electronics and the like were on a par with auto repair; not just limited , but nonexistent. Friends had taken courses at local colleges, and camped out at places like Home Depot. Now, many were trolling lumber yards and paint shops, hauling all sorts of things into mini-vans, jeeps, and trucks. Others were saving the earth, hunting down nurseries and garden supply stores, bamboo shoots, watering cans, and trowels. Regular Martha Stewarts, 1990 equivalents of the old nursery rhyme, "Mary, Mary Quite Contrary."

Shannon admired both Martha Stewart and her friends' resourcefulness, but had no desire to emulate them. Weeds, seeds, they were all the same to her. It wasn't just that she lacked the instincts of a gardener; she had no desire to become one.

Was she out of synch with the times? Probably. But then she'd felt like that often in her life, zigging when others were zagging. She'd returned to work outside the home when her twins were in nursery school, and left her permanent job when they were grown. She'd made tradeoffs along the way, but who had not? When Tony had left her, the twins were off at college and she had a career to fall back on. Overall, it had been a good life. Too late to change now, kiddo.

A co-op and Bronxville suited her needs. About six miles north of her first Bronx home, she'd visited there as a child with her father. They'd taken the train north on Sundays, then walked to the lake a few blocks west of Bronxville's mission-style station. After feeding the ducks, they'd stop for an ice cream or a soda before returning home.

Sweet memories. The peace and quiet of the lake area; the greenness of it all; the sense of neighborhood, and everything was within walking distance of Lake View—schools, hospital, church, shopping, library. The main business district was still on Pondfield Road, the other side of Metro-North's tracks. On one block was an 1890s-type pub, a health food store, a 1990s coffee bar and a nouvelle cuisine restaurant. There were more than a dozen eateries, several delis, and three bagel shops. Great takeout food for every ethnic palate. Shannon's friends were baking their own bread, cooking natural foods in woks, and mixing up tropical health drinks in blenders. Good for them. For her, takeout places were literally manna from heaven.

There was Food Emporium and CVS, a discount sundry store; and several small businesses, medical offices, and shops. With a dry cleaner on almost every block, there was simply no excuse for the rumpled look.

Bronxville was often defined by what it was not. There was Starbucks but no McDonald's or discount clothing store, no bargain shopping or sodium lights. It was simply an enclave of 6,000 people in one square mile, Norman Rockwell's America that had folded gently into the modern era. Even so, some joked that the next century here meant the twentieth, not the twenty-first century.

Most, not all residents, were upper-middle income. About half lived in private homes, the rest in apartments. Villagers were used to making news, not reading about it. They were also trying to hold on to the center, to balance civility and development, tradition and progress, business and community life.

A co-op offered Shannon the security and tax benefits of home ownership, without the hassle.

She'd liked Lake View from the beginning. It stood at the end of a cul-de-sac in a landscaped court, about two blocks from the main road, Pondfield Road West. The rear faced the Bronxville Lake, with superb views of the changing seasons, birds, ducks, squirrels, an occasional turtle or rabbit. A park surrounded the lake with benches for reading, grass for sunbathing.

A sign prohibited picnicking, feeding wildlife, and littering, among other things. Unless trespassers made complete nuisances of themselves, violations were ignored.

She'd been lucky enough to purchase in a buyer's market. Her third floor five and a half room apartment in the rear had two views of the lake, a master bedroom, den, living room, dining area, and eat-in kitchen. For the first time in her life, she'd bought a new refrigerator and dishwasher. Most women did these things when they were brides; she'd waited until her divorce. She'd even bought *Brides' Magazine* for tips on what to buy and where. Apart from product reliability, her main criterion was convenience. She still clung to that old Horn and Hardart's slogan "Less Work for Mother."

But learning about Bronxville and co-op living was mostly on-the-job. She'd once laughed out loud at the opening scene in the movie *Antonia and Jane.* Jane tells her therapist she thinks there's a book on how to function in life, and says, "I never got a copy."

Moving to a new place was a lot like that. Analytical as she was, she'd read copies of everything available. Real estate brochures featured Bronxville's Elizabethan homes on gentle knolls, condos and co-ops with nineteenth century charm and new world convenience, "life the way you've always imagined it." The library stocked books with history, facts, statistics. There were Chamber of Commerce pieces with glowing promotions of business, services, two colleges, the Bronxville School, and the arts.

Shangri-la.

And then there were newspapers. The local weekly had updates on government, crime, and development. Villagers wanted a broader tax base, but less industrialization; more services and parking, but less traffic. Noise was unwelcome; the most favored dogs were those who didn't bark. With low crime rates, moving traffic violations and "lewd acts" in the movie theater made the court report. Any business wanting to open in Bronxville battened down for vetting. One prospective merchant had thrown up his hands in disgust, midway through the process: "If they wanted to move the White House here, they'd demand a five-year environmental impact study."

The national media periodically pulled out the old Bronxville chestnuts: rich, tony, Waspy, conservative, exclusive, Republican. A village whose women's club had once rejected Rose Fitzgerald Kennedy for membership; where Rose's husband Joe had dallied with Gloria Swanson, conveniently living at the now-defunct Hotel Gramatan; where Jews, Italians, and people of color had once not been welcome.

Yes, but...

That was then, when the whole world was different. Now, there simply was no tome on day-to-day living. This was not a town where you knocked on a stranger's door and asked what it was like to live here. That you discovered for yourself.

Shannon O'Keefe found that she liked living here. If the Bronxville Lake area was not the Garden of Eden, it was close. If Bronxville was still working out some bumps, so was she.

The morning was warming up. One more lap around the lake and she'd return to her apartment, change, and meet her sister-in-law Ceecy for breakfast.

10

....

"Pondfield Lunch" coffee shop, three blocks west of Lake View, was open from early morning till midafternoon.

It was just outside Bronxville proper, in Yonkers, with an address in the Bronxville zip code. The local equivalent of the Cheers bar, with one difference. The owners didn't always know your name, but knew your order. Last year when a customer had been hit by a car, Shannon was greeted with: "Did you hear what happened to Grilled Cheese on Rye?"

The food was homemade and delicious, with prices so low you felt you were being subsidized. There was a wide variety of customers, young and old and everything in between; secretaries and truckers, nurses and postal workers, doctors and retirees. They sat, unrushed, on old-fashioned fountain stools that swiveled for group conversations; or at formica-topped tables.

The daily news analysis here was more insightful than PBS, and certainly funnier. Today, one customer was giving the U.S. Postal Service a report card. "How can they deliver the mail when they can't even print decent stamps? That Dorothy Parker was a lush and Elvis Presley a mess. Then they've gone and printed one guy's brother's picture, instead of his. Can you believe it?" A rhetorical question, if ever there was one.

Shannon found herself humming "Don't Be Cruel." A Saturday morning regular, she was known as "Scrambled on a toasted, seeded, buttered bagel." She guessed there were worse things for your epitaph, and it was certainly more chipper than Dorothy Parker's, "Excuse my dust." Coffee was in front of her even before she sat down in a small booth in the back. One day she'd shift to a corn muffin with the eggs, but not today. Why spoil a good thing? Besides, she'd have had to call ahead to stop the bagel en route to the toaster.

Shortly after nine-thirty, Ceecy Caruso Cohen arrived in her usual state, hyperventilating. A snug melon jumpsuit set off a stunning figure. Five feet, eight inches tall. Short, straight, black hair with a single dramatic white streak, dark brown eyes, large nose, and deep-throated, loud voice.

You wanted to evaporate when Ceecy ordered. Today, told there was still no wheat germ or herbal tea, she settled for a bowl of Shredded Wheat, skim milk, and decaffeinated coffee. Well, thought Shannon, at least she didn't order bean sprouts.

Ceecy talked nonstop about her life and problems for ten minutes. Her husband Arthur, a philosophy professor at Sarah Lawrence College, was planning a sabbatical to do research at Oxford in the spring semester: "He thinks maybe he doesn't have chronic fatigue syndrome, he's just sick of students," said Ceecy.

Shannon had once asked Tony, her ex-husband, how his sister kept her clientele. A psychiatric social worker, she seemed to have more problems than anyone else. "That's how," Tony had answered. "When patients hear all her problems, they forget their own."

Today, Ceecy paused for breath: "So, what's new at Lake View?" Her tone implied that anything would pale beside her own sagas.

"Well," said Shannon, "being on a co-op Board continues to be a blood sport. We've been threatened by an applicant the Board turned down. There's an ongoing battle with a shareholder who wants to set up a telescope on the roof, right in the middle of his neighbor's terrace. Oh, and we made an offer for the open super's job." Shannon gave a *Reader's Digest* version of the interview process. By the time she'd gotten past Max Schneible's appearance, Ceecy was cheering out loud.

Among other things, Ceecy Cohen was not just a feminist, but what her detractors often called a flaming, radical one.

"God, and I was beginning to think this town had skipped the 20th century completely. A woman building superintendent here? You gotta be kidding. They'd sooner have a Martian!"

"Well, maybe the guy with the telescope will see the Martian before he lands." With that, Shannon's voice trailed off before beginning again. "Ceecy, the woman who just came in, the one with the tool box. That's her. That's Max."

Max Schneible moved quickly past the two of them. The waitress ushered her to the restroom at the back of the shop. Returning, she refilled their cups and said to Shannon and Ceecy, "A little leak in the john, ladies. Max'll fix it in a jiff!"

"You've had her before?" asked Ceecy.

"Oh yeah, couple of years now. We got to know her when the Con Ed crew was repairing some pipes outside a while back. We had an emergency inside and she fixed it. You know how most plumbers tell you they have to go out for a special tool, then bill you for the time out? She missed that part of the course. She comes with all her equipment, and the thing's fixed for good."

"Omigod," said Ceecy. "All the equipment without the testosterone. What we've got here is the Second Coming. Alleluia!"

A quarter of an hour later, Max exited from the rest room, announced that the leaky faucet was fixed, and said good-bye. Eyeing Shannon, she said: "Hello again. I figured I wouldn't get the job first time out. One of these days I will."

"Of course you will," offered Shannon, after introducing her to Ceecy. "By the way, would you give me your number? I don't have a regular plumber."

"Sure," said Max, reaching into her shoulder bag and removing a business card for each of them.

"See ya, ladies." And with that, she was gone.

"Jeez," said Ceecy. "I can die happy. A woman plumber who brings all the tools, fixes the problem, and business cards to boot."

Shannon laughed. "Well, now you know what we rejected. I just wish I felt better about the guy we didn't. I have that Dr. Fell feeling about him."

"Who?"

"I was remembering the 17th century poem about that English Churchman:

'I do not like thee Doctor Fell,

The reason why I cannot tell;

But this I know and know full well,

I do not like thee, Doctor Fell.'"

Ceecy guffawed. "In other words, women's intuition."

"Whatever," answered Shannon, "though the poet was one of his students, Thomas Brown."

They finished breakfast and walked up front to the cashier. "My turn, Ceecy," said Shannon. A customer was just paying the bill for breakfast and a newspaper. Asked by the owner if he'd done the Jumble or Crossword puzzle, he shook his head.

"Then you don't have to pay for it. Just leave the paper there." The man did just that, and left, astonished but happy.

Out on Pondfield Road West, Ceecy turned to walk a half block to her car, and asked Shannon: "By the way, what's Fell's real name, the guy you hired?"

"Rizzuto. Dominic Rizzuto."

Ceecy's eyes glazed over. No words, just a pause and a thumbs-down gesture. Then she was off.

Shannon got the message. Somehow, in a professional capacity, Ceecy knew of Dominic Rizzuto.

Clearly, he was not a number "10," like his name-sake, Phil. More than likely, a zero.

Walking back to Lake View, she mused to herself: "Dr. Fell, you've served me well." She'd ask Dan if the reference checks were thorough, but lacked confidence that anything would turn up. Her own experience had shown that prior employers were reluctant to give out honest evaluations. No one wanted to risk a lawsuit. Rizzuto had probably come up squeaky clean.

Back in the apartment, she removed Max Schneible's business card from her pocketbook and filed it in her Rolodex. A good plumber was even harder to find than a good man.

11

....

After a day in the city, Dan Horgan stepped into his sixth floor penthouse apartment just after eight that Saturday night.

A long bar association lunch, too long, followed by a boring speaker. When it finally ended, he'd gone to the Museum of Modern Art on 54th Street to re-energize himself. It hadn't helped.

Now he heard someone talking to him. Damn answering machine.

"Dan, it's Margo. Margo Stern. Just wanted to let you know: I'm still at the office, working on a new development on the Meyers case. How about brunch tomorrow? I can fill you in and…"

He grabbed the phone. "Hello, Margo. I just came in the door."

"Great, so…"

"Margo, we've been through this before. It's over. OVER! Please leave the brief on Todd Fahey's desk, and he can finish it on Monday. Then get out of there! Yesterday was your last day. I wish you well, Margo, but you need a new start."

"Give me a break, Dan. Fahey's an asshole! I can run circles around him."

"Margo, I'll say this just one more time. Cut out

the stalling. Go home. Get your act together, then find another job. It'll be better for all of us."

"Like heck it will. Better for you, maybe. What about me? You owe me!"

"Yes, and the firm has paid off, Margo."

"Dan, please listen…"

"Margo, I'm hanging up now. Good-bye."

"You'll regret this, Dan."

He hung up the phone, went to the mini-bar in his living room, poured a couple of fingers of Chivas Regal over ice cubes, and sipped it slowly. Returning to the hall, he picked up the phone and dialed Security at his office.

"Charlie, it's Dan Horgan. If Margo Stern hasn't left by ten, please escort her out of the building. Be sure she hands in her ID and keys."

"Will do, Mr. Horgan."

"One more thing, Charlie. As soon as she leaves, get the locks changed on all the doors."

"Fine. How about the computers?"

"Done deal, Charlie. At midnight, Margo, Brian Palmer and Walter Donohue will no longer have access. The new passwords kick in. I'm sure they won't return, but let's follow normal security procedures."

"O.K., Mr. Horgan. Have a good night."

God Almighty, thought Dan, what trivia we spew out to each other. "Yeah, you too, Charlie."

He sipped the rest of his Chivas, removed a chicken dinner from the freezer, and stuck it in the microwave. While it was heating up, he walked over to his Yamaha baby grand. A Silent Series model. He played Schumann's *Traumerei*, softly and with great feeling. Once, Jake had played its haunting melody of childhood on the violin, with tears in his eyes.

What a world. Jake got his highs from Schumann, his granddaughter Margo from booze. And then there was Schumann, a melancholy genius, dead at forty-six.

A bell signaled that dinner was ready. "We're all connected," they say. Yeah, by the bell from a microwave, grind of a fax, the click of a mouse. Christ, if Schumann were alive today, he'd have killed himself at thirty-six. He rose from the bench and walked to the kitchen. Back to the living room for dinner on a TV table. Once upon a time, it was "a chicken in every pot," he mused. Now, it's chicken in a fiberboard box. Still, it tasted good.

Eating cheered him, and by the time he'd cleaned up, he was again in good humor.

And Margo was right about Todd Fahey. Phi Beta Kappa from Michigan, Yale Law School, and an asshole. But not a drunk. No, not that.

Well, the downsizing was over. Now, if only his other problem were as simple.

The phone rang again. He'd screen the call, having had enough of Margo for one night. "Dan, it's Lou here. Got some bad news."

He picked it up. "Hi, Lou. Margo's been on my case, and I figured it was her again."

"Yup, I understand. I'm calling about Walter.

Walter Donohue. A heart attack last night on the subway. He didn't make it."

A pause. Then, "Lord, Lou, he once said that he'd be carried out of the mailroom, feet first. I wish he'd had a few happy years with Edna. Are the funeral arrangements set?"

"Yes. A traditional Irish wake. Three nights beginning tomorrow, seven to nine, at McKeon's Funeral Home, Perry Avenue in the Bronx. The Mass is Wednesday at ten, at St. Brendan's."

"O.K., Lou. Thanks. That's Shannon O'Keefe's old neighborhood. She'll give me directions. I'll probably hit the wake tomorrow night. Wednesday I'll be on the coast for Thanksgiving with Chip."

"Right. We've got a network of people calling everybody at the office to let them know."

"Thanks, Lou. What would I do without you?"

"Hey, don't ask. I might tell you and you'd have to double my bonus," answered Lou.

Dan had just hung up the phone when Shannon rang the doorbell. He ushered her into the living room and walked over to the bar to pour two glasses of white wine.

"Every time I visit you," she began, "I get a complex about my own place. Yours is so neat. All those modern prints on the wall, sparkling furniture, everything in its place. Disgusting."

He smiled. "Thanks to Rosa. Even with her working part-time with Minnie these days, she manages to keep me shipshape."

"How's Minnie doing?" she asked. Jake Stern's widow had fallen and broken her hip several weeks ago; Rosa Di Carlo, Dan's housekeeper, had been helping her out.

"Well, you know Minnie. She's anxious to be on her own again. For now, she and Rosa are a happy couple. Actually, Minnie's doing better than her granddaughter." He told her about Margo's call and then about Walter Donohue's death.

"I'm really sorry about Walter, Dan. And Margo, what a waste. I was hoping that losing her job would force her to move on, get her act together. I don't have a lot of faith that Fahey will have that brief on his desk on Monday, do you?"

"No."

"Dan, change of subject. Did Rich Kryhoski offer Dom Rizzuto the super's job yet?"

"Yes, and he accepted on the spot. He'll start around mid-December and move his family sometime after the New Year."

"Oh."

"Why do I think you've got this guy pegged as a lemon? Is there something you're not telling me?"

She hesitated a moment. "No, maybe it'll work out. Listen, time for a concert. Play something cheerful," she asked him, pointing to the piano.

"O.K., how's this?" And he proceeded to play a Dixieland jazz version of "The Old Wooden Cross." Then, Shannon asked him if he knew any Scriabin, and he nodded.

What he played was a piece by Scarlatti, not Scriabin. Still, it was lovely. Halfway through, he stopped and looked up: "Sorry, I've just drawn a blank on the rest of it."

"Half a loaf is better than none," she joked. "Thanks. You play so well."

He was pleased. "Now it's a hobby. Once I thought of making a career of it. My father convinced me that the law was more lucrative. There's no doubt about that, but sometimes I wonder What If?"

"Well, we could use a music store in Bronxville. Why don't you open one up when you retire?"

He smiled: "I'm just not sure there's a big enough market for that kind of music, even here."

"Oh, I don't know," Shannon answered. "I can see the store window now: GREAT HITS FROM THE S & M CROWD: Scriabin and Mozart, side by side with Spice Girls and 10,000 Maniacs."

"The village gentry would have a field day," he laughed. "But you're right. It's all in the marketing."

They talked for another hour or so; then Shannon got up to leave. "Oh, I'd like to go to Walter Donohue's wake tomorrow night," she said. "I was fond of him, and it's in my old neighborhood."

"Great. How about meeting me in the lobby at about seven? I'll drive; you can navigate, find us a parking spot."

"Sounds good."

Dan kissed her on the cheek and said goodnight. Then he ambled back to his Silent Series baby grand, put on his earphones, and plugged in the digital feature. Hester Harrington might not appreciate music at this hour.

He played a medley of Irving Berlin, George Gershwin, Cole Porter, Thelonius Monk, and Duke Ellington. As Saturday turned to Sunday, only he heard the familiar strains from days long past.

12

....

"Sure'n, doesn't he look grand?"

On Sunday night, Walter Donohue was being waked at McKeon's Funeral Home on Perry Avenue in the northwest section of the Bronx, a few blocks above Mosholu Parkway.

The question was addressed to Shannon and Dan by Nan O'Brien, who was moving away from the open casket. Nan was the cleaning woman in Horgan & Stern's law offices on Park Avenue. Befitting her station, she was decked out in her Sunday best: navy dress, black pumps, hat cum veil.

"Yes, Nan. It's sad, but he's at peace now." Dan grasped Nan's hand and the two shared a look at the body.

Shannon wanted to scream, "How can he be grand? He's dead!" She didn't. This was an Irish wake. The living recited the litany for the dead, their final good-byes. Before the evening was over, she would hear echoes of the phrases she'd first heard as a child when her grandfather had died:

"Ah, it's himself, all right."

"The casket, just lovely."

"Will ye look at that fine suit? And still a full head of hair!"

"And the white handkerchief in the pocket. Walter always wore a handkerchief on Sunday."

"The Missus is holding up pretty well, don'tcha think?"

"Have ye ever seen so many flowers? Saints preserve us! Even more than Mick O'Grady, and he was a councilman!"

"Good luck, Walter. Put in a good word for me up there, will ye?"

"At least he didn't suffer." Had Walter died after a long illness, the line would have been, "At least there was time to say good-bye."

Shannon knelt and said a short prayer. The "Missus," at least she guessed that was Edna Donohue, was the woman in the center of a large group of mourners off to the right of the casket. When the crowd cleared a bit, Shannon and Dan approached her.

Edna's face bore marks of sudden tragedy; hazel eyes had receded deep into their sockets and her mascara was streaked. Her handshake was firm, however, and she held her stocky, compact body ramrod straight. A white-collared navy blue dress was well cut, and her gray hair was combed in an attractive style. The voice that greeted them was cordial and strong: "Thank you for coming."

Edna Donohue reminded Shannon of feisty Irish and Irish-American women she'd known, of those in Synge's plays, of no-nonsense Earth Mothers played by Colleen Dewhurst, Maureen O'Hara and Brenda Fricker.

Now, Edna introduced them to the very tall, matchstick-slim, dark-haired man at her side. Later, Dan would remark that the man's narrow, long face reminded him of an Alberto Giacometti bronze figure. There was an otherworldly quality about the eyes and face. He looked about forty, and judging by the cut of his carefully tailored gray suit, very successful. "This is Tim, our son," said Edna. "We call him Buddy."

The nickname seemed ill-suited. Buddy was polite but cold.

"It's Dr. Donohue, right?" offered Dan. "Your father was very proud of you."

"He was the best," said Buddy. "Excuse me, but I see a couple of cousins who just came in." Shannon got out a quick "Nice meeting you," but Buddy Donohue had already moved away. She saw no new arrivals at the door.

"He's a neurosurgeon," said Edna, smiling wanly. "Walter always said they're better with people when they're sedated. But he's always been a good son."

"Of course," said Dan, as he and Shannon moved back to allow others to talk to her.

The Horgan & Stern crowd, present and past, was there in full bloom: several attorneys including Lou De Femio and his wife Nina; several secretaries and technicians; the entire mailroom staff; even Brian Palmer, his companion Reed James, and the drone Todd Fahey, who would pick up Margo Stern's work.

Then there was Margo herself, whom Dan had to acknowledge looked sober and well put together. She attempted to corner him and continue discussing the brief she'd been working on. He cut her off quickly. "Not here, Margo. Call me."

Bad move. He should not have encouraged further contact, but Walter Donohue's wake was not the place to square off with Margo Stern.

After a while, Shannon moved away from the group to greet some old friends and neighbors. That was one thing about growing up in the Bronx. Even if you had not seen a friend in twenty years, you could still finish each other's sentences. "It's not the same, Shannon," more than one said tonight. "All the old things are gone. The new people are not like us."

"They threw away the model, right?" she joked. Shannon had loved growing up in the Bronx, and enjoyed returning there. But long ago, her mother had said that you need to move on in life, remember the good times, but look for joy where you are, not where you were. One of the things that had attracted her to Bronxville was that, in many ways, it reminded her of the Bronx, a sense of neighborhood and community.

Tonight, though, was for reminiscing and laughter and memories.

Just before nine, Dan approached and the two said good-bye to Edna Donohue. Buddy was nowhere to be seen, so they left.

The muggy late autumn night had turned chilly and a soft rain was falling. It didn't help Dan's spirits. Shannon felt that he wanted her to say, "It's not your fault. The layoff had nothing to do with Walter's heart attack. It was just his time to go."

She said nothing, and they talked little on the drive home. Too many downsizings had resulted when top executives had over-reached, basked in high pay and perks, overhired, underplanned, whatever. They were quick to act when the rank and file screwed up. Those who'd mismanaged the business were harder to nail.

But people like her had work because companies needed help to reduce staff, and to minimize the legal and business risks in doing it. Lately there was a new buzzword: corporate anorexia. The same experts who'd recommended downsizing were now consulting companies that had cut back too far.

Consultants were the Willy Lomans of the 90s, peddling their wares in a global marketplace, and she was one of them.

No, she didn't think that Horgan & Stern had killed Walter Donohue, but they'd robbed him of a bit of his life spirit.

Let God judge. She would not indict Dan Horgan, but how could she comfort him? She could not even comfort herself on this gloomy November night.

13

On Monday, Dan Horgan arrived in a teeming rainstorm in the lobby of his Park Avenue office.

Terry Hackett, the weekday security guard, assured him that all had gone quietly over the weekend. "Oh, Charlie left me a note. Said to tell you that Margo Stern stopped by last night and wanted to go upstairs. When Charlie said no, she left a package for you. I gave it to Jackie when she came in today."

"Thanks, Terry."

Upstairs, Jacqueline Sheppard, Dan's executive assistant, was already at work. He passed her workstation, waving good morning. Jacqueline was a late 30s light-skinned African-American woman with stunning looks, style, brains, and ambition. In June, she'd complete her paralegal studies; in the fall, she was headed for law school.

On top of Dan's huge Chippendale desk was Margo Stern's brief. He read it through carefully, awed by its structure, research and logic. A superb product. Should he telephone and thank her? Better not. Margo would see that as amnesty, an invitation to return. He was not confident he'd say no. Let Lou De Femio call her later in the week, when Dan had left town.

Jackie came in with plane tickets for Chicago where depositions would be taken in a product liability suit. "Don't forget, Mr. H., the plane leaves today at three, from La Guardia. Remember, you're going to Chicago."

"Yeah, yeah, I know. And I leave Chicago Wednesday morning for San Francisco." He looked up and Jackie was grinning. She'd given him tickets several weeks ago for a La Guardia flight to Dallas. He'd made the flight in time, but called from Cleveland. Said he'd gotten on the wrong plane, and the flight attendant hadn't checked his boarding pass.

Today, after making a few business calls, he walked around the floor, stopping in the mailroom to offer condolences to Walter Donohue's staff. They'd bonded in what could only be called a deep funk.

"See you at the Mass on Wednesday, Mr. Horgan?" asked Myrna Scheflin.

"I'd like to, Myrna, but I've got a court date in Chicago that can't be changed. Will be there in spirit, though."

Myrna said nothing and he left. "Court date, my eye," she mumbled to Tyrone Ferrer, mail clerk. The two had mailed out the material for the depositions and knew they'd be taken in Chicago tomorrow, Tuesday. "If he wanted, he could fly back and leave after the funeral on Wednesday for San Francisco. If that bub hadn't laid off poor Walter, his heart might still be tickin'. Mr. High and Mighty just can't face it." Her co-workers nodded agreement.

Who cared what the higher-ups called it? Voluntary retirement, downsizing, rightsizing, outplacing, regrouping, restructuring, repositioning, repotting, or whatever. To Myrna and her staff, it all came down to the same thing. "More for them, less for us."

"Yeah, but we ain't got no fun," added Tyrone.

And that was that from the mailroom.

14

....

On Tuesday there were six; by Wednesday morning, there was not a squaw in sight.

On Thanksgiving Eve, Luke Plisky was facing a crisis with his fifth graders who were scheduled to put on the school's holiday play at ten. For weeks now, six girls had cast themselves as Indian squaws to commemorate the first Thanksgiving. Now, with showtime less than two hours away, Miranda Brown has arrived early to announce, "squaw is an ethnic slur, and I'm not gonna be one. No way." Miranda was a hefty, brown-eyed intelligent child of eleven, going on twenty-one. Tomorrow's Lani Guinier, not today's Pocahontas.

Luke had helped his class research the history of Thanksgiving and write its own play. Every holiday presented teachers with a unique challenge: how to celebrate the event without offending some student, parent, administrator, clergyman, community activist, civil liberties watchdog, or just plain busybody. Charlotte Weiss had drawn the school play assignment for Columbus Day. Her third graders had deftly managed not to alienate Italians, Spanish, or Native Americans. When Charlotte allowed the children to choose the music, she was not surprised with their choice: "Row, Row, Row your Boat."

The Thanksgiving play should have been a breeze.

It was, until Miranda Brown had taken her stand. When Miranda followed that up by saying she would now be an Indian brave, the other five squaws said they would be, too. At this, Frankie Micelli shouted out: "Mr. Plisky, how can they be braves, ya know what I mean, like they ain't even got no…"

Luke held up his hand, considering whether to first correct Frankie's grammar or his manners, when Miranda interrupted: "That's what you know. Lots of girls play boys on the stage, right, Mr. Plisky?" Luke nodded wearily. Given the nearness of the opening (and closing) performance, he was not anxious to discuss the history of theater or transgender issues.

But Frankie still had a practical problem: "So what's gonna happen to all the little papooses if there be no squaws?" What indeed.

Li Wang, a slim, dark-haired child, raised his hand: "What's the big deal? Why don't we all just be whatever we wanna be? It's all make-believe, anyway, like in the movies. Whoever wants a papoose can just grab one," said Li, pointing at the "prop table," where six rag dolls wrapped in brown bags were piled up on their sides.

Saved by Li. It was quickly agreed that the actors, boys and girls, could be whatever they wished, pilgrims or Native Americans, white, brown, yellow or even kiwi. They would all speak about what Thanksgiving meant to them and to their families. Call it performance art.

The play, retitled "A Virtual Thanksgiving," drew a standing ovation. Li Wang, with two papooses on his back, drew the loudest cheers of all.

At lunch, Harry Reeber congratulated Luke, and asked if he'd consider serving as creative adviser for Harry's fourth graders' play in December. "Harry," he answered, "remember that old line about how you get to Carnegie Hall?"

"Sure. Practice, practice, practice."

"Don't," said Luke. "A waste of time."

15

....

"Bless this house, O Lord we pray."

On Wednesday morning, while Luke Plisky was mediating the details of the Thanksgiving play, Walter Donohue was undergoing his final rite of passage. The Mass of the Resurrection was being sung by Father Sean O'Grady at St. Brendan's Church on East 207th Street, three blocks north of McKeon's Funeral Parlor.

Father O'Grady was young, reverent, red-haired, and silver-voiced. "A darlin' boy and a grand voice to boot," proclaimed the older Irish ladies in the parish. More like a "golden boy," thought the pastor; collections were always up at Father O'Grady's Mass. A Bishop in the making, this lad.

The young curate prided himself on his homilies, though he was known to take poetic license. Funerals brought out the best in him. Today, he'd pirated his verse from the English poet John Keats' "Ode to Autumn." Had the ladies known that, the darlin' boy's star might have dimmed just a bit. Happily, they did not.

Walter Donohue had been a Church usher, Korean war veteran, Rotary Club man, Boy Scout troop leader, member of The Friendly Sons of St. Patrick, and the church choir. Contingents from all those groups filled the Church, along with his friends from the Greentree Bar and Grill and the checkers club in Williamsbridge Oval. The choir was at its best for one of their own, beginning with a spirited "How Great Thou Art" as the casket was wheeled down the aisle. Behind it walked Edna Donohue, dignified and dry-eyed, on the arm of her son, Tim; then, Tim's wife Diane, holding the small hand of a slight, curly-haired girl about five, followed by two teenagers, a boy and a girl. A group of three dozen other family members and close friends followed, filling the front rows of the church.

Shannon had told her boss Burke Parker that she'd be attending the funeral, and would work from noon till eight that night. Parker was a drone, but knew a good thing when he saw it. Shannon did the work of two people. "No problemo," he'd said.

She'd taken a taxi for the six-mile trip south from Bronxville and sat now in an aisle seat in the middle of the Church. By ten o'clock, when Mass began, several of the Horgan & Stern group had joined her: Lou De Femio, a couple of young attorneys, the mailroom staff, Brian Palmer, and Reed James. Midway through the service, Margo Stern arrived. She was elegantly dressed in a mid-weight forest green suit, jewel-necked beige sweater, matching accessories and simple gold jewelry. Shannon recognized the suit as an Anne Klein creation. Margo's gait was steady, her eyes clear. She appeared poised and rested.

Whatever their own beliefs, mourners traditionally work hard to act ecumenical and follow the prescribed ritual at funerals. At Catholic requiems, there is usually a take-charge woman parishioner seated near the front, who will stand, kneel, and sit just a second before the appropriate moment in the liturgy. A cue to the congregation to fall in line. Today, Edna Donohue herself orchestrated this ritual. Good for you, Shannon thought. A gutsy woman, a survivor.

The choir sang traditional hymns: "Amazing Grace," "Panis Angelicus," and Shannon's own favorite: "Let There be Peace on Earth." She'd always thought that John Lennon's "Imagine" was the secular version, and she loved that one too.

Father O'Grady gave the final blessing in his lilting baritone voice: "May the angels lead you into paradise." He then extended the family's invitation to all to join them in the ride to Woodlawn Cemetery, and back to the Greentree Restaurant for lunch. Turning, he led the casket and procession of family and friends down the aisle.

Walter Donohue's casket was carried out on the pallbearers' shoulders, not wheeled out on the dolly. Walter was a large man, and just as the procession started down the aisle, a rather small undertaker stumbled under the heavy load. "Bedad, if he's not dead yet, he will be soon with this bunch," whispered an elderly gent to his wife. For which he received a not-so-gentle poke and a "Shhhh…that's the way Walter wanted it. He always said they'd carried him into the Church in the old country at baptism. The least they could do was carry him out of it in the new one, at the end."

A flutist played "Danny Boy." Was it Chesterton who said that Gaelic songs were so sad and their wars so funny? Shannon thought so. After this one, no one was left dry-eyed.

Outside, the day was uncommonly beautiful and the multi-ethnic neighborhood stirred with happy activity. But, Shannon thought, didn't the sound of life always seem sweeter after a funeral?

The procession of cars lined up behind the hearse, and left for the trip to Woodlawn Cemetery, a few miles north. There, Walter would be laid to rest within walking distance of Herman Melville and F. W. Woolworth. Not too far away were Irving Berlin, Fiorello La Guardia, Bat Masterson, Miles Davis, and George M. Cohan.

Some joined the funeral brigade; others returned home, many to telephone no-shows and give them a full report. A large group of Edna Donohue's Leisure Club friends headed to McDonald's for coffee to review the affair, before heading up to lunch at the Greentree. By tonight, outfits and floral wreaths would be vetted anew.

The consensus was that Walter had gone out in style. "We gave him a fine sendoff," said one. Time to feed the living.

Shannon and Lou De Femio walked together across 207th Street and turned left on Bainbridge Avenue, toward the subway. "You know," said Lou, "maybe it's good that Dan couldn't make the service today. He might have taken that 'Danny Boy' finale to heart."

"Maybe," Shannon countered, "but my guess is that he might have thought they were singing it for him." Lou smiled. They were Dan Horgan's friends, but they also knew he was self-centered.

They left the sunlight and walked down the stairs, through the token booth and onto the subway platform. When the "D" train thundered in and opened its doors, they boarded and settled in for the short ride to Manhattan.

16

....

"Over the River and through the woods…"

On Thanksgiving night, Shannon was humming the old song, driving home from her daughter Maria's house in Scarsdale. It was close to midnight, with few cars out on Route 22.

She had not been looking forward to seeing her ex-husband Tony again. If he felt the same, it was not evident. He looked tired and older than his fifty-four years, when he kissed her on the cheek. Most of a thick unruly head of black hair was gone, and his six-foot frame now sported a definite paunch that even a well-cut blue Armani suit could not hide. "You look great, kid," he greeted her.

She smiled and said softly, "You don't look so bad yourself. How are things going for you?"

"Working most of the time."

"Ah, what a surprise!" But her voice was kind. This was not a day for old grievances. Carol Sherman, the young pediatrician he'd left Shannon for, was long since gone. If Tony was still trying to "find himself," there was no talk of it now.

Her son Ted had arrived in uniform. A New York City cop, he'd pulled a night shift, and left soon after dinner for his mid-Manhattan precinct. "Hey, this is a half day for me," he'd joked. "No classes."

Ted was attending St. John's Law School at night.

More and more, he reminded her of Tony and those early years of hospital internship and residency, years when long hours and constant fatigue only fueled his passion for healing. He would be a surgeon, the best in the country, and would spend one day a week offering care to those who could not afford it.

When did the fire die? Shannon was not sure. What she knew was that somewhere along the way, he'd seen that the real money was in cosmetic surgery, where wealthy clients (even then, they were never patients) were happy to pay whatever it took to restore youth and beauty. No need to depend on cheap and stupid insurance company bureaucrats, or, in recent years, managed care's gatekeepers. Soon Tony's entire practice was devoted to lifting chins, moving nipples and navels, tucking in tummies, removing aging spots and the like.

The recession that began in the late 80s, if anything, had opened up new markets for Dr. Anthony Caruso. Prior to then, most of his clients had been women. Now, many male executives who'd lost jobs in mid-career flocked to plastic surgeons to make them appear young and marketable.

What was wrong with this picture? Nothing at all, except that it was not what Shannon had signed on for. Carol Sherman's appearance on the scene had, in some ways, made her own separation and divorce less painful than it might otherwise have been.

Tony's idealism and passion had faded. Would Ted's as well? She hoped not.

Ah well, not a night for nostalgia. Just one for giving thanks for life's blessings. She'd had many. Maria's dinner had been superb. Shannon's son-in-law, Ken Albrecht, was his usual self, kind, attentive and dull. Ken was an actuary who fit the old description, "an accountant without the charisma." What did it matter? Maria and their son Drew adored him. Drew had hurdled "the terrible twos" at eighteen months, and had kept going. Now four, he was into chaos theory. His father already saw in him a future Fellow of the Society of Actuaries.

When Shannon got out of her car in Lake View's parking lot, Ralph Tierney, the night doorman, greeted her: "A good Thanksgiving, Ms. O'Keefe?"

"The best, thanks. Good night, Ralph."

....

Margo Stern's Thanksgiving was not the best.

Margo woke up at three o'clock in the afternoon in her small upper West Side apartment in Manhattan. She'd staggered in at four from a neighbor's holiday party, and fallen into an alcoholic stupor. Now, her head felt like a bass drum was beating inside it. Disoriented and nauseated, she forced herself to eat a boiled egg and some toast.

She was due at her grandmother's for dinner in Bronxville at five. Forget that. She telephoned and begged off. "Flu symptoms are coming on." Minnie Stern had heard it all before, and just said, "Take care of yourself, Margo. I love you."

Margo then settled down to check the want ads

in last Sunday's *New York Times.* There were a couple
for attorneys with her specialty, taxation and corporate law. She clipped the ads and set them on the coffee table. Tomorrow, not today, she thought.

A football game was on the tube, but she couldn't
focus on it. She spent the rest of the day cursing Dan
Horgan. It was not just the fact that she'd lost her job.
No, her firing had nothing to do with downsizing. Was-
n't she the most seasoned attorney in mergers and
acquisitions, an area where Horgan & Stern was
weak? Before long, they'd be out on the street hiring
a couple of people to replace her.

Dan Horgan had not only dumped her as a lover,
she was certain it was he who'd told De Femio to
dump her from the firm. The downsizing was just a
convenient excuse. And yesterday, the coward had-
n't even attended Walter Donohue's Mass. Too bad
it was Walter they'd buried, not fancy Dan Horgan.
Well, she mused, I'll be around when he goes down,
too.

She'd see to that.

The prospect made her smile and the food had
helped settle her stomach. Walking over to the liquor
cabinet, she took out a liter of 90-proof vodka, poured
herself a double, and toasted Dan Horgan's future...
"A short one!"

....

In Queens, the Rizzuto clan had a calm day.

Dom had accompanied their son Rudy to a high
school football game. Ida was not sure the venture

would succeed; Dom wanted to talk to his son, a sophomore, about transferring to Bronxville High School. Rudy had first greeted the news with the usual, "No way, José!" How could he leave his friends behind? How could the basketball team win without him?

When they returned from the game, however, Rudy had mellowed. An honor student, Dom had told him about the Bronxville School's reputation: "If you want to go to a top college, you'll have a much better shot than if you stay here." Now, Rudy had come into the kitchen while Ida was preparing the turkey stuffing, and asked if he might stay at his grandmother's through June, and finish up his second year at Queens High. She told him that she and Dom would discuss it, and if Dom agreed, they'd ask her mother.

Family peace, a treasured gift for the holiday.

....

In a loft apartment in Greenwich Village, Brian Palmer had prepared a turkey breast with all the trimmings.

His lover was listless and feverish. Reed James had been diagnosed as HIV-positive about two years ago and with full blown AIDS six months ago. He'd lost twenty pounds in that time. Even worse was the loss of his normally buoyant spirit. Reed was a freelance artist, and lately, even his work reflected the despair in his heart.

Brian's layoff could not have come at a worse time. His firm's liberal medical policy included domestic partners. For a time, Brian could continue the coverage by paying full cost, an exorbitant sum which he could not afford for very long. Reed was not a Basquiat, who had soared to fame while still young. No, he was just a painter who'd made a moderately successful living before he'd become ill. Now his royalties and commissions had dwindled to almost nothing.

Brian did his best to cheer Reed on this Thanksgiving. Who knew if they'd have another? This morning, they'd attended a service at Dignity, a Catholic organization for gay people. At Communion time, Brian found it hard to rid himself of anger. Dan Horgan had boosted the firm's reputation on Brian's computer skills. Then, when Brian was no longer needed, he'd tossed him aside like an old brief.

The wrong partner had died. Had Jake Stern lived, Reed would still be ill, but Brian would have a job and be able to give Reed the medical care and drugs he'd need in the months ahead. For the first time he could recall, Brian's own gentle nature was being tested. He found himself wishing that Dan Horgan was having a miserable day, a day with little to be thankful for, like his own and Reed's.

Hope is a precious gift. Dan Horgan had destroyed that when the firm let him go.

....

Brian Palmer got his wish.

At Fisherman's Wharf in San Francisco, Dan Horgan was not having a happy holiday.

He and his son Chip had gone out for dinner. Chip had always been closer to his mother, Julie, than his father. When Julie died six years ago, Dan and he had lost the one thing that bonded them. Perhaps it was Chip's way of rebelling against his father, against his establishment credentials, his Bar Association contacts, his Republicanism, his occasional fling, even when Julie was terminally ill.

Dan had hoped he'd follow in his own footsteps; become a lawyer, a doctor, some profession that would do him proud. The boy was certainly bright enough, an honors graduate from Williams College and Yale's Drama School.

But Chip still hung out on the fringe. Most of his friends were long-haired with rings and studs on parts of their bodies and tattoos on the rest. They had no sense of style or settling down, and seemed destined to sow wild oats for the rest of their lives. Education seemed to have left them with no understanding of how the world works, except when they needed money.

As Chip did now.

Dan wondered how long it would take for Chip to bring it up again. Chip needed "about a hundred thousand or so," seed money to produce a play he'd written. Dan had promised to read the script, and did. He thought it the worst drivel he'd ever read, and told Chip so, probably more candidly than he should have.

His son would not give up, and took up his case again today, between the pumpkin pie and coffee. "A loan, Dad, that's all it is. I'll pay you back with interest, I promise."

Dan punted: "Let me sleep on it." But Chip could see that his father's tired eyes were focused on the fishermen's boats, coming in from the day's catch.

"You won't, Dad. You've already made up your mind. One day, you'll be sorry."

Dan said again: "Chip, let's leave it for now. I told you I'll think about it, and I will." The two drank coffee in silence, as the sun's last rays dipped into the bay.

....

Luke Plisky's car rolled into the driveway of his Crestwood home at eleven o'clock on Thanksgiving night.

He'd spent the morning at Macy's annual Thanksgiving parade. In the early afternoon, he'd served dinner to the homeless at a soup kitchen in the Bowery, on New York's lower East Side. Then he'd driven uptown, navigating through late afternoon traffic on the George Washington Bridge, arriving at the Altieri home just before five.

Bruno Altieri's house was more like a mansion. Two armed security officers manned both front and rear gates. Normally, a visitor required a photo ID, but the guards knew Luke well and waved him in.

Once inside, he was, as always, greeted as family. In 1971 Luke had been a lance corporal in the Army, and Bruno Altieri was his first lieutenant and platoon leader. In the spring of that year, Bruno had received orders to take the small town of An Doai, a haven for North Vietnam intelligence. Two hours before daybreak, he'd led his men across a broad patch of scrubby land just outside the town.

The North Vietnamese had been pre-alerted and the platoon was quickly fired upon from ground and air. Bruno Altieri was the first to be hit and fell quickly, clutching his heart. All but four men fell within seconds of the assault, and those too were down within two minutes. Most never stirred again.

Luke had been hit twice, once just under his right eye, a second time in his left leg. Too weak to move, he remained still. He saw Bruno Altieri about twenty yards away, softly moaning, still alive. Luke looked around and saw none of his other buddies moving. If he were going to get Altieri out, he had to move quickly, before the sun rose.

He did, crawling on his hands and knees, washed in his own blood, and half-pulled, half-dragged a semiconscious Bruno back to a wooded area, behind a rice field. Their only hope was to stay there, avoid capture, and wait until nightfall for help. None came.

At dawn, the Viet Cong came out onto the field, checked the bodies, found two who were still breathing, and shot them in the head. Miraculously, they never discovered Luke Plisky or Bruno Altieri crouched in the underbrush.

It was two nights before help arrived and they were airlifted to an Army hospital. By then, Luke was in critical condition, near death. Bruno's wounds were serious, but he was stable. Stateside, Luke had been a volunteer fireman, trained in basic emergency care. His meager supplies had been used to staunch Lieutenant Bruno Altieri's wounds. Luke had given Bruno all his water, except for a few drops to keep himself alive.

Both survived. In two months, Bruno left the hospital and went back to the front where he was soon promoted to captain. Luke was shipped home to the best rehabilitation hospital in the country, paid for by Sal Altieri, Bruno's father. His recovery took a full two years.

Bruno had been awarded the Purple Heart. He'd recommended Luke for the Congressional Medal of Honor. There had been a spate of recommendations at that time, and Luke was awarded the Distinguished Service Cross and an honorable discharge.

Sal Altieri, Bruno's father, had pronounced Luke "part of our family so long as we all shall live." All these years, he'd been true to his word. Luke, then twenty-one years old, had not seen his own father for many years, and settled happily into the role of adopted son.

Only later did Luke learn that Sal Altieri was reputedly a major player in organized crime. He stuck it in the back of his mind, neither accepting nor rejecting it. Luke had found in life that it was best to judge people by your own experience, not by what others said of them. The Altieris had been kind and generous, to him, to his mother, and especially, to his wife Karen, while she lived.

In his own life, his country had sent him to a war that was fought mostly by the poor and lower middle class. Almost 60,000 had died. Few who lived returned to heroes' welcomes. Decades later, many were still ill, dreadfully ill. Some were alcoholics; many were drug addicts. Two he'd trained with at Fort Jackson in South Carolina now lived in cardboard boxes in New York's Central Park. Good men all. Not perfect, but good. Once young, now old, still haunted by the hell they'd seen in a distant land.

And the men now running the country? They had stayed home, attended fine schools, and snagged the top jobs in government and business. Some now lived in luxury co-ops in upper Manhattan with breathtaking views of Central Park. He wondered if they ever looked out and saw his two buddies, the ones who now lived there in cardboard boxes.

So, Luke turned a deaf ear to "mob" talk from people who had let others fight and die for them.

On this Thanksgiving night, Luke Plisky had gratefully shared a meal and their home with the Altieris, father, son and extended family.

....

On Wednesday, after Walter's burial and the lunch that followed at the Greentree Restaurant, Edna Donohue had gone home with her son Buddy.

Buddy and his wife Diane lived in a stately old pillared brick home in Lawrence Park West, a community once dubbed by *The New York Times* as "a Yonkers locale, a Bronxville pedigree." Technically in Yonkers, but a Bronxville post office and zip code. Buddy had told her of neighbors who were unaware that they lived in Yonkers, not Bronxville. Light dawned with one of two events: trying to register a child in the Bronxville school, or receiving a bill from the City of Yonkers for overdue taxes. Edna wondered why people with so much money were too dumb to find out where they'd be living before moving there.

Even harder to believe was that a son of hers and Walter's could own this lovely home worth more than a half million dollars. Of course, Buddy's medical practice was thriving. And, from all they'd observed, Buddy had, in Diane, the perfect wife and mother to his children. This brilliant but "loner" son of theirs, was now warmer and happier in ways his mother had never thought possible.

On Thanksgiving Day, Buddy had gone to a high school football game with the kids. Edna had promised to help her daughter-in-law with the cooking, but was astonished to awake just after noon.

"Don't worry, Edna, there's not that much to do," said Diane. "Sleeping late was your body's telling you it needed to rest!" Edna found talk of listening to her body too 90ish, but knew that her daughter-in-law meant it kindly.

The dinner went well, even when five-year-old Tricia looked around and noted: "There aren't many men in the family anymore." An icebreaker. Edna joined in the laughter. There would be months, even years to grieve for Walter. Today she was thankful for family around her.

Life, after all, endures. You go on. Edna Donohue

would do what she always did, what her mother had taught her from childhood, "the best you can." It had worked in the past. Now, it would just have to do.

17

On Monday of the third week of December, Dominic Rizzuto arrived at Lake View to begin his new job as building superintendent.

Rich Kryhoski, managing agent and Rizzuto's nominal boss, was there to ensure a smooth entry and introduce him to the staff. Steve Jablonski, Lake View's burly porter, gave Dom a vigorous handshake and pat on the back. Mario La Guardia, the weekday doorman, formally offered his hand but no pat. His face said "You'll have to prove yourself to me, buddy."

When Dan Horgan returned from work at about seven o'clock, the night doorman assured him that all had gone well. Dom Rizzuto seemed like "a nice fella; the little woman's a sweetheart."

Dan walked to the end of the hallway and knocked on the door of the Rizzuto apartment. Loud voices were coming from inside. A family argument? Or maybe just the TV. The sounds ceased with his knock and Dom answered the door.

"Just dropped by to say welcome, Dom. Did everything go well? Anything you need?"

"Smooth as silk, Mr. Horgan. Come in and meet the wife."

The wife emerged from the kitchen, colander in hand. This was no "little woman." A "looker" in her day, thought Dan. Still able to turn a man's eye, if she wanted to. Tonight, though, she looked exhausted. Wisps of mostly auburn hair fell over half-closed brown eyes. Lips pinched in a tight smile; a face with little joy.

"Welcome, Mrs. Rizzuto. I hope Dom told you how glad we are to have you both here."

"Thanks, Mr. Horgan. We're glad to be here." Ida's words belied her expression. She looked like she could use about forty-eight hours' sleep, so Dan wished them good night and left.

Outside, Shannon O'Keefe emerged from the elevator. "Hi, Dan. Just brought a loaf of Zaro's rye bread up to Minnie."

"How is she? Rosa tells me she's making terrific progress."

"Yup, but you know Minnie. Rosa's been manna from heaven, helping her out, but Minnie can't wait until she's on her own again."

Dan smiled. "Well, good for Minnie. I just stopped in to see our new super. Pure gold, well worth the wait."

Shannon smiled. Her employment experience had taught her that hiring people was a lot like betting on horses. You played the odds, but there were always surprises. Applicants tailored their background to say what they thought employers wanted. Those who interviewed well often beat out shy, more qualified people. Long ago her Irish grandfather had taught her that the horse first out of the gate rarely ended up with the roses.

"Let's hope. Better still, let's pray," she cautioned. "The first sixty days should tell."

"Amen. Well, for all our sakes, let's hope he's here for the long run. It's a lousy job. Living where you work is no fun. But just think of the perks, Shannon. Great clients like all of us."

"That's what I *am* thinking about. The clients like us," she smiled, as they boarded the elevator.

18

....

At five-thirty on the last school day before Christmas, the teachers at P. S. 807 were holding their holiday party at Luigi's, an Italian restaurant not far from the school.

Tonight, Charlotte Weiss remarked, "Luigi's is a place where you can never be overdressed." Harry Reeber, nodding, had added: "Looks like a bordello, with all of those red drapes, floor-to-ceiling mirrors, and chandeliers." They spoke softly, lest Selma Einstein overhear them. A few years ago, the Christmas party had almost been canceled. Successive committees had thrown in the towel. Getting teachers to agree on where to have the party, when, what price to charge, and whether guests could be invited, drove more than one group up the wall. When principal Mark Borras had asked Enrique Dupraz, a gentle thirty-five year old third grade teacher, to convene still another committee, Enrique had replied: "I'd rather negotiate peace in the Mid-East, or even worse, do lunch duty."

Borras had then resorted to his back-up plan: Selma Einstein, school secretary. Selma was his contingency plan for everything. When the Board of Education ordered schools to cut staffing by one position, many principals had offered up a secretary.

Mark Borras had given up an Assistant Principal slot to keep Selma. No one second-guessed him.

Selma reluctantly agreed to organize the party, after unilaterally setting three conditions. She would do it on school time, not her own. She'd take one survey of preferred location, dates, prices and menus. When the details were announced, payment was due in cash one week before the party. No checks. No refunds. No exceptions. Period.

She had made certain accommodations, of course, like kosher and vegetarian meals, but drew the line at others. When Jake Cohen asked her to buy the kosher meat from his brother-in-law the butcher, Selma dished out a raspy: "What, you think I was born yesterday? No!"

That had been four years ago. Since then, the staff had happily acknowledged Selma's reign as party queen for life. To the occasional complainant, her response was: "So, you think you can do better? So do." No one did.

Tonight, at the cash bar, Charlotte and Harry were updating each other on the latest rumors about an early retirement offer. Word was that the Chancellor had recommended it, but some on the School Board had balked at the short-term costs. One member had been quoted in the media: "Why should we bribe them to stay home and do nothing?"

"Hah!" screamed Harry, the school's union representative. "That from those Livingston Street louts who've done nothing their whole lives." The reputation of New York City's Board of Education was only marginally higher than the I.R.S.

"Well, if they offer anything decent at all, I'm outta here," said Charlotte Weiss.

"Me too," chimed in Harriet Noble. "And speaking of Livingston Street, the mother of one of my kids had the nerve to call me at home one night. Said she was going to write to the Board and complain about me. What gall! I'd told her smart-aleck Sam that the English language is not limited to four letter words, and he might consider expanding his vocabulary!"

Luke Plisky asked: "What did you say to his mother?"

"Gave her the Board's address. Told her to send it Priority Mail. Next day Sam told me he'd mailed it, and I'd better watch out for my 'you know what.'"

"What happened?" asked Harry Reeber.

"Zilch. That was two months ago. I knew that when that crowd got something marked Priority, they'd figure it meant action, so they'd pass it around indefinitely. The letter probably went out when the last schools chancellor hotfooted it out of there." Harriet basked in the group's laughter.

"Yup, that poor guy had one thing against him," said Harry.

"Competence. They couldn't deal with that. I heard he cleared out his desk and even skipped his own farewell party. Anyway, Harriet, we're all glad you got to keep your 'you know what'."

More guffaws at still another chapter in the saga of bureaucratic incompetence.

Over the next hour, the group moved from the bar to the open buffet. Luke Plisky and student teacher Enid Gomez were already sitting down to platefuls of roasted chicken, pasta and salad. He noticed that she was somewhat somber. "Hey, lighten up, it's Christmas!"

She smiled. "Sorry. I'm just wondering if twenty years from now, I'll feel jaded like them."

"Ah, it comes with the territory. Criticizing the system is one of the perks of our job. It gets us through the bad days. Besides, have you ever been in their classes?"

"No," she admitted.

"Well, Charlotte spends hours of her own time before each semester decorating her classroom. And today, her husband had to drive her to school. She had a small gift for each of her kids."

"No kidding."

"And Harry once played semi-pro baseball. In the nice weather, you'll see him out in the yard after school, teaching kids to hit. On his own time. And they're both superb teachers."

Enid nodded: "Guess I've got a lot to learn."

"Don't we all?" Luke smiled.

The banter lasted well into the night. There were several toasts to Selma for outdoing herself as party CEO. Mark Borras presented her with flowers. The hard-edged Selma was touched, and Harry Reeber whispered: "Good grief, I think she's waxing sentimental. Never thought the woman had tear ducts."

"I wouldn't count on it, Harry," whispered someone across the table. "I'd say it's a one-night stand from our Selma!"

Just before eight, Luke and Enid said good night and walked to her Honda in a nearby garage. Enid had offered to drive him to the White Plains airport for his holiday visit to Michigan. Surprisingly, they made good time on the Cross-Bronx Expressway, and then north onto the Hutchinson River Parkway to the airport. When Luke got out of the car, he thanked her: "You're great. Have a super Christmas."

A quick hug and he was off.

The plane was on schedule when he checked in at the first class window and purchased flight insurance. A half hour later, he was seated near the front of the Northwest jet. The airplane's stereo system was playing "Star of Wonder, Star of Light." The night was completely black, but it didn't seem to matter.

After a smooth takeoff, he'd settled back into his seat and was checking his insurance. A young voice interrupted his reverie: "So, you think this thing might crash?" Luke's seatmate was a handsome, husky African-American boy with short brown hair and jet black eyes, well dressed in a brown leather bombardier's jacket and black jeans.

He smiled at the boy, who appeared to be about twelve: "No, not really. It's just habit, I guess. The rates are so low, I got used to buying it when my wife was alive. Now I do it automatically."

A nod from the boy: "My mom says that when it's

time for you to go, you'll go, whether you're on a plane or on the ground."

"Makes sense to me. My name's Luke. Luke Plisky."

"Hi. I'm Jason. Jason Coburn. Yeah, well…I've asked my mom what if it's the pilot's turn to go and not yours?"

"Good question. What did she say to that?"

"What she says whenever she doesn't know the answer. 'Go do your homework.'"

"Sounds familiar. Anyway, you heading home for Christmas?"

"Nah, I live with my mom in Greenwich. They're divorced, my mom and dad. He's a lawyer, lives in Detroit and gets me for holidays. Lucky him."

"You don't sound too happy about it."

"Could be worse, I guess. So, what happened to your wife? Uh, do I call you Luke or Mr. Plisky?"

"Luke is fine. My wife Karen was killed in a robbery, years ago."

"They catch the guy?"

"Not a guy, but yes, a woman who was high on drugs. They caught her."

"She go to jail or what?"

"Or what, I guess." Luke answered. "No, she didn't go to jail. She had friends in high places and got off with probation and community service."

"Jeez, I woulda killed her, myself," said Jason.

"Guess I didn't want to spend the rest of my life in jail for murder." There was no need to tell the boy that the woman was long since dead, along with her husband. A month after the trial ended, their motorboat had mysteriously exploded off Long Island's shores.

"How about changing the subject?" asked Luke.

"Sure," said the boy. "You got a father?"

"He left home when I was a little younger than you. Sent me this that first Christmas." He pointed to the sterling silver identification bracelet on his right wrist. "We never saw him again."

"Deadbeat dad, huh?"

"They didn't call them that in those days, but yes, I guess he was."

"Why'd he go?" asked the boy.

"He'd lost his job at a small printing company. When automation took over, they went out of business. His note said that he hoped to find work out west, but we never heard if he did or not."

"Wow. Well, that kind of thing won't happen to me. I'm, like, going into business for myself. It's the only way." Jason Coburn spoke with the unique self-confidence of an old head on young shoulders.

"You've got a point, there. What business are you thinking of going into?"

"Well, first I'll go to law school like my dad, then politics. I figure that's how you learn where the big money is. When I leave office, I'll head right there." Jason smiled happily. It appeared that he'd thought all this out carefully. "So, Mr. Plisky, Luke, whadda you do?"

"Well, you could say I'm in business for myself, too. I teach in the South Bronx."

"Hmmm. You any good?"

Luke thought a moment, then looked at the boy's open face, which seemed to demand candor. "Yup, I'd say so. The kids in my classes score pretty well on the citywide exams each year."

"Yeah? My mom says that the public schools are not so hot in the city."

"Well, that may be true in some schools. Not in mine. The teachers work pretty hard; so do the kids. Where do you got to school?"

"Greenwich Middle School. It's tough there, but I do O.K."

Luke nodded. "Bet you're tops on the honor roll."

"Naah." Jason Coburn held up three fingers. "When you're number three, you gotta try a lot harder."

"Amen," said Luke, as the flight attendant came down the aisle with snacks and drinks.

Over juice and crackers, Jason asked, "Where're you spending Christmas?"

"With my sister Lily and her family, in East Lansing. And you, with your dad?"

"Yup, and his new wife and son. Her son. I've seen pictures…looks like a geek. What do you think I should call her?"

"Your stepmother? What's her name?"

"Grace. That might sound a little familiar, though. I sure don't wanna call her mom."

"Maybe you could ask her what she'd like to be called, and just take it from there."

Jason nodded. They chatted like that, this normally taciturn man and his serious, manchild seatmate, for the rest of the hour and a half trip. As the plane prepared to land in Detroit, Jason asked Luke: "So, when you comin' home?"

"The Saturday after Christmas. The flight leaves around noon, I think."

"Hmmm. I leave the next day. Maybe I'll see you 'round again, sometime." Jason stuck out his hand palm up, and they exchanged high-fives.

"I hope so. Merry Christmas, Jason."

"You, too, Luke." As the plane pulled into the gate, the flight attendant helped with their carry-on luggage, and the two walked through the gateway together. In the Detroit passenger terminal, carolers were singing "We Wish You a Merry Christmas."

In a few seconds, Jason was swept up in the arms of a bearish, ebony-handsome man, with huge arms and a hearty voice. Luke waved good-bye and was soon bear hugged himself by his sister Lily Westrum.

They headed for the baggage area, where Luke's suitcase was already waiting. Outside the terminal, his brother-in-law Ned greeted them with ten year old Danny and large golden retriever, Wolverine. "Welcome home to Michigan, Luke," said Ned.

"Woof, woof," added Wolverine.

"He's saying Merry Christmas, Uncle Luke," said Danny.

"Woof, woof, woof," laughed Luke. "That's Happy New Year."

The small party headed happily toward the parking lot, just another family locked in seasonal joy.

19

Peace on Earth. Good will to men.

The holiday season brought out the best in people. At Lake View, Hester Harrington's lobby-decorating committee had outdone itself. Tree, wreaths and plants were proclaimed to be the best of any building in the village. Hester beamed. When the cranky Foster baby giggled at the tree, she grabbed the child from its mother's arms to give him a closer look. When the wailing tot drooled on her new green satin dress from Neiman Marcus, Hester whisked out her linen handkerchief and said, "Don't give it another thought," to the horror-struck mother.

The baby quickly got into the spirit of it all and stopped crying at night. Florence Arnold, the neighbor who had filed several complaints with the Board about the screaming infant, was so delighted, she knocked on Mrs. Foster's door and handed over a freshly baked honey cake. "For the little one," she said. The child's mother was again stunned, but reciprocated the next day with a Christmas stollen.

Observing all this bonhomie, Mario La Guardia said to Steve Jablonski, the porter: "It won't last. I give it till New Year's, when the bloom is off the poinsettias." Steve was not into metaphors and explained to Mario that the plants should last well beyond that time. "We'll see," said Mario, rolling his eyes. "We'll see."

And then it began, on New Year's Eve, the whimper that set everything else in motion.

The whimper was coming from Hester Harrington's radiator. At eight, she telephoned Dom Rizzuto's apartment to complain.

Ida answered: "Mrs. Harrington, Dom stepped out for a few hours. I'll have him call you when he comes in. It may be late, though. Would you rather he called in the morning?"

"I can't sleep with this noise," moaned Hester. "He can call at any time."

Ida's best guess was that Dom had gone to a Yonkers bar with his buddies and would return well after midnight. At nine o'clock, after leaving a note next to the telephone, she left for her night shift at Queens Hospital. Ida had volunteered to work New Year's Eve. With the emergency room short-staffed, she'd receive time-and-a-half pay.

When Dom returned at two-thirty, he saw Ida's note to call Hester. Bleary-eyed and wobbly, he read it through glassy eyes, with enough sense to know he was not up to bonding with either Hester Harrington or her radiator tonight. One was worse than the other. Let the old goat wait until morning, he thought. Lonely residents had a habit of waiting till weekends and holidays to report problems. The hell with her. And off to bed he went.

The old goat had waited up until one o'clock, when she too went to bed. The whimper meant that it took her ten minutes to get to sleep, instead of her usual five. She slept through the night and was awakened by Rizzuto's call at just after ten the next morning. "Apologies, Mrs. Harrington. Happy New Year," he said, charmingly. "Ida just told me you'd called last night. Is it convenient for me to come up now?"

Hester, whose only planned activity for New Year's Day was to watch the Rose Bowl parade on TV, replied grouchily: "Yes, I'll fit you in. I can't spend one more sleepless night with this noise. Come up in half an hour."

Dom was made to feel like a penitent when he arrived. He listened attentively to a complaining Hester for ten minutes before he got to the offending bedroom radiator. Hearing nothing beyond a normal hiss, he stated that the baffler needed a part. He'd purchase it from a local hardware store and install it that afternoon.

At about four o'clock, he returned with a tool box and a small bag. There was nothing in the bag, but Hester didn't know that. He proceeded to open box and bag, banged on the radiator for about fifteen minutes, and pronounced it fixed. Sure enough, Hester now heard nothing. "Well, at least I can sleep tonight," she grumped. Dom Rizzuto, again offering apologies, went out the door, singing "Vincera," from the triumphant aria in *Turandot.*

A few days later, Hester met Ida Rizzuto in the hallway and gave her a grumpy "Good Day." Ida, suspecting that Dom had lied about the telephone message, did not return the snub. Hester would not have believed her anyway.

On Friday, Rich Kryhoski called Lake View and got doorman Mario La Guardia. "Is Dom there, Mario? I'd like him to stop over here at the office and let me know how things are going." Rich liked to meet regularly with his new superintendents. Best to nip small problems in the bud, before they became big ones.

"He's out to lunch, Rich." It was then two o'clock, and Dom had left for lunch at noon.

"O.K. When he returns, tell him I'd like to see him over here at four-thirty."

"Will do," answered Mario.

That afternoon, Dom walked about six blocks to the managing agent's office on Kraft Avenue. Kryhoski thought he looked flushed, but confident. Dom gave a full report on the past week, including the problem of Hester Harrington's radiator. He was sure that she'd called Kryshoski to complain and wanted to be sure that his boss knew it was Ida who had "screwed up." Hester had not called him, so Kryhoski just listened.

"Look, Dom. I don't care what your message system is. Just see that it works. Pleasing Lake View's Board is a big key to your success, and Hester Harrington thinks she's the Queen Mum over there. Treat her well."

"Gotcha. It won't happen again."

When the meeting was over and Dom had left, Kryhoski made a note of the discussion for Rizzuto's file. Overall, the first couple of weeks had gone pretty well. No major complaints from Lake View's residents; a high water mark for most co-ops he managed.

Florence Murano, Kryhoski's administrative assistant, sat at her work station, just outside his office. Florence was a plain, dark-haired twenty-five year old with a pudgy face and short fat fingers that flew over her computer keyboard at lightning speed. Her green squinty eyes now peered up at Dom Rizzuto as he exited the managing agent's office.

"Arrivederci, bellissima," he waved, as he passed by and pinched her cheeks. Florence was temporarily distracted by his familiarity and stared down at the DOS prompt on her computer screen. "Dirty old stud," she mumbled, grabbing her mouse and aiming it like a hand grenade at his back.

20

"Whadda they know? The only time they're accurate is when they look out the window and tell you what it's doing now."

Dom Rizzuto was giving his thumbs-down evaluation of meteorologists to his wife, over a late breakfast on the second Sunday in January. Ida had just driven home after her night shift. Queens Hospital, relying on the forecast for "a blizzard of Biblical proportions," had developed a week's contingency plan for emergency room staffing. A limo would arrive for her in the early evening. She'd just told Dom that she was packing a small suitcase, in the event she had to stay at the hospital for several nights.

Dom regaled her with tales of bad forecasts from his youth, right up to the prior winter, which many had predicted would break all records. The season had turned out to be among the mildest in years.

"Remember all that rock salt the landlord had me haul in? The snow blower he ordered up? Still sitting there, unused."

Even as they were eating scrambled eggs and bagels, heavy flurries were falling and sticking. Ida had been through too much with Dom to argue. "Well, you do what you have to do. I'm going to sleep for a few hours." While Ida slept, Dom watched football and drank a six-pack of Miller Lite.

At four o'clock Ida awoke, dressed for work and walked out to the living room to ask Dom if he wanted something to eat. She was going to make herself soup and a sandwich.

"No, you go ahead. I'll wait till the end of the game," he answered.

While Ida was at the stove, she looked out her ground floor kitchen window. Several inches of snow were already on the ground. She flipped on the radio for the latest forecast: "One of the worst storms in the last fifty years, with accumulations over two feet, temperatures headed for single digits, record wind drifts, and hazardous driving conditions."

"Dom, the weather reports are pretty bad," she shouted into the living room. "Look out the window."

"Yeah, well, when the game's over, I'll walk out and take a look."

Just after five, Ida put on her hooded down coat and storm boots, and said good-bye to Dom. "The limo will be here in about fifteen minutes. I'm going outside, so he doesn't have to wait for me. The radio reports are already talking about hazardous roads. I'll call you tomorrow."

"Whenever, babe." As Ida closed the door, Dom was screaming a slurred obscenity at a wide receiver who had just dropped a thirty-yard pass.

21

Shannon awoke the next morning to a white, white world.

She turned on the radio for the early morning news. More than a foot and a half of snow had fallen, with no end in sight. Drivers were advised to stay off the highways to allow snow plows through. Metro-North's trains and both New York and Westchester County bus systems were either not running at all, paralyzed between stops, or experiencing long delays. Many of the city's businesses had simply declared a snow holiday.

When the assignment with Burke Parker had ended in December, she'd decided to take a few weeks off. Brett Halliday of Halliday Temporary Executives had called a couple of times with offers, but she'd turned him down. Christmas and New Year's had meant lots of togetherness with family and friends. Now she wanted just a little time for herself.

The weather confirmed her decision as wise; reports were increasingly gloomy. A day with no *New York Times,* no mail, no guests. She lingered over a leisurely breakfast of grapefruit, cereal and toast, then dressed in her warmest parka and ventured downstairs.

Lake View's driveway and pedestrian path had not yet been plowed. Now Dom Rizzuto was out there with his snow blower, fighting a losing battle. Drifts were already high; a thick crust of unplowed ice and snow made his efforts all but useless. Seeing Shannon, he shut the machine off and walked over: "Can you beat this? I called the snow plow guy hours ago and he's not here yet." Shannon thought there was liquor on his breath, but couldn't be sure.

She nodded and walked away, leaving him muttering about the unreliability of service contracts.

Many of her neighbors were out taking pictures. A few telecommuters were hoping that the storm would break all records. Others were snow historians. Gwyneth Fielding recalled New York's December 1947 blizzard: "We felt gypped since it fell during the Christmas holidays, and we didn't have a day off. I was in grammar school then, thinking that the nuns must have been happy about that. Little did I know until I became one that they probably felt even more gypped than the kids!"

Elmer Brick laughed. "I remember it very well. I spent hours digging out my car only to find out when I was done that it was some other guy's car!"

People had begun talking about the day being a great time to clean closets, write letters, set up their calendars for the new year, organize tax files. Shannon just listened and waved good-bye. Her own plan was to read a good book and listen to the new CDs she'd received as Christmas gifts.

The phone was ringing when she entered the

apartment. Dan Horgan was calling from Phoenix. "Hi, Shannon. Just got a call from Rich Kryhoski. Is it as bad as he says around there?

""Well, I'm not sure what he told you. Best as I can tell, Dom did nothing until this morning. Now it's an uphill battle. He said he'd called our snow plow contractor, but there was a long waiting list."

"A very long one, according to Rich. Dom only called them this morning, and you have to get on their backs early. Are the natives up in arms?"

"Not quite. Give them a day or two. Today they know that nothing much is moving anyway. They're still in the winter wonderland phase. By tomorrow that will pass, and a few will be grumping up a storm of their own."

"Well, I've authorized Rich to hire a couple of temporary guys to get in there and help as soon as the plow gets through. Best we can do for now."

"Agreed, Dan. No doubt, though, it's a royal mess. Will you be back for Thursday's Board meeting?"

"As of now, I'm scheduled to land at Kennedy early in the afternoon. I should be there in plenty of time."

"O.K. Well, if not, let me know and I'll fill in for you."

"Will do, and thanks, Shannon. See you Thursday."

After hanging up the phone, she made a cup of hot chocolate and settled down in the den to read. She took out a few CDs, starting with the latest one from Joanie Madden and the Irish women's band "Cherish the Ladies." What better way to chase away thoughts of the bungling Rizzuto?

22

....

By Tuesday, snow had stopped falling after accumulations of more than two feet.

The plows had finally arrived and cleared Lake View's walkway. Now, Dom Rizzuto and four men were working in subfreezing temperatures with snow blowers in the parking lot. A few hardy residents were shoveling out their own cars.

Shannon walked out to the main road and met Binky Seagram, a retired attorney and Lake View neighbor. "I'm not sure why they bother," he said. "Anybody who drives on these roads for the next couple of days is a nutter."

Even then, nutters were driving slowly on Pondfield Road West. The plows had pushed as much snow as possible against the curb; still, accumulations and drifts had managed to convert a two-way thoroughfare into a single lane. Most drivers were polite, allowing one car to go in each direction. A few were not. There had already been one near fistfight earlier in the day.

"This is ridiculous," huffed Gwyneth Fielding, who had now joined the small crowd of car-watchers. "Why don't the cops make it a one-way street, before someone gets hurt?" With that, she stalked off back down the cul-de-sac, toward Lake View.

"Gone to find her old habit and push them into line," said Binky Seagram.

A few minutes later, Gwyneth was back, sans habit, cum whistle. Hustling out to the road, whistle in mouth, she shrilled loudly and directed traffic with perfect hand signals. When a woman driver attempted to ignore her and move out of turn, Gwyneth let out a toot like a banshee, and literally stood in front of the car, waving an astonished delivery truck driver past her. "Thanks, Sarge!" he shouted.

"Talk about instant justice," said Val Thomas, who had joined the group. "Our Gwyn is a regular Madam DeFarge. It's a good thing the guillotine is a thing of the past, or that driver might be headless by now."

After an hour or so, Binky Seagram went out to relieve Gwyneth, who walked briskly back to a cheering crowd of neighbors and admirers. She had a small smile on her face and took a mock bow. Someone had brought out a thermos of hot chocolate and she happily swigged down a cup.

"Well," said Shannon, "I'm going to use the next best thing to a car to get around: feet. Anyone need anything? I'm walking over to Palmer Avenue."

She took two orders for bread and one for orange juice, and was on her way. She crossed the street and trudged in the fresh snow, feeling young and happy. Walking around the west side of the village, she noticed that other driveways and pedestrian walkways were in a lot better shape than Lake View's. Clearly Dom Rizzuto had not acted quickly enough to clear the snow. When three or four residents complained about

Dom, she'd defended him: "The storm is probably worse than anyone expected. I'm sure he did his best."

"Well, his best was none too good," was one person's reply. "Amen to that," thought Shannon. She'd defended Rizzuto not because she liked the man, but because she didn't. It was her way, perhaps to please herself; she often gave more leeway to people she didn't like than those she did.

Now, it was clear they were right. This week, at least, Lake View was not la crème de la crème.

Anyway, Dan would be back on Thursday, and the Board could review the situation then. She'd reached Bronxville's rotary, otherwise known as "Prayer Circle." About two traffic accidents a year occurred here. Stop signs, Yield signs and pedestrian crosswalks were routinely ignored. One villager claimed that "at least they had the good sense to put it right across from Lawrence Hospital, so they can whisk the victims right to the emergency room." Today, with reduced traffic, pedestrians able to mount snowbanks had a rare opportunity to cross the street with minimum risk of being run over.

Shannon walked down Palmer Avenue, picked up a couple of hot dishes at an Italian takeout place, and sundries from a Korean produce store. Returning to Lake View, she delivered bread and juice to Minnie Stern, who insisted on making her a cup of tea. Rosa Di Carlo, "my temporary significant other," as Minnie called her, was not able to make it in during the storm. Minnie was delighted to be able to fend for herself for a few days. "Good Lord, it's only a broken hip. I've got two good legs."

"Minnie, the walking will be bad for a few weeks; it's not worth trying for two broken hips," said Shannon. Minnie nodded glumly.

"How's Margo doing?" asked Shannon. She knew that, on more than one occasion, Minnie had tried to talk to her granddaughter about her drinking, with no luck at all.

"Well, she's not doing a whole lot. Keeps thinking that Dan will soon realize they can't get along without her, and ask her back. Wanted me to intercede, but I said no. She's got to stay sober and move on, that girl."

"Amen," said her younger friend.

"Oh, another subject, Shannon. Do you know a good plumber? I've got a toilet that you have to keep jiggling to get it to stop flushing. I had Dom up, but he just took one look and said it was a big job, one for a plumber. He's a good talker, that one, but I had the feeling that almost any job is too big for him."

Shannon laughed. "Matter of fact, I do know one. She comes highly recommended. Would you like her number? I'll give you a call when I return to my apartment."

"A woman plumber? Well, hooray for her! Thanks. I'd appreciate it."

After an hour or so, having noticed that Minnie was tiring, she got up to leave. "It's not that I don't love to see you," said Minnie. "I just wish I could do more for myself."

"You will, Minnie. Just be patient."

23

....

"What we have out here is a filthy sewer."

On Thursday morning Mario La Guardia declared an official end to winter wonderland. Local highways and main streets were now manageable. Beyond the village, though, many Westchester roads had not been cleared. Parking was virtually impossible, with several feet of frozen snow packed against the curb.

At two o'clock, Jacqueline Sheppard from Dan Horgan's office telephoned Rich Kryhoski. Dan had just arrived at Kennedy Airport from Phoenix and would chair Lake View's Board meeting that night. In view of the weather, he suggested that the meeting be held in his penthouse apartment. Would Rich call the Board members?

When he got Shannon, Kryhoski mentioned that he'd had half a dozen complaints about Dom Rizzuto's snow clearance efforts. "And there's more," Rich said. "I just found out that he lied on his application. Never got a degree from Queens Community College, though he did attend courses there for a year."

"Well, guess we'll deal with it tonight, Rich. See you then." Just before four, she left for a beauty parlor appointment at Panache, a few blocks west of Lake

View. Sidewalks and crosswalks were still treacherous in spots, and Shannnon felt good when she arrived for her "do."

At Panache, you could always count on catching up on life's major and minor events: babies, bridal showers, divorces, and neighborhood gossip. Today, patrons announced they were sick of weather updates, then proceeded to talk about nothing else. One insisted on showing Shannon her holiday snapshots of people she would never meet, and had no wish to. "And this bald guy is my daughter-in-law Sadie's stepfather and his third wife Tillie. He met her…"

Shannon welcomed the distraction of a loud horn blowing outside. Customers rushed to the window, cheering. The veterinarian next door had mounted a high snowbank, opened the passenger door to a van, and was lifting a young woman's pooch out. Back over the snow with his charge and into the office for pup repair. "If only managed care were this good," said one customer.

By the time Shannon left Panache at five, she was in high humor that not even icy sidewalks or Dom Rizzuto could chill. Just enough time to relax and prepare for the evening's Board meeting. She arrived at Dan Horgan's penthouse apartment five minutes early. Rosa Di Carlo, Dan's housekeeper, greeted her at the door. "I'ma glad you comma first. Meester Horgan just called and said he'd be a leetle late. Could you starta up without heem? I feex up the dining room table. You serve dreenk at dees parties?"

"Don't fuss, Rosa. We usually have nothing at all, but you might ask people if they'd like a soda. Otherwise, relax. We'll be fine."

Rick Kryhoski came next and mentioned that Evan Doubleday would be absent. He'd been at Westchester County Medical Center since Monday, filling in at the emergency room. To her surprise, Shannon felt disappointed. He'd added a note of sanity and calm to the Board's occasionally testy deliberations.

Within ten minutes, all but Dan Horgan had arrived. The informality of the setting added to the group's bonhomie. Elmer Brick, noticing a Jasper Johns print on Dan's dining room wall, commented that his grandson's kindergarten sketches were better.

Shannon began the meeting. Gwyneth Fielding's minutes were quickly approved, and Val Thomas summarized the preliminary financial report for the prior year: "The final figures, of course, are still unaudited. I think I can safely predict that we'll end up the year about $20,000 under budget." Elmer offered a "Well done, Val," and the Treasurer smiled. Most thought that Val still had the first dollar he ever made.

He then pointed out that the blizzard meant that the new year's budget was already in jeopardy. Val directed a mild frown in Kryhoski's direction, as though the managing agent had deliberately run up a tab for temporary help to clear snow and ice in Lake View's driveway.

Rich, like most managing agents, regularly accepted responsibility for acts of God. It was easier than arguing with co-op Boards. The week had taken its toll, however, and tonight he commented: "Well, the storm will cost us a few thousand in extra manpower costs, but that's still cheaper than defending liability suits for broken bones. Our contingency budget of $50,000 is there for just this type of thing."

"Yes," agreed Val, "but it's only January and we can't dip into that too early in the year." Rich nodded, mumbling that if snow came in July, budgeting would be a lot easier.

"O.K.," said Shannon. "Next item on the agenda is the Arthur Bliss letter. Rich?"

"Yeah, well, you may remember this guy. The Board interviewed him back in September for an apartment and turned him down. He's sent me a couple of angry letters, demanding to know why he was rejected. Sent him the standard reply, simply reiterating the fact that his application had not been approved. As you know, we're not required to tell him why. The Board can turn down any applicant for a cooperative apartment for any reason, so long as you don't discriminate under existing law. In other words, you can discriminate, but you can't discriminate illegally."

"Uh, play that one again, Rich?" Elmer Brick asked.

"Well, as an example, you can't reject someone because of his race or creed, but you can turn him down because of the disruption he might bring to the building. Richard Nixon was once rejected by a New York City co-op. Residents thought the Secret Service would be all over the place, and weren't willing to risk the disruption."

"Maybe they just didn't like him," offered Gwyneth.

Hester Harrington, a leading fundraiser for the local Republican Party, became apoplectic: "Nonsense, considering what we have now, he was outstanding!"

Val Thomas added: "I did read recently that some co-ops are reluctant to admit lawyers."

"Damn right, and good thinking on their part," came a voice from the hall. "Who needs 'em?" Dan Horgan had arrived home, red-faced and breathless. "Sorry I'm late, folks. Metro-North is still running a little behind. Be with you in a few seconds."

"Good example, Val," continued Rich. "With litigation costs increasing, residents see lawyers as inviting the enemy in. Back to Arthur Bliss, the record producer. The info we picked up from contacts in his current building is that he installed a sound-recording studio without getting the Board's permission. His clients rehearse at all hours of the day and night. The Board told him to tear it out or they'd sue, and he told them to go ahead. In the interim, however, they've made life miserable for him and he's looking to move."

"Just what we need," said Elmer. "Hip-hop and rap-hip."

Dan entered the dining room and took a seat near Shannon. "Your show now," she said, pointing to the current agenda item.

"Ah yes, our friend Arthur Bliss. Well, he's claiming that the reason we turned him down is because he's African-American, and of course, that has nothing to do with it. Our attorney continues to respond to him, but he won't go quietly." There was general agreement on that point. Hester mentioned that Whoopi Goldberg had once been turned down for a Manhattan co-op, so the group seemed mollified. In a pinch, the "Whoopi" defense would do fine.

"O.K.," continued Dan. "On to Dom Rizzuto. I hear we have a few problems."

Kryhoski offered a quick summary. First, the report from Queens Community College, indicating that Dom had taken about thirty credits there, but had not graduated. "And then there's the storm. Dom should have contacted our snow plow contractor on Sunday, and been out there with the snow blower himself. You've got to get to this stuff early. He claims he was at his brother's in Astoria, and had a tough time getting home. By the time he did, it was too late to call." Rich's tone implied that he was not vouching for the story, only for what Dom had told him.

"By Monday, all the plows in the county were tied up, and he was at the end of a long line. I don't need to tell you, I've chewed his…uh, ears off about all this. Told him we'd be covering the incident tonight at our meeting, and I'd let him know your reactions."

Kryhoski glanced over at Dan, who looked at Shannon. Since no one else seemed poised to speak, she began: "Lying on an application is not uncommon, especially in a tight job market. Surprisingly, there are just as many cases where people omit mentioning advanced degrees and special training. They don't want to be thought overqualified, likely to leave when a better job comes up."

"So, the employer's supposed to just ignore the lie?" asked Jay Shapiro. His exasperated tone implied that Shannon was aiding and abetting a felony.

"No, just that it's a judgment call once you find out. If you're hiring a doctor and discover he has no medical degree, that's one thing. Seems to me the issue here is that now that Dom has been around a month and we've seen his performance, are the lie and the lack of a two-year degree important enough to fire him?"

"And having to start from scratch to find a replacement," added Kryhoski, his weary voice telegraphing his own position.

Gwyneth Fielding piped up: "Normally I don't countenance lying, but I'll admit to doing something similar along the lines Shannon discussed. Not being forthright about my entire background. I needed the job." The group waited for more, but Gwyneth had said all she planned.

It was enough. Dan looked around: "So, is there a sense that we should give him another chance?"

"Yes," said Hester. "And the delay in getting the snow plow meant that we were inconvenienced for a day. We weren't going far anyway."

Elmer Brick nodded: "Good call, Hester."

Kryhoski agreed to talk again with Rizzuto, to let him know the Board's displeasure, and to shape up. "Or ship out," mumbled Shapiro, glaring at Kryhoski.

"Anything else?" asked Horgan.

Val Thomas proposed a motion to officially thank Hester Harrington and her committee for the "outstanding job of decorating Lake View during the holiday season." It was quickly seconded and unanimously approved. Jay Shapiro interjected: "Best of all, no one got bopped on the head!"

"Bopped?" shrieked Hester.

"Bopped," said Jay. "My firm got a contract to oversee the decorations in a Park Avenue co-op last month. They wanted not only the full treatment on a tree and plants, but a stable and menorah as well."

"Oops, asking for trouble," said Dan. "What happened? Did the Muslims want a crescent?"

"Nope," said Jay. "The Board told us to put up a menorah. By mistake the decorator put up a seven-branched one. An orthodox Jewish guy went nuts when he saw it. Grabbed it and hit the Board president, a rabbi, over the head with it. The Hanukkah candelabrum has nine branches."

When the laughter subsided, Horgan once again thanked Hester "for sparing me a bump" and proceeded to schedule the next meeting. "I'll be on the road for a couple of weeks, a messy malpractice case. How does the second or third week of February look?"

They settled on Thursday of the second week, and adjourned just past seven-thirty.

24

"Bad timing. I picked the wrong day to tell him."

Ida Rizzuto was sitting in a soft leather recliner, talking to her therapist, Ceecy Caruso Cohen, on the day after Super Bowl Sunday. Ceecy's office was on the ground floor of a large old gabled house on Woodland Avenue in Bronxville. Earlier that day, a tearful Ida had called and made an appointment. Ceecy was leaving for London the next day and had notified her clients that she would not be available until June. Ida had sounded so distraught on the telephone, Ceecy made an exception for her.

Now, Ida was trying to compose herself: "You see, Dom bet on the underdog, hoping to make a killing, make up for the losses he'd had lately. When the favorite won big, he knew he'd have to pay up and soon." At this point, her voice trailed off, and eyes filled up. Ceecy said nothing for a few moments, then stood and reached for a box of tissues she kept near her own armchair, just across from Ida's. "Take your time. I've got no more appointments today."

Ida removed her dark glasses and wiped her eyes. The swelling on the right one had gone down, though the color of the skin around it was now blue and purplish. In a few minutes she continued. "So I guess he figured he'd go to the bank's ATM machine before I got home, and use my card to withdraw the money he owed his bookie."

"And?" Ceecy prodded gently.

"That's when he found out I'd canceled the card. I'd opened a new one, but of course he still doesn't know that. Anyway, when I came home from work, he was angry and drinking heavily, screaming about moving all our accounts to another bank on Monday. That's when I told him what I'd done on Friday. I'd tried to tell him about it Sunday before I left for work, but he wouldn't listen. Said he had to place a bet, and dashed out of the house."

Ida paused again and poured a glass of water from a carafe on a small coffee table. Between sips, she continued: "So that's when he lost it and hit me in the face. Just once with his fist. I fell against the sharp edge of the kitchen table, so the bump on the side of my head was my own fault." Ida looked up at Ceecy, who said nothing but raised her eyebrow.

"O.K.," said Ida wanly. "No Dom, no bump. I just don't want to make him out to be worse than he is."

"And how bad is that, Ida? How willing are you to stay with him until the next time it happens?"

"I don't think I am. We're scheduled to move the rest of our stuff from Queens later this week. Our lease there expires in two weeks, so the new building superintendent can move in. I haven't told Dom yet, but I'm not moving to Bronxville. I'm filing for divorce."

"Where will you stay?" asked Ceecy.

"For a time, with my mother. She's been taking care of Rudy, our son, until the school year ends. I called her just before I came here. I can go there tonight, after work, if I want. Just for a short stay, until I get my own apartment. More than once, I've heard from my mother that a wife's place is with her husband. I'll only be there for a day or so before she starts it again, the old 'for better or for worse' speech. She stayed with my father, who brutalized her and us. Why should I be different? Except that it's always Dom that gets the better and the rest of us the worse."

"Well, it seems that you've thought things through," offered Ceecy. "Do you think he'll come after you?"

"Oh, yes. First with roses, then with threats."

"Then you may want to think about getting a restraining order to keep him away."

"Well, I don't want to cause him any more trouble than I have to. I just want him out of my life."

They talked like that, Ceecy and Ida, for another half hour. Finally Ida asked for and Ceecy gave her the name of a local attorney with experience in handling battered wives. Ida called her from Ceecy's office, and the two agreed to meet later that night.

After Ida left, Ceecy swiveled in her chair and looked out of her bay picture window. As day faded into dusk, her client was walking slowly to her Saturn. Was it her imagination, or did Ida Rizzuto seem taller than when they'd first met?

Madonna the cat slithered across the wooden floor and jumped, purring, into Ceecy's lap. She stroked the animal's soft white fur, offering a silent prayer that Ida would not lose her resolve.

25

....

"Where did you find her? My toilet has stopped flushing and I'm joining the computer age," Minnie Stern greeted Shannon in Lake View's lobby on the first Sunday in February.

Shannon was just returning from twelve o'clock Mass and Minnie was carefully navigating her walker. "Whoa, you mean Max Schneible?" asked Shannon, laughing.

"Yes, after she did her plumbing, I asked her if she'd like a cup of tea. We started talking and I told her that the worst thing about a broken hip in this awful winter was that you're cut off from the world. I'm not cut out to be a couch potato, and the only news in the papers is bad news. So Max suggested I get a computer. Funny, but I'd been thinking about it on and off, mostly off. Figured they'd think I was a senile old lady."

"Well, Minnie, you're certainly not senile and I never think of you as old."

Minnie smiled. "Well, it's funny meeting you. Max said there were lots of people on the job market these days who might be willing to work with me: choose the machine, set it up, and get me started on the Internet. I thought you might know someone."

"I do, Minnie. Let me make a call or two. I'll get back to you."

Shannon was thinking of Brian Palmer, the technology manager laid off by Dan Horgan's firm. She'd given him a reference to Halliday Temporary Services, and Brett had since mentioned that Brian's client was highly satisfied. Shannon dialed Dan Horgan's number, first. Dan just might not welcome running into Brian so close to home.

He, however, had no problem with the arrangement, agreeing that Minnie and Brian would be a good team. She then called Brett Halliday, who promised to call Brian at home, then asked her about returning to work.

"I'm just beginning to congratulate myself on taking the winter off," she answered.

"Yeah, so you said. But the groundhog says we've got six more weeks of winter ahead. Why hang around the house? Besides, I've got a super opportunity with your name on it. In the spring you can quit and fall in love again."

"Like you, right?" Brett had been married to his business since a messy divorce a few years back.

"Hey, just do as I say, not as I do. Really, this slot is perfect, practically in your own back yard here in White Plains. A two-month stint to run the administrative operation at a start-up women's magazine. They're desperate for someone with your background. Really top rates. Only one catch: they need somebody fast."

"I don't think so, Brett. I have plans for the first

couple of days this week." He groaned.

"Will you at least think about it?" he asked.

"Of course." When Shannon hung up, she noticed there was a message on her answering machine. "Hi, Mom. It's Maria. Need a favor. Ella broke her arm and can't mind Drew for a few weeks. I know you planned on staying home for a time, but Ken and I are desperate. What would it take to get you to come up here and play a real nanny for a month or so? Call me. Thanks. Luv'ya."

Decisions, decisions.

Shannon did not really want to return to work nor mind Drew. One of the perks of being a Temporary Executive was that you got to decide when to take off. The weather during the past month had made her happy to be home. Driving was out, and the evening news reported disastrous performance on Metro-North's trains. A couple of nights, thousands of commuters had been stranded at Grand Central Station for hours.

And then there were all those catch-up things to do: an apartment to paint; a car to service; a computer to upgrade; new books to read; an exercise program to begin; Christmas notes to answer; friends to call.

Of course, if she extended her vacation, there was a good chance that Lake View's affairs would intrude on her personal plans. Dan Horgan had mentioned some upcoming business travel and residents were not apt to let problems, even minor ones, sit for weeks. Rich Kryhoski was perfectly able to manage

things, but many expected the Board to stay personally involved. The worst prospect of all would be to
stay home, complete none of her own work, and
become a complaint service for a few pesky neighbors. Given a harsh winter, some would have little
else to do except complain.

Even less appealing was the thought of minding
Drew, who had been reared to expect that others'
mission in life was to entertain him. Unlike her
friends, Shannon tried to avoid critiquing her daughter's child-rearing habits. It was something her own
mother had done, and it had driven her crazy. During
her few brief babysitting stints with Drew, she'd
read, sung, danced, and played with Mighty Mor-
phins. Fun for a night; a few weeks of that, she
thought, will land me in the looney bin.

Besides, too many of her friends had filled in for
nannies temporarily. Months, even years later, they
were still doing it and still complaining. "How can I
pull out now? My son says if I do, they might just get
a nanny from hell," said one. Nonsense, she thought.
There were thousands of wonderful nannies out
there. Maria and Ken could afford to hire a good one.
If she played nanny, it would be like Alice going down
into the black hole. Who knew when she'd surface
again?

Her sister-in-law Ceecy told her regularly that
she should have been able to just say no, without
explaining why. With business associates and salespeople, she'd learned to do that; family and close
friends were something else. She often wanted to fall

back on the old W.C. Fields line: "I'd rather be in Philadelphia."

She made a light dinner and called Brett Halliday back, half-hoping that the job had been filled. It hadn't. When they talked further, she understood why. Pressed for details, Brett acknowledged that this super opportunity was one that three people had already bombed out on. "The record stay is two weeks. The first hire was fired after a week; the next was a guy who quit at the end of two; the third, a woman who stayed through orientation, then took a coffee break and pulled a Judge Crater. Hasn't been seen or heard from since."

Shannon laughed. "So tell me, Brett, why would an independent woman like me even consider jumping into this swamp?"

"Two reasons. They'll pay about twenty-five percent above the market to hire you, sight unseen. They've read your application and checked you out. And the place is really a great learning experience, Shannon. State-of-the-art technology, top-notch staff, great location, right near Metro-North's White Plains station. You can just roll off the train and into the office. I'll even buy you lunch one day." Brett's office was just across the street from The Westchester, a new White Plains mall for upper-income shoppers.

"Terrific. So why did all those people leave?"

"Well, the editor's a bit of a hellion. L. Jayne Grey's smart as hell, but a workaholic who thinks that anybody working only fifteen hours a day is goofing off. But you're up to her, Shannon. You've got brains and energy to burn, and you've seen her type before."

The old Everest pitch. It's there, so you've got to take on the challenge. Brett knew her so well. It worked every time.

She looked out the window. A steady stream of cars was again cruising on the Bronx River Parkway. Metro-North's trains were running close to schedule. Her "to do" list could wait. Shannon agreed to take the job, starting on Wednesday. Two months guaranteed; no more; no less.

Brett Halliday was a happy man.

Maria was an unhappy woman when Shannon called to say that she'd need to make other arrangements for Drew. He, however, was philosophical: "So, Mom, who'll take me to play school and pick me up?"

Maria was now downright miserable. Silly questions were not her strong suit, especially those from four-year olds.

26

....

"Did you see today's *New York Post?*" the voice asked Shannon O'Keefe.

It came from the man who had just sat down beside her on Metro-North's eight o'clock train from White Plains to Bronxville. The question momentarily distracted her. She'd just settled in for a relaxing ride, after a second week working for L. Jayne Grey, dubbed "Lady Jane" by her troops. It was not meant as a compliment. Most wished her the same fate as the original Lady Jane, first beloved, then beheaded.

Now, looking up, she was surprised to see Evan Doubleday: "Sorry, didn't mean to interrupt your reverie. Tough day?"

"Not really," she smiled. "New job with a boss who's finally broken the glass ceiling. Wants to be sure that every other woman experiences the pain she did in cracking it."

"No 'She's my sister,' huh?"

"Nope. So what gives in *The Post?* They were all sold out at the station."

He handed her the paper, pointed to a small article on the bottom of page seven, headed, "Former Building Superintendent Arrested at Queens Hospital." The story reported that the police had been called by the hospital's security officers just after midnight the previous day. "Dominic Rizzuto, a former building superintendent, was seeking to enter the emergency room and talk to his wife, Ida Rizzuto, supervising nurse there. Mrs. Rizzuto, after filing for a divorce, got a restraining order against her husband last week. When asked to leave the hospital's premises, Rizzuto allegedly screamed racial obscenities and punched Pedro Cortes, a security officer who had denied him entrance to the building. Rizzuto will be arraigned today on charges of disturbing the peace, assault, and violating a court order. This swift action represents a crackdown by local enforcement officers following two recent cases where husbands, after posting low bail, violated restraining orders and later killed their wives."

"Well," said Shannon. "Looks like our Dom may set a record for the shortest stint as Lake View's building superintendent."

"Yes," said Evan. "Of course, no one in Bronxville, except us, reads *The Post.*" Shannon looked up and he was smiling. "You're one of the few people anywhere who admits reading it," he added. "If you see someone buying it, guaranteed they'll say it's for their mothers, grandmothers, or girlfriends."

She nodded. "I once met a guy buying it on a rainy night. Said he'd forgotten his umbrella and needed it to cover his head."

Evan laughed. "Good thing I'm an oncologist, not a heart specialist. Hester Harrington will get arrhythmia or worse over this dirt."

"Well, we'll find out tomorrow night at the Board meeting." As the train approached the Bronxville station, the conductor was cautioning departing passengers to walk carefully on the slippery platform.

"Sometimes I think Metro-North is run by unemployed orthopedic surgeons," groaned Evan. "Why don't they clear the stuff away, instead of warning us about it?"

They stepped out on the ice-slicked platform, Evan first, then Shannon. He turned, took her arm and they walked slowly across the stairwell, to navigate still another obstacle, black ice. Once outside, the night was frigid but clear. The tree branches on Pondfield Road West were wrapped in thin crusts of frozen snow. Icicles hung from some. The sky was dotted with stars. There were few people out, and only an occasional car on the road. Evan started humming "Silent Night."

Well, thought Shannon, not for long.

27

....

"Angie baby, boobie! This woman has no coupon. Get her one!" It was five-fifteen the next evening, Thursday. A cheerful middle-aged cashier was shouting to a gum-chewing girl who was lazily re-stocking the shelves in CVS, Bronxville's chaotic sundry store on Pondfield Road. Shannon had walked over from Metro-North's station to purchase a few items before the Board meeting. Dozens of other commuters apparently had the same idea. Lines were long and tempers short.

Now she was the center of attention, attempting to buy a sale item without the additional discount from a coupon. When she turned to the customer behind her to apologize for the delay, the woman said: "Glory be, what a lot of shenanigans for nothing! I don't shop here often. Coupons, schmoupons! Far as I can see, there's lots of sales nowadays but no bargains." The two looked at each other, and then Shannon recognized her: "It's Edna, right? Edna Donohue. I'm Shannon O'Keefe. We talked briefly at Walter's wake."

"Of course," said Edna. "How are you?"

"Well, considering the weather, not too bad. And you?"

"The same. There was lots to do after Walter's

death, but most of that was over a month ago. I'm really not much for senior citizen clubs. Then my Church group wanted me to go on a bus trip to Washington for a big protest. The anniversary of Poe and Cade, was it? Something like that. You know, the abortion thing."

"Sure. Roe v. Wade," said Shannon.

"Them's the ones. Anyway, I said what does an old lady like me want to go down there and tell all those young ones what to do? Let them figure it out for themselves! But my friends said that's not why they go. They go for the lovely hot lunch. Thank you very much, I said, I'll make me own lunch right at home." Edna laughed in the telling, and her face lit up.

"Sounds good to me," said Shannon.

"Then my daughter-in-law Diane got pregnant and the flu at the same time. I'm not sure which is worse. My son Buddy asked if I'd come up and stay for a few weeks, till she was back on her feet again. Their house is not far from here. Lawrence Park West."

"I know the section. A lovely area."

"Yes, but I'll be leaving soon, thanks be to God. I don't drive and I'm used to being able to walk to things. Feet, they're more dependable."

Just when it appeared that the stock clerk had taken a safari, she slouched up to the cashier with the coupon. A good thing, too. The line had doubled and so had the grumbles. The cashier was totaling the bill when Dan Horgan came up to Shannon, and gave her a bottle of shaving lotion. "Add this to your stuff, will you? I'll pay you later."

He smiled at Edna Donohue, and Shannon quickly said: "It's Edna, Dan. Edna Donohue."

A puzzled look, then: "Of course. Edna, how are you? How are you adjusting?"

"We'll make it through, Mr. Horgan. We always do."

"I'm glad. Walter was looking forward to retirement. He'd want you to go on with your plans, even without him."

Edna stared for a moment, then nodded. "My Buddy will be picking me up soon. I'll be on my way home next week."

Shannon asked Edna if she'd like to have lunch one day in the Bronx. "I work four days a week, but am usually free one day. I often visit friends in the old neighborhood. May I call you?"

"Lovely. As they say, I'm in the book."

After saying good night, Shannon and Dan left CVS, turned right at the corner, then right again to Kraft Avenue.

"Do you think that's wise?" he asked her.

"What?"

"Seeing Edna for lunch," he answered. "She thinks Walter elected retirement. Why not let sleeping dogs lie? Something might come up and the truth would come out. Be a bit awkward."

"Awkward for who? Look, Dan, most of us don't wake up in the morning thinking about you and the firm. It's just lunch. Besides, I thought Edna looked drained and thinner."

"Really? Didn't notice," said Dan.

No, you wouldn't, thought Shannon. You never do.

They walked in silence, arriving at the managing agent's office a few minutes later.

28

....

"He'll have to go," announced Hester Harrington, sweeping into the Board meeting a few minutes later.

The others had all arrived, and Dom Rizzuto was already on their informal agenda. To no one in particular, Hester added: "Well, at least the news about him came out too late for the Bronxville paper. No sense washing dirty linen in public. No one will want to buy our apartments."

Elmer Brick looked up from reading the "Court Report" in the weekly newspaper. "Righto, Hes, but that green-eyed feller that's been running naked around the college campus was spotted again. Compared to our Dom, he'll soon be small potatoes. Seems like they have a good line on him, though. White, over six feet, and green eyes."

Gwyneth Fielding said: "Well, he wasn't quite naked, Elmer. He was wearing a bandana this time."

"The wind-chill factor," added Elmer.

Dan interrupted: "O.K. We need to resolve the Rizzuto problem tonight. Let's get started. Any corrections to Gwyneth's minutes?"

There were none. With limited discussion, financial and maintenance items were covered.

Dan commented that Arthur Bliss had now filed

a racial discrimination suit against Lake View, naming all eight Board members as defendants. The co-op's lawyers had filed a motion to dismiss, of course. While there were no guarantees they would be successful, case law was on their side.

"So we could all end up bankrupt or in jail," moaned Jay Shapiro, "for doing this job with no pay, no perks, and daily abuse."

"Theoretically, yes, Jay. But we're covered for Directors' liability insurance, so that's unlikely." Jay was still muttering when Shannon suggested they move on.

"O.K.," Dan began. "By now you all know that Dom Rizzuto was arrested on Monday night in Queens, charged with disturbing the peace, violating a court protection order, and punching a cop. This was his first arrest, and his brother bailed him out. He's due back in court in three weeks."

"Figures," said Jay.

Dan nodded to Kryhoski: "Rich, will you pick it up from there?"

"Sure. Dom called me right after he got out of jail. Said the charges were all trumped up. Admitted he'd had a beer or two that night. He'd seen a marriage counselor and wanted to talk to Ida about getting back together. Said he just got carried away when she wouldn't see him."

"Romeo, wherefore art thou Romeo?" mumbled Val Thomas.

"Yeah. Anyway, bottom line is that he wants another chance," said Rich.

"Dan," asked Evan Doubleday, "are we at risk if we fire him? You know, the old 'innocent till proven guilty' thing?"

"Well, there's always some risk. I'd say it's minimal, Evan. I had one of my guys research the spousal abuse charges Ida brought against him, and the order of protection. The judge is no pushover; he doesn't award those things easily. Rizzuto's appealed, but the word is he's got no case. It'll stick."

"Then I'd vote for terminating him," said Evan.

"The sooner the better," added Jay Shapiro.

"Any dissents?" asked Dan. There were none.

"O.K., then. Rich, take care of it. Give him the usual two weeks in lieu of notice. See that he's gone by then."

"Done," said Rich. "Now, what about his replacement? Go back to the drawing board, or make an offer to one of the two we saw in November? It's not a good time for hiring. Any super who's proved his worth this winter will get a counteroffer from his current Board."

"Hank Gonzales had no takers in November," said Val Thomas. "I liked Max Schneible then; now, she looks even better."

"She certainly has the qualifications," said Gwyneth. Dan asked: "Any other thoughts? No? Then let's vote."

Shannon made a motion; Evan seconded it. After unanimous approval, Rich Kryhoski was authorized to offer Max Schneible the job.

"Just one question," interjected Hester Harrington: "Should we tell her that the first three months are probationary?"

"Why?" asked Shannon.

"Well, she's a woman, of course. There's never been a woman building superintendent here in Bronxville!"

"Hester," said Elmer Brick, "we've never had a naked man running around a college campus either. If the town hasn't gone to pot over that, I'd say they can survive Max Schneible."

Laughs and agreement from the others. Hester, seeing no support, simply shrugged in "don't-say-I-didn't-warn-you" fashion.

The meeting was quickly adjourned, and Shannon walked out with Rich Kryhoski. "Well, it'll be a new challenge for me," he said to her.

"I'm sure it will, Rich," she said. "But just think, you'll be hailed by the feminists as a trail-blazer!"

"Yeah," he said wryly, "Maybe I'll make the Bronxville Centennial Book of Records. What a way to go!"

The rest of the group got into their cars after leaving the meeting. Shannon said she'd walk the few blocks back to Lake View. Gwyneth and Evan joined her. "I'm still puzzled," said Gwyneth, as they crossed the Bronxville rotary.

"About Max?" Evan asked.

"Good lord, no," said Gwyneth. "That naked man. Who got close enough to see his green eyes?"

29

On Wednesday of the following week, Principal Mark Borras entered the Computer Room at P.S. 807.

A few years back Borras had been a short, squarish, fifty-two year old man who wore ill-fitting suits. More than one teacher had remarked that both Mark and the school had seen better days. The Principal himself had said he was just marking time till early retirement.

Now, Borras was still short and even broader. While he would never make anyone's "best-dressed" list, his suits, if not elegant, now fit. His shoes were shined and he walked with a certain air and confidence. Last year, when the school board had offered an attractive "early-out" package to supervisory personnel, Borras had tossed it in the waste basket.

"Poor Charlotte" Noble, second-grade teacher and chronic complainer, had commented at the time: "He's lost it completely, not getting out while the going's good."

Well, Mark Borras was now a different man and P.S. 807 a new school.

Take today, for example. His school was open for computer classes. Most other city schools were closed for February vacation week.

A month ago, Luke had asked him to open the computer room for three afternoons that week. The school's Foundation had recently purchased a new generation of computers; Luke would recruit volunteers to teach the kids how to use them. Borras was no longer astonished by anything Luke proposed, and immediately set out to tackle the usual bureaucratic layers. The local Community Board was first and easiest. This was the same crowd, of course, that had once called him a nutcase, after he'd proposed a Foundation.

Then, Community Board President Felix Mendoza had said: "Now, look here, Mister Borras, just who do you think is going to donate money to folks in the South Bronx? They sho ain't gonna get no building named after them like those rich men at Hahvad." The morning's *Times* had run a story of still another multi-millionaire graduate who'd donated several million to his alma mater.

Mendoza was a polished, highly successful attorney, who wore custom-made suits and was known to have high political aspirations. A superb public speaker, he liked nothing better than to mimic the establishment. Tonight, several parents and guardians began laughing and punching each other. One man shouted, "You tell 'im, Felix! Will they settle for their name on a piece of coal in the furnace?" The school's heating system, like more than one-quarter of the city's, was antiquated. Replacement was on a very long list of capital expenditures that the Board of Education regularly presented to the

Mayor's office for funding, and got routinely rejected. Borras smiled too, as though he shared the absurdity of it all.

But this, after all, was theater. Early in his career, Borras had been frustrated by the bureaucratic game; now, he'd mastered it. He'd grown up as a middle-class kid, the son of a Puerto Rican father and an African-American mother, not too far from the school. The neighborhood, called Highbridge, was now lumped in with the broader community, under the heading "South Bronx." To some, the name was still a metaphor for urban decay and broken promises.

Borras and Mendoza had known each other well as students at Manhattan College. When Borras became P.S. 807's principal and Mendoza the Community School Board president, they renewed their friendship. They dined in out-of-the-way restaurants between Board meetings. After discussing the school's needs and challenges, they'd negotiate and plan strategy and tactics.

That night, Borras followed the planned script. "Look, Mr. Mendoza, those were my sentiments exactly. Luke Plisky changed my mind. How about having him address the Board briefly? You've got nothing to lose." Borras put out his arms in a you-tell-him-why-it-can't-be done gesture.

Mendoza nodded, waving Luke forward. "Ten minutes, Mr. Plisky. We've got a long agenda."

Luke took five. He quickly outlined the school's needs, highlighting those which were unlikely to be funded during the lives of anyone in the room. Suburban communities had set up private foundations. Why not P.S. 807? Luke knew of at least one anonymous contributor who would provide seed money and an initial contribution of $100,000. He thought other businesses would contribute as well.

Luke then walked back to his seat near the rear of the auditorium. It was noticed that he walked with a very slight limp.

Mark Borras again took the microphone and thanked Luke, being sure to let the audience know that this was one of the school's most dedicated teachers, one who "like Felix Mendoza is a Vietnam War hero." Luke cringed.

And so the Foundation was born. It had taken more than a year to get the proposal through the Board of Education, the Teachers' Union, the Mayor's Office and a host of other minefields. Felix Mendoza made it happen. Over time Felix had cultivated a whole network of media contacts. Now, he played them like a maestro, pulling them in whenever the Foundation proposal was stalled. It was good press for the Chancellor, the teachers, the kids, and, not least of all, for Felix Mendoza.

Luke Plisky, true to his word, had provided the seed money and the initial $100,000 from a donor "who wished to remain anonymous, so he won't be besieged by every school district in the city." Many of the city's business people responded with enthusiasm and contributions. Here was a chance to both do good and get a skilled work force in return.

Felix Mendoza rode the publicity to a seat on the City Council. Word was out that he'd run for Congress in the next election.

The school began to prosper. Reading and math scores had improved a year after the Foundation was set up, and each year since. Mark Borras was pleased and Luke Plisky became a neighborhood hero. From time to time, there was talk about the mysterious donor who got the whole thing started, the one who periodically made big donations. But why look a gift horse in the mouth?

So, last fall, when Luke had proposed opening the school for a few afternoons during winter vacation, Borras made a few phone calls. Obstacles surfaced and magically disappeared. Higher-ups at the Board of Education in Brooklyn were not enamored of the idea. The union expressed "principled opposition." There were questions galore: What about liability insurance? Building security? How would other schools and parents react?

But all of these nay-sayers looked to Felix Mendoza for funding by the City Council. Mark Borras later explained it to Luke: "Principled opposition met unprincipled pragmatism. Pragmatism won."

"It usually does," answered Luke.

Now it was three o'clock on a sunny, late February day. Luke and seven or eight other adults were in the room, giving the kids hands-on lessons at the computers. Borras recognized Enid Gomez and Enrique Dupraz, along with a few older teachers who'd retired the previous year, and a parent or two with computer skills.

"How's it going, Luke?" he asked, after greeting and thanking the others.

"Well, Mark, we've got at least a couple of Bill Gates clones in this crowd, guaranteed!"

"And Grace Hoppers, too, Mr. Borras," chimed in Enid Gomez. Enid had told him about the legendary woman who later became a navy admiral. Dr. Hopper had worked on the original ENIAC computer in the 50s, and taken it apart when the machine malfunctioned. There, somewhere in the middle of a motherboard and wires, was a dead moth. "Eureka! The computer bug was christened and buried on the same day!"

Borras laughed: "And Grace Hoppers, too." After a while he dropped a couple of boxes of Dunkin' Donuts on the table and walked down the hall to his office to catch up on paperwork.

Luke decided to check his own E-mail for messages. There were a couple, including one from "Loot." It read:

LUNCH AT 22?

Luke replied: "O.K." and signed off.

Lunch meant that Bruno Altieri wanted to discuss a contract. He and Luke regularly had dinner, but never to discuss business. Bruno, himself a gourmet cook and wine connoisseur, liked to dine at expensive restaurants. Lunch, on the other hand, was for business. They'd prearranged the day and time, always meeting on the last Saturday of the month at two-thirty in the afternoon. Only the restaurants varied. They'd developed a list of noisy fast-food places where conversations were unlikely to be overheard.

Bruno Altieri and Luke Plisky would meet at Restaurant #22, "Nathan's" on Central Avenue in Yonkers, on the last Saturday in February.

Good, Luke thought. If P.S. 807 was to really get going on the Internet, the Foundation would need an infusion of cash. Perfect timing.

30

"Dom Rizzuto has resigned as building superintendent for personal reasons," said Rich Kryhoski's letter to Lake View residents.

It was Thursday of the third week of February. Rosa Di Carlo had just brought up the mail and Minnie Stern was sitting at her kitchen table, reading it aloud.

"Whatsa mean, personal reasons?" asked Rosa, who was stirring the sauce for lasagna.

Minnie hesitated. Dan Horgan had told her the circumstances, but she was not sure how much of this was confidential. Rosa answered: "I teenk I know. He jomp before he was pooshed."

Minnie nodded.

"Itsa good he go," added Rosa. "I lika his wife, notta heem so much. He no treata her verra good. I read about it in da Post. A *cafone,* datta guy. I donna care what parta Italee he say he comma from. *Cafone,* dattsa heem."

Minnie smiled and continued reading: "We are pleased to announce that Ms. Max Schneible will be replacing Mr. Rizzuto, and will be on the premises in about four weeks."

"Thatsa the ladee who coma here to plumb?"

asked Rosa.

"Yes."

"Verra nisa ladee."

"I think so, too, Rosa," said Minnie.

"I hopa she soop as gooda she plumb," said Rosa.

"You're not the only one," laughed Minnie.

Rosa continued stirring the sauce, while Minnie looked out her kitchen window. The Bronxville Lake was starting to thaw. "If winter comes, can spring be far behind?" she said, half to herself, half out loud.

Rosa, unlike Shelley, was emphatic: "Only a coupla weeks, itsa gonna comma," she answered. "Eet's a gonna be a verra interesting, dees place."

About that, Minnie had no doubt at all.

....

Later that afternoon, Dom Rizzuto walked into the reception room at the offices of Horgan & Stern.

A young woman with milk-chocolate skin and hazel eyes looked up: "Yes, how may I help you?"

Dom paused a moment. Not the time for a snappy response. "Dominic Rizzuto. One of Dan Horgan's employees. I'd like to see him. It's personal."

"Mr. Horgan is tied up at the moment," she replied. "Can someone else help you?"

"Look, Miss…"

"Ortega, and it's Ms." answered the hazel-eyed girl, in a firm but pleasant tone.

"Look, Ms. Ortega," he continued, raising his voice. "Don't give me that. I'm going to sit here until he comes out."

With that, she calmly asked him to sit down, then rose and walked down the hall to Dan Horgan's office. Dan was standing in the doorway talking to Jacqueline Sheppard, his executive assistant. Ms. Francine Ortega said that Dominic Rizzuto was in the reception area and unlikely to leave.

"Guess I'll have to see him and get rid of him, then. Jacqueline, call Security. Have them standing by."

"Well, what is it, Mr. Rizzuto?" asked Dan, standing formally behind his desk, as Dom entered the door. "Please don't sit down. I'm a busy man," he added. "Rich Kryhoski told you all you need to know."

"I want another chance," said Dom. "My lawyer said the charges won't stick. Ida and I are trying to get back together."

"Mr. Rizzuto, kindly leave. There's nothing to discuss. The Board's decision was unanimous."

Dom was prepared to whine, beg, even apologize. One look at Horgan told him that nothing would work. He stood up, walked closer to Dan and eye-balled him across the desk: "Why, you..."

He got no further. Two husky Building Security guards appeared behind Rizzuto, strong-arming him. "Please leave, Mr. Rizzuto, before I call the police," said Horgan.

Dom pushed the guards away, straightened his tie, and turned his back on Horgan, shouting over his shoulder: "I'll go, bud, but you'll be hearing from me. You and all your rich friends will be sorry."

"Good-bye, Mr. Rizzuto," said Horgan.

Dom Rizzuto was escorted out of the reception area and out of the building, after a final leer at Ms. Ortega.

Best not to wish him a nice day, she thought.

31

....

In 1916, "Famous Nathan's" opened up near Coney Island's boardwalk. Over the years Nathan's hot dogs had achieved the same aura as quiche in France or Beef Wellington in England. Legend had it that FDR and Eleanor Roosevelt once served them for lunch to King George VI and the Queen on a royal visit.

Now the signature garish yellow sign hung out in hundreds of malls, airports and shopping thoroughfares all over the country, a cheerful, randy invitation to check high fat, high cholesterol, and high sodium angst at the door.

On this last Saturday in February, it was just before two-thirty in the afternoon. Luke Plisky had walked the mile and a half from his Crestwood home and arrived early at Famous Nathan's on Central Park Avenue in Yonkers, just south of a sprawling Caldor's discount department store. It was a sunbaked day, cloudless sky, with temperatures well above normal. Throngs of weary shoppers were barreling into the huge seating area for a late lunch. Families followed the drill: find a table; stake out ownership with coat or a body; take meal orders; get in line. Squealing kids were piling out of vans, howling out orders for large orders of french fries, pizzas and sodas, even as they ran toward the restaurant.

Luke was just opening Nathan's front door when he saw Bruno Altieri get out of his two-door silver '88 Mercedes. His friend waved and walked toward him. Casually dressed in a tan canvas sports jacket, dark jeans and running shoes, Bruno still had an aura of command. A neatnik; well over six feet; stiff-backed, with a quick walk, and rock-hardened jaw, a mediterranean-skin, and an appearance that might have been called handsome, save for a nose with a conspicuous bump. His friends called him Beaker.

Bruno had once told Luke that he'd gotten the lump in a gang fight at about age nine. A group of older kids had called his father "Mafioso." Bruno had thrown the first punch at the gang leader, three years older and thirty pounds heavier. He was then pummeled by three boys and ended up in the emergency room with a broken nose, mild concussion and several broken ribs. The bones had healed, but his nose was never the same and he refused plastic surgery. Bruno regarded it as his badge of honor, a talisman that marked him as a worthy firstborn son. A Princeton graduate, he now functioned as president and chief operating officer of his father Sal's far-flung businesses in real estate development and contracting. No one doubted that "Beaker" Altieri had the old man's confidence.

Entering Nathan's, they queued up behind an older couple, the man thin and squirrelly, the woman shaped like an inverted two-stemmed pear. Jack

Spratt and his wife. "Oy, Sarah," said Jack, pointing to the wall menu: "Vill you look at that? Healthy Choice meals!" The man shook his head sadly. "Vot's the world coming to when Nathan's serves Healthy Choice?"

Round-faced Sarah, who looked five years younger and forty pounds heavier, but in better health than her frail partner, shrugged: "Not for us, Iz. Get the usual…corned beef on rye, two extra slices of bread. Large fries. And pickles, he shouldn't forget the pickles. Two coffees. Decaf for you, Iz. Extra cream; no sugar; sweetener for me. I'm dieting."

Iz parroted her order. Just then a hefty young Hispanic woman with a badge marked "Assistant Manager" appeared and began talking to the deli man, whose carving knife was suspended in midair. A short lecture followed on how to set up huge slabs of corned beef, turkey, roast beef and pastrami for maximum appeal in the display case; then, how to slice efficiently on the butcher block cutting board. Deli man looked nonplused until she walked away with a satisfied smile: "Her," he gestured with his large knife, "been here six days. Thinks she's running Maxim's. Me, I've been slicing meat for thirty years."

Customers on the line nodded sympathetically. Who had not had a similar experience with a stupid boss? Deli man now wielded his knife like Damocles' sword. Thick lobs of corned beef rained on rye bread. At least a half-pound. An extra plate and two more pieces of bread, with enough pickles to start a business. Thanks to management, Nathan's would make little profit on this deli man's shift.

Bruno said to Luke: "It's almost enough to make me change my order, but I can't resist the hot dogs. Do you think he'll squeeze two on the bun?"

Luke laughed. When it was their turn, Bruno ordered a hot dog, large fries and Coke; Luke, a roast beef sandwich and root beer. The sandwich seemed to contain at least half a steer. "If I get Mad Cow Disease, you'll know why," Luke told Bruno.

After paying, they headed for the condiments table, where customers drowned food in sauerkraut, mustard, and relish. One woman had brought along a small plastic bag into which she was scooping out a large portion of hot sauerkraut. "For my dog," she explained to Bruno, who was waiting for the ladle. "He likes it with his dinner."

Bruno smiled. "Take your time," he said.

Luke and Bruno headed toward the rear, and sat down at a table near the noisy video arcade, the best place to discuss business.

"So, how's the family?" asked Luke, as they began eating.

"Good," said Bruno, knocking on the wooden table. "Great wife, good kids, I'm a lucky man. And you? Ready to try again?"

Luke smiled. "Nope. When you've flown first class, you're not about to go tourist. Besides, I'm set in my ways. Who'd want me?"

"Dumb question, so I won't answer it." Bruno

dropped the issue. Though his friend's wife Karen had been killed more than fifteen years ago, Luke was still locked up in her memory.

"Romance is all around us," said Bruno, nodding to the left. A sixtyish hair-challenged man and a prune-faced woman of about the same age were sitting at adjoining tables. The man had just finished reading *The Daily News* and asked her if she'd like to read it. Woman said, "No, thanks," and continued munching her cheeseburger slowly. Man babbled on about the weather, the upcoming baseball season, and the stock market. Woman initially answered in polite monosyllables, then ignored him. She stared straight ahead with a don't-bother-me-look that was obvious to all but this pest. Finally, announcing he was leaving, he dropped the newspaper on her tray, stating: "I'm done with it; you can have it." Woman shoved paper back at him, screaming loudly: "I told you I didn't want it!"

Luke said to Bruno, "Not a good place for trolling babes. Maybe he should read that book about when No means No!"

They talked and laughed that way, back and forth, the way old friends do, for another half hour. Finally, when both had finished their sandwiches, Bruno looked around to be sure they could not be overheard. No problem. All around them, hassled parents were coaching small tykes to finish gargantuan orders of fries and sodas they'd demanded. Tykes were now shouting for frozen yogurt and video games.

"O.K., here's the deal," Bruno began.

Quietly, he outlined the murder-for-hire in usual fashion. No names until Luke agreed to take the job. Just background on who wanted it done, to whom, and why. Bruno knew Luke's ground rules. This was not your usual contract killer. Luke would not kill randomly, for money or simple revenge. The situation had to be unique, where the normal rules hadn't or wouldn't work. Luke had set boundaries and Bruno honored them.

Two of his contracts involved drug dealers where a child had died from an overdose. In another, a parolee had confessed to killing an elderly woman during a robbery; when his lawyer was able to show that the man had not been fully advised of his rights, the killer had walked. A fourth was an anesthesiologist who'd been drinking, accidentally killing a young mother during routine gall bladder surgery. The man had gotten probation when his wealthy father had bribed an attending physician to say that the patient's occasional drug use was a contributing factor in her death.

Vigilante justice? Not to Luke. Not after Vietnam, where so many had died in a legal war. When computer systems crashed, only people could fix them. It was the same with government. He saw his work as a way for ordinary people to get simple justice. A righting of wrongs, when all else failed.

He had long since lost faith in an afterlife. For him, the only refuge from personal despair was to do what you could to make this one better for the living.

It was why he killed, and why he taught in the South Bronx.

This case was different from all the rest. Interesting, but different. When Bruno had finished the briefing, Luke had questions, lots of them. Bruno's answers satisfied him. The final test was always a letter, which Bruno now handed him. The letter was handwritten and signed by the person who wanted someone killed. The letter sealed the contract. Luke had no illusions about his work. One day, things might go wrong. In the event they did, the client could not turn him in without risking his own involvement.

Normally the letter was sufficient. But this case had a novel twist. Luke wanted something more from the client before he'd take the job. "I don't think that'll be a problem," said Bruno. "I'll see that you get it."

Luke nodded. "On that condition, it's a deal." The client could afford the usual fee of $100,000.

Bruno's investigators would do the legwork, provide a detailed description and photos of the victim, his residence, business, daily routine, and the rest. A third party would deliver the packet of information within ten days. Luke would then execute the contract. When the job was done, the money would be wired to his Swiss bank account. There would be no connection with Bruno Altieri or his father. He and Bruno would never again discuss it.

When they'd finished talking, Bruno got up, shook hands, and exited by the rear door. Luke, leaving his jacket behind, went and bought a cup of coffee. Returning, he noticed the woman at the nearby table, the one who had earlier shunned the pesky man's advances. She was still sipping coffee. Nathan's was now crowded and tables for one or two were nowhere in sight. A short, homely blondish man with a paunch approached her. He looked about ten years younger than she, and had searched for a place to sit down and eat. Finding none, he walked over and asked quietly: "Would you mind if I sit here?"

"Of course," said the woman, smiling, her face lighting up like a Halloween pumpkin.

When Luke left Nathan's twenty minutes later, the man was chatting about the latest Jim Carrey movie, and his companion was laughing. Good for you, lady! Better an interesting young geezer than a boring older one.

32

By St. Patrick's Day, Bronxville was ready for spring.

At Lake View, Mario La Guardia had arrived at seven-thirty for his doorman's shift, resplendent in emerald tie. Forty-five minutes later, a van came to move the last of Dominic Rizzuto's furnishings from the building superintendent's apartment. A great day not only for the Irish, thought Mario, but for the Italians as well. "Arrivederci, bum," he mumbled as the van finally pulled away at noon.

That afternoon, Max Schneible and her two brothers arrived to move her things in. More than the usual number of residents hung around the lobby and the mailboxes for a look. By now, word had spread that Max was a she. Given Dom Rizzuto's short, unsuccessful stay, most were curious to see how this one would turn out. Max was not the first woman to benefit from succeeding a failed male.

A few withheld judgment, pending evaluation of skills, ranging from the replacement of light bulbs in the early morning to fixing the boiler before the heating system croaked. The early line was that Max was friendly without being familiar; that she brought an arsenal of computer equipment; that her furniture came from a consignment shop; and that her wardrobe could use a little sprucing up. Hearing that comment, resident Binky Seagram said to Mario La Guardia: "When she's putting a new washer in my faucet, I'm not sure I'll notice if her scarf and shoes match."

Overall, not a bad first day, according to Mario. He'd been overheard telling Rosa Di Carlo: "If any woman can make it here, she will." The fact that Max had bought him a green carnation on St. Patrick's Day hadn't hurt.

Later, Rosa reported that to Dan, adding one of her own: "Thatta Mario a pretty good judge. Lika me, he no lika da last guy from day one. I teenk dissa woman gonna do good."

Dan laughed. "Maybe the Board should just let you and Mario hire people in the future."

Rosa quickly shot back: "We couldna do mucha worse than you with the udder soop."

Dan gamely nodded agreement.

33

....

"April in Paris…" sang Minnie Stern to no one in particular.

It's still March, she thought. Why am I wishing my life away? On this late afternoon, an hour before sunset, she was sitting out on the open terrace of her Lake View penthouse apartment. The day had brought the first signs of spring, and cool evening air would soon move in. Beyond the trees and the Bronx River Parkway, a bright sun still clung to sky, reluctant to surrender the day. Tree branches, freed from winter's snow, sprouted very tiny buds.

Late afternoon was Minnie's favorite time of day. She liked to sit and rock, reflect on life, sing the songs she and Jake loved best. Often she'd bring a book and read aloud. When she and Jake were very young, they'd pack a picnic lunch and go to Coney Island on the subway, swim, eat, read poetry and make sweet love in the moonlight. Sometimes it would be Orchard Beach in the Bronx on the bus. "A cheap date," Jake had called it.

After marriage and two children, the venue changed but not the ritual. There was still the journey, the beach, home-cooked food, and always poetry to suit the day, the night, the season, or just the mood.

The seasons passed so quickly. At seventy-two, Minnie figured she'd had her share of good ones. When friends told her she didn't look her age, she'd laugh. "I don't look a day older than seventy-one, right?" Until last October when she'd broken her hip, Minnie hadn't felt old at all. She'd always been "well-rounded," her mother used to say. "Stacked," her first boy friend had called it. Her five-foot four-inch frame had a few pounds more than what the life insurance charts recommended, and they were on the generous side. Still, she'd been healthy most of her life, and planned to outlive the tables. Who were the old male actuaries or the young women at Jenny Craig to know what was best for her? Two of her friends, Emily Dolan and Effie Bingham, had joined a seniors' Weight Watchers program about five years ago. Emily was later killed by a hit-and-run driver, and Effie died of Alzheimer's the following year. No, Minnie planned to eat what she liked for as long as she lived. Whose tombstone read, "She died thin?"

Still, there had been no more walks into the village for a while; no more long walks at all, she thought, without a companion. She smiled at the phrase. At one time, it meant simply "friend." Now, it popped up in obituaries to describe a homosexual's lover. A nurse or aide to a senior citizen or disabled person had always been called "companion." Would Rosa be listed as a "longtime companion" in Minnie's obituary? Good, she mused. Give them something to talk about when I'm gone!

Minnie was teaching English at Stuyvesant

High School in Manhattan when she'd met Jake, who'd returned to his alma mater for Career Day. She thought him the homeliest man she'd ever met. Then he spoke and his face was transformed into John Barrymore's. A brief courtship was followed by a long marriage with as much passion at the end in Antigua as in the beginning in the Bronx. Despite a broken hip, Minnie felt blessed. The first in her family to attend college, she'd graduated from Hunter with a teacher's degree, 50 years ago. It was much later when she realized the sacrifices her parents had made to send her. Just last night before dinner, she and Rosa Di Carlo had drunk a glass of red wine, and Minnie proposed a toast: "To Harry and Ruth, wherever you are. Save a good seat for me!"

Her parents, Harry and Ruth, had always seen "good seats" as a sign of making it in life. The week after graduation, Harry had taken Minnie, a baseball fan, to the Polo Grounds for a Giants-Dodgers game. They'd seen dozens of games before, always from the bleachers. This time her father had purchased two box seats, right on the third base line. A uniformed man ushered them there, wiped the clean seats with a big cloth, tipped his cap to Harry, and gave Minnie a friendly wink. She remembered thinking this was the poor man's equivalent of the debutante's ball. Rich girls came out in the main ballroom at the Plaza Hotel; poor ones at a field box in the Polo Grounds. Who else had thirty thousand people cheering at their debut? Too bad it wasn't today. The electronic scoreboard would have had a greeting: WAY TO GO, MINNIE!

Harry had given the usher a dollar that day, saying "Don't tell your mother." She never did. She didn't tell Harry, either, that Ruth had taken her to a Broadway matinee of "Finian's Rainbow" that week; that they had sat in third row orchestra seats on the aisle; and that Ruth had given the usherette not one dollar, but two. And the woman hadn't even wiped the seats.

The lesson was not lost on Minnie. Don't buy cheap seats. That meant she didn't get to see as much, but what she did see, she saw well. "Up close and personal," they called it today. Long ago, Minnie knew that was the place to be.

Now here she was in a balcony seat on her terrace. No matter. There were no more box seats at the Polo Grounds, either. No more Polo Grounds at all. She'd read this morning that good seats at a major league game were around thirty dollars. She'd been young at a good time.

Minnie liked to look out on the Bronx River Parkway at rush hour and hear the whoosh of the cars. Why did they go so fast? When would there be too many cars on the road? She wondered if there would ever be an organization for car control, like the one for population control. It was nice that someone was trying to save spotted owls. Why wasn't someone trying to save pedestrians? In her son Michael's family, there were three people and four cars. Well, that was a problem for someone younger, someone with two good hips.

She enjoyed watching the games that drivers

played on the Parkway. They were like school children. Some were peeved that a car had entered the Parkway at Paxton Avenue, forcing them to slow down a bit. They gunned the motor, moved to the left lane and passed the offender in no time at all, tooting their horns. What did they want, a gold star?

Now, traffic was moving more slowly than usual.

Minnie first noticed the convertible because it reminded her of her first date with Jake. This car, too, was dark-colored; maybe navy. It was moving slowly in the right lane. Someone on the passenger side, a tall, gangly figure, stood, eyed a target, raised an arm and hurled a light package to a person standing near a large oak tree on the park's grass. The pitcher was a strong southpaw with a good overhead curve like Warren Spahn's. When the catcher effortlessly caught the object with a smooth, breadbasket catch, Minnie wanted to cheer. Then the driver speeded up and the car rounded the curve, continued north on the Parkway and disappeared from view.

Her first thought was that the person was tossing out trash. What would the Bronxville Beautification Committee think? But the tall, thin figure who retrieved the package appeared to have been awaiting it. The man (she was now sure it was a man) tucked it carefully under his arm, left the lake area, and walked back toward the main road, Pondfield Road West.

If this was a new form of express mail delivery, she hadn't heard about it. It did seem that the package was expected, though. Minnie thought about it for a time. Then evening set in and she grew tired.

She navigated the short walk back into the apartment on her cane. Careful, she thought. She'd make dinner, then watch a little TV, maybe a Miss Marple movie, to keep the mood going.

Minnie Stern knew she'd already had a good run, but it was not over yet. Wasn't she now taking computer lessons, thanks to Max Schneible? And Brian Palmer was a good teacher. The poor man needed more "get up and go," of course. But who was she to talk? Hers had got up and went!

Extra inning games were always the best. Minnie wanted one in life, too. Soon she'd be chatting it up with all the other nerds. Oh Jake, dear heart, if you could see me now.

34

....

A week after lunch at Nathan's, a fax had arrived at Luke Plisky's Crestwood home.

It contained simple instructions on how and when Luke would receive the investigative report on the victim. On March 18, at four o'clock, a car traveling north on the Bronx River Parkway, just after the Pondfield Road West exit, would deliver it.

Now, Luke was sitting in his den reading the file that had been tossed to him from the Parkway. Good throw, good catch, he mused. Often it seemed like they were kids playing at Murder, Inc. It was the simplicity of it all, that made it work. One meeting in a busy fast-food restaurant, thorough research on the victim's lifestyle and habits by Bruno's organization, and delivery to Luke. There were few chances for leaks. No telephone conversations that could be taped, no bills that might be traced, no computer files to be searched. Not foolproof, but what was in this world? Now, he had his fifth contract.

Luke had begun reading the file at about eight o'clock. Then, he reread it three times from cover to cover. When he was finished, he knew all that was important to know about Dan Horgan. Most important of all, he'd discovered that Dan, like himself, was an early morning jogger.

Over the next two weeks, Luke left his Crestwood apartment just before dawn and headed for the Bronxville Lake. Sometimes he drove, occasionally he biked, but usually he walked.

Most joggers fell into a predictable rut. You could set your clock by the time of day each one ran. A weekday jogger who started at dawn rarely began a half hour later.

Weekends brought new runners with their own routines. The early morning group was young and fast. The late morning and afternoon crowds were older and slower; sometimes Luke wanted to stand by with an oxygen tank. Early evening brought a mixture of young and old, all focused on completing their runs before dusk.

Joggers ran in their own worlds around the Bronxville Lake Park, ignoring all around them: walkers, bikers, roller-bladers, ducks, dogs, an occasional squirrel that skitted across the path. Each had a distinct, if limited, wardrobe. In mild weather, some wore short shorts and sleeveless tees; others, longer boxy pants and tees. The white-shorted group rarely wore colored ones. The length of the shorts was usually inverse to the wearer's figure; short, boxy runners favored long boxy shorts. Those who favored headbands and caps wore them every day.

There were not many fat runners. Most were angular. Their strides differed, though. Some ran friskily like young antelopes; others took small, measured steps like puppies. The track around the Bronxville Lake was about two-thirds of a mile, and runners were fairly consistent in the time they took to circle it.

On weekdays, Dan Horgan had a fairly predictable routine and Luke Plisky soon knew it by heart. On days when he was not traveling, he usually exited from the rear door of the Lake View complex at daybreak. He loped a short distance down a grassy hill to the lake, picking up the pace when he hit the pathway. Five times around the lake, with a short diversion to the road just north of the pedestrian crossbridge, then back to the lake path. He started out slowly before hitting his stride in the second lap. White short-shorts; a New York Athletic Club tee-shirt; blue headband; NIKE running shoes, white with blue trim; white socks. Horgan ran like he did everything else: alone, with single-minded purpose and precision. No Walkman. Luke Plisky watched morning after morning. In two weeks, he'd mastered the routine. Luke arrived at the lake before dawn, always varying his outfit and appearance. Sometimes he'd shaved; sometimes not. Occasionally he'd wear a hat or headband, never the same one twice. The key to a hitman's success was to be invisible, like a good teacher.

When he reached the lake, Luke would start jogging around it. Invariably, Horgan appeared. There was never an acknowledgment, but then joggers never noticed each other. After two weeks, Luke Plisky knew where he would kill Horgan and how. That weekend, the first in April, he filled out two plan books. One for the next week's classes, and one for the murder of Dan Horgan.

Planning was 50 percent of success; execution, the rest. Luke Plisky worked very hard at both.

35

....

On Tuesday of the second week of April, Shannon was in her small office at *Westchester Woman* magazine in White Plains. On Friday her assignment with L. Jayne Grey, Executive Editor, would end.

It was now a quarter to eleven and after just three hours of work, she felt bushed.

Her boss had scheduled a crisis staff meeting at ten but had still not arrived. Just outside, Shannon could hear the din of writers, editors, and support staff scurrying back and forth, lugging huge piles of paper into the conference room. Word had gone out that L. Jayne was unhappy with virtually everything for the next issue, and final proofs were due at the printers by the end of the week. Until today, everything had been on schedule, except for Jayne herself.

The woman often made Shannon wish that she'd minded her grandson Drew and played Mighty Morphin Power Rangers for several weeks. At times, Jayne made even the evil, purple-bearded Ivan Ooze look good. She worked long hours, but usually did not arrive before ten. She then schmoozed with the publisher, power brokers, and potential advertisers behind closed doors. At one she left for a two-hour "power lunch," returning for six or seven hours' more work. Had she been able to communicate with the staff by osmosis, that would have been fine. Unfortunately, by the time she was ready to meet with them, it was dark; most had gone home.

Just last night, she'd asked Shannon to hang around to do some copy editing. When it was done by nine o'clock, she seemed shocked that no one was around to check out the final art specs, due at the printers by noon the following day. When Shannon announced that her own talents as an artist were zilch, and that she was leaving, Jayne moaned: "Once again, I have to do everything myself." Which she invariably ended up doing. Before Shannon left, Jayne had asked her to schedule an emergency staff meeting the following day at ten. "Heads will roll this time," she said.

Was this horror what feminists had worked so long and hard to produce?

This morning, just as Jayne swung by her office, Shannon heard the phone ring. It was her own line. She picked it up, surprised to hear Rich Kryhoski's voice. Rich had never called her at work, even when Dan Horgan was on the road. He was good at handling Lake View's day-to-day problems, leaving the Board to handle policy issues and exceptions. What prompted his call now?

Rich's voice was breathless: "Morning, Shannon. I know you're busy, but I thought you should know as soon as possible. Got some bad news. Dan Horgan died this morning."

A pause, then he continued, rambling almost incoherently: "Apparently jogging around the

Bronxville Lake, just before seven. A doctor found him. Tried CPR, but no use. He was already dead."

"Heart attack?" asked Shannon.

"Nope, shot." said Rich. "Murdered. As of now, no one knows who or why."

Shannon was shocked into silence. "You still there?" asked Rich.

"Yes. I'm still finding it hard to believe."

"We all are. Look, things are moving pretty fast around here. Technically the murder happened in Tuckahoe and the whole lake park area is roped off with cops doing their scene-of-the-crime stuff. The Tuckahoe Police Chief is Paul Martino. His guys have started to interview people, but he asked me to set up a meeting of Lake View's residents tonight. Figured it was a good way to brief everybody and ask for their help."

"Makes sense," said Shannon.

"How does seven-thirty sound? I figure that'll give most of the commuters time to get home from work."

"Fine," said Shannon.

"Oh, and I know I don't need to tell you this," Rich continued, "but you're now president of the Lake View Board. I think you should chair the meeting, introduce Martino, get the thing going on the right track."

"Of course."

"O.K. then. See you tonight. And Shannon, I'm really sorry. I know you and Dan were close."

"Yes. Thanks, Rich. Till later, then."

After hanging up the phone, Shannon remembered the old saw, that Vice Presidents do little but attend funerals. She was just collecting her thoughts and emotions when Jayne came shrieking down the hallway. "O.K., everybody, let's get going. We've got a week's work to do and one day to do it in!"

Jayne's motivational skills were not the best. What was it Shannon's mother used to say at times like this? "Pull yourself together, girl!" Now, headed for the conference room, she did just that.

36

....

It was standing room only at the stockholders' meeting in Lake View's lobby that night.

Max Schneible had set up and checked out the lectern and microphone. Now she stood with Rich Kryhoski in the rear of the room. Shannon began the meeting promptly at seven-thirty, with stragglers still arriving. Faces in the audience reminded her of those old sepia photographs with gravely serious stares frozen in time.

"I appreciate your coming on short notice," she began. "This is an extraordinary night. The loss of a good friend and neighbor has affected all of our lives. By now you probably all know that Dan Horgan was fatally shot early this morning, while jogging on the Bronxville Lake path. The murder occurred on the Tuckahoe side of the lake, so Tuckahoe Police Chief Paul Martino is heading up the investigation. He's here tonight to tell us about that and ask for our help. I know he'll get it. Chief?"

Paul Martino moved slowly to the podium and adjusted the microphone. A short, squat, barrel-chested man, with sallow complexion, a creased face, thin lips and thick black hair. He looked about fifty, but might have been younger. Shannon sized him up quickly as a person she wouldn't want to meet in a dark alley.

Martino spoke from notes for about ten minutes. Deep bass voice. Plainspoken, direct. No wasted words.

"Every available officer on my staff is working overtime to solve this murder. Mr. Horgan was murdered on the Tuckahoe side of the Bronxville Lake. Technically, it's our case, but we're enlisting the aid of the Bronxville and Yonkers Police, and the Westchester County D.A.'s office. We'll also be working with New York City's Homicide squad, since the deceased worked in Manhattan."

"Several of you have already been interviewed by my officers. Before the week is out, all of you will be. Despite what you read, it's often not great police work that solves crimes. It's people like you. Please think about anything you saw or may have seen, over the past several days or weeks. Any strangers around the property. Anything at all out of the ordinary. No detail is too small. We'll make the decision if it's important or not."

"Do you have any leads?" came a voice from the rear.

"Lots," answered the Chief. "Horgan was a nationally known attorney. As you can guess, he probably made enemies in the course of his career. We're contacting people who knew him, worked with him, argued against him, all across the country."

"So you think it had nothing to do with Lake View?" asked a plaintive Hester Harrington. "Things like this don't happen here. Not in Bronxville!" Her tone implied that the murderer had committed not just a ghastly crime, but a social gaffe to boot.

"Maybe yes. Maybe no. Too early to tell," answered Martino calmly. "As I say, we're looking at every angle. This I promise you: We *will* get the person who did this."

A few more questions and answers. No, it did not appear to be a random killing. No, there were no witnesses so far. Every indication was that this was a planned act and that Dan Horgan was the intended victim. There was no evidence of robbery or even a struggle.

Jay Shapiro's hand shot up: "Have you called in the Feds?"

The Chief said that, for now, only local enforcement people were involved. As the investigation progressed, he would certainly be working with the FBI, as needed.

Finally, sensing waning interest, Martino thanked the group and turned the meeting back to Shannon. She asked that they all stand for a moment of silence in Dan's memory. That done, she adjourned the meeting just after eight-thirty.

Paul Martino came over and told Shannon his officers would like to interview her tonight. She was not looking forward to it, but thought it best to get it over with. She asked that they give her about fifteen minutes, and then come up to her apartment.

Shannon rode up on the elevator with Minnie Stern and Rosa Di Carlo. Rosa broke the silence: "A gooda man, thata cop."

Shannon and Minnie nodded yes. When the door opened at the third floor, Shannon waved good night and exited. Not before she overheard Rosa continue: "Too bad he donna have no clue."

Right again, Rosa. But he would, she thought. Tomorrow or the day after, or the one after that.

37

How to dress for an interview with the police?

Back in her apartment, Shannon's first order of business was to change into something comfortable. Within minutes, she'd donned jeans and an aqua sweatshirt, trading in low-heeled black pumps for aerobic walking shoes. A quick look at the mirror, a flick of a hairbrush, and she was set.

She walked into the den and saw an incoming fax from her daughter Maria: Could she mind Drew on Sunday afternoon for a few hours? Hmmm.

Out in the kitchen, she opened the refrigerator door. Maybe there was something she could stick in the oven while the cops visited. Shelves overflowed with juice, Snapple, seltzer, soda, tonic, bottled water, low-fat milk. A fridge with lots to drink, little to eat. She closed the door just as the doorbell rang.

When she opened it, two cops stood there: "Good evening, Ms. O'Keefe. May we come in?"

"Of course. Please sit down." She ushered them into the living room, where they seated themselves on a hunter green leather sofa near a triple window that looked out on the Bronxville Lake.

They introduced themselves. The ranking officer, Detective Sergeant Dave Corrigan, appeared to be in his late 30s, just under six feet; he had a slim, well-scrubbed altar boy face, receding hairline and an open, earnest manner. His partner, Officer Lee Quaglio, was several years younger, maybe twenty-seven or so, dark-complexioned, good figure, healthy skin. She wore her red hair in a short pageboy; a little blush, no other makeup. Her manner was serious, focused, intense. All edge. Pen and paper were poised to take down Shannon's statement, word for word, she was sure.

Corrigan led off: "Ms. O'Keefe, how well did you know the deceased?"

"Let's see. I met him about four years ago, when I moved to Lake View."

"And what exactly was your relationship?"

"For starters, we were neighbors, then friends. Later I did a consulting assignment for his law firm. When I joined the Lake View Board two years ago, we worked closely on…"

"Did you have a personal relationship with him?" Lee Quaglio interrupted.

"If you mean, did we see each other socially? Yes. Did I sleep with him? No."

Corrigan colored briefly, and seemed embarrassed at his junior partner's bluntness. Or maybe that was how they worked. Quaglio, ignoring him, plodded on: "Did you ever consider it?"

This was beginning to sound like dialogue from an old "B" movie. Shannon, torn between admiration for the young woman's chutzpah and annoyance at the invasion of her privacy, took a deep breath before answering: "No. I'm divorced, with no current plans to get seriously involved with anyone."

"Do you mind if I ask why?" Quaglio asked.

"Yes, but I'll tell you anyway. I'm Catholic. My husband got the divorce. I've filed for an annulment and am waiting for it to come through. Is all this relevant, Officer?"

Corrigan jumped in: "I'm sorry if we seem intrusive. Frankly, we're grasping at every straw at this stage of the investigation. For starters, I'm guessing that Horgan made some enemies as Board president. Anyone you can tell us about?"

"Detective, when you join a co-op Board, you enlist in a mini-war. At virtually every meeting, we're resolving some kind of conflict. The usual stuff."

"Define 'usual,' Ms. O'Keefe." Quaglio seemed to have been born with an obnoxious gene.

"Well, last year we had a resident who played an instrument several hours a day, and well into the night. He thought it was music; his neighbors called it noise."

"Piano?"

"Tuba," said Shannon.

"What happened?"

"The woman he was going with said he'd have to choose between the tuba and her, if the relationship was to continue. He moved out when they married."

"Where to?" asked Quaglio.

"I don't know. The managing agent might." She gave them the tuba player's name, along with Rich Kryhoski's address and telephone number.

"Any other problems that come to mind?" asked Corrigan.

Shannon thought a moment. "A few months ago, a resident hired an unlicensed building contractor to redo his kitchen. The ceiling collapsed and he wanted the co-op to pay for it. We refused. Then his lawyer wrote us a few outraged letters, threatening suit. When the co-op threatened to evict him for violating the terms of the proprietary lease, he backed off. At least I think he did; we haven't heard from him in several months."

"Anything else?" said Quaglio.

"Well, there's a woman with a dog. Pets are forbidden, but we know she has one. She swears that the barking that people hear is her toilet on the fritz."

"What have you got against animals?" asked Quaglio. Her tone implied that Shannon was leading an "Act Up" crusade against pets.

"Look," said Shannon, "this is not a personal thing. Most of the people here love animals; many had to give one up to move into the building. But there are trade-offs in co-op living, and this is one of them. Animals involve work, care and consideration of neighbors. Easy to say; tough to enforce. One co-op prohibits dogs taller than eighteen inches. Ours decided long ago to stay out of the dog-measuring business. It's easier to prohibit them. Trust me, many co-ops that do allow them are rethinking their house rules."

Shannon knew she was becoming tired, irritable, and, worst of all, preachy. "Trust me" was a particularly annoying phrase when someone said it to her.

Lee Quaglio, however, seemed not to notice. If anything, she seemed mollified by the riposte. "And there's a record of all these problems somewhere?" she asked.

"Yes," said Shannon. "The Co-op Board's secretary prepares minutes of our meetings. You'll find them at Rich Kryhoski's office."

Quaglio asked: "How about rejected applicants? Did the Board turn anyone down recently for an apartment?"

"Just one that I recall. An African-American record producer."

"Wrong color?" Quaglio pressed on.

"Of course not. Color was never an issue. We checked with some of the tenants in his former building. Without telling anybody, he'd converted his apartment into a recording studio. His neighbors were treated to so-called music, heavy metal, hip-hop, rap, you name it, at all hours of the day and night."

"How did he react to being turned down?" asked Corrigan.

"Not well. Kryhoski had a few nasty phone calls and letters threatening a discrimination suit. Dan Horgan said the man, Arthur Bliss, telephoned him once at home. Dan hung up when the man persisted in screaming obscenities at him."

"You worked for Dan Horgan for a while, right?" Corrigan inquired.

"Yes. Technically I work for Halliday Temporary Executives. Brett Halliday runs it, hires professionals and managers for short-term assignments. Dan's law firm retained us as business analysts to review their operations and staffing. I stayed on for about four months."

"And you downsized the place?" asked Quaglio.

"That was one result. Our charge was to review the business, decide if the problems were in growth, expenses, or both. Examine resource allocation, see if the resources themselves were being used efficiently."

"Downsized it," murmured Quaglio, scribbling something on her pad, and underlining it twice. "How many people lost their jobs?"

"About forty or so. Some of those were voluntary retirements."

"Voluntary, like if you don't go now, we'll make your life miserable and fire you in the next year?" Quaglio asked.

Time out, signaled Shannon, holding up her hands. "Look, I'm thirsty. Can I offer either of you soda or juice?"

A "yes" from Corrigan, and a "no" from Quaglio. The interruption clearly upset her sense of control.

Shannon returned with three Cokes, one for Corrigan, one for herself, and one for the table in front of Lee Quaglio: "In case you change your mind," Shannon murmured.

"Look," she continued: "I was there to make recommendations to Dan and his partners. That I did.

There were three choices: increase revenue, reduce expenses, or do both. The firm chose the third, and that meant staff reductions. I'm not claiming that we didn't impact the layoffs. But the choices as to who and how were the firm's, not mine. Overall, the severance arrangements were generous. It was not a bloodbath."

"So you're saying there were no unhappy campers?" asked Quaglio.

"No. You're saying that. I suggest you talk with the people themselves. Long ago I learned not to talk about how other people feel."

Quaglio nodded.

"Did you know Horgan's son, Chip?" asked Corrigan.

"Yes. The three of us had dinner once, and I met him a couple of times when he came in from the coast."

"Is it true they didn't get along?" asked Corrigan.

"I'd say there was tension from time to time, but I know Dan loved him."

"What was the problem? Money?" asked Quaglio.

"Partly that, partly the career he'd chosen. Chip is a playwright. He wanted Dan to lend him some upfront money to produce a play he'd written, then adapt it for a movie."

"And his father said no?" asked Corrigan.

"Right. He felt Chip had no talent."

"And did he?"

"I don't think so. Then again, I'm no theater critic. I never did understand Beckett and he won a Nobel Prize."

"Me neither," offered Quaglio, barely concealing a grin, before continuing: "O.K. Just one more item, Dom Rizzuto. The Board fired him. I understand that Horgan got a couple of threatening notes from him. That right?"

"Yes. Well, we don't know for certain that they were from him. The notes were sent to Dan at Lake View. They appeared in the open magazine slot of his mailbox downstairs. Anonymous, of course. They began after Rizzuto visited Horgan at his law office. Dom knew that Kryhoski fired him on the Board's orders. He wanted to appeal the decision, said that the alleged spousal abuse was all 'much ado about nothing.' Dan refused to discuss it with him."

"And the Bronxville Police were notified when the threatening notes began?"

"Yes, they checked them out both times. Anyone with access to the building could have placed them there. They were written on cheap stationery, enclosed in self-stick envelopes. No other clues. The police patrol cars have been swinging by Lake View regularly. Rizzuto hasn't been seen in the area since he moved out. I think he's still out on bail."

"Yeah, we'll be following up on that angle," said Corrigan. "O.K., it's getting late. I think that's it for now, unless you can think of anything else."

Shannon thought for a moment. "Look, this may have been my imagination, but Dan appeared to be preoccupied lately, as though something were bothering him."

"Can you give us an example?" asked Corrigan.

"Yes, last Saturday night. Unless one of us had plans, we had a standing arrangement to visit each other's apartment for an after-dinner drink. One week I'd go there; the next, he came here. I saw him in the hall last Friday, coming in from work. Said he'd see me the next night. He never showed up."

"And you didn't call?" asked Quaglio.

"No. When he hadn't arrived by nine, I figured he'd gotten delayed. I got caught up on the phone and next thing you know it was almost eleven. I thought he'd tried to call and the line was busy. It was unlike him not to have called the next day, though. I never saw him again to ask what happened."

"O.K.," said Corrigan. "And you have no idea at all about who or what may have been bothering him?"

"No," said Shannon. "As I say, the Saturday night incident may have nothing to do with all this. And maybe it's wishful thinking, but I don't think the murder is connected with Lake View. Rizzuto's a wife-basher and a braggart. I didn't like the man, but I doubt he's a killer. Yes, I think he sent the threatening letters. But he was always big on talk, small on follow-through. Apart from his personal problems, that's why we fired him."

A pause, then: "And the other stuff that's gone on is nothing special for co-op living. There are always a few people who feel that rules aren't made for them. People who flex their power from time to time. There are doctors, lawyers, judges, politicians, CEO's and other 'big shots.' You name it. Then there are the rest of us. Some of the 'shots' don't understand that in a co-op, you check your title at the door. The same rules apply to all. You have only as much voting power as the shares you own, based on the size of your apartment. Anyway, when these people go too far, the Board pulls the plug, gives them a warning. The violators stomp and rant. Some drive the Board nuts with phone calls and letters. Others threaten lawsuits. Most of them eventually give in until the next thing that makes them unhappy. Then the cycle starts all over again. People either cope or move. They don't kill."

"And that's it?" Quaglio asked. She was back to original form, making Shannon feel like a schoolchild who'd turned in a shoddy assignment.

"For now, yes."

"O.K. Thanks," said Corrigan, standing and nodding to Quaglio. "We may be back to you again. Please call if you remember anything else at all. Here's our card."

"Right." Shannon gave them each her own business card and they left. Returning to the living room, she picked up three empty Coke cans. Well, who would have thought it? The woman's human after all.

Back in the kitchen she scrambled a couple of eggs, to jell with her scrambled brain.

38

....

While Shannon was being interviewed by the Tuckahoe police, Luke Plisky was watching the local news on cable TV.

Since early morning, there had been nonstop coverage of the Bronxville Lake murder. Tuckahoe Police Chief Paul Martino had been interviewed at the crime scene around noon, and the tape was replayed throughout the evening.

Tonight, a reporter was interviewing Dr. Timothy Donohue, "a prominent local neurosurgeon," just outside his home in Lawrence Park West. Her questions began with the inane: "How did it feel to find a body on the jogging track?" Then, "How did you know he was dead?" Finally, "Do you think it's safe to jog tomorrow?"

Luke thought that Dr. Donohue responded with quiet dignity and professionalism. He explained that he had found Dan Horgan lying prostrate while jogging around the Bronxville Lake early that morning; that Horgan had had no pulse or any other vital signs, and that all attempts to revive him were futile. The doctor had then asked another jogger to stand by while he went to dial "911" for help. Police and an ambulance had arrived within minutes, and Dan Horgan's body had been transported to the Westchester County Medical Examiner's Office.

"While the apparent cause of death was a gun-shot wound to the heart, we should all await the results of the autopsy," Tim Donohue added. As to the safety of the Bronxville Lake Park, he had confidence that the Bronxville and Tuckahoe Police would do whatever was needed to safeguard their citizens. To his knowledge, this was the first murder in recent history to occur in the park.

Luke smiled wryly. The man could have been a politician or a real estate agent. When he'd seen enough, and was reasonably confident there were no immediate clues to the killer's identity, Luke shut off the TV and went up to bed.

He found it hard to sleep. Looking over at the night table, a black and white wedding photo smiled back at him. He talked to Karen now as he did each night. "If only...if only I hadn't been hurt in Vietnam. If only you hadn't nursed me back to health at that New Jersey hospital, given me hope again. If only you hadn't been killed in a robbery. If only the judge hadn't let her off. If only Bruno's guys hadn't killed her, to save me from doing it."

Bruno had never admitted orchestrating the boat explosion on Long Island Sound. Not before, not after. Some things were best left unsaid. Let it be. Luke had saved Bruno from death in the scrubby forest outside An Doai. When Karen died, Bruno had snatched him from madness, from the jaws of despair.

Think of something positive. Like Paris. They had honeymooned there and had talked of going back one day with their children. Now there was no Karen. There would never be kids.

Still, there were memories. Their twentieth anniversary was coming up in July. Why not go back over summer vacation? Rent a car, take a side trip to the French countryside, search for peace again. Maybe it was time to move on, begin somewhere else.

Finally, at three o'clock, he drifted off to sleep, dreaming of Karen, Paris, and things forever lost.

39

....

Some days start out badly and go downhill from there.

On Wednesday, the day after the murder, Shannon's quirky alarm clock went off at eight-thirty, three hours late. She'd hoped to get off to an early start. Her clock seemed to have a mind of its own, though, and while she should have been grateful for the extra sleep, she was not.

First things first. Call L. Jayne Grey and say she'd be late. An exercise in futility, since Jayne rarely arrived before ten.

Wrong. Jayne picked up her own phone, honeyed voice dripping with sweetness: "Oh, I understand, dear. The murder, how awful. Don't rush." Bad sign. Either her ladyship had overdosed on Prozac or she wanted something.

Shannon would take her at her word about getting in. She went into the den, scribbled "Yes" on her daughter's request to mind Drew on Sunday. Better to fax back than call, since by today Drew might need minding next week as well. Maria knew that the *Westchester Woman* assignment ended on Friday.

When Shannon finally walked down to the lobby and out Lake View's door, it was ten-thirty and Mario La Guardia was fending off a news cameraman:

"Bub, you've got ten seconds to drop that and get off the property." Just before the bulb popped, Mario moved forward and "Bub" was rubbing his arm, wincing with pain. The camera was at his feet.

Seeing Shannon, Mario said: "Don't worry, I've got things under control here."

She smiled. "I can see that. Thanks."

Walking down the long cul-de-sac and out to Pondfield Road West, she brushed aside several reporters and headed for the Metro-North station.

Spring had sprung. After a night of heavy rain, the streets were awash in color and the smell of growing things. Benches in small nooks were filling up with nannies, toddlers, and seniors, people-watching, chatting quietly. The air hummed with quiet life.

This glorious morning, though, there were also small groups of villagers on street corners with newspapers, pointing in Lake View's direction, shaking their heads sadly.

Once on the half-empty train to White Plains, Shannon pulled out *The New York Times.* Dan Horgan's murder had made the front page of the Metro section. No new developments since last night's briefing. She read that the Tuckahoe Police were working with New York City's homicide detectives, exploring "a possible Manhattan connection."

There was a background story on the downsizing at Horgan & Stern, with quotes from current and former employees. By tomorrow, she was sure the whole Dom Rizzuto affair would also be grist for the mill. Poor Ida and her family.

There were the usual trite bromides about the victim. The head of the city's Bar Association called him "a gentleman and a scholar;" another colleague said, "he'll be sorely missed." Shannon hoped that when she died, no one would say that about her. No style.

Bronxville and Tuckahoe residents who'd been interviewed had commented, predictably: "We don't even lock our doors here," and "Where is it safe anymore?"

When the train pulled into White Plains, she walked four blocks to the offices of *Westchester Woman.* A beaming Jayne followed her in.

"Everything made it to the presses on time," she greeted Shannon. "How about a late lunch today around one-thirty at The Galleria?"

Since Jayne never ate with underlings, Shannon had no illusions. Something was up, and it was not good.

The Galleria was a huge enclosed shopping mall with several floors and a sprawling International Food Court. Once there, Shannon ordered pizza "with everything" and lemonade; Jayne, a humongous green salad and bottled water.

As soon as they found a table, Jayne, just under six feet and bordering on anorexic, announced she was dieting: "I'm growing out of all my size 6 clothes," she complained. Shannon smiled agreeably, determined not to add, "You don't need to."

Somewhere between the third and fourth forkfuls of rabbit food, Jayne folded her arms and asked conspiratorially: "So, how would you like to write a first person story about it for the magazine?"

"About what?"

"The murder, of course. It's got everything. The Bronxville angle, old money, murder in the park. And every day you pick up the paper, there's another story about the hassles of co-op living. What can top this?"

A red-hot pepper picked that moment to stick to the roof of Shannon's mouth, making it difficult for her to shout: "Are you crazy?" She hoped someone nearby knew the Heimlich maneuver; she might well need it before lunch ended.

While Shannon was choking, Jayne nattered on: "The publisher's demanding something unique. Says it's time for the magazine to break out of the pack, carve its own niche."

Shannon wanted to carve Jayne herself, or at least stick what looked like an olive in the mystery salad up her boss's nose. Finally she sputtered: "I don't think that's something I could do."

"Shannon, I wouldn't ask if I didn't know you could do it. You're a superb writer."

"Thanks," said Shannon. "I should have expressed it better. I know I can do it. I don't want to." Why beat around the bush?

Jayne seemed deaf: "But you'll at least think about it? The publisher will pay big bucks for an insider's scoop on this one."

"Of course I'll think about it," said Shannon. For half a nanosecond, she thought. "I'll let you know tomorrow, but please don't plan on it."

Jayne smiled happily and reached over to pat Shannon's hand, before delicately eating the rest of her salad. When they were done, Shannon noticed that Jayne's makeup was still perfect. Not a blotch in sight. Nor were there stains on her elegant watermelon silk suit.

Back in the office, Shannon congratulated herself for handling the incident with poise and self-control. When she went into the ladies' room, however, there were pepperoni smudges on her yellow blazer, and pizza sauce below her right eye. So much for image.

At eight that night she arrived home to find many of the same newspeople in the parking lot. She moved past them briskly and reached the entrance to the building. Rob Guinan, an elf-sized retired mailman and nighttime doorman, looked up and was just about to whisper "Private Property" when he recognized Shannon. "Sorry," he blushed: "Tough night."

"I'll bet," said Shannon. "Looks like you're holding them off, though." It looked like nothing of the kind, but the poor man was nervous enough. Reassurance seemed best at the moment.

"Thanks, I'm doing my best," said Rob. "They've had a day with no news and are getting antsy."

"I'm sure. Well, hold the fort, Rob." Shannon made a mental note to talk to Rich Kryhoski. If Lake View were under siege for any prolonged period, Rob might quit. Good doormen (why were they usually men?) were in short supply.

Upstairs, she played back several messages on the answering machine. Residents wanted an update on "this awful business." Most could not even call it murder. Maria had called to say that she would deliver Drew "Sunday afternoon at ten." So much for her daughter's sense of time.

Then, Evan Doubleday's voice: "Hi, Shannon. Give me a ring when you come in? Thanks."

Well, at least the day would end on a high note. First things first, though. She was starved. She heated some leftover macaroni and defrosted a shell steak in the microwave. By ten, having polished off a rare home-cooked meal, she was in high-cholesterol heaven.

Evan answered immediately when she dialed: "Hi, how goes it?" he asked.

"Well, Dan's death puts everything in perspective. Still, not a banner day. How about you?"

"Same here," he said. "Look, I wanted you to know before it hits tomorrow's paper. Dan's autopsy results were inadvertently leaked to the press. He died of a single gunshot wound to the heart."

"No surprise there."

"Uh-huh, but this may be. He had a progressive brain tumor. Would have died anyway, within a year, tops."

40

Evan Doubleday was wrong. Word of Dan Horgan's terminal illness first broke on the eleven o'clock news that very night.

In his Greenwich Village apartment, Brian Palmer was just about to flip off the TV and head for bed when the anchorman announced: "This just in. The Westchester County Medical Examiner's office has refused comment tonight on a report leaked earlier today to the press. Reliable sources have confirmed that the immediate cause of Daniel Horgan's death in the Bronxville Lake Park yesterday morning was a single shot to the heart from a small caliber handgun. Reports are now that the autopsy has also confirmed that the victim was seriously ill, with no more than a year to live. No further details are available at this time."

Brian had spent most of the day at St. Vincent's Hospital, where Reed had been rushed earlier that morning with viral pneumonia. He had shed no tears yesterday when Dan Horgan had died. So it was all for nothing. The old guy would have gone anyway. He laughed out loud. Reed would enjoy hearing about it tomorrow.

Edna Donohue normally listened to the ten o'clock news and then went to bed after the weather report. Since yesterday, though, she'd become a Bronx celebrity and the phone had not stopped ringing.

It began with her friend Mary Kenneally who had called at noon, just as Edna was heading out the door for a Leisure Club meeting at the parish hall. "Wasn't that your Buddy who found that poor man's body in Bronxville?" Mary had asked, before saying "Hello." Edna had barely gotten out a "Yes," when Mary had continued: "Imagine that. Moving away to that posh place and finding a dead man on the jogging track. What's the world coming to?"

Later, at her meeting, Edna was the center of attention. Did Buddy know the man? At what hour had he been killed? Didn't it just go to show that no place was safe anymore? The school's janitor came by for a cup of coffee, and summed it all up: "We might as well stay here and be mugged, than pay all that money, move and be murdered."

There was general agreement on that point. Muggings and purse-snatchings were recurring events in the area. A few years ago, the Leisure Club had even had a party to celebrate the victims' heroism. Each muggee had received a corsage.

Murder was something else. If killers were out there, let them head for the suburbs and knock off the rich.

Edna had tired of all the fuss and was greatly relieved when Buddy had finally called her last night. Yes, he was fine. Yes, he'd told the police he knew the victim, though not well. No, he was not a suspect, though he'd been in the police station for several hours giving a statement. "That's well and good," said Edna, "but I've been watching 'Law and Order.' Look out for entrapment. If I were you, I'd call John Cronin. If they want to talk to you again, your own lawyer should be there."

"Thanks for the advice, Mom. I think you're overreacting. Have a cup of tea and I'll talk to you soon."

Edna said good-bye, thinking: Tea, me eye. Glory be to God, how could Walter and I have produced such a smart boyo without a bit of common sense?

That was last night. Twenty-four hours later, she tuned in to hear any late-breaking news on the Horgan murder. When it came, she hurried out to the hall to call Buddy again.

Diane answered the phone. "He's not home yet, Edna. A meeting with John Cronin."

"Thank God for that," said Edna.

"It may be late when he comes in. Can he call you tomorrow?"

"That'll be fine," said Edna. "It's nothing important."

"Like heck it's not," said Diane to the TV screen, after hanging up the phone. Last night when Buddy had told her of his mother's advice, Diane had said: "She's right, Buddy. Your mother doesn't know that Horgan forced your father out. You did. You said you'd never forgive him for that. That's called motive. Call John."

"So, let me get this straight," Buddy had answered. "You're saying that if I was going to kill Horgan, I'd shoot him in the early morning on a public running track, make the gun disappear, give him CPR, then call the police?"

"Of course not, but that's because I love you, and know that the whole idea is nonsense. The police don't. Call Cronin. Please. Do it not just for your mother, but for me."

He'd looked at his wife, who was three months pregnant. She rarely worried about anything, but was clearly troubled now. Walking over, he'd kissed her. "You win."

Then he'd gone into the den and dialed his attorney. Edna might thank God for Buddy's seeing the light. Diane was more inclined to thank Edna and herself.

....

The next morning, Margo Stern was reading *The New York Times* on her grandmother's Lake View terrace. When she'd told Minnie about a job interview in New Rochelle, Minnie had insisted she come for dinner on Wednesday and spend the night. Now Minnie was sitting across from her, reading a computer manual.

Margo had finished the first part of the paper, and came to the Metro section with the update on the Bronxville murder. "Good grief, Grandma, listen to this!" She read aloud the first paragraph, which summarized the autopsy report and Dan's terminal illness. When Margo looked up, her grandmother was simply nodding. Why did she not seem surprised?

....

The teachers at Luke Plisky's school were definitely surprised.

They were less shocked at another story that had made the news that day. Still another child, this time a nine year old girl, had been abused for several months, then murdered by her stepfather in a Brooklyn tenement apartment. The Mayor's office was "appalled" at the breakdown between the school system and the social services agencies: "Where were the teachers who should have noticed this, and taken action to stop it?"

Murder, of course, was an outrage. But teachers were sick and tired of being fingered as principals in these events. "It's like we're co-conspirators or something," said Charlotte Weiss, over lunch in the cafeteria. "*Cherchez les parents!*"

Several others agreed. It was, by now, an old story. Everyone who had never taught had ideas about how to do it better than those who did it daily. A visiting psychologist had once explained it to them at an educational conference: "They've all been students, so they're experts. Worse, they've all had at least one teacher-from-hell. Years later, when anything goes wrong in a school, they remember that person and take it out on you. It's called displacement. If you want to remain in this job, you'll have to learn to live with it."

None of them had.

Sadly, the Bronxville murder was more interesting if only because it was different. Was it a random killing? If not, and the killer knew the victim, did he also know he was terminally ill? If he didn't know, wasn't it ironic that the murderer had killed for no reason at all?

Good questions all. By the end of lunch, no one had offered a satisfactory theory. Walking back to the classroom, Enid Gomez asked Luke Plisky: "Do you think they'll ever find out who did it?"

Luke paused a second before replying: "One day, yes. My guess is that it will be later rather than sooner."

Enid would remember the moment months later, not just what Luke said, but the gentle matter-of-fact way in which he'd said it.

41

On Saturday morning, Shannon did a few slug-gish laps around the Bronxville Lake.

The immediate crime scene on the north end of the lake was roped off, with two uniformed police officers standing by. Media ghouls and just plain neighborhood ghouls hovered nearby, comparing notes and theories. Only joggers seemed immune to the unusual commotion.

Shannon felt like she'd survived a week in hell. Residents continued to pester her for updates on the murder, even though she'd told them she knew noth-ing more than they did. Asked to call the police, most answered: "Oh, we'll just get a runaround. We fig-ured you'd tell us what's really happening."

She was sure what many now wanted to know, but hesitated to ask, was why Chip Horgan had stopped into her apartment Thursday night. He'd knocked on the door about eleven, and after apolo-gizing for the late hour, told her about the funeral arrangements for his father. There would be a Mass and private burial service on the following Wednes-day for family and close friends at Gate of Heaven Cemetery in Hawthorne, about a half hour's drive north of Bronxville. Would she be free to come?

He'd looked dreadful and declined coming in for

a cup of coffee or just to talk: "Thanks, anyway. I'm beat tonight."

Chip's normally cheerful thin face seemed on the verge of collapsing into itself. Bags under his eyes had added at least a decade to his thirty-odd years. Shannon told him that of course she'd be at Wednesday's service, and, since she'd be around the following week, to holler if there was anything she could do for him. "Thanks. Bringing him back to life would be nice," he'd said sadly.

This was a first, thought Shannon. I've never been invited to a funeral before. Dan must have been a Catholic. Funny, he'd never mentioned it.

The week's only good news was that L. Jayne Grey was now part of Shannon's employment history. Jayne was not pleased when told there was no way Shannon would consider doing an investigative feature on "the Bronxville co-op murder," nor did she know anyone who would. Then, on Friday, Jayne had suffered still another blow. The magazine's owner-publisher had sold it to a Canadian media monarch. A frenzied Jayne had quickly communicated to the staff that "heads would roll," but promised each a superb recommendation from her.

Hearing this, a copyeditor next to Shannon had whispered: "Is she wacky? Hitler would be a better reference." For a long time, they'd speculated about the "L" in Jayne's name. Loopy and Leadbelly had been favorites. On Friday, the smart money was on "Lopped."

Shannon's own departure date came at an ideal

time. Waiting for severed heads to roll was not her idea of fun. Neither was following Dan Horgan as Board president, especially if the murder was connected with Lake View.

Rich Kryhoski had called and scheduled a breakfast meeting on Monday, for an update on the co-op's affairs. With another Board meeting in ten days, they'd also plan the agenda.

But first, there would be a weekend to catch up with family. Her son Ted had invited her to an early Saturday night dinner with him and his new girlfriend "Red." Ted and Red were catching an eight o'clock film at the Bronxville Movie Theater, after supper at Craven's Pub.

Shannon had never met Red. Her twins had always checked out each other's opinion before entering a serious relationship. Maria had mentioned that Ted seemed serious about Red, and had given it her own blessing. "She's terrific. Just what he needs to lighten him up. You're gonna love her, Mom!"

Things were looking up.

42

She didn't love "Red."

Early Saturday night, Shannon left Lake View and walked five blocks into the village. The prospect of a good meal on a perfect spring night almost caused her to forget the past week's horrors.

Arriving at Craven's Pub early, she asked for a booth since the Saturday night church crowd would soon be arriving. The pub's soft, comfortable red leather booths and tables were ideal for informal dining. Kids were welcome and burgers cooked to order. With daily specials on a board, you don't get to listen to waiters spew out a litany of options with odd-sounding sauces. Best of all, the congenial staff did not frown at substitutes.

She was sipping a ginger ale when Ted and a young woman came through the door. "Let it not be," thought Shannon.

But it was. "Red" was Lee Quaglio, the cop who'd acted as Grand Inquisitor in her apartment the night of Dan's murder.

Ted was smiling and, oblivious to the women's mutual shock, began introductions.

"Uh, we've already met," said Red.

"You two know each other? And you left me in the dark?"

Shannon smiled awkwardly. "We just met this week, under slightly different circumstances. Officer Quaglio interviewed me the night of the Horgan murder."

"Right," added Red. "Ted mentioned his parents were divorced, but I never made the connection since your last names are different."

"Of course," nodded Shannon. "Who'd guess that an O'Keefe is mother to a Caruso? Anyway, what do I call you now?"

"My friends call me Red. You can probably guess why," she laughed, with a toss of her dark red mane. "My father was Italian, my mom Irish."

"The best combination of all," said Ted. "Well, let's start with a drink."

"Good idea," said Shannon. To Red, she added: "And my friends call me Shannon."

Red Quaglio ordered a vodka tonic. Shannon wanted a double martini, very dry and neat, but settled for a vodka tonic, too. Ted ordered beer on tap.

"Well, here's to us," said Ted, when the drinks arrived. "You guys both look like you've been through the wringer this week."

Bless him, thought Shannon. Ted always had the knack of smoothing things over. She'd once worried about whether he was tough enough to make it as a cop. No more. In his first few years on the job, he'd received several commendations for valor. He'd always aced exams, and hoped to get his detective's shield in record time. Ted was one of the few people Shannon knew who really loved his work. Looking over at this handsome, dark-haired, six-foot-two son of hers, she was proud. She and Tony had raised a couple of great kids.

Red and Shannon compared the week's experiences and agreed it was a tie for "worst." Still, Red was upbeat, explaining to Shannon that she was a recruit from New York's Police Department. "Ted and I met at the 52nd Precinct in the Bronx. Now I've worked in Tuckahoe for a couple of months. I grew up there and decided to work closer to home."

"Isn't it tough questioning people you know?" asked Shannon. Forget about those you don't, she thought.

"Absolutely. Some are annoyed to be questioned at all, and go ape when I double-check their stories. Others drive me nuts at home, wanting the inside scoop. Since the O.J. Simpson case has died down, the snoops need something to replace it. This is it."

"Tell me about it," nodded Shannon. She filled in with her own stories of neighbors checking in daily for gossip. "Then there's the crowd I haven't heard from since my divorce. All of a sudden, they want to chew the fat, get together, renew old times, and make up for the lost years."

Ted had been looking at the menu, the board specials, and his watch. Now he interjected: "Hate to interrupt the sleuth talk, but let's give it a break while we order." In a few minutes, having read the entire menu and the blackboard specials, he ordered his usual medium-rare cheeseburger with everything on it.

"Did I raise a gourmet or what?" asked Shannon.

"Or what," said Red. "I'm going for the meat loaf and mashed potatoes." Shannon opted for breast of chicken.

Over dinner, the talk settled into humdrum stuff. Unlike Ted, Red had never expected to become a cop. "I majored in psychology, hoping to find out what made people tick."

"And you couldn't?" asked Shannon.

"Yup, I could," answered Red. "Decided I didn't really care about a lot of it. All that sharing. When someone says they want to share with me, it's never good. Makes me want to head for the hills."

"Amen," said Shannon, laughing.

"The final 'aha!' came when I fell asleep during a group therapy session," continued Red. "What I like about being a cop is that you control the results. Not always, but usually, if you do the job right, you get closure. I like that."

"So, dear girl," said Ted, "are you telling my mom you'll get your man in the Bronxville case?"

"Or woman," answered Red. "Of course. It may take a while, but we'll get him. As they say, '*cui bono?*' Who benefits?"

"Some might say the whole world does when the victim's a lawyer," laughed Ted.

"And that from a lawyer-to-be," said Shannon,

raising her coffee cup. The time had flown, and it was now seven-twenty. "You two better get going. On Saturday nights, the line forms early at the theater."

"Righto," said Ted. He paid the check, and the three walked out onto Pondfield Road. Ted kissed his mother, who said good-bye to them both. "If I pick up any clues, I'll be in touch," she told Red.

"Thanks. Even Holmes had his Watson," laughed Red. Ted took her arm and they walked companionably down the block and around the corner to the Bronxville movie theater.

Well, whaddayouknow, thought Shannon. Red did have a nice smile, even a sense of humor. How bad could a meatloaf-and-mashed-potatoes woman be?

That night, Shannon dreamt of several carrot-topped grandchildren running around her apartment. She woke up sweating.

43

Zoo with Drew was not to be.

Sunday was mild, grim and rainy. Great, thought Shannon, over a second cup of coffee. The zoo would have to be in her apartment.

At nine-thirty, she was checking her videos for kid-friendly films when the phone rang. Someone was downstairs: "Hi, Mom," said Maria on the speakerphone. "We got here a bit early. Didn't think you'd mind."

Maria and Drew arrived with enough gear for a two-week camping trip. "Drew likes to nap in his sleeping bag. He packed a couple of his own things so you won't have to entertain him."

"Great," said Shannon. "I'm just getting ready for church, though, so that'll be our first stop."

"Drew loves Mass, right, honey?" Maria said, giving him a fast hug and even faster good-bye. "Have fun, you two. Thanks, Mom! The matinee should be over at five, so we'll be back at six, six-thirty at the latest."

"We'll do fine," said Shannon.

With his mother out the door, Drew announced that he hated church unless there was music, nor did he like to walk. Would she drive? And when would he have his morning snack?

Promised both music at church and a snack afterwards, he cheerfully checked out Shannon's video collection while she got dressed. They drove the short distance to St. Joseph's, since the day was not only rainy but raw.

On most Sundays, finding a parking space in the village was easier than during the week. In the rain, however, no one wanted to walk, not even a block. She was lucky enough to find a spot in the Cedar Street lot across from The Food Emporium, just down from the church.

St. Joseph's was a lovely old English Gothic building with some modern touches. In the 1980s, its interior had undergone major repairs. High above the altar, bright-colored beams of blue, green and red now braced an angular ceiling. At the time, tradition-alists were not pleased. Now, many had died, moved or simply adjusted.

In the 1930s, Rose Fitzgerald Kennedy had wor-shipped at St. Joe's, and her youngest son Ted mar-ried Joan Bennett here in 1958. In the spring of 1994, Richard Nixon attended a friend's wedding at St. Joseph's; the following week the ex-President died of a massive stroke.

The congregation was family-oriented. Pastor and parish staff worked tirelessly on outreach pro-grams for every age group, and generally succeeded. There were still some who found the pipe organ too loud, and electric votive candles too modern. "Give us back real candles, wicks and all!" The fact that those were fire hazards was lost in the dialogue.

Today, the ten forty-five Mass had organ music and a full choir, but Drew whispered: "No guitars?" They took a couple of seats just off the aisle, near the front. Best for a quick getaway if he became restless.

Drew behaved admirably. Only when the priest began his homily on the shortage of vocations to the priesthood, and the importance of celibacy, did he give Shannon a tug: "What's cebilacy?"

"Celibacy. I'll explain it after mass, O.K?"

At Communion, the choir sang "Be Not Afraid." Drew joined in, with slightly modified lyrics: "Be Not a Pain." Well, thought Shannon, even better.

After mass, walking back to the car, Drew looked up at her and said: "Cebilacy?"

Dear God, why couldn't four year olds have the same memory lapses as their grandparents? "It's celibacy," she began. "And it means that priests can't marry or have girlfriends."

"Why not?"

"They need to spend their time working for God."

"Hmmm. But then they have nobody to sleep with."

"Right, but lots of people sleep alone." That should end it.

Fat chance.

"So why don't they have lady priests? If there were ladies, they could sleep with them, and there'd be enough priests. Wouldn't that be an idea?"

"It sure would. Maybe one day it will happen."

"I think I'll write and tell them," said Drew.

"Good," she answered, as they navigated her Buick Skylark out of the lot.

"We can do it after my snack."

In five minutes they were home. Getting out of her car and approaching Lake View's lobby, she noticed a few media types in the parking lot. The rain had stopped, and the weekend doorman would not arrive until two. Seeing a young woman with a microphone approaching, Shannon put up a hand, waving her away.

Drew asked, "What did she want?"

"She wanted to interview me, but we need to go upstairs for your snack."

"Maybe we could've been on TV," said Drew.

"Maybe." Up in her kitchen, she'd just gotten milk out of the refrigerator when the doorbell rang and a voice shouted: "Pizza Man!"

"It's Uncle Ted," shouted Drew happily. "I know his voice!"

"In the flesh," said Ted, as Drew opened the door. "Max Schneible recognized me and let me in. How are you, tiger?"

"Hungry," said Drew. Had Uncle Ted arrived with the Golden Fleece, he could not have received a warmer welcome.

"Well, I was in the neighborhood and hungry too. It was close to lunchtime, and I thought you might be here. Good thing, since otherwise I'd have to gorge on two large pizzas."

Drew ordered up one piece of plain and one with sausage for starters, "and then I'll see." Shannon set up Cokes and paper plates in the kitchen, where they made quick work of the two pizzas.

After a while, Drew tired and announced he'd have a nap now, "and my snack when I wake up."

While Drew napped, Shannon made coffee for Ted and herself. She waited for an opener, knowing he had not come just to deliver pizza.

"Look," he began, "about last night, I'm really sorry. I had no idea you and Red had met and hit it off badly. It wasn't a set-up, really!"

She frowned for a moment, then burst out laughing. "Hey, I believe you. Maria's the one with guile in this family, not you. Anyway, forget it. We'd both had a long day on Tuesday and were wound up a little tight. It's not like we got into a hair-pulling contest. We reached a kind of truce at the end."

"Good. With a couple of Type A personalities like you, I'm not sure who would win."

"Change of subject," she said. "I didn't want to talk shop last night, but what's happening on the investigation? The media hasn't had anything new to report in a few days."

"That's because there's not much to say. We're slogging through dozens of interviews. There's the local crowd, of course: joggers and others who might have seen somebody strange hanging around that morning, or maybe before it, staking out the place. Then there's the Lake View angle. Some of your older neighbors can't get out much, so they welcome anyone, even cops. They haven't given us a whole lot, though. Red said that some old lady reported seeing a guy, I think she called him Warren Spain, throw a package from a moving car on the Bronx River Parkway a couple of weeks ago."

"Have they finished talking to the residents?" Shannon asked.

"Just about. They've also waded through the managing agent's minutes for the past couple of years, trying to identify possible suspects."

"That's got to be a long list."

"It is. Dom Rizzuto, the superintendent you fired, and Arthur Bliss, the applicant you rejected, are probably at the top. Both have alibis we're checking out. Horgan also alienated a couple of people before you knew him. About five years ago he pushed the Board pretty aggressively for an assessment to build up its reserve fund. There hadn't been one in twenty years, and it was justified, but not everybody was convinced. According to Kryhoski, one guy had to be hauled into court to pay up. Another, who had lost a prospective buyer for his apartment when maintenance charges went up, tried to punch Horgan out."

"What happened?" asked Shannon.

"The guy picked the wrong spot. They were in the lobby. Mario the doorman saw what was happening and took him on. The guy backed off."

Shannon laughed. "Good for Mario. What about Dan's firm? Any leads there?"

"Lots. That's where the Manhattan Homicide Division has lent a hand. We've been doing those interviews. Lou De Femio gave us a list of people laid off, and we're going through it. It's ironic that Tim Donohue, the guy who found Horgan on the track, had met him before at his father's wake. Walter Donohue was apparently one of the people terminated, right?"

"Yes," said Shannon. "It wasn't as hard-nosed as you make it, though. Walter was sixty-eight and had really slowed up. They were able to merge the mail unit with some other administrative services and eliminate his job. He left with severance, a pension, and his medical plan intact." She tried not to sound defensive, but knew she'd failed.

Ted nodded. "But not with his dignity, according to Buddy, as his friends call him. His father had told Tim he was forced out, but not to tell his mother. Buddy admits he had no use for Dan Horgan, especially after his father died. He also acknowledges that Walter had a bum ticker, but feels the firing helped bring on the heart attack. He asked that we not say anything to Edna, his mother, about that. She still thinks Walter elected retirement."

"Yes. Dan and I met her in CVS one night a couple of months ago. She was cordial to us both. In fact, I'd planned to call her this week for lunch. I don't think any of this should change that, do you?"

"Not at all. We've already talked to Edna Donohue. Nothing there."

"No wild card theories?" she asked.

"Well, Chief Martino's right. I walked by the lake today to get a good look at the crime scene. There's no way this was a random hit. This guy was very careful, knew exactly what he was doing. No fingerprints, hair fibers, blood, or anything we could trace. My guess is he's a pro."

"Hmmm," said Shannon. "So even with airtight alibis, you can't eliminate people. Almost anyone could have done it, right? Hired a killer?"

"Uh-huh. You got any hunches?"

She hesitated a moment, then asked: "Did Dan know he was ill?"

"Don't know yet. His personal physician doesn't think so. Horgan hadn't seen him in a year. Why do you ask?"

"I'm not sure. You don't really put a pattern together until you know someone's ill, and then things start to fit. When I first joined the Lake View Board, Dan was sharp as a tack. He ran every meeting smoothly, decisively."

"And lately?"

"He often vacillated, seemed to lose his energy level and concentration. He'd put things off if he could. Last year, when Brett Halliday and I did the consulting assignment at Dan's firm, we saw the same thing. It was hard to believe that its reputation had once been so high."

"But wasn't Jake Stern the real manager there?"

"Yes," she said, "but several months after Jake's death, Dan did take charge. Even when his wife was ill, there was no doubt at all about who was the managing partner. It was only in the last year or so that he seemed to drift, lose the will to fix things. Lou De Femio as much as admitted that to me. Somebody as good as Lou and not quite as loyal might have just walked. Lou said he would have, too, if Dan hadn't brought us in."

"Yeah, De Femio seems like a good guy. Of course, Horgan and he had keyman insurance on each other's lives. If either one died, the policy paid off enough to allow the survivor to buy out the other's interest in the firm. So De Femio himself benefits from Dan's death."

They were interrupted by Drew's shouting from the living room, where he'd napped in his sleeping bag: "O.K., I'm ready for my snack now!"

"And I've gotta run," said Ted. "I'm off today, picking up Red in half an hour."

"Give her a peace sign from me."

"Will do. And if you pick up any vibes about the case around here, give her a call, will you? She'd really appreciate it."

"Sure," said Shannon, kissing him good-bye. Ted high-fived his nephew and left.

Drew followed her out to the kitchen to assess snack offerings. "Then we'll write the letter about the lady priests, O.K?"

"Sure, and fax it to the Curia in Rome," she mumbled, opening up the refrigerator door.

"Let's send it right to that nice old man, the Pope. Wouldn't that be an idea?" asked Drew.

"Best I've heard all day," she answered.

41

....

On Monday morning Rich Kryhoski was sitting in a booth at the Village Cup and Saucer Coffee House, just across from Bronxville's train station.

When Shannon arrived just before eight o'clock, the morning's newspapers were spread out on the table. He greeted her with: "Well, at least we've moved off page one for now. I'll be happy the first day we're not in the papers at all."

She nodded. "At least the crowd in front of the building has thinned out. Last week, I felt like I had to dress for TV every morning."

The waitress arrived with pad and pencil, and quickly took two orders of large orange juice, scrambled eggs, bacon and toasted buttered bagels. "Good for you," she said. "Phooey on all those reports about cholesterol. Look at that poor Mr. Horgan. Always worried about staying fit. What good did it do him?"

They smiled uneasily.

Rich pulled out a thick vinyl folder bursting with papers of every sort. Stick-it notes of all sizes and colors clung to the inside of the folder and to each other. He removed a palm-sized computer organizer. "Great little gadget. Stores over five thousand records, addresses, to-do lists, and memos."

Pushing it aside, he added: "There's nothing in the damned thing. Never use it. Wife gave it to me for Christmas. Makes her happy to see it in my folder every morning when I leave the house."

"I wondered who bought those," said Shannon. "Now I know."

He nodded. "O.K., first I want to tell you something." A pause. He was obviously uncomfortable. Then, "I'm going to retire."

Shannon had just swallowed a mouthful of steaming coffee. "Today?" she gasped.

"No, no, sorry! It's been a tough decision, so I wanted to get it out fast. The end of the year. Lucy, that's my wife, Lucy and I decided to sell the house, buy a condo in south Jersey to be near our daughter and her family. We're both in good health, but the real estate business is a roller coaster ride. Figured it was time to make the move while things are up."

"Well, good for you," Shannon answered.

"I told Dan two weeks ago. He'd planned to discuss it at next week's Board meeting. I wanted to give Lake View time to plan ahead."

"Are you selling the business?" she asked.

"Yup. The outfit's called Peters and Hartung. They're growing pretty fast in the Northeast, and want a Westchester branch. They'll move into our offices once I go, maybe add some of their own people. It's a good deal for both sides."

"Do they also manage co-ops?"

"Oh, yeah. One option for Lake View will be to

negotiate a new contract with them. They don't come cheap, though. But we'll have plenty of time to talk about that before the Board has to decide."

"Good."

"O.K. That's out of the way. Let me brief you on some other stuff." Breakfast arrived, with minimal effect on Rich's briefing. He talked expertly about Lake View's budget and pipes; of trees to be pruned; of a front walk needing repaving. When he was done, his yellow tie was stained with orange juice, and his blue shirt had bits of scrambled egg on one cuff. Every scrap of paper now had a small check mark on it, and had been stuffed back in his folder.

"And that's everything, I think."

"Now I know why Dan was impressed with you. Thanks."

He smiled. "Yeah, I'll miss him too. But you'll do fine, don't worry."

"Thanks. One thing before we go. How's Max Schneible working out? Any complaints from residents?"

He looked down, grinning: "Not from my end. In this business, no news is good news. Even Hester Harrington seems to be impressed. Struts around like the peacock who hired her!"

They laughed, getting up to leave. "I'll sure be glad when they find this killer, and not just because I liked Horgan," said Rich. "The cops are still hunkered down in my office going over board minutes. Kind of dumb, really. Any Board with a little sense doesn't write down all the nasty stuff. Dan always told the Board secretary to record what action was taken, not everything that led up to it."

"Good thing, too," said Shannon. "Otherwise it might read like *Animal House* and no one would buy our apartments!"

He chuckled and paid the bill. "My treat, to celebrate your elevation to Board president."

She smiled wanly and they parted, promising to stay in close touch. Across the road, a Metro-North express train roared by. Suddenly, she wished she was on it, off to somewhere tranquil and humdrum.

45

The private Mass for Dan Horgan was on Wednesday morning at ten o'clock at St. Francis of Assisi Church, on the grounds of Gate of Heaven Cemetery in Hawthorne.

The short graveside ceremony was now ending and Chip Horgan had invited the group for lunch at a nearby restaurant. Shannon had driven up with Evan Doubleday, who wanted to be dropped off at Westchester Medical Center for an early afternoon lecture. About thirty others were in the funeral party, so she and Evan felt comfortable declining the luncheon invitation.

Lou De Femio, his wife Nina, and Jacqueline Sheppard, Dan's executive assistant, were there, along with Margo Stern, and Rosa Di Carlo. The rest of the group seemed to be relatives.

Shannon and Evan were talking to Jacqueline when Lou came over and introduced his wife Nina, a tall, regally handsome woman with a French twist of ash blond hair and a friendly manner. She was elegantly dressed in a dark brown linen suit. A woman of style and grace, thought Shannon.

After hearing they would not be attending lunch, Lou asked Shannon: "Are you working these days?"

"Just finished an assignment last week. Thought I'd take a breather," she answered.

"Good. I'll call you."

Before she could reply, he'd turned and walked quickly to catch up with Nina, who had headed for their car.

About a half block away, Shannon noticed Dave Corrigan and Red Quaglio of the Tuckahoe Police Department, standing beside an unmarked car. Just behind them were three local cops who had taped off the burial site, to allow the family some privacy. Even now, flash bulbs were popping and reporters were running after Chip Horgan, trying to interview him.

Turning to Evan, Shannon asked: "Ready to go?"

"Would you mind taking a walk down the hill with me first?" he asked.

"Why not?" she answered. It was, in fact, a perfect April morning. Strong sun, low humidity, mild spring breeze. "Where to? Babe Ruth's grave? Billy Martin's?"

"Nope," smiled Evan.

The two walked slowly down the hill, past many gravestones with well-known names. There, near the road, was Mike Quill's. The voice of the fiery Irish-American head of New York's Transport Worker's Union was stilled only by death. Mike had died of cardiac arrest during a particularly angry bargaining session with the City of New York. "My father once told me they waited three days before burying him, to be sure he was dead," said Shannon. Evan laughed.

Not too much further down was a simple, small stone with an inscription: John Sullivan. In even smaller letters at its base was a second name: Fred Allen. This time it was Evan who recalled the legendary comedian's remark about radio: "I don't trust furniture that talks."

"I wonder what he'd think of all those home entertainment centers these days?" Shannon asked.

They had continued about a hundred yards further when a couple of joggers in tee-shirts and shorts passed by. "A funny place to run, no?" asked Shannon.

"Maybe they figure it's safer than the Bronxville Lake track." He took her arm and turned right at a long row of headstones. About a third of the way up the hill, he stopped at a slate one, somewhat taller than the rest. There were fresh flowers at its base. The inscription read:

Mary Teresa Doubleday
1957-1987
Cherished Wife

"We'd been married only two years," said Evan softly.

"I'm so sorry," she answered. "An accident?"

"No. Breast cancer. She was in remission when we married. About eighteen months later, it resurfaced. She lasted just four months."

"I can't even imagine the pain," said Shannon.

"Here I was, thirty-two years old. The world at my feet. A great wife who was pregnant with our first child. Then, nothing."

"How did you pull yourself out of it?"

"Went camping. Mary and I loved the outdoors, and had planned on doing Yellowstone that summer. In the fall, I was set to join the Central Park West practice of one of my medical school professors who wanted to retire in two years. Chance of a lifetime."

"And Mary? What were her plans?"

"She was an interior decorator, who already had a thriving business on Manhattan's upper West Side. We'd moved there after our marriage."

"And you stayed for a time?"

He nodded. "That fall, when I came back from the camping trip, I knew that I needed to do something different. I just wasn't up to dealing with patients for a while, so I sacked the plans to go into private practice. Got a job at Sloan-Kettering doing oncology research, and discovered I liked it. They seem to like me, so I'm still there. It took longer to leave the apartment. Two years after Mary's death, I sold it and moved to Bronxville. Fewer memories."

"I understand," said Shannon.

They left Mary Doubleday's grave and walked quietly back to Shannon's car, near the chapel. The setting reminded her of Yeats' Innisfree, where "peace comes dropping slow." The silence was broken when they reached the pond, where ducks were quacking away. A "No Fishing" sign stood on the grass. Pointing to it, Evan laughed: "That wouldn't have stopped Mary. She loved to fish."

They got into the Buick and drove slowly out the cemetery's gate and south on the Taconic, onto the

Bronx River Parkway. Just before exiting at the Westchester Medical Center, Shannon asked Evan: "When you called the other night with the autopsy results, you sounded like you'd known Dan was ill. Or am I mistaken?"

He hesitated a moment, then answered: "One night in early October, we came home from the city together on Metro-North. Dan looked terrible and I asked him about it. Said he'd been having some problems, but was sure it wasn't a big deal. Blamed it on working too hard, traveling too much, downsizing his firm. Felt that he'd let the troops down. Anyway, he was having short lapses of memory, finding it hard to stay awake at meetings, stuff like that."

"And your diagnosis?" she asked.

"I said it could be something that a couple of weeks off would cure, but it could also be serious, even life-threatening. The symptoms were too general. The next day I called him with the names of three good neurologists and recommended a full checkup. Told him I'd be glad to speak with them first if he wanted."

"And did he follow through?"

"Not so far as I know. Two of the three guys practice locally and I've run into them at local medical meetings. They always appreciate referrals, and neither of them mentioned him to me. I gave their names to the police."

It was close to one o'clock when they drove into the Medical Center. Getting out of the car, Evan thanked her for the lift: "Sorry I can't even buy you lunch. Lucky me. Today I dine with a couple of kidney specialists. Can I call you soon and make it up to you?"

"Sounds good. Break a leg at your lecture."

"A good place to do it," he smiled, waving goodbye.

46

Two days later, Luke Plisky was watching the twelve o'clock news over lunch in his fifth grade home room.

Harriet Noble, whose classroom was next door, stuck her head in the door: "Excuse me, do you have any Grey Poupon?" He waved her in.

Harriet reminded Luke of that short, stout teapot with a small lid. Always cold, she wore an all-season hat. More often than not, she forgot to take it off during the day, earning the name "Mad Hatter" from her classes.

Today, she was characteristically hatted, and uncharacteristically happy. Waddling over, she grabbed a chair near Luke's desk, sat down and opened her brown-bag lunch.

"What's up? You win the lottery?" he asked.

"Even better. The Board of Dead finally came up with that early retirement package. My days are numbered here!"

He raised his Coke can in a toast: "Hey, I'll miss you. Who'll fill us in on all the plots and plans from the Livingston Street mob?"

"Don't worry," said Harriet. "The grapevine liveth forever!" She took an enormous bite from a small tuna fish sandwich, and joined Luke in watching the twelve o'clock news on his small TV. The anchorman announced a short commercial break: "And when we return, a live report from Gate of Heaven Cemetery in Hawthorne, where Bronxville murder victim Dan Horgan was laid to rest today. Stay tuned for an update."

"Doesn't sound like they're making much progress on that one," said Harriet, chomping away at a piece of celery. "That's not far from where you live, right? What're the locals saying about it?"

"Not much," said Luke. "Most are relieved it's not Yonkers, for a change. Bad for business."

Harriet nodded. "I heard the reward money's up to fifty big ones now. That should bring somebody out of the woods."

They sat silently through a phone company commercial. Several jovial rubes, one of each color, were promising to switch long distance carriers. "Where do they find those jerks?" asked Harriet.

"Livingston Street," said Luke.

"Figures," laughed Harriet, now searching for dessert at the bottom of her lunch bag. She pulled out a package of Yankee Doodles and groaned: "Someone's eaten one! I left my desk for one minute to go to the rest room and a kid must have stolen it from my bag!"

"Are you sure they were all there when you packed your lunch?" asked Luke.

"You bet I am. Picked up a fresh pack on my way to work."

"Well, if you think it's a kid who took it, you might try what I did to flush out the thief."

"What's that?" asked Harriet.

"One day I'd packed a Dunkin' Donut with my lunch. Came time to eat it, and it was gone. When the kids came back from the cafeteria, I said that someone had probably taken my donut by mistake, and I'd just heard on the news that there were reports of botulism in Dunkin' Donuts. I just hoped whoever stole it hadn't eaten it."

"Good grief, you can get botulism from a donut?"

"Who knows?" he answered. "Anyway, a quiet girl, Kerry Egan, ran up, said she was ill and had to see the nurse right away. Case closed."

Harriet laughed. "Who would have thought that little slip of a thing would steal a donut? Anyway, I like your method. I'll try it on my class, see if it works."

"It will," said Luke. "It might be good to post the nurse in advance, though. She didn't speak to me for months after that."

"Good advice," said Harriet, polishing off her dessert. "Well, it's back to work I go. Thanks for the advice, Sherlock."

After she left, Luke got up and looked out the grimy window. He was not thinking of the missing Yankee Doodle, but about that $50,000 reward offered for information leading to Dan Horgan's murderer. He thought he'd covered his tracks well.

Then again, Kerry Egan had probably felt she
was home free after her donut caper.

47

Early in her career, a mentor had given Shannon some advice: "When moving to a new job, put your own stamp on it fast. Do something dramatically different from your predecessor."

At six o'clock on the last Thursday in April, she began Lake View's Board meeting. Elmer Brick mentioned that Val Thomas had not yet arrived. "Right," she said, "he can catch up when he does. I don't like to hold up those of you who are here. A foolish question, but does anyone have any corrections to Gwyneth's minutes of our last meeting?"

There were no hands. "Good. Next, the managing agent's report: Rich, you're on."

Kryhoski placed the several sheets of paper in front of him in some kind of order known only to him. "Apart from the murder," he grimaced, "it's been a good month. Max Schneible is doing well." He paused and looked up for reactions. Experience had taught him to speak modestly about new employees until the Board made up its own mind. Tonight, though, the room was wreathed in smiles, Hester Harrington's widest of all.

Rich moved confidently into more routine items, including the replanting of the small garden behind Lake View, which was finally awash in flowers a year after the new gardener had promised them. Nothing more had been heard from Arthur Bliss, the rejected applicant who had filed suit against the co-op. "I'd guess that Dan's murder shut him up for a while," commented Jay Shapiro.

"Or maybe he shut Dan up," added Elmer Brick.

"Could be, though I doubt it," said Rich. "It's too obvious. Anyway, there's just one new item. Hannah Green, a new resident, has been parking in the fire lane near the building on more than one occasion. Mario has spoken to her about it, with absolutely no effect. When he calls her on the intercom, it's often hours before she comes down to move it."

"What's her reason?" asked Evan Doubleday.

"Guess. What else? Said she's a doctor, and is entitled to special consideration."

"Nonsense," said Evan. "She's a pediatrician with a practice in Manhattan."

"Right," said Rich. "Anyway, I want to send her a letter telling her that the next time it happens we're calling the police and her car will be ticketed or towed. Just want to be sure I've got the Board's blessing."

He got it. "Good," said Rich. "I wish we could do more to protect residents from our media friends. The police are doing all they can."

"Agreed," said Shannon, "and we couldn't ask for more from Mario and Max. They're guarding Lake View like the Alamo!"

Val Thomas had now arrived, surprised and mildly flustered to see the meeting in progress.

"Val, would you like to give your report?" Shannon asked.

He did, and it was mercifully short. For once, he skipped warning of a financial crisis that was always one "Act of God" away.

The next order of business was to fill the Board's open vice president slot. Shannon announced that the rules called for her to move into Dan's job as president for the remainder of his term, a year and a half to go. "Would someone like to begin the nomination process?" she asked.

Jay Shapiro quickly nominated Evan Doubleday, who was seconded and voted into office unanimously, despite his caveat: "I don't do funerals."

That still left a vacant spot on the Board. They decided to post it on the laundry room's bulletin board. Anyone interested could submit a note with a "CV" (no one in Bronxville called them résumés) to Rich Kryhoski within two weeks.

"They'll be hanging from the rafters to sign up," said Elmer.

"Yeah, right," said Shannon. "Oh, there's one announcement before we go. Rich?"

The managing agent announced his plans to sell the business and retire at the year's end. He was telling them now, so they could decide whether to go with the new firm or search for another one.

Elmer slapped him on the back with a cheerful,

"Good for you, young feller. Git while the gittin's good! The secret to a happy life."

On that note, the meeting was adjourned just after seven o'clock. "A record," proclaimed Gwyneth Fielding, noting the exact time on her digital watch. The rest applauded, saying that if Shannon guaranteed one hour meetings forever, she could be president for life.

"A fate worse than death," she answered, but her pleasure was evident as they swept up their papers and walked out into the chilly spring night.

A light rain had begun to fall, but Shannon said she was walking home. "My hair needs washing anyway." Evan joined her. The others accepted a ride from Elmer or Val, who had driven.

Crossing the Pondfield Road West rotary, Evan looked up at a checkerboard sky with dark clouds. "Spahn and Sain, and pray for rain," he said. Seeing Shannon's questioning face, he added: "An old baseball line. Major league pitchers need several days' rest between outings. In the 50s, the Boston Braves had two superstars, Johnny Sain and Warren Spahn, and not much behind them. Somebody came up with that line. It worked for a short time."

Shannon smiled. "You know, one of the cops mentioned that an older resident had said something about a guy hanging around the lake. She mentioned a name, but I think it was Warren Spain. The cops didn't give it much credibility."

"It wasn't me who saw him," said Evan. "The only one who can beat me in Baseball Trivia is Minnie Stern. If Minnie told them, I'm sure she called him Spahn, not Spain."

"Maybe the cops wrote her off as a doting old lady and didn't really listen."

"Worth checking out," said Evan.

"Absolutely."

48

....

On Friday, Shannon awoke just after seven to a warm, clear day.

She dressed quickly and walked out Lake View's rear door down to the path around the lake. The ground was damp and muddy after a heavy rain that had lasted through the early morning hours. Not a good day for jogging.

At the north end of the path, the yellow tape roping off the crime scene was gone. Two cops were still standing by, and one appeared to be Red Quaglio. She walked over to talk with them.

Red saw her first and waved hello. Shannon greeted her and her partner Dave Corrigan: "Still at it, I see."

"Yup," said Red. "We'll be out here for at least a couple more days, looking for anybody who might have seen a stranger hanging around the track prior to the murder. By now, I think we've probably talked to all the regulars. We're hoping that maybe someone who's been away will come forward and remember something."

Shannon nodded. "Evan mentioned something to me last night. It may be nothing at all."

Corrigan interrupted: "Well, nothing is all we have so far. What's up?"

"Warren Spain," Shannon began, before Red interrupted: "Right, the old woman in the penthouse apartment who talked about a guy throwing something from a car back in March. Reminded her of Warren Spain. You know him?"

"No," said Shannon. "But could she possibly have said Warren Spahn?"

"Could be," said Corrigan. "Matter of fact, I think that's what she did say. Does it matter?"

"Maybe," said Shannon. "The woman is Minnie Stern, who happens to be a longtime baseball fan. If she said the guy threw like Warren Spahn, there's a chance she might remember something else about the incident."

Red nodded sheepishly. "I've gotta tell you, we were both working double shifts that day. Lots of pressure to get through as many interviews as possible while memories were fresh. Maybe it's worth another try."

Corrigan asked: "Her name again?"

"Stern," said Shannon. "Minnie Stern. A former school teacher. Apartment 6E, top floor. Don't be thrown by her bad hip. Her brain is intact. Pretty sharp lady, I'd say."

"O.K., we'll follow up as soon as we're done here," said Red.

"Good. Take care," said Shannon, turning away.

Red called after her. "Hey, thanks!"

"Sure. Keep in touch."

When Shannon returned to her apartment, she

dialed Minnie Stern's number: "Thought I'd warn you. The cops are coming back to see you, and I'm to blame." She explained what had happened.

"They thought I had an addled brain, right? I'm old, but not stupid. Anyway, it's Rosa's day off. I'll just act a little dithery, get out a little veiled hat, pretend I'm Miss Marple."

Shannon laughed: "Humor them. They're young. Cheerio, Jane!"

49

....

On the first Sunday of May, Shannon returned to her apartment at ten o'clock, after her first major league baseball game at Yankee Stadium. Evan Doubleday had invited her and they'd dined at Palmers, a local restaurant, following the game.

The red light was flashing on the telephone answering machine.

In simpler times, there was only a mailbox to check. Now, there was so much more: telephone answering machine, fax, and E-mail. Still, she had to admit that she felt a bit sad when there was nothing on any of them.

She turned on the recorder. "Hi, Shannon. Lou De Femio here. It's bedlam at the office. Walter's death, Dan's murder, the reorganization. Could you please think about working here for a couple of months, to get us through? At least let me try to convince you over lunch? Call me. Thanks."

What did he think she was, a masochist? Horgan & Stern had just gone through massive layoffs. Even without two deaths, the place would be a battlefield. She'd vowed never to work in a company that had just been downsized. Survivors were like the walking wounded. Many were doing more work or learning new jobs. You breathed stress when you opened the door.

Shannon had put all that behind her. Now, she could choose her assignments. Besides, as Lake View's new Board president, she needed time to dig in quickly: help the police as best she could, find Dan's murderer, and ease her neighbors' fears.

This was a no-brainer. She picked up the telephone and dialed De Femio's number. Her answer would be a clear and unequivocal "No."

No lunch. No job. Thanks but no thanks.

50

....

She said "Yes."

Not at first, of course. But when she called Lou back, he'd suggested lunch at The Four Seasons in Manhattan on Wednesday, and she'd agreed. It was one of her favorite restaurants, with chocolate cake to die for. A day away from Bronxville couldn't hurt, right?

When Shannon arrived at the restaurant, the maitre d' said that Lou was already there, and ushered her to a corner table. When he rose to greet her, there was a rare smile on his square, lived-in face.

Dan had told her that De Femio was one of Jake Stern's early recruits from St. John's Law School in Brooklyn. The son of Italian immigrants, he was the first in his family to attend college. He was also bright, hardworking, and hell-bent to succeed. After twenty years at the firm, Lou was respected and liked by his professional colleagues, though some bristled at his tough and direct manner. More than once, Dan had urged a softer approach to him: "For Pete's sake, you've got all the charm of a pit bull. Can't you add a few adjectives to your vocabulary?"

To which Lou had responded: "Sure, but you wouldn't like them."

Since his record as a litigator was among the best in the city, Dan had long ago given up trying to change him. When Jake Stern died, Lou had become an equity partner in the firm and Dan's right arm.

Today, he greeted Shannon warmly: "You're one of the few bright spots in my appointment book this week."

"Hey, life in Bronxville is no picnic, either. I go out the back door to dodge a gaggle of reporters, and run into my snowbird neighbors, back from winter in Florida. They want a blow-by-blow version of all they missed."

"Not much different at the office," answered Lou. "Everybody's antsy. Some are afraid that whoever killed Dan had a grudge against the firm, that he was just the first victim. We can forget about new clients. Until this thing's solved, we'll be lucky to hold on to those we have."

Shannon nodded. "Look, I'm starved. How about we order first, talk later?"

They did. Two tossed salads, salmon for him, well-done steak for her. Perrier for both.

Over the salad course, Shannon asked: "What's the party line? Do you think the murder was work-related?"

"I'm not sure. Dan won a whole lot of big cases for some wealthy clients. In the past few years, he defended a couple of hospitals and wealthy physicians against multi-million-dollar malpractice claims. He won all of them, leaving more than one injured plaintiff in the dust."

"How about the downsizing as motive?" Shannon asked.

"Maybe, but the last three people had left almost five months before the murder."

"Margo Stern, Walter Donohue, and Brian Palmer, right?" she asked.

"Yeah, and we know it wasn't poor Walter, unless he rose from the dead."

"What's your take on Walter's son Tim? He was obviously pretty bitter at his father's wake. Odd that he was the one who found Dan's body, wasn't it?"

"Yes. A week after Walter died last November, his wife Edna called to make a date to come in and review the death benefits. The day before her appointment, Tim called to say that Walter had told Edna he was retiring voluntarily. Tim wanted to be sure that nobody here let the cat out of the bag. He felt his mother could never deal with the truth."

"And did they?" Shannon asked.

"Nope. I personally walked around the office to talk to people. The day Edna came in, she spoke with the human resources counselor first. Later she stopped by to say how well things had gone. She was surprised that his insurance death benefit was over $100,000, double Walter's final salary. He'd also elected a joint and survivor option on his pension, which continues until she dies. Financially, she'll be O.K."

The waiter served the main course, and they began eating. Lou had a remarkable ability to chew and talk at the same time. "So," he continued, "that leaves Margo Stern and Brian Palmer. Both took the leaving hard. Hardly a week went by that Margo didn't call Dan or me to take her back. Finally, neither of us took her calls."

"I heard she threatened Dan."

"Yes. Half the time, she was three sheets to the wind, so I held back telling the cops about it. But good old Margo told them herself. She also said she was innocent."

"Do you believe her?"

"Yes. Margo's more likely to self-destruct than to kill somebody else. What a waste, that woman. The smartest damn lawyer we've had in the shop in years."

"What about Brian Palmer?"

"No threats that I know of. Too weak-kneed. He's still looking for a job where he can get medical benefits for his uh, friend Reed. Won't happen. Reed's running out of time. Still, I feel for Brian, poor bugger. Did I hear he's been getting temporary jobs?"

"Yes, he's been tutoring Jake's wife Minnie Stern. Things are going pretty well. O.K., Lou, change of subject. Why do you want me working for you again?"

"Thought you'd never ask. Look, I'm putting in fifteen-hour days. Nina's said that either it stops or she's filing for divorce."

"No decision there. Nina's worth holding onto," said Shannon.

"Don't I know it. Problem is that I'm trying to

run the whole damn show, and something has to give. Dan used to supervise the firm's outside stuff, while I watched over the business end. Now I'm trying to do both and end up doing neither well."

"Wasn't the plan to consolidate a lot of the administrative stuff under an office manager?" she asked.

"Yes," he said sheepishly. "Problem was that I was reluctant to give some of the stuff up, and Dan didn't push me. We still haven't got around to it."

"It happens," she said. "So you want me to do that temporarily, then hire someone permanent, right?"

"Something like that. Or," he smiled, "you might just get to like it and stay."

"No dice. Look, if I do consider coming to work for you, I've got some conditions."

"Shoot."

"A four-day work week. Flexible hours. You hire me through Brett Halliday's Temporary firm, at twenty-five percent more than you paid us last time. My top priority is to find and train a replacement, work myself out of a job."

"Deal," said Lou.

She was unprepared for the fast response. "O.K., I'll think about it and get back to you before the weekend, but don't get your hopes up."

"That I can't promise you. Anyway, here's the reason you came today." The waiter was arriving with two orders of cappuccino and chocolate cake.

"How did you know?" she asked, seeing the cake.

"Dan told me. I may look like a pit bull, but I've got a memory like an elephant."

Soon they'd finished lunch and were out on the sidewalk. Shannon looked at her watch. It was just after two o'clock. "You sure don't waste much time. A one-hour business lunch must be a record."

He smiled, waved and said *"Ciao,* see you Monday," and dashed off.

Back in her apartment by three-thirty, the red light was flashing on the answering machine. One message, from her daughter Maria. Could she sleep over next Wednesday night while Drew's nanny was on vacation? He would be thrilled.

Bad sign, the first sleepover. On Tuesday, she called Maria and said no. On Friday, she called Lou De Femio and said she'd take the job.

"Great. Got your office already set up."

51

....

That Saturday night, Luke Plisky telephoned his sister Lily Westrum in East Lansing, Michigan.

His nephew Danny answered the phone: "Hey, Uncle Luke, what's happenin? My dad just bought a small plane. How 'bout comin' out here this summer to go flying?"

"Sounds great."

"Mom says that Dad better find lots of friends to fly with him, cuz she gets airsick."

"Well, we'll set a date in August. Put your mom on, will you?"

Lily came to the phone a few seconds later. "Sounds like you already know about our new addition. A plane."

"Yup," he laughed. "Should be less work than a kid, anyway."

"I wonder," she said.

"Anyway, I just wanted to say Happy Birthday."

"Oh, gee. I was hoping it was Stevie Wonder calling to say he loves me."

"Ned might have a problem with that."

"Maybe not. Right now he's married to his plane."

They talked for ten minutes about what was going on in their lives. Finally, Lily asked: "How are you really, Luke?"

Good old Lily, the only one who really knew him. Knew about their father's desertion, Vietnam's horrors, the long hospitalization, storybook marriage to his nurse Karen, her hit-and-run death, his despair. Then, the miracle, picking up his life, becoming a teacher.

"Good," he answered. "Really good. Guess who's going to Paris in mid-July? I'm making final plans with the travel agent this weekend."

A pause. He knew why. Lily was wondering if this was a good idea. Would it renew the old pain?

"Look," he said quietly, "it's something I need to do."

"Well then, do it. I wish I could join you while Ned and Danny are off flying. Too bad I have another job, one I get paid for." Lily was an information specialist in the local library.

"I promised Danny I'd come out there in August when I get back. O.K. with you?"

"Anytime. Just let me know when. Give me your flight number and plans before you leave for Paris, O.K? Just in case I decide to meet you there."

"Will do, little sister. Talk to you soon."

"Yes. And Luke, take good care, please. You're my favorite brother."

"And your only one, kid. Talk to you soon."

After hanging up the phone, Luke turned on the TV and caught a ten o'clock station break: "There are new developments tonight in the Bronxville Jogger murder case. Stay tuned for our exclusive report on the eleven o'clock news."

Luke stayed tuned. At eleven, the anchorwoman led off with not one, but two new developments. The first: "A Lake View resident has reported seeing a stranger retrieve a parcel thrown on the Bronxville Lake Park from a moving vehicle on the Bronx River Parkway. The incident allegedly happened in the late afternoon on March 18, a few weeks prior to the murder. The witness gave a sketchy description of the person: Caucasian male, over six feet tall, who walked with a slight limp in his left leg. Police have confirmed this report, but are still unable to corroborate any connection with the murder of prominent New York lawyer Daniel Horgan."

The second bit of news was that Horgan & Stern and the New York Bar Association had contributed a total of $25,000 for information leading to the arrest and conviction of the person or persons responsible for the murder. "The total reward is now up to $75,000."

Well, thought Luke, that should send lots of rabbits up the hole.

Turning off the TV, he went upstairs to the den and worked on the itinerary for his summer trip.

52

By mid-May, Mario La Guardia and Max Schneible were media darlings. Early on, someone had tagged them "the M & M's" and the name had stuck.

As Lake View's chief doorman, Mario was not only the gatekeeper, but an ex-cop with friends still on the force and an insider's knowledge of murder investigations. Rumors were that he'd declined a slot on "Hard Copy," an exclusive interview with a tabloid's ace investigative reporter, and a monthly column with his own web site on a true crime zine. Capping it all was a book offer, tentatively titled *Bronxville's Hidden Secrets: The Centennial Edition.*

The more Mario said no, the more popular he became. His *'bon mots,'* like Forrest Gump's, were achieving cult status. Asked if he saw himself as a Kato Kaelin, O. J. Simpson's "houseman," he answered: "Nope, I never have a bad hair day," doffing his doorman's cap to reveal a bald pate.

Newer residents worried that he'd succumb to pressure, and that Lake View would become a second Brentwood, where Nicole Brown Simpson and her friend Ron Goldman had been brutally murdered in 1994. One shareholder actually drafted a code of ethics for Lake View's employees, specifically outlawing conversations with the press under penalty of dismissal. Shannon swiftly circulated that to the Board with a note: "I don't favor this. We've hired people for their integrity, competence, and loyalty. This is no time to question that." No one disagreed.

Older residents knew that Mario enjoyed the spotlight, but that he regarded the Fourth Estate as riffraff. Dan Horgan had once tagged him "the biggest snob in the building," and Mario now lived up to that billing. He refused to allow reporters to park or remain on Lake View property: "You must have official business here. Tell me what it is and you will be announced." He was immune to flattery, bribes, and threats; more than once he'd called the Bronxville Police to complain that trespassers were disturbing the peace. The cops arrived quickly and dispersed the crowd.

It was, Mario said to Steve Jablonski, Lake View's porter, "a defining moment."

"Is that good, Mario?" Steve had asked.

....

With Mario guarding Lake View's front entrance, several creative reporters had attempted to enter the building from the rear. The door would be locked, of course, but they'd hoped to tag along behind some resident returning from the lake.

That strategy was equally doomed, since Max Schneible could usually be found there. Not so crusty as Mario, she was equally adept at keeping

them out. A few investigative types were shocked to
discover that Max was the building superintendent.
In no time at all, her own story appeared in background pieces on what was now called *"The
Bronxville Jogger's Murder."*

Until now, her predecessor Dom Rizzuto's short,
unhappy stay at Lake View had been minor news that
had not even made the Westchester papers. With Dan
Horgan's murder, everything changed. Rizzuto's history resurfaced from court files; he was profiled as
"an accused wife-abuser, a man who was recently
fired by the Lake View Board, and who subsequently
threatened the victim, its president. Westchester's
District Attorney and the police will only confirm that
they are continuing to interview Mr. Rizzuto, along
with several other witnesses."

Max Schneible, his successor, was no stranger to
the press. As a Con Ed construction supervisor, she'd
had numerous opportunities to give briefings on
power outages and water main breaks. Now, she
called many reporters by their first names.

On fine days, Max came out Lake View's rear
door, and set up a table with a huge coffee urn on the
lawn, just down from co-op property. Still, she told
them no more than Mario about anything they
wanted to know. "You don't want me to lose my job,
do you?" she'd ask, when pushed.

As the investigation dragged on, with little new
to report, Max too became hot copy. One paper dubbed
her "Mother Jones for the New Millennium;" another,
as "Bronxville's own Roseanne." An upcoming issue

of a women's magazine was preparing a piece on "the new wave of feminism," featuring college graduates who were now doing jobs once held by men. Max Schneible, who "declined to be interviewed," would appear on its cover, supervising a Con Ed line crew. The caption read: "Breaking New Ground, Not Glass Ceilings."

All very heady, thought Max, but sure to pass. As her grandfather used to say: "That and a token will get you on the subway." Best focus on the job at hand, keeping the managing agent and Lake View's Board happy.

It was there, at the rear of the building, that Max was watering the garden on a Friday morning when Steve Jablonski approached her and asked if she had a free moment.

"Sure thing, Steve. Let me just finish up this row of impatiens."

That done, she walked over to the chunky porter and asked: "Now, what's up?"

"I want to confess," said Steve.

The first rabbit had popped up the hole.

53

....

A half-hour later, when Shannon's doorbell rang, she was reminded of Dorothy Parker's line: "What fresh hell is this?"

It was Friday, her day off from Horgan & Stern. She'd just hung up the phone from talking to her son Ted and getting a cryptic update on the murder investigation: "Dead-endsville."

Now Max Schneible and Steve Jablonski stood at the door. Max was her usual relaxed, confident self, while Steve was anything but, staring at the floor, repeatedly wiping his work-stained shoes on the doormat.

Max led off: "Apologies for bothering you, Shannon. Steve has just told me something related to the murder. I thought we should talk with you first."

"Rather than the police?" asked Shannon.

"Right. He knows he'll have to tell them eventually, but can you give us a few minutes?"

"Of course. I've got a half hour before I leave for a lunch date in the Bronx. Come on in." Max entered the apartment. Steve continued to wipe his boots. Shannon was not sure whether they needed wiping, or he was just prolonging the inevitable. Finally, she said: "Don't worry about my rugs, Steve. They need a good cleaning, anyway."

Now he raised his round, pudding face to Shannon and blurted out again: "I want to confess."

"O.K., the confessional's in here," she answered, leading them into the living room.

As soon as the two sat down on the leather sofa, Steve blurted out quickly: "It's about the letters."

"What letters?" asked Shannon.

"The ones in Mr. Horgan's mailbox. The ones from Dom Rizzuto."

"You mean the two threatening letters? What about them?"

Steve nodded unhappily. "It was me. I put 'em there. Dom told me they were just asking Mr. Horgan to change his mind, give 'im his job back. Then he could get his wife back. Dom couldn't get in the building, so he asked me to do it."

"Why didn't he mail them?" she asked.

"Said that on really important stuff, you can't trust the post office." Steve's head was again down, and he said nothing further until Max prodded gently: "Tell her about the money."

"Oh, yeah. He gave me $25 each time," he said shamefacedly.

"Steve," Shannon began, "you know the house rules. No one is allowed to put anything in a resident's mailbox without checking with Max first."

"I figured there was no harm; it wasn't a bomb or nothin' like that. I felt 'round the envelope to be sure."

"Well, that's something, I guess," said Shannon.

"So I won't be fired?"

"Look, Steve. First, you need to tell the police. Then we'll talk about your job."

"I thought maybe you or Max could tell them."

Max said: "No way, Steve, you've got to tell them yourself."

"Right," said Shannon. "You can call from here, if you like."

"Could you do it?" asked Steve.

"O.K." said Shannon reluctantly. If she didn't, he wouldn't.

"If you need to go up there, Steve, I'll drive you," said Max. Shannon was already on the telephone with Red Quaglio.

Returning to the living room, she said: "Officer Quaglio wants you to come up to the Tuckahoe Police Station as soon as possible. They'll take your statement for the record."

"Not a CD?" asked Steve.

"Time's up. Out," said Max, standing up and hustling him out the door. Not before Steve asked Shannon: "Do you think I might get some of the reward money?"

"I don't know," she said.

"Well, if I get the reward, I won't need the job. But I won't leave you and Max in the lurch, Ms. O'Keefe. I'll find someone good as me," said Steve.

"That's comforting to know, Steve," she answered wearily.

54

....

At eleven-thirty Max and Steve left Shannon's apartment. A half hour later, she walked out into the late May sunshine for the short drive to the Bronx for lunch with Edna Donohue.

She parked near the Mosholu Library on 205th Street, arriving at The Chariot Restaurant just around the corner and down the block on 204th Street. It was almost twelve-thirty, and Edna was walking up the hill from Perry Avenue. Wearing a fashionable emerald pant suit, black ribbed sweater and low-heeled shoes, she waved hello. "Let's go in and get a table, then we'll talk. They fill up fast."

They were seated quickly and a cheerful Irish-American waitress came with menus and took beverage orders: iced tea for Edna, Coke for Shannon.

"It's good to see you, Edna. You look well."

"I am," said Edna. "I've become the toast of the neighborhood, since my Buddy found poor Mr. Horgan's body in that park of yours. Imagine that."

"Yes," said Shannon. "I saw him interviewed on TV the day it happened."

"I was expecting them, the press, that is, to interview me too." said Edna. "Thanks be to God, they've stayed away so far. Count your blessings, my mother used to say. Maybe Tim just told them one member of the family is enough to pester at a time. Who would have believed that he'd be the one to find the body?"

The waitress returned for their orders: a medium hamburger and fries for Edna, a BLT on whole wheat toast for Shannon. "The BLT is for old times' sake," she told Edna, when the waitress left. "Remember Adolph's ice cream parlor and luncheonette on this block? I thought Adolph had the patent on the BLTs. The world's best."

"And well I remember it," smiled Edna. "I can still taste them. When the place was mobbed, he practically skated around the marbled floor, down the aisles with that big heavy, round tray on his shoulder, zigzagging this way and that between the baby carriages. Speedo we called him. Adolph, God rest his soul, has gone to his eternal reward now."

"He never made a mistake, even when it wasn't what you wanted," said Shannon. "In grammar school, I usually went home for lunch, but sometimes my mother went downtown shopping and gave me money to come here. I'd sit at the fountain and order up a tutti-frutti ice cream soda and a banana split. Adolph would nod, then bring me a grilled cheese sandwich and milk, instead."

Edna laughed. "In those days I don't remember whole wheat toast. And who ever heard of pita bread? White for toast and rye for sandwiches. That was it."

"And no diet sodas," said Shannon. They laughed and reminisced about old times and new. Looking around at the happy multi-ethnic lunch crowd, she added: "And if you'd asked me what a minority was in those days, I'd have said a Protestant. Almost everybody I knew was either Catholic or Jewish."

The sandwiches and beverages arrived in about ten minutes, and Shannon asked: "So how are you getting along?"

"Pretty well," said Edna. "Up until the murder, that is. My friends think that since I knew Mr. Horgan and my poor Buddy found the body, I have an inside scoop. The cops did interview me the first week. Said they were talking to everybody with a connection to Horgan & Stern, those who'd been let go and them that's still there."

Edna took a small bite of her hamburger, then continued: "I told them Walter left on his own. He was retiring at the end of the year. With vacation time, he was able to leave just before Thanksgiving. I didn't have much to say, so they didn't stay long."

"His death at the holiday season must have been difficult for you," said Shannon.

"It was, but when's a good time to go?" asked Edna.

"Of course. There is none," said Shannon, blushing. Not for the first time, she thought that making inane comments like this was a sure sign her youth had fled.

"So, how's the BLT?"

Shannon smiled. "Hate to say it, but it's the best I've had in years. Maybe Adolph left the patent in the kitchen."

"Wouldn't surprise me."

"How are Tim and his family doing?"

"Good, praised be Jesus and Mary. Diane's pregnant, you know, so I've been back there a couple of times helping out. Nice girl, but drives me to drink sometimes. Said she wants to come down and organize my kitchen, alphabetize the condiments, things like that. All I've got is salt and pepper. Not much alphabetizing there. These younger ones, they make life so complicated."

"Tell me about it," said Shannon. "My grandson Drew graduates from pre-kindergarten soon. By the time he's in first grade, we'll have attended three commencements."

Edna laughed. "Everything's changed. In my day, the nuns went a little overboard on diagrams. Now it's all diaphragms, and the kids don't know a noun from a verb!"

When the waitress returned, Edna ordered coffee. "By chance, do you have tutti-frutti ice cream?" asked Shannon.

"No," said the waitress, "but we have lots of other flavors."

"Thanks. I'll just have decaf."

"No decaf in those days either," said Edna.

When the check arrived, Edna insisted on paying, "so we'll do it again, but in Bronxville. You can pay for all those little green leaves and sprouty things on your plate for twice the price."

"You've got a deal," said Shannon.

They left and walked up the corner past the storefront that was once the Jay-Dee bakery, home of the world's best Jewish rye bread. "Remember that?" asked Shannon.

"Remember it? I can still taste it," said Edna, "with lots of butter. And sugar-glazed jelly donuts that left a wonderful big lump in your stomach. Those were B.C. days. Before cholesterol."

They turned the corner and reached Shannon's car. "How about a lift home?" she asked.

"No thanks. I need the exercise."

"O.K. Thanks for lunch. I'll call you soon."

"Do," said Edna. "That'll be lovely."

The lunch had cheered Shannon. Arriving home at Lake View, Max Schneible greeted her in the lobby: "Well, Steve had his day in court, or at the police station, anyway. I think the cops believed him when he claimed he knew nothing about the threats in Dom's notes."

"Good," said Shannon. "I do, too. I'll have to cover the Board, but my guess is that they'll agree. He made a mistake, but it's no reason to fire him."

"He'll appreciate that, although when we drove home, he was more interested in the reward than his job. He told Mario he'd had a defining moment, too. Talking to the police."

Shannon laughed. "Good for him. My guess is that Dom Rizzuto will have one, too, before long."

"Righto," said Max.

55

On Tuesday before Memorial Day weekend, Shannon approached the window of Bronxville's Metro-North station for a monthly commuter's ticket.

It was nine o'clock. With rush hour over, civility prevailed. The cheerful young Asian-American agent processed her check quickly, adding that the nine-fourteen train to Grand Central Station was on schedule.

How times change. When Shannon had first moved here, Alice, a feisty middle-aged woman, had staffed the booth like some diva in a Wagnerian opera. Regulars could count on at least one loud, punchy verbal attack on anyone who broke the line or simply asked her to hurry: "Buddy, you in a rush? Take a plane!"

Once, Shannon had been standing across the tracks on the north side platform with two other commuters when Alice barked through the microphone: "Are you people deaf? I TOLD you the next White Plains train will arrive on the south side today!" Shannon had turned to dash down the ramp when she noticed the other two hadn't followed. They were having an animated conversation in sign language. She ran back, tugged on the man's shoulder, pointed frantically across the tracks, and shouted, "other side!" Happily, he also read lips. After signing to his woman friend, the three dashed down the ramp together.

She missed Alice, and had once told Dan that Bronxville had character, but few characters. Alice was a character, a remnant of life in the Bronx. People like the crusty cashiers in the exchange and adjustment department of Alexander's Department Store, or the salespeople in Jay-Dee Bakery on Sunday morning. Dan had replied that Bronxville had characters, too. She'd just have to live here a little longer.

Today, Shannon walked over and bought *The New York Post* at the stand. The front page headline was "Duped by Supe?" with side-by-side pictures of Steve Jablonski and Dom Rizzuto below. Once on the train, she read the inside story, headed: "Bronxville Jogging Murder: New Evidence Points to Building Superintendent."

The article reported that the police had confronted Dom Rizzuto, Lake View's dismissed building superintendent, with a porter's statement that Rizzuto had lied to the police; that Rizzuto was the author of threatening notes which the porter, Steve Jablonski, had placed in the victim's mailbox several weeks before the murder. After rigorous questioning, Rizzuto had now confessed to writing the letters, but not to murder. "Mrs. Ida Rizzuto, the alleged suspect's wife, stated that she believes him innocent, though she can't give him an alibi for the day of the murder. The couple is separated. Mrs. Rizzuto has filed for divorce and has a restraining order against her husband for alleged abuse."

There was an additional statement that Tuckahoe Police Chief Paul Martino now had testimony from at least three early morning joggers about a man sighted on the track for several days prior to the murder, but not since. "The description matches one given by a Lake View resident who had seen a stranger near the jogging path in the late afternoon on March 18. The witness reported seeing a man retrieve a package thrown to him from a moving car on the Bronx River Parkway. The person was a Caucasian male, just over six feet, with a slim build and a slight limp in his left leg." Asked if the police were now working on the theory of a deliberately planned murder, possibly by a hired killer, Martino said: "We haven't ruled that out."

The chief also acknowledged that the $75,000 reward had resulted in several calls, but no new leads.

"Dr. Tim Donohue, who discovered Horgan's body, continues to be questioned and today referred all inquiries to his lawyer, John Cronin. Mr. Cronin categorically stated that his client has fully cooperated with the police and that Dr. Donohue is not now, nor has he ever been, a suspect."

The piece concluded: "The insularity that many associate with tony Bronxville is evident at every level. Even Steve Jablonski, the porter who directed the police to Rizzuto, has refused media comment."

When reporters had asked Jablonski for additional details about the threatening notes, the porter read from a prepared statement: "Mum's the word for me. Categorically. See my spokesman."

The spokesman turned out to be Max Schneible, whose only comment was that she had none.

Shannon smiled, finished reading, and settled back in her seat, determined to erase all thoughts of the murder for the rest of the ride to Manhattan.

56

....

Forty minutes later, Jacqueline Sheppard was poring over job applications in her workstation at Horgan & Stern.

Looking up, she greeted Shannon, who had just placed a container of coffee on her table. "Hey, thanks! When did bosses start doing this? I like it."

"Well, you're not exactly a secretary and I'm not exactly a boss."

"Right, now they call us executive assistants. As they say, 'a rose by any other name…'"

Shannon smiled. "Anyway, thanks for screening all those apps. Found anyone to replace me permanently?"

"Well, there seem to be lots of qualified people in the bunch. Maybe they're moles, hoping to get hired, solve the murder, pocket the reward, quit, and write a book about it."

"Hadn't thought of that. Even I'm amazed at the number, though. Lou was afraid the murder might keep applicants away. Dan always said your street smarts got him through some jams. If there's a mole in the pack, you'll find him. Or her," she added.

"Will do my best. God knows, I miss Dan. He left me alone. Lou's great to work for, but edgy. A workaholic. Wants to check everything himself."

"So I've noticed. I'm going to mention it to him next time he does it to me. It's one of the great things about being temporary. You can tell the boss off," she laughed. "Look, there's something I've been meaning to ask you. Did you know Dan was ill?"

After a long swig from her coffee cup, Jacqueline said: "That he had a brain tumor? No. That he wasn't what he'd been? Yes."

"For instance?"

"Little stuff. Like forgetting things I'd told him yesterday, losing focus, getting on the wrong plane. Dan was a lot like me, a stickler for detail. It's what made him a great lawyer. One day last fall, he was headed for Dallas, but called from Cleveland. Said the departure gates at La Guardia were side-by-side, and the ticket agent didn't even notice when he gave her the wrong boarding pass."

"Guess I can see that happening to me," said Shannon.

"Oh, me too. But Dan? No. I'm a princess of minutiae. He was king. We'd kid each other about being obsessive-compulsives."

"And you'd worked for him for five years, right?"

"Yes. Good years," added Jacqueline, whose lavender eyes were now filling up.

"O.K. I didn't mean to upset you. When you've had a chance to sort through this pile, just pick up the top five applicants and stick them on my desk, O.K?"

"Sure, but I've never worked in personnel."

"So you have no biases. You know this place better than anybody. Give it your best judgment. Look for gaps in experience. Eliminate those on bright-glow paper, or any with spelling errors. Cross off anybody who loves people, wants to work in a win/win environment, or has a vision for the new millennium. That should cut the pile in half."

Jacqueline laughed: "At least. My mother always said that a vision meant you were either a saint or a nutcase. Now you're a sage."

"Smart mother," said Shannon, leaving for her own office down the hall. There, she took a memo pad from her bag and jotted herself a note: Call Evan tonight.

57

There was no need to call.

At ten that night, Shannon was standing on the platform at Grand Central Station, awaiting the Bronxville train. She and Jacqueline Sheppard had worked late to finish sifting the job applications for office administrator. Then they'd walked uptown and east to Parnell's Restaurant on 53rd and First for a late night supper.

Now, a man walked up behind her and said quietly: "A quarter for your thoughts."

"Believe it or not, they were about you."

"Good," said a smiling Evan Doubleday.

"Well, not exactly about you. I planned to call you tonight and ask you something about Dan. It's probably way out in left field, though."

"See, you're already using baseball lingo! What's your question?"

"Remember when I asked if you thought Dan knew he was ill?"

"Yes."

"You mentioned giving him the name of a couple of specialists he might want to have check him out."

"Right again. To the best of my knowledge, he never did."

"But you also said that two of them practiced in the New York area. That must mean that one doesn't."

He nodded. "I thought that would give him the option of doing it quietly. But Dan said he had a heavy travel schedule and couldn't fit in a detour. I gave him the guy's name, but he never even asked for the number. Said if the symptoms continued, he'd see somebody local."

"This neurologist, the one from somewhere else. Do you remember where?"

"Sure. Cleveland."

"Bingo."

"What?"

"There's a chance Dan might have seen him after all." When she told him the wrong plane story, he agreed to check it out. "I'll give Clyde a call. His name's Clyde Green. I'll also let the cops know, unless you'd rather do it."

"No, it would be better coming from you. Thanks. It might just be a coincidence."

"Or it might not. It's a little late tonight. I'll call Clyde in the morning."

He did, and got the office nurse. "I'm sorry, Dr. Doubleday. He went to a medical conference in Zurich, and stayed over a few days with his wife. They'll be back on Sunday. Is this an emergency?"

Evan knew that Clyde Green rarely took time off. "Good for him," he said. "It's nothing that can't wait. I'll catch him next week. Thanks."

He then telephoned Paul Martino in Tuckahoe. The Chief called in Dave Corrigan and Red Quaglio, and passed on Evan Doubleday's message: "It can't wait. Get on it fast."

They did.

58

On Saturday of Memorial Day weekend, Evan Doubleday dialed Shannon's number and had started to leave a message when she picked up the phone.

"I'm here, Evan. I was sure it was one of those awful telemarketers calling. They seem to favor the dinner hour."

"No kidding. Anyway, just got a call from Chief Martino. Clyde Green's in Zurich, flying home tomorrow. They faxed him about Dan Horgan."

"And?"

"He never saw Dan Horgan."

"Oh well, it was worth a try. Thanks."

"He did see Craig Clinton."

"O.K., Evan. Help me out. Who the heck is Craig Clinton?"

"Guess."

"Come off it, Evan. Tell me, or are you saying that Dan Horgan and Craig Clinton are the same person?"

"Either that or clones. The cops faxed Clyde a description of Dan and his picture. Clyde remembered a man who fit the description, but used a different name. His nurse checked the files and came up with Craig Clinton. They're ninety percent sure it was Dan. The cops are flying out over the weekend to see Clyde Green Monday morning."

"So, if Dan did see him, the chances are he knew he was ill."

"Yes."

"And that places a whole new spin on the case."

"Spoken like a media maven," said Evan. "Anyway, I thought it was worth interrupting dinner to call you."

"Absolutely. And I really haven't even thought of dinner yet."

"Me neither," said Evan. "How does Italian take-out sound? If the maven sets the table, I'll get the food."

"Best offer I've had all week. See you around eight?"

"Eight's good."

59

"All units prepare to move out!"

It was nine-twenty on a sun-splashed Memorial Day in Bronxville. Shannon joined a festive crowd near Leonard Morange Square on the village's west side. Her sister-in-law Ceecy Caruso Cohen promised to meet her there at nine, but was nowhere to be seen.

A small girl standing next to Shannon tugged on a man's arm, whispering, "Where do we move out to, Daddy?" The father patiently explained that the Grand Marshal was telling marchers to line up for the parade. "Oh," said the child. "How come if she's a marshal, she has no badge?"

Shannon smiled as the father turned to her, saying: "I think the kid's a future "Jeopardy" candidate."

"A champ, I'd say."

People from every generation were assembling in the street, on foot, bikes, roller blades, in strollers and cars. Two bands were tuning up, prompting a comment that the littlest people always played the biggest instruments. There were veterans, senior citizens, police, scouts, Lawrence Hospital volunteers, a crack unit of women Marines, Daughters of the American Revolution, and the League of Women Voters. There was at least one large dog wearing a red, white and blue ribbon. The dog had even stopped barking during the laying of wreaths ceremony and the minister's benediction.

"A Bronxville-trained dog," said a raspy voice next to Shannon. Ceecy was back.

She hugged Shannon, who greeted her with: "Welcome home! How was London?"

"Well, I came home with a terrible cold after the rainiest spring in English history. Then Arthur found out that another scholar's been doing similar research on Wittgenstein, and he's been working on it for five years."

The din drowned out both Arthur and Wittgenstein. A band struck up a Sousa march, and a boy of about five pointed to a contingent of veterans and shouted to his father: "You mean all those grandpas won a war?"

An elderly woman nearby screamed to her friend who was riding in the leather rumble seat of a vintage blue Ford convertible with a Senior Citizens banner. "What are you doing in there?"

"Rumbling, what else?" shouted the passenger to a cheering crowd. "I got in, but they'll need a derrick to pry me out!"

The child next to Shannon now wanted to know: "What's rumbling, Daddy?" Father removed a handkerchief from his pocket to wipe his brow before attempting an explanation.

Finally, the "move out" command was given and the parade began. "The great thing about Sousa is that people know the tunes, so the bands don't have to be good," said Ceecy.

The spirited marchers soon passed, heading east under Metro-North's tracks, and on to the business district and the Bronxville School's grounds. Shannon and Ceecy walked across the street to buy take-out coffee at The Village Cup and Saucer and sip it on a nearby bench.

Once seated, Ceecy demanded that Shannon "start from the beginning and give me chapter and verse on the murder."

Shannon started. When she was done, Ceecy said: "Sounds like you're the only one who's not a suspect."

"I'm not sure about that, unless becoming president of a co-op board is a motive for murder."

"Sounds like a perfect insanity defense. Does Dom Rizzuto head the list of suspects?"

"Well, the locals are betting on him," said Shannon. "His wife Ida says he's innocent, though she can't give him an alibi. Dom's living with his bachelor brother, who was out of town on business the morning of the murder."

"Yeah. Ida called me yesterday and said that Dom had called, wanting her to lie for him, say he was with her. The putz told her she'd have to explain it to their kids if he was arrested. Ida hung tough and said no."

"Good for her," said Shannon.

"Amen. Change of subject. What's new in the romance area? I was talking to Ted."

"You mean Ted and Red? Sounds like a vaudeville act. Well, Ted's never really had a serious relationship before, and he does seem smitten with her. He probably told you we got off to a rocky start."

"Something like that. He also told me about your fling. Am I hearing what I'm hearing? You've fallen for another doctor?"

"Evan? Hey, it's not that serious. Just a baseball game and a couple of informal dinners."

"So what's he like? A Tom Cruise twin?"

"Not exactly. More like short, shy, skinny, with glasses that cover half his face. What little there is of his hair is mousy brown. Oh yeah, he does have a Tom Cruise smile."

"That's something, I guess," said Ceecy, warily.

"And he's six or seven years younger than me."

"Mr. Perfect! I've always thought women should marry younger men and reduce the number of lonely widows."

Shannon laughed. "Think of your business. You wouldn't have all those women in therapy."

"Not to worry," said Ceecy. "There's always a new phobia around the corner. Right now, it's computers."

"People afraid to use them?"

"Nope. People who can't stop. They're glued to E-mail and the Internet bulletin boards, day and night. This is the same crowd that used to complain about their retired parents who did nothing but wait for the mailman."

"Oh, right," laughed Shannon. "I read that some-one's christened them Internuts."

Coffee finished, they rose and said good-bye. Ceecy jumped into her car and Shannon walked back to Lake View, humming "Stars and Stripes Forever."

When she arrived there, Steve Jablonski was at the door. Mario La Guardia was on vacation. Nor-mally that meant hiring a temporary doorman, but Max Schneible had suggested a realignment of duties and hours to allow the porter and the night doorman to cover the door at peak times. Steve was delighted at both his temporary elevation in status and the hol-iday pay. When Rich Kryhoski had submitted the pro-posal to the Board, some had reservations. When Val Thomas whipped out his calculator and estimated a savings of several hundred dollars, there was quick agreement to give it a try.

Now, Steve looked and acted like a Plaza-trained concierge. Sharply creased grey slacks, navy blazer, blue shirt, red bow tie and poppy in his lapel.

"Like it, Ms. O'Keefe?" he asked, pointing to the tie. "Nice touch for the holiday, right?"

"Spiffy. How's it going so far?"

"Good. Don't worry. I won't let any lowlifes in."

"I've no doubt about that," said Shannon.

And she didn't. Wasn't Uncle Sam guarding the door?

60

....

At eleven on the third of June, New York City cop Ted Caruso called his mother at Horgan & Stern.

"What's new?" Shannon asked.

"Thought you'd like to know. Dave Corrigan and Red are back from Cleveland. You were right. Dr. Clyde Green confirmed that the man who said he was Craig Clinton was really Dan Horgan. The doc had done a bunch of tests, and the blood samples match Horgan's. Everything else checks out."

"So Dan knew he had a brain tumor."

"Yup, and that it was inoperable. Probably wouldn't have been able to stay in his job for more than six months. The doc's best guess on the time he had left was a year, fifteen months at the outside."

"And he told Dan that?"

"Yes. Horgan wanted to know everything."

"How did Dan react?"

"Green said he'd never seen anyone so cool. It was eerie, like they were discussing someone else. Horgan thanked the doc for his honesty, asked him for a bill, and returned that afternoon with a personal money order."

"Wasn't that unusual?"

"Green said it never happened to him before. It tipped him off that Craig Clinton was probably not his patient's real name. He offered to refer him to a couple of specialists in New York, for another opinion. Horgan said no, he'd checked Green out, knew he was tops in his field. The doc said to call him if he changed his mind or just wanted to talk. Horgan said he'd think about it, but Clyde Green never heard from him again. Didn't even know about the murder till the cops told him. Said he didn't have much time to keep up with national news, and even if he had, the name Dan Horgan would have meant nothing to him."

"I can believe that, having been married to your physician father."

"Uh-huh. Anyhow, if Horgan had been found hanging from a rope or overdosed from pills, we'd figure it was suicide. Harder to say that when he's been shot in a public place and there's no weapon in sight."

"Unless someone got rid of it before Tim Donohue reached him," said Shannon.

"Or Donohue was the shooter and ditched the gun himself."

"But why would he hang around and give him CPR?"

"Who knows? Maybe he saw someone coming, didn't have time to run. Pretended he was trying to revive Horgan."

"And the gun? What happened to it?"

"No problem. Donohue was the one who left the track to call the cops, once he knew Horgan was dead. He could have hidden it somewhere along the way. Retrieved it later."

"When will this hit the media?" she asked.

"Tomorrow morning. The Westchester D.A. wants a full briefing from the cops before going public."

"Ted, there's a Lake View Board meeting tomorrow night at six. Usual spot, at Rich Kryhoski's office on Kraft, near the movie theatre. What are the chances that Corrigan or Red can brief the Board on what's going on? Nothing more than what's public information, but it would help if we could say the cops are doing everything possible. You know Bronxville. A little personal attention goes a long way."

"It's a bit unusual, but I'm guessing that Martino wouldn't have a problem. I have to call Red now about dinner tonight. I'll ask her to talk to the chief, and let you know either way."

"Great."

When Shannon returned from lunch, Jacqueline Sheppard told her that an Officer Red Quaglio had called. "Said that she and Sergeant Corrigan would see you tomorrow night at six. Make sense?"

"Sure does. Thanks."

61

The following night, Shannon arrived at the offices of Kryhoski and Davidson at five forty-five.

Dave Corrigan and Red Quaglio were already there, talking to Rich Kryhoski. Both cops looked tired and thinner than when she'd first met them in April. Ted had mentioned they'd been working many extra hours on the Horgan case. "Thanks for doing this," she greeted them.

"We're happy to," said Corrigan.

"Besides," said Red to Shannon, "Rich just gave us some good news."

"Oh, no! He's confessed?"

"No, though at times I've considered it," said Rich. "Dan Horgan's murder has been tough on business. No, I just told the officers that the Board of Realtors and the Association of Co-op Owners in this area have just kicked in $25,000 reward money. The pot's now up to $100,000."

"Good," said Shannon. "Look, about tonight's meeting, let's have the officers speak first. Then they can leave whenever they like."

"Fine," said Rich.

One by one, the Board members arrived. By six, when Shannon opened the meeting, all but Val

Thomas were there.

"By now you all know Tuckahoe Police Sergeant Dave Corrigan and Officer Lee Quaglio. You've probably also read or heard the latest information on Dan's murder. I've asked them to give you a quick update on the investigation, and answer any questions. Sergeant Corrigan?"

"Dave. Thanks," he answered. "Red Quaglio and I will each talk for about five minutes. Then we'll take questions."

The two were well prepared. Val Thomas arrived, mumbling his monthly apology, just as Dave was finishing his remarks. Red Quaglio then spoke about the Cleveland angle, their conversation with Dr. Clyde Green, and the discovery that Dan had in fact known he was terminally ill.

"So where does that lead you?" asked Jay Shapiro.

Corrigan replied: "We're not sure. If the victim knew it, then there's a good chance that others might have, too."

"How about suicide?"

"Well," answered Quaglio, "that's a possibility. The physical evidence makes it unlikely, unless someone helped him."

"Are you sure this was a deliberate hit, and not just some creep who was out to kill the first guy he saw?" asked Val Thomas.

"No, we're not sure," said Corrigan, "But all the physical evidence points to a carefully planned execution of this victim, no one else."

Rich Kryhoski interrupted to say that the reward money was up to $100,000.

"Well, that's something," said Elmer Brick. "Still, it's a lot less than the lottery."

Hester Harrington complained that the case was now two months old, without much visible progress. "I certainly hope it gets solved before Bronxville's centennial."

"Look, we're all working overtime, doing our best," said a testy Red Quaglio.

Dave Corrigan added smoothly: "Mrs. Harrington, I've never seen resources like those we've committed to this case. Some things can't be hurried. We want to be sure not only that we find the killer, but that the charges stick. I promise you that we'll get this perp."

"Please make it soon," pleaded Hester.

There were several more questions: Was Dom Rizzuto still a suspect? How about Dr. Tim Donohue? Why hadn't the police circulated a picture of the stranger seen by several witnesses on the jogging track?

"Mr. Rizzuto and Dr. Donohue continue to be questioned," said Red Quaglio. "No one has been eliminated as a possible suspect," she added, grimly. "As to the stranger hanging around the track, you're right. We did have fairly consistent descriptions from three joggers and your neighbor, Mrs. Minnie Stern, who saw him from her terrace. A slim, white male, about six feet tall, with a very slight limp. That's it.

No one saw or remembered his face. Mrs. Stern was too far away, and joggers rarely notice another runner's face, only his feet. All they recalled was that he ran faster than they did and that he owned several brands of running shoes."

Sensing waning interest, Corrigan said: "O.K., I think that's it. We'll say good night and get back to work."

The group thanked them and the two cops left at six forty-five. "Well, it looks like they're still traveling down several roads," said Evan Doubleday.

Gwyneth Fielding nodded: "But, as we used to say on the farm, none of them leads to town."

"That says it all, 'Toots,'" said Elmer Brick.

Shannon guided them through the rest of the agenda fairly quickly. Relative to the murder, everything else paled. Rich Kryhoski reported that he'd received a letter on behalf of Arthur Bliss, the rejected applicant, from his attorney. He read the final paragraph to the Board: "Given the circumstances of Mr. Horgan's untimely demise, my client has graciously declined to pursue his case. Mr. Bliss feels that the exclusionary policies of many co-ops are now public knowledge, and he has made his point."

"Pap!" said Jay Shapiro. "He just didn't like being in the limelight as a suspect."

There was general agreement that Steve Jablonski had more than distinguished himself as part-time doorman while Mario was on vacation. Val Thomas thought the red bow tie "a little over-the-top," but was quickly drowned out by the rest. One could never be too patriotic in Bronxville. Shannon had once wondered if the entire audience at Independence Day concerts by the Boston Pops came from Bronxville.

Before a seven-thirty adjournment, the Board elected attorney Binky Seagram to fill Dan Horgan's seat, and agreed to one meeting in the summer. Routine matters would be handled by phone.

When the group walked out onto Kraft Avenue into a still-bright June sun, Gwyneth Fielding said: "Look, it's like an orange lollipop in the sky."

And so it was. "Toots" was hot tonight.

62

....

Minnie Stern had invited Shannon to a Mets-Braves baseball game on the second Sunday in June.

Minnie was now walking unassisted, but her orthopedic surgeon had said that Shea Stadium in Flushing was pushing it a little. Why not watch it on TV? Minnie was disappointed, but was not prepared to challenge the woman's advice. Break another hip, and she'd be under the knife again. Risky business. TV it would have to be.

When Shannon arrived at one, Rosa Di Carlo answered the door. Rosa had stayed on to help Chip Horgan clear out his father's apartment, and now cleaned for Minnie once a week. Sunday was her day off, but her husband had gone to visit his sister in Manhattan. According to Rosa, her sister-in-law was "een a beega funk deesa time. Mostly she's een a little funk. I seek of her!" Facing a day with no one to talk to or cook for was Rosa's idea of hell, so she'd called Minnie and said she was making lasagna. "Woulda you lika some?"

An hour later, Rosa had arrived with what looked like the fixings for a five-course meal for twelve. When Shannon handed over a bottle of Chianti, Rosa said: "You watcha game first."

For the last few weeks, Minnie had been tutoring Shannon on baseball fundamentals. "I felt like Evan was talking in a foreign language at the game," she'd told Minnie.

Now, Minnie was explaining the difference between a curve ball and a breaking ball. Mets star Bobby Jones was pitching. "This Jones boy has a good curve," said Minnie. Rosa had just come into the living room to check where the oregano might be, and overheard her.

"That Jones girl, she's gotta pretty gooda curves, and she breaka balls too," said Rosa, pointing to a newspaper on the coffee table. The headline was about Paula Jones, who was suing the President for alleged sexual harassment. "I teenk she's a-pitch woo!" added Rosa, just as the intercom buzzed.

A laughing Minnie said: "That's my granddaughter Margo. She was doing some research at Pace law library and said she might stop by."

When Rosa went to answer it, Minnie confided to Shannon: "We had a bit of a brouhaha a few weeks ago, about her drinking. This is her way of making up."

It was, in fact, Margo, looking better than Shannon had ever seen her. Her tiny, trim body sported stylish Donna Karan white shorts and top, set off by Easy Spirit running shoes, matching headband and thick imperial purple leather belt. After hugging her grandmother, Margo greeted Shannon and Rosa cordially, settled into a family-heirloom rocking chair and told Rosa: "I'm not staying, just stopped by for a short visit."

Shannon sensed that Minnie and Margo might like a few moments alone. When Rosa asked if anyone wanted a cold drink and snack, everyone did. "I'll help in the kitchen," offered Shannon.

Rosa's idea of a snack was more like a plowman's lunch. In twenty minutes, Shannon returned to the living room with a tray of iced tea, several kinds of cheeses, cold meats, small rolls and crackers.

All four were surprisingly hungry. After an hour of dining, baseball, and light-hearted conversation, Margo got up to leave.

"I'm redoing my résumé," she told Shannon. "I want to send out a bunch of letters this week."

"Good for you, Margo. I'm sure you'll land something soon."

"Thanks." Margo then kissed her grandmother, said good-bye and left.

When Rosa returned to the kitchen, Minnie said to Shannon: "She wanted me to know that she joined AA two weeks ago, and has been dry since."

"Good for her. It's a beginning. That's what counts."

"She also wanted me to ask you for a favor."

"Sure."

"Would you recommend her to that temporary firm you work for? She needs a jump start to get going again."

Shannon thought a moment, just as "the Jones

boy" attempted to throw a fast ball by another Jones boy, Braves' infielder Chipper Jones. Chipper blasted it into the center field seats.

When Chipper had rounded the bases, Shannon said: "Minnie, I'll be glad to talk to Brett Halliday, but I'd also need to tell him about Margo's drinking problem."

"I was afraid you'd say that. Won't that kill her chances?"

"Not necessarily," said Shannon. "My Irish grandmother always said that the devil you know beats the one you don't. I'll also tell him she's a heck of a smart lawyer. That's more than he'll know about strangers. Who knows what their problems are?"

"Never thought of it that way," said Minnie. "Where would we be without our *bubbes?* I'll tell Margo. Thanks."

They continued watching the game, a tie until the bottom of the thirteenth inning, when Mets catcher Todd Hundley homered into the upper right field deck for a Mets victory. "Gooda for heem!" shouted Rosa. "Now, *mangia!*"

63

On Monday morning, the ringing phone at Halliday Temporary Executives in White Plains was answered by Halliday himself.

"Hi, Brett. It's Shannon O'Keefe, calling from Horgan & Stern."

"How's it going?"

"No complaints. Lou's terrific to work for, but doesn't delegate enough. I'm on the case. A couple of good lawyers are ready to walk unless he gives them more breathing room. But that's not what I called you about. Got a favor to ask."

She gave him Margo Stern's background. Would Brett consider hiring her?

"Matter of fact, we've had a couple of calls for attorneys that I haven't been able to fill. Didn't I meet her briefly at Horgan & Stern?"

"Probably."

"So why did they let her go? My recollection was that she was one of the brightest young lawyers in the place."

"You're right. Actually, her termination had nothing to do with our study. Dan Horgan just used that as an excuse, and Margo knew it. She had a drinking problem."

"And what's happened since to change that?" asked Halliday.

"She's clean, now. Joined AA a couple of weeks ago and has been sober since. The word's out about her past, though, so she's having a tough time getting something permanent."

"And you're willing to vouch for her?"

"Yes. I think she's worth the risk. Lou De Femio called her first-rate, and I've heard the same thing from others at Horgan & Stern. The lawyers still call to sound her out on complex cases."

"Two weeks' sobriety isn't much of a test," said Brett.

"Look, I know that. I don't want to put you in a tough position. If you can't, you can't."

"Who said I can't?"

"Then you'll think about it?"

"Don't need to. Have her call me, set up an appointment. No promises. I'll decide for myself."

"Thanks, Brett. I owe you one."

"Fair enough. Just one thing, though. Remember she's still an alcoholic, always will be."

"Isn't that a little harsh?" she asked.

"Takes one to know one," he answered gruffly. "Haven't had a drink in ten years, but can't swear I won't, tomorrow. 'Bye."

Shannon shook her head as she hung up the phone. Who would have guessed that Brett Halliday had a problem? They'd shared several business lunches and at least one dinner over the last year.

He'd always ordered Perrier or tonic with a twist, but
that meant nothing anymore. Many people had eliminated or cut back on alcohol for a variety of reasons:
health, smaller entertainment budgets, stiffer sentences for drunk drivers.

Well, so much for this devil she thought she
knew. She picked up the phone again, called Margo
at home and left Halliday's number on the answering
machine. "Call him for an appointment."

She hoped it was not a mistake.

64

"Now they'll all be walking around Bronxville with a cup in their hand."

That was the locals' view on Bruegger's, when it had opened several months before. The third bagel store in town, it joined two coffee bars, all of which were now thriving. At nine-thirty on this last Friday in June, Margo Stern parked her Toyota Camry in a metered parking space right in front of the store. She'd driven up from her Manhattan apartment to join Shannon for breakfast.

"Talk about luck, pulling up and finding a parking spot with your name on it," Shannon greeted her at the door.

Margo smiled wryly. "Yeah, luck's my middle name. Hope you haven't eaten yet."

"Are you kidding? When you're treating?"

Bruegger's has a dozen kinds of bagels, and even more choices of fillings, twelve for cream cheese alone. Shannon decided on a sun-dried tomato with butter; Margo ordered pumpernickel with cream cheese and smoked salmon. Two orange juices and coffees, a newspaper for Margo, and they were set, moving down the line to pay.

The arrival of trendy new stores in the business district had been a culture shock for some. Their salespeople were young, fast and hip. Today, a prime-of-life woman ahead of them was telling the cashier she'd been shortchanged a quarter. He rapped a closed fist against his head and cheerfully apologized: "It's tough when you're born with half a brain."

"Oh, dear," said the sympathetic customer, "you do very well, considering."

When the woman left, he rang up Margo and Shannon's orders and said: "Normalcy is overrated."

"And underpaid," added Margo.

They sat down at a rear table, and eagerly began eating. Between bites, Margo said: "Thanks again for calling Brett. Saw him on Wednesday. Thought it went well, but I was still surprised to get a job interview in Yonkers this afternoon. It's with a small real estate outfit. Their attorney had a massive stroke last week. It's not really what I'm looking for, but they need someone fast, and I need a job fast. We'll see if it's a match."

"Great. Not that the man had a stroke, but that it's a shot for you."

Margo nodded. "Speaking of deaths, what's the latest on Dan's murder? I hear the cops are still on Tim Donohue's case."

"Seems a little farfetched to me," said Shannon. "Still, he made it pretty clear at the wake that he blamed Dan for Walter's death."

"Sure did. Guess I've been hoping all along that this had nothing to do with Horgan & Stern," said Margo. "We're all trying to put that behind us. You probably know it, but none of us is off the suspect list yet. I was so hung over I didn't roll out of bed till noon that day. Not the world's best alibi."

"I wouldn't think so," said Shannon. "Lou De Femio said the worst part of Tim's now leading the pack of suspects is that Edna Donohue will find out about Walter's retirement."

"What about it?"

"That it wasn't voluntary."

Margo, who had stopped chewing, looked up. "Lou thinks she didn't already know that?"

"Right. Before Edna came in to go over Walter's insurance and pension benefits, Tim called Lou to be sure no one spilled the beans. His father had told him, but asked him not to say anything to Edna. There was no reason for her to know. In fact, I had lunch with Edna a few weeks ago. She made a point of saying that Walter was not like the others. The decision to retire was his."

"No," said Margo.

"No what? You think she's lying?"

"I know she is."

"Are you sure? Did someone tell her?"

"*Moi,*" Margo answered calmly.

"When?"

"The night Walter died. Edna telephoned the office when he wasn't home by eight, and I was still there. The mailroom was empty, so I called down to security. The guard said Walter had left around six, so I told Edna not to worry. He'd probably stopped off at Rosie O'Grady's with a couple of people, and would walk in the door any minute."

Margo paused, wiping a smear of cream cheese from her chin: "Anyway, Edna and I talked for several minutes. Brian Palmer, Walter, and I had gone out to lunch that day. A cry-in-each-others'-beer thing. Brian mentioned the worst part of being let go was having to tell Reed, who was ill. Walter said he was lucky. Edna was glad they'd forced the issue, told him that things happen for the best. She was looking forward to having him home. I said that one good thing about being single was that there was no one I had to tell. So, I thought Edna knew. I was trying to make small talk that night, let her know how valuable Walter was, keep her from worrying. Said that of all of us who'd been screwed, he deserved it the least."

"And she never said anything to contradict you?"

"Nope. She let me babble on, which I was happy to do."

"So why is she lying now?"

"Beats me. But why would a nice old lady hire a hitman to kill somebody?"

Maybe, Shannon thought, for the same reason a nice young one might drink herself to death. She asked: "Remember the nice old ladies in *Arsenic and Old Lace?*"

"Sure," laughed Margo, "but things like that don't happen in real life."

Shannon suddenly felt the generation gap between them, and answered, "Oh, but they do, Margo. They do."

65

....

After breakfast with Margo, Shannon walked home and decided to walk a few laps around the lake.

It was now close to eleven-thirty, with temperatures in the high 70s. Sunbathers sprawled on the grass; grandparents, parents, and nannies pushed carriages; toddlers fed the ducks. Baby rabbits scooted back and forth across the path, like fleet-footed ball boys at Wimbledon.

Good company for sorting things out.

What to do about what Margo had told her? Why had Edna lied? Her first instinct was to forget about it. Edna was a friend, not a close one, but still a friend.

But wasn't Dan a friend, too? How could she ignore a possible clue to his murder? She could call Chief Martino or Red Quaglio, let them decide whether to pursue it. Maybe run it by Ted, first.

Or, she could talk to Edna herself. It wouldn't be easy. Edna might say it was none of her business, or that Margo Stern was confused, or that Margo had been drinking when they'd talked. Or…or…or.

Tuckered out after the third lap, she entered Lake View by the rear door. Her dilemma was not unlike Macbeth's:

"If it were done when 'tis done, then 'twere well

It were done quickly…"

She hadn't realized she'd been talking out loud until Steve Jablonski's flummoxed expression greeted her near the laundry room.

"Excuse me, Ms. O'Keefe?"

"Sorry, Steve. Just trying to make up my mind about something."

He nodded. "Just do it," he said.

"Shakespeare couldn't have said it better. Thanks!"

His broad face broke into a wide, lopsided grin. "You're welcome."

Back up in her apartment, she showered, changed clothes and picked up the car keys. Half an hour later she was driving down Parkside Place in the Bronx. Just down from Edna Donohue's building, a car was pulling out of a space. Good, she thought. God still lived in the Bronx.

She entered the building's spotless outer hall and buzzed the apartment. In a few seconds, Edna was on the intercom. Too late to run.

"Edna, it's Shannon. Shannon O'Keefe. Can I come up and see you for a few minutes?"

"What a surprise! Second floor. I'll buzz you in."

Edna was standing at her apartment door, just across from the elevator. "Come in, come in! Lovely to see you. I'm just making lunch. Join me?"

"Thanks, no. Had a late breakfast. I'll have something cold to drink, though. Iced tea, soda, anything at all."

"I've just made a fresh pot of iced tea. We'll sit in the kitchen and visit there."

"Fine."

Within five minutes, Edna was making a cream cheese and jelly sandwich, and both were drinking iced tea. Shannon pointed to the repast. "Reminds me of my mother's first rule of life: Always use a different knife for dipping into the cream cheese and jelly."

Edna laughed.

"Edna, you said to tell you if anything came up on Dan Horgan's murder. Something has."

"Apart from the fact that they're driving my Buddy crazy?"

"Yes. Look, it may be nothing at all. I'd like you to tell me that. It's about Walter's leaving Horgan & Stern."

"You mean his retirement," said Edna cautiously.

"Not exactly. Edna, you said he'd left on his own. But he didn't, did he? And I think you may have known that all along."

"Who says?"

"Margo. Margo Stern. We had breakfast this morning and it just came out."

"Who came out, Margo?" said Edna, laughing nervously and beginning to pile dollops of jelly over cream cheese.

Shannon plunged ahead. "Margo said she'd talked to you the night Walter died. You see, he'd told her you were glad he'd been forced to retire, that things happen for the best. But Margo wanted you to know how sorry everyone felt about what happened to Walter; that he deserved better, after all those years."

Edna nodded, saying nothing, finishing her sandwich. A few minutes later, she rose, put the cream cheese and jelly back in the refrigerator, dishes and silverware in the sink, and began wiping the table slowly. Up and down, up and down. Finally: "Let's bring our drinks into the living room. It's cooler there."

Shannon followed her in, where Edna sat on a beautiful old cherry wood rocker near the two-paned window facing the street. Once, looking out, you could see and hear the El train running high above Webster Avenue. No more. Today, happy shrieks of children on bikes and skates still came through the screens.

"Look, I'm sorry about this, Edna." Shannon was sitting directly across from her, on a maroon, upholstered princess-style chair. "I thought about saying nothing, or even telling the cops. Let them decide what to do. I didn't want to hurt you."

A film appeared over Edna's eyes. Fighting back tears, she looked out the window and said quietly, "Yes, I knew. I never let on, though. Stiff upper lip and all that. Walter wanted to spare me, maybe spare himself. Put a better face on it with his friends. When he died, I thought, why tell anyone now? Let my poor man be."

"I might have done the same thing," said Shannon.

"He'd told Buddy the truth, and of course, he went along. He wanted to protect me, too. Glory be to God, both of them needed protectin' more than me!"

"I believe you," said Shannon. "So, if it were not for Margo, you'd still be in the dark?"

A long pause, then: "Oh, no. Tell her it's not really her fault. She just…," and now Edna stopped and looked directly at Shannon. "You see, I was pretty sure before that."

"You were? Had someone already told you?"

"Yes."

"Who?"

"Walter. It was Walter himself who let the cat out of the bag."

"When?"

"Saturday night, a week before he died. I'd gone out with a neighbor to a movie. Walter hates, hated movies. When I got back and rang the doorbell, the phone was ringing. His hearing wasn't what it used to be, so I used the key to get in, then went into the kitchen to make a pot of tea. He was on the phone talking to someone about…"

"Take your time," said Shannon.

"Getting back at Mr. Horgan, for what he'd done to him."

"Did you know who the caller was?"

"He never called him by name. After a minute or so, I slammed the refrigerator door and Walter hung up. Came out to the kitchen, said he was going out for *The Sunday News.* When he came back, I asked for the comics. Walter said they were all out, he'd get one in the morning. I didn't believe him, though. You see, the paper's never sold out at that hour."

"You think he went out to use a pay phone?"

"I'm sure of it. When he returned, he seemed at peace with himself, like he'd just settled something, taken a load off his mind."

"And he never said who he was talking to."

"No."

"And you never asked."

"No. He'd have said if he wanted me to know, now, wouldn't he? Of course he would. I once told him he wasn't a very good liar, so he better never try it with me. He never did, until the end. Even then, he got caught." A sad smile crossed her face before she continued. "No, I didn't know then who it was, but when Walter left I found out."

"Walter had written down the telephone number?"

"No."

"So how…"

Edna pointed to the phone on a small corner table in the hall. "We'd been getting a lot of crank calls at odd hours. Ended up being kids, of course. Anyway, when Walter went out, I was worried. so I dialed that number that puts you through to the last caller. I already had a pretty good idea of who it would be, and I was right."

"Who was it?"

"It was 'Knuckles.' Knuckles O'Callaghan."

"And you never told Walter?"

"No, nor Knuckles that it was me. I hung up the phone when I recognized his voice. Walter died the next Friday, so there was no need to protect him from himself, anymore. You had to know Walter. I'm from Dublin, but he and Knuckles grew up in Belfast. Their parents felt that if they didn't move, their boys would either be killed or kill someone else. They hung out with a rough crowd, not really IRA, but on the fringes. When their families came here, Walter cut the old ties. Not Knuckles. For a long time, Walter and he lost touch with each other. Are you sure you want to hear all this?"

"Yes, if you don't mind telling me."

"I don't mind. Well, Knuckles built a pretty good business here, but he still went back to Belfast to see what they were stirrin' up. He was there in the thick of all the troubles in '69. When he came back here, he was always into some kind of IRA fundraising."

"And he looked up his old friend Walter again?"

"Yes. First it was just a drink on a weekend. Then Knuckles and his friends started coming to play cards. I could see they were into the same old shenanigans. Not just raising money and giving the same old silly speeches, but going to rallies, stirrin' up decent people, singing fighting songs. By now, Kunckles was rich and respectable with a fine business of his own. Hung out with the beautiful people, as Walter called them. But Walter always said that

Knuckles never forgot his old friends. He was still the one to see, if you had a grudge against any man."

Edna was wilting. "How about I get us a refill on the iced tea?" asked Shannon.

"That would be lovely."

When Shannon returned and Edna had taken a sip, she continued: "Anyway, our Buddy was growing up and I didn't want him seeing the likes of Mr. Knuckles O'Callaghan and his friends, beautiful or not, on our doorstep. Money or no money, he was not welcome here. It was the only time Walter and I really fought. But from that day on, Knuckles never came again. They stayed in touch, though, and saw each other in the city from time to time. And there were always Christmas cards. As the years passed, though, I think even Walter realized that he was too old for this stuff."

"And that's all you know?" asked Shannon.

"Yes, except that Walter once said that Knuckles never actually killed anyone, though he could always be counted on for a kneecapping or a good thrashing for a worthy cause." Edna smiled at the irony. "Oh, when he wanted to, Knuckles could charm the knickers off the Queen Mum. And he had a heart. At the wake he told me that Walter was like a brother to him, the best man he'd ever met. If I needed anything at all, he'd come running. And he would have."

Shannon wondered if Edna didn't also have a soft spot in her heart for Knuckles O'Callaghan.

After a deep breath, her friend said, "That's everything, Shannon. Do you have to tell the police all this?"

"Edna, they need to know. They won't let up on Tim till they do. But no, I'm not going to tell them. It's your story. I think you need to call Tim first, then the cops."

Edna said nothing, just rocked slowly. Finally, Shannon walked over and placed Red Quaglio's card in Edna's lap. "I know you'll do the right thing. Call Tim."

Of course Edna might not call at all, and if she didn't, what should be done about it? Placing her hand on the older woman's shoulder, she gave it a gentle squeeze and said good-bye. When she opened the apartment door, a tall, thin man practically fell into her arms. Recovering, he smiled awkwardly. "Sorry! Didn't mean to frighten you. I was just about to ring the doorbell."

He stuck out a thin, bony hand and said, "Tim Donohue." It was obvious he did not remember their short meeting at his father's wake. Now he brushed past her, entered the apartment, and shouted to Edna, who'd remained in the living room. "Hi, Mom. It's Buddy. How's my favorite girl?"

Shannon, shocked at the warmth of his greeting, finally saw him as a "Buddy." She quietly closed the door and left the building.

66

....

While Shannon O'Keefe and Edna Donohue were sipping iced tea on Friday afternoon, Luke Plisky and Enid Gomez were driving down to the South Bronx, for P.S. 807's end-of-the-year party.

With the Yankees playing away from home, traffic was light on the Major Deegan Expressway. Arriving in the area just past four-thirty, they found a parking spot on Shakespeare Avenue, about two blocks from Alphonse's Restaurant, where the cocktail hour would start at five. Enid suggested a quick tour of the neighborhood, "to see how much it's changed."

And changed it had, thanks to a major rebuilding effort by the Federal, State and City governments, working with the support of churches and community leaders. In the 1970s, a good part of Highbridge was a hilly wasteland of burnt-out homes and gutted rubble. Now, there were new and renovated apartment buildings with almost a thousand units; nonprofit health and social services, including day-care centers; job opportunities; new brick, two-family homes. "There's hope again," said Enid to Luke, "and we're a part of that."

At five-fifteen, they were back at Alphonse's. Most of P.S. 807's teachers and support staff were already there, crowding the bar. Hearing that the Community School Board, headed by Felix Mendoza, was paying for the cocktail hour, Enrique Dupraz said: "He's lost it, our Felix, but let's drink up till he finds it again!" Several teachers were holding two drinks, one in each hand, chugalugging anything that flowed.

"Speaking of losing it," said Charlotte Weiss, "I almost did that with my kids yesterday. If I'd remembered what the last day of school was like I'd have brought in twenty-five bottles of Ritalin. The whole class had Attention Deficit Disorder. Finally, I just screamed out 'Jesus, Mary and Joseph'!"

"What happened?" asked Enid.

"Three kids stood up," said Charlotte.

Boffo.

Enrique was now reading aloud an article in that day's *New York Post*: "The City of New York and the Board of Education have still not announced plans to hire staff for lunch duty in the city's schools next September." As part of the prior year's union negotiations, the teachers' union had won a no-lunch-duty clause in their contract.

"Maybe they'll hire a nutritionist to tell parents that lunches are unhealthy, so there'll be none," said Enrique.

"Better still, why don't those oafs from The Board of Dead do something useful for a change and do lunch duty themselves?" hooted Harriet Noble. "See how they like it when a kid steals a Yankee Doodle from their lunch bag!"

"We'll miss you and your hat, Harriet!" came a voice from a dark corner. Harriet, Harry Reeber, and Charlotte Weiss were in rare form tonight. All three were taking The Board of Education's recent offer of a liberalized early-retirement package.

The banter continued through the meal, and well into the after-dinner speeches. When Principal Mark Borras toasted the retiring teachers, Felix Mendoza lifted his glass and said: "Hear, hear! You'll all be sorely missed."

"Sure, like pimples on his bum," laughed Charlotte Weiss, downing her third martini. Charlotte ("bad nerves, poor thing") was well liked by students, but less so by teachers. She regularly brought her mental health problems to the principal's attention. As a result, Mark Borras always gave her the best classes, and routinely transferred problem students to other teachers. Sadly, neither principal nor teachers would miss "poor Charlotte" Weiss for very long.

Still, the dinner party was a great success, and at nine o'clock, a happy band of party-goers headed for the door. Selma Einstein, school secretary, was walking just ahead of Luke and Enid and was now pointing to the right, mumbling "I don't believe it." Charlotte of the bad nerves had approached Mark Borras, and was now asking to be placed at the head of his substitute teacher list in September.

"Well, let poor Mark get himself out of that can of worms," said Enid to Luke. The two walked past the bar and out into the muggy June night. Selma waved good-bye. "Bring us back something lovely from Paris, Luke!"

"Better still, someone lovely!" shouted Mark Borras.

P.S. 807's teachers had weathered another year, and summer's stardust was in their eyes. Their reward, a peaceful summer, now beckoned.

67

....

When Shannon had left Parkside Place on Friday, she decided to wait a few days to see if Edna did in fact tell Tim, then the police.

On Sunday, she'd just returned to her apartment after one o'clock mass when the phone rang. It was Edna Donohue.

"I'm glad you called," said Shannon.

"Yes, well, I wanted you to know I talked to Tim, told him everything."

"I'm glad. It would have come out anyway, Edna."

"Little did I know, part of it already had. Tim said that when the reward money went up to $100,000 a police snitch had gone to the cops. The man hangs out around Williamsbridge Oval, and said he'd heard talk from Walter's checkers crowd. The word was out that a man named Donohue had talked to someone, he didn't know who, about teaching Dan Horgan a lesson."

"This hasn't hit the papers yet, right?" asked Shannon.

"No. The cops were keeping a lid on to see if they could flush out something from Walter's friends. No luck and little wonder about that! Knuckles isn't the kind of man you'd want as an enemy."

"I wouldn't think so," said Shannon.

"So that's when they started pestering my Buddy again. They were sure he was the one who got someone to kill Mr. Horgan. Friday, he finally told me. He was worried I'd hear it on the news. Poor Buddy wouldn't even know how to find Knuckles if he did want to hire him. Besides, Walter had said Knuckles himself had retired from the enforcement business. He'd have had someone do it for him."

Shannon asked, "So, you told Tim about the phone call?"

"I had to then, didn't I? It explained everything. It was Walter himself the men were talking about, not poor Buddy. Anyway, on Saturday we talked with John Cronin, Buddy's lawyer. I gave John Officer Quaglio's card, said that I'd call her first, her wanting to be in on things and all. John said we should all meet with the district attorney together, that it's best dealing with the top on these things. So I told him men have been dealing with the top for all these years, and just look at the puddle we're in. I was calling Officer Quaglio on my own, and telling her my story. John and Tim could tell theirs to the Pope, for all I cared."

Shannon laughed. "Good for you!" Having told Edna of her own delicate relationship with Red Quaglio, she wondered if that had weighed in her decision. She hoped so, and not just because it might preserve her still slightly shaky relationship with Red. Her own friendship with Edna might even survive this rocky patch.

"So," continued Edna, "we compromised. I called Officer Quaglio, John called the district attorney, and we're meeting with the whole bunch on Monday morning. John wanted to go today, but I told him not on the good Lord's day. It was Monday or nothing."

A Hobbesian choice, thought Shannon.

"Maybe now they'll let poor Buddy alone. Even if Walter had lived, he wouldn't have wanted Mr. Horgan dead. A good thumping would have been fine."

"Well, I'm glad you told them, Edna. I'm sure it wasn't easy."

"No. Sometimes I laugh just so I won't cry. I was thinking about the old days when we'd ask those poor nuns in religion class: If you wanted to kill a man, but found him dead when you got there, was it still a mortal sin?"

"And what was the answer?"

"Who remembers?" said Edna. "I always thought it was just the luck of the Irish!"

They both laughed, but Shannon was no longer smiling when she hung up the phone. Nor was Edna.

Edna and Tim were in for a week of rough questioning. And Knuckles O'Callaghan? That man would need more than Irish luck to pull him out of this pot of stew.

68

....

Three days later, Minnie Stern was sitting on the terrace of her Lake View apartment, drinking iced coffee and reading *The New York Times*.

The temperature at eight o'clock on this sultry early July morning was already eighty degrees, with the heat-humidity index expected to exceed a hundred by day's end. Minnie felt about this index the same way she did about the wind-chill factor. What good were they, except to make people feel warmer in July and colder in January?

Heat or no heat, she was looking forward to a rare treat, a day by herself. Last night Brian Palmer had called to say that Reed James had died, and Brian would not be coming for computer lessons for several days. Minnie had expressed regrets at Reed's passing, but told him no one could have done more than Brian to ease his friend's (she could not quite get out "lover's") last days. She was sure that Reed was now at peace in a better place. Where, she had no idea, but the pedestrian thought always seemed to comfort the bereaved, as it had Brian.

Later today she'd wire flowers. Brian was a kind, patient, and thorough teacher. Along with Max Schneible, hadn't he gotten her addled brain going, while an old hip was mending?

The fact was, though, that Minnie was a quick study. Had Brian not needed the income, she'd have ended the lessons some time ago. After the first few weeks, she suspected he'd always been a student who'd received attendance awards, took copious notes in class, and turned in homework on time. On imagination and intellectual curiosity, the poor fellow came up short. Worse, he failed to see it in others. A fatal flaw for a teacher. When Brian had suggested she sign on to "Senior Citizen Chat Rooms" on the Internet, she asked why. "So you'll be able to talk to people with the same interests as you," he'd said.

Fiddlesticks, thought Minnie. If this group of chatters was anything like many of her friends, they'd be gossiping up a storm about Medicare, Social Security, the ingratitude of children, and their own aches and pains. Who needed cyberspace for that? She could get the very same menu at The Food Emporium every day of the week.

Even worse, when she'd asked Brian to recommend a computer text, he'd mentioned *Internet for Idiots.* Now why would she want to read anything that assumed basic stupidity? No wonder they called it dumbing-down. She was not out to break into national security files, just to become computer-literate. Now that she was, she could teach herself what she didn't know. As Casey Stengel said, "Ya could look it up."

Before tackling the computer this morning, she'd finish *The New York Times.* There, on the first page of the Metro section, was an update on Dan Horgan's murder:

"Mr. Francis Xavier O'Callaghan, according to reliable sources, is now regarded by Westchester law enforcement authorities as a key witness in the murder of Manhattan attorney Daniel Horgan, on the Bronxville jogging track, last April. Mr. O'Callaghan, a prominent Long Island businessman, known as 'Knuckles' to friends, is reported to have talked with Walter Donohue, a mailroom supervisor at Horgan & Stern, several days prior to Mr. Donohue's death of a heart attack. Mr. Donohue, a thirty-year employee, had been forced to take early retirement when the law firm was downsized last year, and allegedly blamed Daniel Horgan for his dismissal. According to his widow, Edna Donohue, her husband had talked with Mr. O'Callaghan about getting back at Mr. Horgan. The story is further complicated by the fact that it was Doctor Timothy Donohue, son of the deceased Walter Donohue, who discovered the victim's body on the Bronxville Lake jogging track. Police have continued to investigate whether this was, in fact, a coincidence or part of a conspiracy to commit murder."

The story was accompanied by a biographical sidebar on Mr. O'Callaghan, from birth in Belfast, Northern Ireland, through a hugely successful, though controversial, business career. Now president of his own construction company in Nassau County, he'd emigrated from Northern Ireland in the late 1950s, and become a prominent lobbyist for Irish causes. A Knight of Malta, Mr. O'Callaghan had just last year been considered for Grand Marshal of New York's annual St. Patrick's Day parade, only to lose out to a more moderate Irish-American leader.

Minnie laughed when she read O'Callaghan's reaction to all this. His attorney, Mr. Philip Kaplan, had acknowledged his client's conversations with Westchester authorities, and released a one-sentence formal statement: "Mr. O'Callaghan has been interviewed in connection with the death of Daniel Horgan, and has promised to assist the police in every way possible to find the person or persons responsible."

Mr. O'Callaghan had not responded to *The Times'* several telephone and fax requests for comments. One enterprising older reporter had, however, followed Moira O'Callaghan to the local supermarket, and confronted her at the butcher's: "Is it true that your husband once said of Dan Horgan, 'He'll get *his?'*"

To which Mrs. O'Callaghan had fired back: "Probably, but don't be daft, girl. If all of us who ever said that acted on it, the sun would have set on the British Empire long ago."

Hooray, thought Minnie. Just when plain speech seemed to be going out of style, Rosa Di Carlo and Moira O'Callaghan kept it alive. Minnie just hoped that feisty Mrs. O'Callaghan's husband was not also a killer.

69

....

Luke Plisky was worried.

It was early Wednesday morning, the third week of July. His flight to Paris would depart from Kennedy International Airport at eight o'clock that night. He'd put on the TV for the first weather report of the day. Not a cloud or raindrop was predicted until the following day.

But the weather was not the only reason he watched the news. Last night, reports were that Westchester police were close to an arrest in the murder of Bronxville resident Dan Horgan. "Virtually all speculation revolves around Dr. Timothy Donohue, prominent neurosurgeon who lived less than a mile from the victim, and who discovered his body on the jogging track last April. Dr. Donohue's father Walter had been forced into early retirement by Mr. Horgan's firm, and died of cardiac arrest on the way home from his last day at work. One possible theory alleges that Dr. Donohue either killed Dan Horgan himself or was involved in a conspiracy with Francis Xavier O'Callaghan that resulted in his death."

This morning, another story had preempted the news: a multi-car collision in the Holland Tunnel. "Two dead and dozens injured." The Horgan case was temporarily on the back burner, pending further developments. Watching and waiting.

What if Tim Donohue were arrested? Worse, what if he were tried and convicted? The circumstantial evidence was strong. How could Luke have guessed that someone with a motive would have discovered the body?

The whole thing was becoming his worst nightmare, what he'd always feared. An innocent man might be accused, charged, and found guilty. Would Luke intervene, and at what risk to himself? Until today, he hadn't been sure. Now he knew that he could never let that happen. If he did, his own life would lose what little meaning it had. He would be no better than the rest of them.

He shut off the TV and went upstairs to his den. There, he put on gloves, opened the wall safe, and pulled out a business-size envelope.

He walked back downstairs and stuck it in a zippered leather portfolio, directly on top of his packed luggage.

70

....

Forty years ago, New York's Kennedy Airport was viewed as a gateway to the modern age. Now, it functioned like a creaky athlete long past her prime.

At 5:45 in the early evening on Wednesday, the third week of July, Luke Plisky checked in at TWA's bustling ticket window. After purchasing flight insurance, he ordered a Coke in the First Class Lounge. His nonstop eight o'clock flight to Paris was on schedule. "Perfect flying weather, *Monsieur,*" the reservations agent had said.

Around him were harried business people with thick reading folders, laptop computers, and cellular phones. He got up, walked outside and sat in the general lounge. Higher decibel levels, but happier sounds. Just across from him was a French family with rambunctious children wanting to know how soon they could board, and whether there would be inflight video games. Two young well-dressed African-American men were talking quietly about the sights they would see first, one pushing for the Louvre, the second for the Folies-Bergère. Several high school students with backpacks, cameras, and guide books were walking up and down, restlessly passing time. One unisex person finally sat down, removed a new paperback from its wrapping, and began reading avidly, *French in Fifteen Minutes a Day.*

"Hope she's a speed reader," said a middle-aged man sitting next to Luke, who nodded and smiled. "Chuck Cook," the stranger added, putting out a beefy, work-calloused hand. "This is my wife Rosemary," pointing to a sparrow-like brunette sitting beside him.

"Luke Plisky. Hello," he said, shaking hands with both.

"We were scheduled to go last night," said Rosemary, "but Chuck had to stay over for business."

"Special occasion?" asked Luke.

"Silver anniversary," said Rosemary, one hand in her pocket, the other in her husband's. "He always said if we made it to twenty-five years, we'd celebrate at Notre Dame Cathedral, then on to the Left Bank for lunch. Our anniversary's tomorrow. He's not off the hook yet."

"Good for you," said Luke.

"Anyway, I'm hedging my bets," she said, pulling a red rosary out of her pocket. "Are you married, Mr. Plisky?"

"It's Luke. I was once. Her name was Karen." He told them about her death.

"How awful," said Rosemary Cook. "How did you get through it? Are you a religious man, Luke?"

"No. Once, maybe. No more."

"Well, when we do get to Paris, we'll say a prayer for her at Notre Dame."

"Thank you."

"And one for you, too," she added.

"I could use more than one."

They continued to talk until the boarding announcement for First Class passengers. Luke stood up: "That's me," he said to the couple. "Happy Anniversary!"

"Thanks," said Rosemary. "Maybe we'll meet again at Orly Airport."

"I hope so, but don't look for me at Notre Dame."

"Hey, ya never know," said Rosemary. Luke turned, waved *"à bientôt,"* and walked slowly to the boarding gate.

71

Later that night, Luke Plisky's brother-in-law Ned Westrum walked into the kitchen of his East Lansing home, and got a can of beer from the refrigerator.

Ten year old Danny was finally in bed and his wife Lily had not yet returned from work at the local library. A new computer system had been installed, and Lily was conducting classes for the staff. Ned went down the short flight of stairs to the den, where he flipped on the TV and settled into the recliner with Coors and chips.

At 9:55, the network's news hour had already begun, and an anchorman was speaking gravely: "For those of you who've just tuned in, TWA flight #800 from New York's Kennedy International Airport to Paris crashed shortly after takeoff just after eight o'clock this evening. The plane, according to several witnesses, exploded in the air before dropping several thousand feet into Long Island Sound. Full details are not yet available, but reports are that over two hundred people were on board. There appear to be no survivors. New York State Governor George Pataki and City Mayor Rudolph Giuliani have rushed to the scene, along with the Red Cross, ambulances, police and fire personnel."

The network would be broadcasting throughout the night. "Stay tuned for late-breaking details."

Just then, the front door slammed and Lily walked down the short flight of steps into the den. Ned's face was ashen.

"What's wrong? Are you all right?" she asked him.

"I'm fine," he stammered. "It's your brother. Luke was flying to Paris tonight, right?"

"Yes, I talked to him yesterday," she said, her eyes now riveted to the TV screen.

"Omigod, no! It can't be!" she shouted.

"TWA Flight #800. That's Luke's flight?"

A weak nod. Ned, seeing her crumpled face, got up and gently led her to the sofa. She laid her head down on his shoulder and sobbed quietly as he rocked her like a small child.

72

....

Lockerbie, Scotland. Waco, Texas. Oklahoma City. Places where mind-numbing images of violent death had fractured the nation's sensibilities forever.

When TWA Flight #800 plunged into the ocean, East Moriches, a small coastal Long Island town, joined the list.

Throughout the night, relatives and friends were calling and arriving at the airport's Ramada Inn. Could a procrastinating husband have missed the plane? Could a daughter have changed her mind at the last minute? Could a healthy young man have survived the crash and be adrift somewhere in the Atlantic?

For several hours, there were few answers. When, on the night of the crash, the airline was unable to produce a manifest of passengers, anxiety levels increased, but slivers of hope remained.

The next day hope died. There would be no miracle. Coast Guard boats had searched through the night, finding no sign of life. Several people on shore and in nearby aircraft reported seeing something in the sky prior to the plane's exploding, breaking in two, and crashing into the ocean. Some described it as a fireball, while others thought it was more like a blazing shaft of light. A missile? A

terrorist act? Mechanical failure? Officials from the
National Safety Transportation Board and the Federal Bureau of Investigation were already on hand,
organizing what would become a long, exhaustive
and painful search for the cause, the wreckage, the
bodies.

When the manifest finally was published, families checked for names. Finding them, they now
focused on recovering loved ones' bodies and bringing them home.

Lily and Ned Westrum had driven to Detroit early
Thursday, the day after the crash, and left their son
Danny there with Ned's mother. In the afternoon,
they'd taken a direct flight to Kennedy Airport. Upon
arrival at the Ramada Inn, they received a copy of the
manifest. Luke Plisky's name appeared midway on
the list.

There were two other names on the manifest,
names that meant something to another family, but
nothing at all to Lily or Ned Westrum. They were:

Cook, C., New York

Cook, R., New York

For the next several days, Lily and Ned
Westrum, along with hundreds of other victims' families, attended investigators' briefings. Grief counselors, chaplains and health workers had all
descended on the scene to offer help and support.

The Westrums had been given time off with pay
by their East Lansing employers. By Sunday night,
however, the two were physically and emotionally
exhausted. They were satisfied that everything that

could be done was being done, and that no amount of counseling or grieving in this sad place could bring Luke back. Nor was it clear when, if ever, his remains would be retrieved.

And, while Ned's mother had said that ten year old Danny was fine, they felt that one of them was needed at home.

On Monday morning, Ned flew back to Detroit. Bruno Altieri, Luke's best friend, had called them several times at the airport motel, and asked what he could do to help. Told that Lily would stay on for a time at Luke's house in Crestwood, he promised to send a chauffeured car out to the airport to take her there.

On Monday at noon, an hour after Ned's plane had left, Bruno's silver Mercedes arrived at the airport hotel, with Bruno as driver. He and Lily drove north to the Crestwood section of Yonkers in just over an hour.

It was late July, but Luke's front lawn looked like a small cemetery after Memorial Day. There were masses of bouquets of every color, yellow ribbons, and notes. All the flags on Scarsdale Road were at half-mast. A large group of people stood back quietly to allow Lily and Bruno to enter the house. A small red-haired boy shyly went up to Lily and offered her a rose, "from all of us." When a reporter and TV cameraman approached, Bruno attempted to push them away, but was gently restrained by Lily. She took the microphone and said simply, "Thank you. Luke was the world's best brother. Knowing you loved him too means so much." That night, the scene was televised on local cable TV.

Over the next several days, Bruno left Lily alone to go through the house, sort things out, see what needed to be done. Each morning, a neighbor knocked on the door, offering a car ride or simply a kind word. She needed little. There were daily deliveries of food: a tuna casserole, some oatmeal cookies, a basket of fruit, a bag of fresh bagels, a loaf of home-cooked bread, a breast of chicken already cooked.

One by one, she sifted through Luke's personal things, photos, memorabilia, deciding what should be shipped home to East Lansing. Occasionally, she'd even smile. Unlike her, Luke was such a neatnik! Selling anything, other than the house itself, seemed crass. What she did not want, she would give away.

The following week, Bruno returned and helped her to get Luke's finances in order. Putting the house on the market was too final an act, too soon. When Luke's principal, Mark Borras, had called to invite her and the family to a memorial service at P.S. 807 in September, she promised to return. The house could wait till then.

In early August, Lily returned to East Lansing, to Ned and to Danny. Neither Luke's body, nor anything of his, had been found on the ocean's floor.

73

....

In the weeks that followed, the crash of TWA's Flight #800 continued to dominate the news.

The victims seemed to be not just a microcosm of the nation, but of its best. Young, old, and in-between; married and single; students and teachers; coaches and cheerleaders; businessmen and women, their smiling faces haunted the country every day. For all, Paris still symbolized life, romance, history, beauty, a thoroughfare of great happenings, a place many of the crash victims would never get to see.

There were no passengers from Bronxville, but several from Westchester. On the weekend after the crash, local newspapers ran a feature on Luke Plisky, a New York City school teacher from Crestwood in Yonkers. He was a Vietnam war hero, beloved teacher, widower, devoted brother, friendly, quiet neighbor. Felix Mendoza, Community School Board president in the South Bronx, had announced that a memorial service would be held at P.S. 807 when school reopened in September.

In Westchester and across the country, the public was mesmerized. The media quickly trotted out the usual experts, who talked exhaustively about what might have happened and why. Soon, details of aeronautical engineering, missiles, and explosives were the stuff of everyday life. Fuel tanks, wind shear, static electricity, black boxes, explosives detectors, all became fodder for Internet chat lines, radio talk shows, Food Emporium conversations, bridge clubs, Senior Citizens' meetings, and kindergartners' "Show and Tells."

A massive, heroic effort by Navy divers to locate bodies and wreckage had begun a few days after the crash. Each day that someone, or a part of someone, was found, the tragedy was renewed. Evidence continued to mount as each new piece of the plane was salvaged from the ocean's floor. Still, for all the expertise in place, the cause of the crash remained a mystery.

For weeks, local news was relegated to the back burner. Such was the case with the ongoing investigation of Dan Horgan's murder. Tuckahoe Police Chief Paul Martino was not unhappy about all this. His team could focus on solving the crime, not talking about it.

The truth, however, was that when Shannon O'Keefe had called him today, he'd said there was little to report. There was still a consensus that this was a carefully planned, efficiently executed murder-for-hire. There were no fingerprints, fibers, or other critical pieces of evidence from the crime scene. The reward had turned up nothing important other than Steve Jablonski's testimony that Dom Rizzuto had lied about threats to Horgan. Rizzuto, however, under advice of counsel, had quickly admitted the lie. "But murder? No way," he'd said. While no one could back up Dom's alibi, no one could connect him to the crime scene, either.

Martino was not a betting man. Had he been one, he'd have put money on the Donohue-'Knuckles' O'Callaghan connection, a murder for revenge. But which Donohue was involved? Was it Walter who, from the grave, had his old friend Knuckles kill Horgan? Could his widow Edna have known what O'Callaghan was planning, and done nothing to stop it? Or, did his son the doctor conspire with O'Callaghan to honor his father's last wish?

The Chief found himself identifying with the investigators working on the TWA crash. Bone tired after thousands of man-hours of work, plodding through lots of theories and evidence, with no answers to show for it. One step ahead, a half step back, often a whole one back. At the start, he'd promised his team and the public they'd find an answer to the Horgan murder. The men heading the TWA investigation had made a similar commitment.

It was now mid-August, four weeks after the plane crash, and more than four months after the murder. There were no solutions in sight for either.

For the first time, Paul Martino wondered if there ever would be.

74

"So, who did you like the best?"

"Whom," said Lou De Femio to Shannon O'Keefe. It was a muggy August morning, the day after her conversation with Tuckahoe Police Chief Martino. She and Lou were discussing applicants for the office manager job at Horgan & Stern. During the week, Lou had seen the three top candidates that she and Jacqueline Sheppard had screened from hundreds of applications.

"Picky, picky," she answered. "Just tell me if you liked any of them. All three can do the job."

"Agreed, but I think the guy had the best qualifications."

"Fine. Then he's your choice?"

"There's just one problem."

"What?"

"He buffs his nails. Can't stand men who do that."

Shannon laughed. "Well, you're the lawyer, but I don't think nail-buffers are a protected class. Look, once you're talking about qualified people, it often gets down to personal chemistry. Chances are if you don't like his nail-buffing, you'll soon find some other reason you can't relate to the guy, like his after-shave lotion."

"Yeah," said Lou. "Come to think of it, I didn't like that or the cheap rug on his head. Why can't the guy buy a decent hair-piece? You know what, though? Seeing these three gave me a chance to compare them to our own people."

"Just remember I'm not available."

"Right. You've told me often enough. No, I was thinking about Jacqueline."

"Jacqueline Sheppard?" she asked.

"You think that's nuts?"

"Not at all," Shannon answered. "Hard to think of a better person. This isn't an easy job. Whoever gets it will be trampling on someone's turf, every day. Somebody who already has your confidence will have a leg up."

"Watch it there, kid. You're talking sexual harassment," he laughed.

"You know what I mean. Anyway, Jacqueline's earned a promotion."

"Agreed. But she's starting law school at night in the fall. Maybe she won't want to take on a new job as well."

Shannon wondered why the issue of too much responsibility rarely surfaced when males were candidates for promotion. She said, "You'll never know if you don't ask her."

"I will."

"Great. Oh, I called the Tuckahoe Police Chief yesterday to see if there was any progress on Dan's murder. We've got a Lake View Board meeting tonight. Not much new. Sounds like they've moved off Dom Rizzuto as the leading suspect. Martino's zoning in on the Donohue-O'Callaghan connection."

"So I've heard. If you ask me, that's nuts. Hate to say this, but I'm beginning to think they may never catch the guy," said Lou.

"If it's a guy."

"Well, the only two women with motives are Edna Donohue and Margo Stern. I can't see one of them as a killer, can you?"

"No, but then neither did Lizzie Borden's nearest and dearest. The problem is that we don't see anybody as a killer, but Dan is still dead."

Lou nodded glumly.

"Anyway, back to Jacqueline. Can you see her now about the job?"

"Sure. Ask her to come in."

When Shannon left Lou's office she was happy for Jacqueline, and just a bit sad that the nail-buffer would never know why he lost out.

75

....

Lake View's Board meeting that night was memorable.

Val Thomas had arrived before six. Good, Shannon thought, starting without him had finally taught him a lesson. Her balloon was quickly pricked when Val announced that his idea of a perfect day was "finding a parking meter with unused time on it."

This was Grant ("Binky") Seagram's first Board meeting. When he'd applied for the slot, his "CV" ran to several pages. The first traced Binky's early life in Andover, Massachusetts, through prep school and Amherst College. The final page had him as the "Honorable Grant S. Seagram," former State Supreme Court Justice. In between there was a law degree from Columbia, a highly successful career as a corporate litigation attorney, and seven years on the bench.

In answer to the question, "What special qualities would you bring to Lake View's Board?" he'd written: "A reputation for integrity in my personal and professional life. I do not tolerate fools gladly." Reading that, Shannon wondered if he thought the rest of the world did.

Binky had retired from the judiciary in his mid-fifties, and now worked out of a small office on

Palmer Avenue. The sign on the door read "The Honorable Grant B. Seagram, Attorney at Law."

Along the way, someone had christened him "Binky." Seagram himself said he didn't recall why, but Dan Horgan had once told Shannon that in prep school, Seagram was dubbed "Finky." It was Grant himself who'd said his middle initial was "B," and he preferred "Binky." The Honorable Grant Seagram was thought to be reasonably intelligent, autocratic, and fair. An acerbic wit took the edge off a case of mild stuffiness. Those who still called him "Judge," however, were friends for life.

When the meeting began, all except Jay Shapiro were there. Jay's architectural firm was bidding on a new design for New York's Coliseum, and he would not be home until late.

Binky Seagram had quickly eyed the only armchair in the room, moved it to one end of the rectangular table, directly across from Shannon, and settled his ample frame into it. Shannon welcomed "Judge" Seagram to the Board. Elmer Brick chimed in, "No gavels here, Binky!" Seagram smiled benevolently and raised his right hand, palm forward. "I swear to leave it home. I'm delighted to be part of this distinguished group."

The preliminaries of approving prior minutes and reviewing the financials took ten minutes. Rich Kryhoski announced that there had been no resident complaints since the last meeting, a first in recent history.

"The biggest cranks are away on vacation," explained Elmer Brick.

"Could be," laughed Shannon. "Anyway, let's move to the two presentations by firms that want to be our managing agents. Rich?"

"Right." Kryhoski then gave some background on the two he'd selected to address the Board. "The principal difference is style. One outfit is traditional, the other is not. Both are well regarded in the industry."

"How much more will they charge than your fee?" asked Val Thomas.

Rich smiled. "That's the bad news. Plan on roughly a twenty-five to thirty percent increase, no matter who you pick."

Val groaned, "Well, let's see their dog and pony shows."

Each firm had agreed to take no more than a half hour, including questions. Rich was right. The choice between the two was more style than substance. The first presenter, F. Clark Holden, was a trim, hair-sprayed man who was pushing forty. He arrived with old-world Southern-style charm and vinyl binders. They contained the firm's history, colored pictures of the principals, a list of specialized services, including certified accountants and lawyers, and blurbs from ecstatic clients. His presentation included several "if you will's." The closer was that the company was now global, and the principals spoke a total of eight different languages.

"Which one have you been speaking tonight, sir?" asked Binky Seagram. A nervous twitter from sir, giggles from the rest. Binky said, "An old Groucho Marx line, couldn't resist."

The second presenter, Ms. Greta Taylor, was a more typical real estate type, a bubbly, extroverted prime-of-life woman. Full-figured, dyed red hair, heavily braceleted, and short-skirted, with spindly high heels. She had the aura of a Ziegfield Follies girl, who'd vaulted voluptuously into a grand middle age. No vinyl folders, but ballpoint pens emblazoned with the firm's logo. She was cheerful and straight-forward, and when Binky asked what languages were spoken by the firm's principals, she said slyly, "Da Bronx, sweetie," with an accent that was pure Arthur Avenue.

"Touché, madame," laughed a delighted "sweetie" and the rest.

After the woman left, there was a consensus that while either firm could do the job, the increased fees would mean a jump in maintenance charges. Was Rich satisfied that there was no one else available?

"There are, but you get what you pay for. I wouldn't recommend them. Look, I did get another proposal from left field today. It's not fleshed out yet."

"Give us a clue, Rich," urged Shannon.

"It's from Max Schneible."

"Max knows someone?" asked Evan Doubleday.

"Yes. Her."

"She's up and leaving to join the real estate business?" gasped Hester Harrington.

"Not leaving," said Rich. "Max thinks that, with some rearrangement of tasks among Lake View's staff, she can absorb the managing agent's role herself. Says the building superintendent's job is not full time. In fact, she's been studying for her real estate license at night."

Elmer said, "In all my years in business, I never had anyone volunteer for more work! Is she well?"

"Hasn't missed a day since she's been here," said Rich.

"What will it cost us?" asked Val.

"As I said, the plan still needs work. Best guess is that the net result could be an annual savings of maybe ten to twenty thousand bucks."

"Let's look into it," said Val, eagerly.

"Absolutely," said Gwyneth Fielding.

"Are you sure we're not moving too fast?" asked Evan. "She's done a great job, but she's only been here since March."

"Exactly what I told her," said Rich. "I've gotta tell you, though, she's done a hell of a lot of thinking about it. She's even talked to Minnie Stern about setting up financial spreadsheets on a computer. You'll still need a C.P.A. on retainer, but apparently Mrs. Stern thinks she can do the basics, what my office does now."

"Let's have her work out the details," said Hester.

The group agreed.

It was now past seven-thirty and energy was fading. Shannon announced that she had just one more item, an update on the Horgan murder investigation. She reported what little information Chief Paul Martino had told her yesterday.

Rich Kryhoski added that the murder had put a temporary damper on co-op sales since the spring. "Two Lake View apartments have been on the market for months, even though they're priced to sell quickly."

"Well, how can we prove we're innocent?" asked Hester. "This is outrageous!"

Binky Seagram answered, "Outrageous or not, Hester, until the murder is solved, no one is going to move here. I'm going to put in a call to the A.G. to see it they can't put more manpower on this. They know me there."

"Who's the A.G?" asked Elmer.

"The Attorney General, of course," said Binky, as he jotted a note on his Letts calendar.

Shannon asked if there was any other business to discuss. There being none, the meeting was adjourned at seven forty-five.

Walking back to Lake View with Evan Doubleday and Gwyneth Fielding, Shannon asked, "Which A.G. do you think Binky will call? County, State, Federal?"

"I'd guess all three," said Evan. "Binky loves to have something to do when he goes to work in his three-piece suit every day."

"And there's always lunch with Madame Greta Taylor to look forward to," said Gwyneth.

Evan rolled his eyes. "Really?"

"Really," echoed Gwyneth. "Just you wait."

76

....

The week after Labor Day was bedlam in Bronxville's business district.

Vacationers had returned, schools had reopened, the summer's languor was replaced by a cacophony of street sounds. Children greeted friends as though they'd last met in another lifetime. Sidewalk excavation was still underway, limiting parking on one side of Pondfield Road. Horns screeched loudly at double-parked cars as a grinding crane scooped up concrete in its giant maw. A small girl was running from her nanny, shouting "Eeeek, it's coming for me!"

It was eleven-thirty on Wednesday morning. Shannon and Minnie Stern had just come out of "Forever Green Natural Foods." Another recent addition to the business district, it featured a full selection of organic foods and produce, vitamins, breads and such. "When I stock up here with that healthy stuff, I don't feel guilty about wolfing down a pint of ice cream," said Minnie.

"Amen," laughed Shannon. "One of my favorite things about the store is that one end of their plastic bags is clearly marked *open*. It beats the pulling, biting, and licking I usually resort to."

Crossing Park Place, they walked behind a couple of older women, with shopping bags from "Alexander's," once a mecca for Bronx bargain hunters. The women were navigating with difficulty through a crowd of schoolkids on lunch break. "They call this a posh little town?" grumbled one to her friend.

"I seen better," said she.

Minnie and Shannon laughed. "They talk about Bronxville's snobs. The Bronx threw away the mold."

"You said it. Think of Calvin Klein, Ralph Lauren, and, best of all, Reuben Mattus!"

"Who's he?"

"Häagen-Dazs' founder. Only someone from the Bronx could jack up the price of ice cream by sticking an umlaut in the name."

They'd now reached Shannon's car and tossed their bags inside. "The only tougher thing than finding a parking spot here is getting out of one," said Shannon. Just as she'd started up the motor, a passing Range Rover stopped abruptly, shifted into reverse, and blocked her. The woman was now signaling aggressively to those behind to back up, which they obligingly did, about two feet. The driver now shouted to Shannon: "There's lots of room!"

There was not, without risking an accident. Shannon's mood was not improved when a boy screamed from the car, "C'mon, Grandma, get your horse in gear!"

"Grandma," said Minnie, "there's a half hour left on the meter. I'm low on ice cream. How about picking up some?"

"Brilliant," said Shannon, shutting off the motor,

leaving the parked car wordlessly, and sending the other driver into an apoplectic fit. "Are you crazy, lady?" Cars behind her were now tooting up a storm.

"Sounds like a John Cage street concert," smiled a male passerby.

"Maybe they're honking for Jesus," answered Minnie. The woman finally zoomed off, but not before her teenager shouted a parting obscenity. The car's rear bumper sticker read: "My child is an honor student at North Central High School."

They walked down Park Place to Häagen Dazs and bought two pints. There was no tutti-frutti, so Shannon settled for vanilla and Minnie for coffee chip. Back on Pondfield Road, they left the parking spot without incident. Mario La Guardia met them at Lake View's door and carried their purchases into the lobby. "Good shopping trip, ladies?"

"We seen better," said Shannon, as the two headed for her apartment, where Minnie was joining her for lunch. Upstairs, Shannon prepared a tray of grilled cheese sandwiches, fresh tomatoes and tall glasses of lemonade. She carried the repast into the living room. Minnie had turned on the TV to a local cable station. The news anchorwoman was reporting a human interest feature:

"Last night, P. S. 807 remembered Luke Plisky, a school teacher from Crestwood, at a special meeting of the Community School Board in the South Bronx. Plisky, a Vietnam war hero and dedicated teacher, was one of the victims in TWA's plane crash this summer. His body has not yet been recovered. Community School Board President Felix Mendoza, Principal Mark Borras, parents, teachers, students, and hundreds of people from the community attended, as did Luke Plisky's Michigan family. The most moving tributes, though, came from his fifth grade students."

Shannon was returning to the kitchen for dessert when she heard one speak: "Mr. Plisky, we called him Duke, cuz 'ya know, he always dressed nice. And he caught a baseball funny, like 'ya know, breadbasket, like Willie Mays." A parent's video film clip showed a smiling Luke coaching the kids on base-stealing. He had the body of a much younger man, tall, fair, slim but muscular. And he ran with remarkable speed and grace, despite an obvious limp in his left leg.

When the anchorwoman led into another story, Shannon looked across at Minnie, who was now staring straight ahead. "You're not thinking...?" she asked.

"It's him," said Minnie. "The man by the lake. The one who caught the package thrown from the car."

"Are you sure?" asked Shannon.

"Positive. Of course I never saw him up close, but the way he caught the package, the way he moved and ran, the limp. It's him all right."

"Then I guess we should call the Tuckahoe Police," said Shannon.

"Yes."

"They'll figure we're a couple of lunatics, but so what?"

"They seen worse," said Minnie, as Shannon entered the kitchen and began dialing.

77

Red Quaglio had long ago realized that Shannon and Minnie were not lunatics. But five months after an unsolved murder, she'd have pursued a lead from the Mad Hatter.

After talking with Shannon, Red dialed the local cable TV station to request a copy of the tape. A cheerful telephone receptionist answered: "No problem. You can pick it up this afternoon." Probably a new employee. Too accommodating.

When she and Detective Sergeant Dave Corrigan arrived at the studio, there was definitely a problem. Station Manager Rex La Faye was neither new nor inexperienced. "What's up, guys?" was his wary greeting. "The cops don't normally drop by to tell us we've run a great human interest story."

Red was noncommittal. "Too early to say. Probably nothing. Look, if anything develops, you'll be the first to know, O.K.?" It was not O.K., but La Faye knew it was the best he could get. Why alienate the police over something so minor?

After leaving, the cops stopped at a video store to order several copies of the tape. Back at the station, Red researched the Horgan files and made a list of every witness who might possibly have seen Luke Plisky in the vicinity of the park. At the top were the three joggers who remembered a man fitting the description given by Minnie Stern.

After hearing their preliminary report, Chief Paul Martino agreed that the tip required checking out. "Keep a lid on it for as long as you can. This guy Plisky sounds like the male version of Mother Teresa."

On her way to work the next day, Red picked up the videos. The Chief instructed his officers to deliver copies to the Bronxville Police Station. Their officers had agreed to help in re-interviewing witnesses.

Initial calls were made to the three joggers. By Saturday morning, all had seen the video. The first two now thought the man was strikingly similar to the one they'd seen, but couldn't swear to it. "When you're jogging, your pace is a lot different from when you're trying to steal a base," said one. "Seemed to me the guy I saw had a more pronounced limp than the one on the tape," said the second.

The third was positive the two were the same. "Until I saw the tape, I'd forgotten he wore a silver ID bracelet. It jangled one morning when he passed me. It's him. I'd stake my life on it."

Over the next week, the cops showed the video to several other early morning visitors to the park. About half a dozen now thought they'd seen the runner in early spring, but not since.

Reporters quickly zeroed in. After ten days of "no comment," Chief Martino contacted Rex La Faye and held a brief televised press conference. With the District Attorney's help, his remarks were carefully scripted: "This is one of several different leads we continue to pursue. Even if Luke Plisky did jog on the lake path, there's no evidence at all that he ever met Dan Horgan, much less killed him. Given that Mr. Plisky's body now lies on the ocean floor, we may never know."

It was enough to prompt outraged statements from virtually everyone who had ever known Luke Plisky. They came from veterans' groups, teachers, Crestwood neighbors and friends, and what, according to Martino, "must be every kid he ever taught, and all their parents and guardians."

In the South Bronx, Community School Board President Felix Mendoza, running for Congress called his own press conference; "I'm here to speak out against the slurs on our fallen brother Luke Plisky's name and the subsequent investigation of P.S. 807's Foundation. This is another vile attempt by our political enemies to remain in power. It's time for the little people of every color to unite, to rise up and take back our communities. Together, we shall triumph!" It was the diciest show in town in a dull election year.

The media questioned whether the Horgan murder investigation was in competent hands. One editorial characterized it as a "Suspect-of-the-Week" shell game. "The only people happy with that," it continued, "are last week's suspects who are happy to surrender their titles."

By mid-October, the cops were disheartened, but not Paul Martino. Nicknamed "Tortoise," he promised never to retire with an unsolved murder on his patch. "All we need is a little miracle or a big cartful of luck."

The answer came ten days later, and was more graphically described by a tart-tongued Edna Donohue to Shannon O'Keefe. "A fine kettle of fish, that's what 'tis. Considerin' what my poor Buddy went through."

It began on a Friday evening with a telephone call to the Tuckahoe Police Station. An FBI agent assigned to the Flight #800 investigation asked for Paul Martino. "Is it important, or can I help you?" said Red Quaglio. "He's just heading home for the weekend."

"You decide," was the answer. "Navy divers pulled up Luke Plisky's luggage from the ocean today. We found a letter in it."

"And it's connected with the Horgan case?"

"I'd say so. It's the murder contract."

Red dropped the phone and dashed out to the street, where Martino had just started up his car.

When he finally did arrive home, it was Monday night, and the mystery had been solved.

78

....

On Tuesday the media was alerted that "the Bronxville jogger" murder investigation had ended, and that federal and local law enforcement officials would hold a televised briefing at noon in the Westchester County District Attorney's office.

Shannon's son Ted had called her at ten with a capsule summary. "Red wanted to tell you herself, but might lose her job if word got out before the official briefing."

"Tell her thanks. The news has left me numb, so I'll stay off the phone till noon."

At eleven-fifty she entered the den, flipped on the TV and settled down in a lounge chair to read the day's paper. A front page story in the business section caught her eye: L. Jayne Grey, former executive editor of *Westchester Woman,* had been "elevated" to vice-chairman of the publisher's holding company. "Ms. Grey will focus on external affairs and special projects," stated her mogul boss. In other words, thought Shannon, she got the boot. Unless L. Jayne was even stupider than she looked, her first external affair and special project should be to find a new job.

The noonday news began with an anchorman's cryptic announcement: "We're now going live to the District Attorney's office in Westchester, where the

FBI and local investigators are set to announce what may be an answer to the murder of Bronxville attorney Daniel Horgan last April."

The camera zoomed in on a cast of several zombie-like staff people lined up behind a lectern, clutching portfolios. A portly, pompous assistant district attorney approached the microphone to say his boss was "arguing a case in the Supreme Court, but wanted you to know that this is still another example of superb police and investigative work by Westchester law enforcement officials, working in concert with the FBI."

"Hey, cut to the chase. We got deadlines, man," a front row reporter mumbled, somewhat louder than intended.

"Right," said the speaker gamely. "Special Agent Todd Winkler and Tuckahoe Police Chief Paul Martino will take it from here."

Winkler and Martino each spoke without interruption for ten minutes. When they were done, the public now knew there was overwhelming evidence that Luke Plisky was hired to kill Daniel Horgan last April and that he'd fulfilled the contract; that Mr. Plisky himself had died when TWA's Flight #800 had crashed in July; and that two pieces of his luggage had been retrieved from the ocean floor. Inside one was a zippered leather portfolio with a letter signed by the man who had hired him.

"And that man was Dan Horgan himself," said a calm chief to his spellbound audience. "Mr. Horgan was despondent, having seen his wife through a long and painful terminal illness. When his own brain tumor was diagnosed, he was unwilling to go through the same thing or to put his son or his firm through the emotional and financial consequences of his illness."

Martino stood aside and Todd Winkler again stepped up to the podium. "The chief and I will be happy to answer any questions that we can."

The two now did a graceful *pas de deux* with reporters:

Q: "So why didn't Horgan just kill himself?"

A: "We'll never know for sure. Best guess is he hoped it would never come out. He wanted to spare his son and his law partners any scandal. We think he was also reluctant to drain his assets for treatments that offered no cure. This was a very proud man who had just put his own law firm through a major downsizing. The illness on top of that may have been too much to handle. He cracked. The contract he gave Luke Plisky suggests a man close to the edge."

Q: "Will a copy of the note be released?"

A: "At his son's request, no."

Q: "You still haven't found Plisky's body, right?"

A: "Right."

Q: "What are the chances you'll ever find it?"

A: "More than 200 have already been recovered. As time goes on, though, the odds against finding the rest will drop dramatically. We'll keep searching."

Q: "For how long?"

A: "Several more months, at least."

Q: "But you're absolutely sure he's dead?"

A: "With a reasonable degree of scientific certainty, yes. We know from the travel agent that he bought a ticket for this flight, that he'd told family and friends he was on it, and that one actually drove him to the airport. There is evidence to show that he checked in at the first class window with his ticket and passport and had a drink in the lounge. Several witnesses saw him on a line to board the plane. And, of course, we found his luggage at the bottom of the ocean, near other remains from the crash."

Q: "But wouldn't you still feel better with a body?"

A: "Wouldn't you?" shot back Paul Martino, getting a laugh from the crowd.

And so it went until one-fifteen when the press conference ended and the station switched back to its anchorman. Shannon pressed the Off button on the remote. The next news feature, tips on making your own Halloween costume, paled by comparison to what she'd just heard.

Later that afternoon and well into the evening, the telephone rang nonstop: First was Red Quaglio to offer thanks for Shannon's help, and then Minnie Stern to say she was only mildly surprised that Dan had opted for a unique brand of suicide. "Jake always said that he knew him as well as anyone, and that wasn't very well. Anyway, I'm happy that Margo and Brian Palmer can get on with their lives."

On Wednesday, Ceecy Caruso Cohen called to say that Ida Rizzuto was grateful Dom had been cleared, but would still divorce him. "Oh, and at least one positive thing may come out of this whole affair," added her sister-in-law.

"I'm all ears."

"It's Arthur. Remember I told you that some other philosopher was doing the same work as he was on Wittgenstein?"

"Yeah. Rotten luck."

"Well, Arthur's on to a new tack. You know all those people who swear to speak the truth with a reasonable degree of scientific certainty? But half of them often contradict the other half?"

"Sure. You see it all the time on TV."

"Well, Arthur says there's got to be some kind of philosophical contradiction there. Kind of makes you wonder, right?"

"Not anymore, with Arthur on the case."

"Anyway," said Ceecy happily, "It should get him a better buzz than Wittgenstein. Oh, one more thing. Tony may give you a ring one of these nights."

"Tony? Not your devoted brother, and my philandering ex-husband?" asked a surprised Shannon.

"That Tony."

"Guess I'll deal with it when he does. It's been a rough time for us all."

For many it was not over. Friends and

colleagues of both Dan Horgan and Luke Plisky all weighed in with theories on what each did and why. Former murder suspects had a final moment of fame. Dom Rizzuto announced he would file suit against the police and certain members of the media for defamation of character. Knuckles O'Callaghan was more forgiving: "As a good Christian gentleman, I say may their two poor souls rest in peace."

His wife Moira was of a different mind: "Sod their souls, I say dig up the two buggers and fry 'em!"

Then there were those whose paths had never crossed either Dan Horgan's or Luke Plisky's, but who now used the case as a vehicle to trumpet their own causes: treatment for depression, the morality of downsizing, father-son relationships, the sanctity of life, the culture of death, the complexity of us all.

That Saturday night, drained and mellow, Shannon had just set the clock back for the end of daylight savings time when the phone rang. It was Tony. After talking for a half hour, he asked if she'd like to have dinner with him sometime soon. She didn't say "Yes."

Or "No."

79

....

At twilight on Sunday, Shannon walked around the Bronxville Lake Park. October was her favorite month of the year, one she loved for itself, not for what was past or for what was to come.

At four o'clock, a hazy sun was already spinning its final rays on leaves that were still changing color. On the footbridge at the north side of the lake, a smiling wedding party posed for pictures. Nearby, children somersaulted in the grass. "Watch this, Mommy!" And again, after sustained applause, "Wanna see me do it again?"

Natch.

An older couple approached, cum baby carriage. She recognized Binky Seagram and Greta Taylor, the woman who'd hoped to be Lake View's next managing agent. Last week, over Binky's objections, the Board had voted to give Max Schneible the job and a new title, resident manager. Binky had argued that "this is a job for an experienced professional like Ms. Taylor, not a novice, however talented." To which Hester Harrington had responded: "Binky, don't be an old stick-in-the-mud. The new millennium is coming!"

Today, Binky looked dashing in a raspberry windbreaker and tweed cap. He and Greta, in a white silk poet's blouse, wide-bottomed citrus pants and high open-toed heels, stopped to introduce Shannon to ten-month-old Trevor. "My first grandchild. Isn't he a sweetpea?" cooed Greta. When Binky tickled him under the chin, a wailing sweetpea nipped at his finger.

The spurned tickler quickly recovered: "Oh, Shannon. Greta has some wonderful ideas about redecorating Lake View's lobby. She's thinking Art Deco. I'd like to present them at the next Board meeting."

"I'll add it to our next agenda, Binky. If the Board agrees, you can head the committee."

"Delighted," said he.

"Time to go, Beanie Baby," said Greta. "Trevor's hungry. Toodle-oo!"

Beanie Baby? Guess there's life in the old dog yet, thought Shannon. He'd need it to redecorate Lake View. Dan had once told her that the last Board that had tackled this had resigned en masse, "choosing life over lamps."

Several yards ahead, she stopped to read the small memorial plaques at the bases of the trees. Victor would always love Norma. Lee and Bob would feed the ducks all day. B-Man had given Gina the love of a lifetime, and Theodore had always had a twinkle in his eye. For Karen, gone at fifteen, someone had written: "Look for me and I'll be there." And then there was Patsy, who had once "danced with the wind and reached for the stars."

Shannon thought of Dan. Chip had called her and talked about planting a tree in his father's memory.

What would it say? What could be said about anyone in a few words? And one day, who would remember?

On April 19, a sad anniversary in Waco, Texas, and Oklahoma City, Bronxville would celebrate its centennial. During the year, there would be a ball, commemorative books, historical exhibitions. Would there be an event in the park? She hoped so. Something for everyone in the surrounding community. Dancing, balloons, jugglers, a clown, puppet and craft shows, a magician. Kite flying and yo-yo contests, a carousel, an art show. And music, all kinds of music, a calliope, a string quartet, a blues guitarist, a rock group, stride piano.

Approaching her now was a small girl riding a trainer bike, a tired turbaned man running beside her. When he gently let go, the bike continued shakily, straightening only when rider seemed to forget she was a beginner and began pedaling for the Tour de France. Shannon caught a glimpse of the father's smiling, moist face. Sweat or tears? Maybe both. "She go! My little girl, she go!" he shouted to cheering passersby.

She gave him a "thumbs-up" and turned back toward Lake View, leaving brides and bikes, babes and babies behind. What was it the Irish musician Eamonn McGirr had said after an accident confined him to a wheelchair? "Forward we go."

Just so.

Epilogue

....

Early on All Souls Day, the second of November, a spare, middle-aged man entered Notre Dame Cathedral in Paris.

He was neatly dressed in khakis, a lightweight ecru turtleneck sweater, herringbone blazer, brown loafers. After walking slowly down a side aisle, he stopped to light four candles. Turning back, he looked up at the enormous stained glass rose window, and then sat down in a pew off the main aisle.

Luke Plisky still believed in nothing. Maybe one day he could pray, but not yet. Now he simply spent time remembering: his wife Karen, buddies left in Vietnam, Chuck and Rosemary Cook. A bell rang, the priest entered the sanctuary, and he stayed for Mass. The day's liturgy, bonding living and dead, brought its own peace. Giving up his seat that July night had been a spur-of-the-moment thing. After he'd talked with the Cooks for a time, Rosemary had mentioned that they still had only one ticket for that night's flight. Even at that late hour, she was praying for a miracle, a last minute cancellation.

Getting to Paris the next morning meant everything to the Cooks, little to him. He could still see Rosemary Cook's face when he'd left the line to tell them. She'd hesitated before accepting; then, perhaps realizing that the gesture meant as much to him as to them, her eyes had misted. Kissing him on the cheek, she'd said: "God bless you, Luke Plisky. We'll never forget you. Thank you." Rosemary Cook had gotten her miracle, and the smiling couple had walked hand-in-hand into the bowels of death.

It had still been early evening when Luke called Bruno Altieri from the airport. Bruno, who rarely left his Manhattan office before eight, had answered the phone himself. Was he free for dinner in the city that night? He was. By the time they'd met at St. Patrick's Cathedral, Bruno had booked a table at a small French restaurant on Eighth Avenue and West 52nd Street.

Later, Bruno persuaded Luke to spend the night at his Fort Lee home. A limo driver picked them up in front of the restaurant and drove them there. Arriving at midnight, they headed for bed. Since Bruno had an early morning business appointment in the city, he'd told Luke to sleep in, use the pool and gym, make himself at home. During the day, he could call the airline and reschedule his flight, remaining with Bruno until departure.

The next morning, Luke had dressed, shaved and breakfasted at ten. At his plate was a message to call Bruno's office immediately. By the time the two talked, Luke had scanned the local paper's front page story: "JFK flight to Paris crashes off Long Island. More than 200 feared dead."

After the initial shock, Luke told Bruno two things. First, he'd need to call his sister Lily Westrum to say he was not on the flight. Second, when he'd relinquished the seat, it was too late to retrieve his luggage. The agent had said the airline's baggage crew would store it at Orly until his arrival there.

"So the problem is?" asked Bruno.

"The letter Dan Horgan wrote to me. It's in a zippered leather folio in one of the suitcases. I'd planned to take a side trip to Switzerland, stick it in my safe deposit box."

"And it's now at the bottom of the ocean," said Bruno.

"Yes." Luke's brain was in overdrive, and Bruno sensed it. "Look," said his friend, calmly. "Give me a couple of hours. I'll get back to you. Till then, stay in the house. Talk to nobody, not even Lily."

When Bruno called back, he said: "You're a dead man."

"Almost," said Luke.

"Nope, really. The airlines released the manifest of passengers and crew on the plane. You were on it."

"But the Cooks?" gasped Luke.

"Them too. My people have checked it out. Looks like somebody planned to change it later, never got to it. Could be he was on the plane that went down."

"My God!" said Luke.

"Yeah. Look, I've called the airport hotel. Lily's on her way here. You sit tight. I'm going out there."

"Then you'll tell her I'm O.K?"

"No, Luke. Can't risk it," he said sharply. Then, more softly: "Look, buddy, you're not thinking straight. Ever wonder why secrets get out?

Everybody interprets 'tell nobody' as 'tell nobody except one other person.' It's like a party line. Trust me to handle it." Luke did.

When Bruno returned that night, the two talked. "We know one thing they don't," said Bruno. "You're alive, so they won't find a body. What we don't know is whether your luggage will surface, so we assume the worst. It will, and if the letter's intact, the FBI will find it. They'll sift through every bit of evidence looking for the cause of the crash."

"And they'll make the connection with the Horgan murder," said Luke.

"Yes."

"So I've got to stay dead."

"Uh-huh," said Bruno, "so here's what we'll do."

For several weeks, Luke never left the Fort Lee mansion nor picked up the phone. Bruno's wife and children were vacationing in Cape May. Apart from a maid, chauffeur, gardener, and Bruno's father Sal, Luke saw no one. The three employees had worked for the family for over a quarter-century, and were totally trustworthy. More, they had known and liked Luke Plisky for much of that time. The fact he was alive was cause to rejoice. They asked no questions.

In mid-August, Luke took an Air France flight to Paris. He now had a shaved head, a four-week beard, an earring, another passport, and a new identity. He was Peter David, an American researcher for a large private foundation.

At Orly, he was met by a woman named Francoise Marriott and driven to her family home in a Paris suburb. He'd met Francoise and her husband Jacques several years before at Bruno's, where they'd been weekend guests. Jacques ran a global import/export business; Francoise was a full-time physician.

Since then, Luke had stayed with the Marriotts, tutoring their two sons in English. The boys were unenthusiastic about this until their father mentioned that Monsier David was also a computer whiz. Jacques himself had been delighted when Luke offered to redesign his company's antiquated systems. The arrangement had suited them all well. Peter David had quickly been accepted by the family and their small circle of friends.

In time he'd move on. For now, this was as good a refuge as any. His French was fluent and he'd spent the happiest two weeks of his life in Paris. Then too, it was easier to live a lie here than in America. The French, he'd always thought, were grand masters of deception. In the wake of Vichy, Indo-China, and Algeria, France not only considered itself a world power, but expected everyone else to, as well. Amazingly, most did.

Though Bruno had coached him well, Luke realized that one day the ghosts from his past might confront him. Till then, he'd do what he could with the day at hand.

The priest was now ending his homily: "Life and death are mysteries, all part of God's plan." Was there a reason why his own life had been spared? He didn't know. This he did: that he'd never kill again.

Or catch a baseball like Willie Mays.